WHERE THE
GHOST HORSE
RUNS

ALSO BY ALFRED SILVER

PUBLISHED BY BALLANTINE BOOKS

RED RIVER STORY
LORD OF THE PLAINS

— ALFRED SILVER —

WHERE THE GHOST HORSE RUNS

BALLANTINE BOOKS

NEW YORK

Copyright © 1991 by Alfred Silver
Maps copyright © 1991 by Anita Karl and James Kemp

All rights reserved under International and Pan-American Copyright Conventions. Published in the United States by Ballantine Books, a division of Random House, Inc., New York, and simultaneously in Canada by Random House of Canada Limited, Toronto.

Library of Congress Catalog Card Number: 90-93513
ISBN: 0-345-36734-0

Cover design by James R. Harris
Cover painting by Alan Daniel
Text design by Mary A. Wirth

Manufactured in the United States of America
First Edition: August 1991
10 9 8 7 6 5 4 3 2 1

———————————— • • • ————————————

This book is for all those foolish friends and family
who ignored signs that I was headed straight for
the nearest gutter or gray building with
no doorknobs and who have since turned into
my ace, continent-wide sales and
promotion machine.

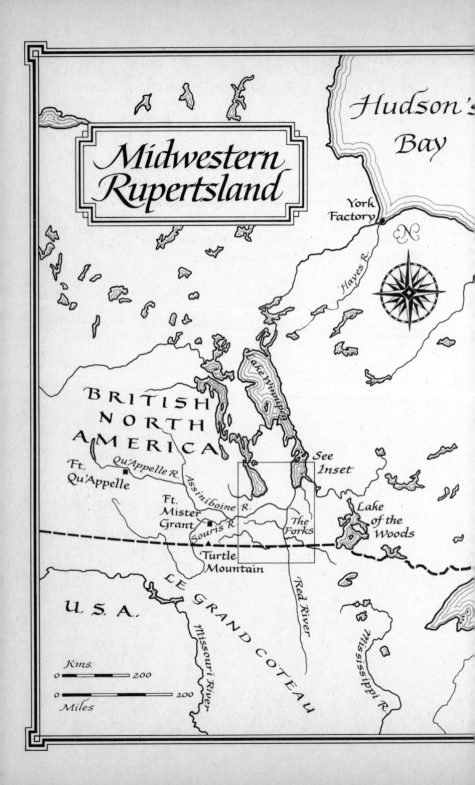

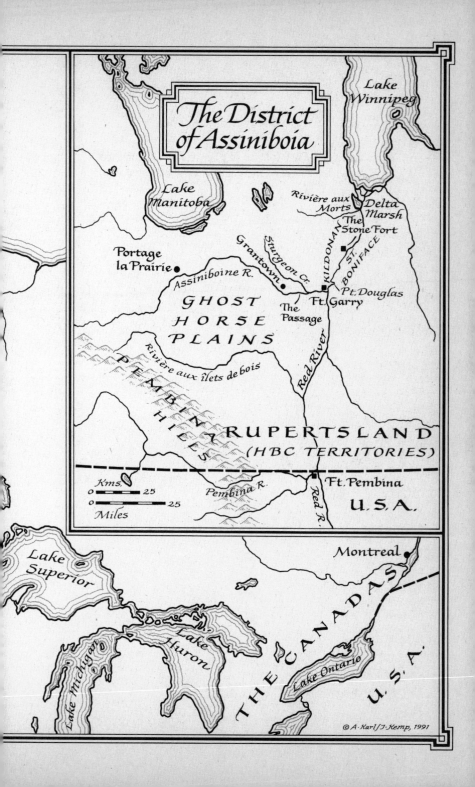

Where the Ghost Horse Runs

PROLOGUE

In the summer of 1821, the Assiniboine Nation decided to hold a Sacred Lodge on the rim of the Qu'Appelle Valley, looking down on The River That Calls. Marie McGillis's father was a trader at the Hudson's Bay Company's Fort Qu'Appelle, so the Sacred Lodge meant that Marie was seeing her grandmother again for a few days. Her grandmother was a medicine woman named Mnaja-Wintko, Unpredictable Loon.

Marie and her mother and Loon were riding around the edge of the bustling camp. The sounds of singing warriors and booming drums and clattering rattles thundered out of the brush walls circling the sacred tree. Women and children and dogs milled within and around the circle of vermilion-daubed white buffalo-hide tents. The horses of the massed herd scampered and whinnied and flirted with the strange horses of other bands. Two long lines of boys were jumping and whooping in the kicking game.

Two young women went giggling by with their faces painted orange with ocher to make them beautiful. Marie's grandmother said to her mother: "If your daughter painted her face like she should, maybe she could get a man."

"Who says she can't get a man?"

"Well, she hasn't got one, has she? And no sign of one as far as I can see. And how many summers old is she?"

"Sixteen."

"Sixteen summers, with a laugh like a meadowlark and smart hands and breasts like pumpkins and still no young men coming around to offer her father horses. She better start painting her face."

"Maybe she doesn't want an Assiniboine young man. Maybe she doesn't want any man at all yet."

"Sixteen summers!"

"It's different for whites."

"She ain't white."

"She ain't Assiniboine, either, and neither am I."

"You got to be one or the other, better make up your mind. You got to be something."

"We are. Métis. We're the New Nation."

Loon just snorted at the conceit that a batch of mongrels could make a separate tribe. Marie was just as glad to have the conversation switch subjects. If it had gone on much longer, she wouldn't have needed ocher to put color in her face. Even if she'd been able to think of something to say in her own defense, she still would've had to suffer in silence. Loon refused to speak any language except Assiniboine, and it always took Marie a while to recover the grasp of it she lost between visits.

But then her mother went and started up again with: "The priests have a school at Red River. Angus says since we're moving there anyway Marie should spend a year or two going to school before she thinks of getting married."

"She won't get herself a man among the Black Robes."

Fortunately the subject was cut off by a boy's voice shouting: "Look out!"

The parallel lines of the kicking match swirled apart, and through the gap came one of the Sacred Lodge devotees, wailing and dragging four buffalo skulls roped to skewers through his back. Marie had never imagined human skin could stretch that far. She started to gag and turned away. Her grandmother said offhandedly: "He made a vow to the Manitou that he'd do that at the next Sun Dance if his son lived through the sweating sickness. But it was juniper and kinnikinnick boiled together that saved his son."

They left the camp behind and kicked their horses into a trot out onto the undulating green sea of grass with shadows of little clouds boating across it. It was a blazing bright day, which was the reason they were leaving the camp and the fort for the prairie. Although it was barely the start of the Red Berry Moon, Loon had announced that the speargrass was ripe and that meant the saskatoon berries would be, too. Marie's father was supposed to catch up with them soon at a coulee a few miles to the south, with his rifle. Grizzly bears liked saskatoons almost as much as they did people; in fact, the bears seemed to be of the opinion that the two tastes complemented each other well.

As the drums of the Sacred Lodge faded under the thudding of their ponies' hooves, Marie's grandmother said, "Red River's a long way from the Quiet People," which was the name of the band she traveled with.

Marie said: "It isn't that far."

"When you get to be my age, child, everywhere's far."

Marie's mother said, "It's a lot closer than Scotland," which seemed unnecessarily cruel. That's where Loon's husband—the grandfather Marie had never known—had gone. Back in the days before there was a Red River Settlement, a trader who lived long enough to retire had nowhere to go but back across the ocean or to the Canadas, neither of which was a good place for people with black eyes and wild ways.

Loon chirped back unfazed: "Maybe you wouldn't find it such a sad thing if *your* fur man went back where he came from." It was taboo for an Assiniboine to refer to a son-in-law by name or speak to him directly. "It's a good thing to have a man when you're young, but once you get old enough to have a mind of your own . . ."

They were almost at the coulee when Loon tugged back on the halter to bring her pony to a halt and slid off the saddle pad with a litheness not at all like an old woman who found every journey far. She pointed at a clump of plants with thick, ribbed leaves and bent spears of white-clustered flower stems. "I see something I want. What is it?"

Marie said, "White man's foot," which was the Indian name for plantain, since they'd never seen it until the white man came and then suddenly it was everywhere, as though it grew out of the white man's footprints. There was another name for it, due to the stiff white spears poking out from the leaves, but Marie didn't want to embarrass her mother.

"And what do I want it for?"

"To mash up the leaves for poultices for burns or cuts or snakebite. Or a tea for trouble in the bladder. Or a wash for sore eyes."

Loon grunted and nodded. "And they make good eating, too." And she proceeded to stuff fresh leaves into one of her dangling profusion of beaded leather pouches.

After the sun forge of the open prairie, the coulee seemed cool and dark and dank with the smells of mud and wolf willow. The thin-leafed shrubs tangling its banks were, sure enough, bowed down with red-purple berries. Marie's mother spread out a couple of blankets in the sun to dry them on. Back at the fort, Marie had caught her grandmother looking askance at her mother bringing out new blankets instead of old buffalo hides to lay on the ground. It was only recently that Marie had begun to notice that her father was a rich man.

The three of them kept up a constant chatter about nothing in particular as they filled their shoulder bags and mouths with juicy berries and poured them out to patter on the blankets. That was the way of things: men kept quiet in hopes that the first sign their brother animals would have of them would be the arrow or the bullet; women talked and sang songs so that mother bears or wolves who wanted to avoid them wouldn't be surprised. Of course there was the occasional grizzly who didn't want to avoid them, the thought of which made Marie increasingly nervous as Sun marched farther across the sky without shining on her father and his gun. Every rustle in the bushes made her start.

When her heart was making more noise in her ears than the drums of the Sacred Lodge, there was finally a sound of approaching hoofbeats. Her mother started back up the slope of the coulee to see who it was. Loon stopped her with: "It's that man with the gray hairs on his face—no Cree or half-breed rides that clumsy. I swear, girl, you're losing your hearing living in wooden walls."

The hoofbeats came to a halt, and Marie's father hallooed from up on the prairie. Marie's mother called: "We're down here!"

As Marie's father came crashing through the undergrowth, holding his long-barreled rifle over his head, Loon turned away so as not to touch her eyes on her son-in-law and said to her daughter: "If the man who trades furs took much longer, he would've met us coming back, or more likely seen us trotting away in a grizzly bear's stomach."

Marie's father said to her mother: "If you happen to be talking to a crazy water bird someday, you might tell it that I was on my way out of the fort when Cuthbert Grant stopped in on his way out of the country. We won't be seeing him again until he's back from England, if he comes back at all. He was sorry he missed you."

The name called up a hundred stories Marie had heard around winter hearths or across summer campfires. Depending on who told the stories, Grant was anything from the kindliest of elegant gentlemen to the most brutal of butchers. She'd been introduced to him once, when she was ten years old and he was drunk, stooping down from his great height to kiss her hand. And she'd seen him from a distance several times, once when her father called her up to the parapet at Fort Montagne à la Bosse to watch the army of the New Nation gallop by with Cuthbert Grant at their head, riding down to Red River to uproot the colonists the Hudson's Bay Company had planted there. A week later the news had come that Grant had massacred half the men of the colony at a place called Seven Oaks.

Loon chortled at Marie's mother. "So much for your 'New Nation.' Without a chief they ain't no tribe at all." Then her voice grew softer. "I saw him the day he captured the Hudson's Bay Company brigade.

"I'd had a dream that I could find good milkweed along the top of the valley near where the Qu'Appelle flows into the Assiniboine. I didn't find any, but when I looked down I saw a big man in a white shirt standing on a rock in the middle of the river. His arms were crossed. The rock was right at the foot of the rapids. Up at the top of the rapids were the big boats of the Hudson's Bay brigade, getting ready to shoot down one by one. The man on the rock and the men in the boats couldn't see each other from where they were, but I could see them both, and I could also see there were a lot of horses grazing out behind the woods on the riverbank. The first boat ran the rapids, and when it came out the other side the man on the rock uncrossed his arms. He had a short gun in each hand. The men in the boat started laughing, that one man could be so crazy—I could hear them all the way up at the top of the valley. And then all of a sudden the woods on both banks were filled with men pointing guns at the boat, and they stopped laughing. The men in the woods dragged the boat out of the river and took the crew prisoner and then hid again while the man on the rock waited for the next boat. They took all eight boats that way, and then I heard *real* laughing."

She let out a sigh that was somewhat more lascivious than Marie would have expected from an old woman. "People can say what they like about that Grant, but there's a *man* for you." She turned to Marie. "Not for *you*. You want a young man, and one that's not so crazy. And you want him soon."

Marie's father said: "Marie, if a diving bird happens to be shrieking in your ear sometime, you should tell it that you're still a very young girl and that you're going to meet plenty of eligible young men at Red River—young men that can give you more of a home than a tent out on the prairie. You can also tell that bird that *when the time comes* you're going to have to beat them off with a stick. On top of all the other good reasons why they'll come chasing after you, the man that gets you also gets five hundred pounds dowry."

Loon said to Marie: "Someday you should tell a white man who don't seem to know any better that it's the young man who's supposed to give horses to his sweetheart's father, not the other way around."

Marie said: "I think I'll wade across the creek and see if there's more berries over there."

PART ONE

RED RIVER

Grant . . . proposes going to England to make some En-
quiry after his private affairs. . . . His object seems to be
[to] deposit his money in safe hands & re-enter the Service,
but if not admitted I suspect he will be inclined to form
an opposition & if he does so he will be a very dangerous
man. . . .

JOURNAL OF GEORGE SIMPSON,
GOVERNOR OF THE NORTHERN DEPARTMENT,
HUDSON'S BAY COMPANY

CHAPTER 1

The streets of London in 1822 were no place to go rambling after dark. There were few street lamps and no police force. Odds on, if the professional thieves and cutthroats didn't get you, the Mohocks would.

It was a grand old London tradition for the sons of earls and marquises to while away a few years of their youth roistering about the streets of London, beating and robbing people whose annual income wouldn't pay their bar tabs for a week. Each succeeding generation coined a new name for themselves—Macoronis, Scourers, the Hellfire Club, the Mohocks—but the tradition of thuggery for the fun of it was handed down intact like Uncle Osbert's pocketwatch.

On a foggy autumn night, a pack of Mohocks prowling the maze of twisting lanes on the cheaper side of Waterloo Bridge came across a perfect target. It was a lone, top-hatted gentleman swinging his walking stick along as jauntily as though taking his evening constitutional through the rose garden. He did appear to be somewhat larger than average—the top hat and the half-cape on his coachman's-style coat couldn't entirely account for his height and the breadth of his shoulders. But there was only one of him and four of them—a baronet, a duke's second son, a Guards subaltern of uncertain origin, and the heir presumptive to a large block of shares in the East India Company.

As if the top-hatted fool weren't tempting fate enough, he veered off to take a shortcut through Fishbone Alley. The duke's son was told to skulk along behind him while the other three circled around to head him off. They flattened their backs against the soot-blackened face of one of the warehouses flanking Fishbone Alley, adjusting their masks and choking back their hoots of anticipation. The baronet flicked the catch on his sword stick and listened to the loudening clicks of boot heels and walking stick on cobblestones echoing in the narrow canyon. When he judged they'd grown loud enough, he leaped out into the mouth of the alley, unsheathing his sword with a flourish. The other two took up positions on either side of him, brandishing a lead-weighted cudgel and a theatrically curved Hindoo dagger.

The top-hatted fool halted in front of them. The incoming fog hadn't coalesced enough yet to blot out the moon. The pale, blue-white light showed a distinct coppery tinge in the complexion of their victim. Above a pair of heavy cheekbones and below the rim of the top hat were a pair of large black eyes with a Mongolian fold to the corners.

The baronet extended his blade and growled through his mask: "Hand over your purse."

The Guards subaltern drawled, "And your walking stick," drawing the baronet's attention to the extravagantly carved silver knob on the head of the Oriental gentleman's cane.

The black eyes tracked slowly and deliberately along the barricade of Mohocks, then returned to the baronet. The compressed line of the mouth opened just wide enough to say: "No."

The baronet blinked to make sure he'd heard that right. Beside him, the subaltern sniggered: "Chinee man givee-pursee." It bought a round of guffaws from all except the Chinee man and the duke's son, creeping up soundlessly behind him with a sandbag poised to crunch the back of his neck without leaving a mark, just like the professionals. It was all too delicious.

The inscrutable expression on the copper features didn't flicker, but the arm holding the silver-headed cane whipped down and backward. There was a loud crack and a scream. The duke's son dropped his sandbag and fell to the cobblestones, clutching his shin. The baronet took that in and then lunged with the point of his blade at the target's broad chest. The Oriental gentleman sidestepped so the sword only passed through the cape between the chest and arm. Before the baronet could draw back for another lunge, a hand like the jaws of a mastiff closed around his sword wrist and twisted, yanking him around to bump up against his oncoming fellow Mohocks.

A series of sounds and images registered on the borders of the baronet's consciousness—the silver knob of the walking stick crunching into the Norman nose of the East India Company's heir, the subaltern's bludgeon whistling in at a copper cheekbone and encountering a wool-padded shoulder instead—but most of his attention was directed toward fighting against the vise clamp that was twisting his wrist and elbow in a direction they were never intended to turn. There was a horrid snapping and tearing sensation, and the fog closed over the moon.

When the baronet's eyes came open again, the moon was still there after all, with only enough mist drifted in to give it a mustache and beard. There was no sign of his fellow Mohocks, beyond a distant whimpering sound that bore a very distant resemblance to the voice of the Guards subaltern.

The round white face of the moon was suddenly eclipsed by an oval, copper-colored one. The top hat had been replaced by a Napoleonic cap of thick black hair. The silver-headed walking stick appeared as a pointer to the slanted corner of one of the black-irised eyes. A crisp-edged baritone said: "Not 'Chinee'—Cree. You should be thankful that the real Mohawks haven't heard that their name is being blasphemed on this side of the ocean by a batch of 'footpads' who couldn't sneak up on a deaf porcupine." The copper man stooped down and disappeared, then reappeared, dusting off his top hat. "I would love to stay and chat, but I'm afraid I'm late for a dinner engagement. Were I you, I'd get that arm seen to immediately. Doctor Mortimer of Harley Street is rumored to be the best bone man in the city."

The dinner engagement was at an elegant town house in Lancaster Square, on the other side of Waterloo Bridge. If the butler was at all taken aback by the complexion of the man rapping on the front door, he didn't show it. "Mister Grant? . . . Mister MacGillivray and the ladies are waiting for you in the library."

"Thank you. Perhaps you'd be so good as to give the head of my walking stick a bit of a wipe when you have a moment—my handkerchief couldn't quite do the trick."

"Certainly, sir."

"And if you happen to know the name of a good reweaver"— waggling a finger through the slit in his coat as the butler moved to help him off with it—"I'd appreciate it if you could jot it down for me."

"No need, sir. Our Martha can see to it while you're at dinner. This way, sir. Spot of trouble along the road?"

"Nothing worth mentioning. The world is cursed with amateurs."

"Just so, sir."

As the butler ushered Grant into the library, a very large man with a very frilly shirtfront pushed off from the mantelpiece and advanced with his hand thrust out, booming: "Cuthbert, lad! It's grand to see you again!"

"And you, sir." Grant started to extend his own hand, then realized the palm was beaded with sweat. He brushed it across his trouser leg on the way up. The last time he'd shaken hands with William MacGillivray, Grant had been a prisoner in a jail cell in Montreal, a situation MacGillivray had engineered. That didn't alter the fact that it was William MacGillivray, as executor of Grant's father's estate, who'd taken a certain shoeless Cree orphan and turned him into a graduate of Inverness College and a rising star of the North West Fur Trading Company.

The hand enveloping Grant's had grown soft and puffy. The formerly resplendent mane of copper curls was yellowing and thinning. Mister MacGillivray released his hand and flourished his arm toward a grayer version of himself shuffling forward from the other end of the room. "You remember my brother? . . ."

"Of course. How do you do, sir?"

"Oh . . . well enough, I suppose," said Simon MacGillivray.

With the handshaking out of the way, it was on to greeting William MacGillivray's dainty daughters, who had both filled out in several interesting directions. They set aside their needlework to stand up and curtsy. Grant bowed and said: "I can hardly go bouncing you one on each knee anymore." They blushed and giggled with their hands over their mouths.

William flourished Grant onto a chair by the hearth and poured him out a tumbler of good Highland malt, hoisting his own glass with: "Shlanje fha!"

"Shlanje mhor." Grant was glad of the whiskey for several reasons. The shoulder that had taken the bludgeon blow was starting to ache and stiffen up. And the drink also helped him endure an aperitif course of small talk. All four MacGillivrays chattered away about their life in London, salting in a few form's-sake questions to Grant about the *pays d'en haut,* the fur country northwest of Lake Superior.

Grant would have found it a lot easier to be convivial if they could have got business out of the way first, but the brothers MacGillivray seemed to believe in prattle first and business later. He reminded himself that he'd already waited eight years and traveled five thousand miles to get this resolved; he could grin and wait a half hour longer.

The ladies kept giggling and shushing each other and shooting gleaming glances in his direction. He had just begun to modestly accept that he was an irresistible magnet for female eyes, when he realized there was something behind him. He peeked back over his shoulder. There was nothing there except the fireplace—a marble mantel with a mint-bright heraldic crest gleaming against the smoke-yellowed stone. He said offhandedly: "I couldn't help but notice the mantelpiece. Did the house come with a coat of arms?"

The ladies wriggled and giggled and tried to cover up their faces with their hands. William MacGillivray attempted a diffident shrug and drawled indulgently: "Oh, the ladies are still a bit giddy over an event that took place several weeks ago. The College of Arms has matriculated a coat of arms for the MacGillivray family."

The ladies sprang off the love seat and ran to a cabinet in the corner. They came bouncing back to Grant and thrust a parchment scroll into his hands. He unrolled it and found himself confronted with a riot of clashing colors. It was a crest built around a quartered shield that somehow managed to contain a cat, a glove, a stag's head, a swimming fish, a ship with all sails set, and a number of stylized daggers and spearheads. The shield was surmounted by a canoeful of paddling voyageurs trailing the old North West Company flag. Hovering over the canoe was a boulder with an oak tree growing out of it.

Grant wrenched his eyes off the parchment and turned them toward William MacGillivray, who was leaned back in his chair pretending to be studying the ceiling, with a hint of a pink flush feathering his cheeks. Barely four years ago Grant would have been looking at one of the most powerful men on the North American continent, the chief superintendent of the North West Company. Now he was looking at a puffed-up old man who warmed a chair at the foot of the Hudson's Bay Company's board table and preened himself betweentimes with this gimcrack.

Grant said: "Congratulations." William MacGillivray blushed deeper and waved it off. The butler announced that dinner was served.

Over the fish course, Simon MacGillivray wheezed: "I'm surprised, Cuthbert, that you took a ship so late in the season. You're going to be stranded here all winter."

"Oh, there's no shortage of diversions here to occupy my time." The ladies giggled. Their father glared. "I've apprenticed myself to a doctor at Guy's Hospital."

William softened. "That's a noble thought, Cuthbert. I've seen too many good men buried in the *pays d'en haut* for lack of a bit of rudimentary medicine."

Grant didn't consider it a noble thought at all. The Hudson's Bay Company substantially increased its salaries for clerks who knew a bit of medicine. "I don't imagine I'll learn a great deal over the course of one winter, but—as you say—even a little knowledge would be useful there. On the other hand, I might not go back at all. Once we've settled the matter of my inheritance, I might stumble across a business to buy into here. Speaking of which . . ."

"Tut tut, no need to bore the ladies with talk of nasty old money. We'll sort it out over the port and cigars."

The conversation shifted to Marie Anne's pianoforte teacher and to the young hussar who'd been paying calls on Magdalene. Grant listened stoically to the ladies' twitterings and chirpings and wondered that there'd ever been a time when he'd daydreamed of growing up to marry one of the great man's daughters and stepping into his shoes.

He knocked back the rest of his claret to wash away the taste of memory and extended his empty glass to be refilled. He diverted his attention to the soup and to Magdalene's delightful décolletage.

After the beef and Yorkshire pudding and the orange trifle, the ladies retired to the drawing room and the gentlemen leaned back, unbuttoning their waistcoats. Grant had just got his cigar alight and was about to get down to business when William MacGillivray took the floor with: "It always seemed to me a great injustice, Cuthbert, that you should have been left out in the cold when the two companies amalgamated."

"We're in agreement on that."

"You know, it just might be possible"—lining a fat finger along the bowsprit of a nose and tipping Grant a wink—"that I could get you back on the lists. Perhaps as a clerk in one of the northern posts."

Grant had every reason to suspect that those wheels had already been set in motion. And he expected a good deal more than some ramshackle scurvy trap perched on the edge of the Arctic Circle. But all he said was: "Thank you."

"Tut tut, my boy—given your abilities, I'd be doing the Company a favor."

Simon said: "Of course, it wouldn't be easy."

His big brother sighed and said: "No . . . no, it wouldn't. I'm afraid in some quarters the name Cuthbert Grant still denotes . . ." He trailed off diplomatically to denote the Seven Oaks massacre and various other killings, kidnappings, house burnings, and so on. "But I believe it could be done."

"In the meanwhile," Grant put in, "there is a small matter of some thirteen thousand pounds."

Simon coughed delicately and shifted to his wheedling business voice. "Oh . . . I shouldn't expect it comes out to that round a sum. . . ."

Grant nodded. "Naturally—after twenty years of expert nurturing I should expect it's grown considerably."

William put in: "And naturally you understand that your education didn't come cheap. And what with tuition and board in Montreal and Inverness, first-class passage back and forth across the ocean, incidental expenses such as books, pens and ink, clothing—" The yellowing copper mane flung back in a burst of laughter, and a soft paw slapped Grant's knee. "By God, Cuthbert—you could grow out of a suit of clothes before the tailor'd sewn in his label."

Grant just nodded. "Naturally."

"Not to mention," Simon added, "the cost of your defense in Montreal and the bail bond you forfeited."

It was Grant's turn to laugh. "There is a case to be made, gentlemen, for those particular expenses being on your own accounts, but let it pass."

Simon licked his lipless mouth, pointed his gimlet eyes at the ceiling, and said: "The difficulty is, you see, Cuthbert—we don't have the figures."

"The figures?"

"Yes, the exact figures, of the amount we had to expend from your father's estate—"

"For your upkeep and education and so forth."

Grant looked from one to the other of them with his mouth open. Did they think he'd traveled halfway across the world for a bit of beef and Yorkshire pud? He said: "Well, send a footman to fetch them. Hell, I'll go myself. Where are they?"

William shrugged and said regretfully: "In the vault in the Company's offices in Montreal."

Something red started pulsing behind Grant's eyeballs. He said: "I took a ship from Montreal. I could have . . ."

"Exactly." Simon smiled like a mackerel on ice. "If you'd only thought to inform us in advance—"

"There seemed to be damned little sense in sending an advance letter that would have been traveling on the same ship I was on."

"Exactly. . . ." William sighed. "If you'd only thought ahead instead of leaping in a boat on impulse—" He cut himself off with another thunder roll of convivial laughter, slapping the table. "But there—you were always one for the heat of the moment, just like your father. And thank God for it when the rest of us needed someone to seize that moment in the affairs of men, eh, Simon?" Simon nodded his deep appreciation for the presence of a Grant at times when hotter heads were needed.

Grant cooled his with another sip of port and said: "I should think we can take it as a given that, whatever my upbringing cost, it was less than three thousand pounds—considerably less. So if you give me a bank draft for ten thousand now, we can settle up the rest when we have the exact figures."

"Why couldn't we do that, Simon?"

"I'm afraid it isn't possible to partially settle an estate. The law doesn't allow for arrangements that are neither fish nor fowl. An estate must be either settled finally on the heirs or still be in the hands of the executors."

"But I'm sure it would be within the bounds of the law for us to provide Cuthbert with an allowance for his upkeep while he's in London, and passage money when it comes time for him to go back home? . . ."

Simon pondered and then nodded. "The law does make allowances for allowances," allowing himself a wheezy chortle at the end.

His brother turned back to Grant and said: "Say . . . two or three hundred pounds to start? If that runs out, we'd be more than happy to extend another hundred. Plus, as I said, your passage home. Simon has to go back across in the spring, to attend to some business. Perhaps you could both take the same ship and settle it when you land in Montreal."

Simon clucked and shook his head gravely. "You're forgetting, William . . ."

"Drat!" William smacked his forehead. "Of course—there's still a murder charge hanging over Cuthbert's head in Montreal."

"I *told* you—" Grant had to pause and pry his teeth apart before carrying on in a relatively level voice. "I took a ship from Montreal. Not one officer of the law took the least notice of my presence."

William slapped the table again. "That's good to hear. I suppose the authorities in the Canadas realize there's been enough water under the bridge to let sleeping dogs lie. So, Simon, when you go back across in the spring, you and Cuthbert can simply root out the figures."

"Certainly, William. Unless, of course, the London Committee demands I stay on here for the summer audit. That is a possibility. And when the committee demands . . ."

The ends of Grant's fingers were digging trenches in the mahogany. It would be so easy and pleasant to grab the scrawny neck with one hand and the pudgy neck with the other and squeeze till the MacGillivrays either coughed up his father's money or their eyeballs popped out. But all that would accomplish would be news broadsheets headlined: MURDEROUS HALF-SAVAGE BROUGHT TO JUSTICE!

Grant stumbled back out into the soot-furred, stinking streets of

London with a bank draft for two hundred and fifty pounds in his pocket and a stomachful of bile pushing against the back of his throat. The fog had settled in. He had to tap his cane against the walls and the fences to make sure he didn't blunder out under the wheels of a passing carriage. He navigated toward the bridge over the Thames by sound and smell—the sound of a big, running river and the smell of sewage. As he fumbled across the gap of an alley mouth, he heard scuffling sounds and surreptitious whispers. He stopped and called out hopefully: "I'm here; come out and play." But no one did.

He was almost at the bridge when his tapping cane encountered something soft instead of brick. He jumped back, whipping his walking stick up in front of him in a parrying position. A voice whined out of the fog: "Please, guv, we got no money or nothing else worth stealing!" A baby began to make half-wakened complaints, and a woman crooned to shush it.

Grant said: "What are you doing here?"

"A person has to sleep somewheres, guv. There's a stove on the other side of this wall they keep burning all night. If we go to the workhouse they'd take away our kid."

Grant delved into his pocket and found a few coins. "Here."

A hand groped up out of the fog and took them from him. "God bless you, guv, you're a very kind gentleman, you are."

Grant didn't feel particularly kind. It was probably barely enough to buy them a hunk of rank sausage and a pint of beer.

Halfway across the bridge he stopped and stood leaning on its rampart, gazing out at the few discernible lights of the capital city of the world. Some of the lights were down below, fog-haloed flickers of fires along the riverbank. From under the bridge came a twittering of children's voices and the smell of roasting potatoes.

In the savage wilderness of the *pays d'en haut*, the poorest man in the country need only borrow an axe and find himself a stand of poplars, and within a week his family would have a snug roof over their heads. Grant muttered to the fog: "Ain't civilization grand."

CHAPTER 2

Five thousand miles due west of the city of London there was a line of rough-hewn farms and hunters' cabins along the banks of the Red River, anchored at the downstream end by a log-palisaded fort on the point of land where the Assiniboine flowed in from the west. For well over a thousand miles in any direction, the only other human habitations were buffalo-hide tipis on the plains, reed-mat wigwams in the spruce woods, a few ramshackle wintering shanties in the hill country, and the occasional farther outpost of the Governor and Company of Adventurers Trading into Hudson's Bay.

On a rainy August evening, one of the houses on the east bank of the Red was raucous with music and singing and the stomping of moccasined feet on a clay floor. Outside, a few heartier or drunker souls cavorted around a sizzling bonfire. The firelight showed all the household furnishings stacked in the yard to suffer through the rain: four handmade chairs, a table with the bark still on the legs, and two tea-chest blanket boxes. It was a métis wedding. The English term *half-breed* had become ridiculously simplistic after five or six generations of stewing races together.

Inside the house, Marie McGillis was dancing in the midst of a jostling mob in approximate time to three fiddles, a concertina, and a Cree ceremonial drum. She was now seventeen, not as tall as she'd hoped to grow, and preoccupied at the moment by her breasts. They were a bit large for her height, and several hours of enthusiastic jig-time jouncing had brought the fact home rather painfully—not to mention the chafing effect of a coarse-woven homespun blouse. If those physical sensations weren't enough, the gap-toothed boy who was her current dancing partner had fixed his bouncing gaze somewhat below her chin and appeared to be drooling.

The music ground to a halt in midmelody. One of the fiddles tried to carry it alone and then gave up. As all the dancers around her stopped confusedly, Marie gratefully followed suit and took the opportunity to nonchalantly cross her arms beneath her breasts. Everyone was looking toward the door. Marie went up on tiptoe and craned her neck.

Filling the doorway was a man in a quillwork-decorated antelope-skin coat and a linen shirt. The rain had plastered his black hair into a tight caul, and his wet face reflected the firelight. His black eyes seemed as self-contained as polished stone. Cuthbert Grant had come back to the *pays d'en haut*.

As he made his way across the room toward the bride and groom, people clapped him on the shoulder or shook his hand or called out his name, some boisterously, some shyly. He passed smoothly through the crowd, trading banter without breaking step and greeting everyone by name. But it seemed to Marie that there was something held back, something lurking behind his easy manner that wasn't comfortable at all. She told herself that she was imagining things. He was a full-grown, war-tested man and the uncontested Chief of the Métis Nation.

The music started up again. Marie waved off her partner and worked her way around the jostling mob of dancers, sidling along with her back against the wall. An arc had drawn itself around one corner of the room that the dancers didn't intrude on, where Cuthbert Grant was standing talking to a grizzled veteran of the fur trade—Marie's father. She got close enough to pick out Cuthbert Grant's crisp-edged baritone from the surrounding riot of whoops and music: ". . . and found a letter waiting for me at Norway House. Simpson has offered me a position as chief clerk at the new fort."

"Which one?" her father asked. "They've been throwing up new forts and tearing down old ones all the way from here to the Athabaska."

"Fort Garry." The fine-carved monument of a head nodded toward the doorway and the monumental new Company headquarters on the other side of the river.

Her father scratched his side-whiskers and growled: "Do you think that's wise?"

Grant laughed, catching her by surprise—larger-than-life-size heroic sculptures weren't supposed to erupt into laughter. "Well, it is true it's been some time since I actually practiced the trade I was educated for, but I don't think the Company'll go broke in the time it takes me to work the rust off."

"You know that's not what I meant. Highlanders have long memories."

"You should know, Angus."

"It isn't to be brushed off." It was her father's turn to nod his head at the doorway, this time to indicate a few of the wedding guests who'd come over from the Kildonan colony on the other side of the river. They were making a pointed exit from any house that harbored Cuthbert Grant. "The ones who lived through Seven Oaks won't forget."

"Well, then they won't forget that if I hadn't been there, none of them would've lived through it. But if they do choose to forget that part of it . . ." The straight-lined mouth and opaque eyes blossomed into a grin so unabashedly boyish that Marie felt a quiver in the pit of her stomach. "I have had unpleasant words muttered behind my back before and lived to tell the tale."

"Well, it's your back. Oh, there you are, Marie. Grant, you remember my oldest daughter? Must've been six or seven years ago, up along the Qu'Appelle? . . ."

The oval stone mask angled to look down at her. She felt herself starting to drown in the black wells of his eyes, then snapped her gaze to the floor. "I certainly should remember, but I'm afraid those were somewhat tumultuous times. . . . Perhaps, Marie, you'll be kind enough to grant me a few minutes on the dance floor, to give my feeble faculty of memory something substantial to hold on to."

She didn't think he could possibly have meant it, but a big warm hand enveloped hers and drew her out into the jouncing mob. She snatched back her sweat-slick hand before it squirted out of its own volition.

The only dance in her repertoire—or in the fiddlers', for that matter—was the Red River jig. The stance was of arms dangled rigidly straight down; a little bouncing of the hands was allowable if it was only a limp reaction to the body's bounce. The steps could be flat-footed or heel to toe, as long as they were energetic and in time with one or another of the musicians. Couples traveled in circles or side to side, depending on personal inclination and the opening of gaps in the press of other jiggers. All in all, the effect was rather like a clog dance in moccasins.

The atmosphere inside the cabin had felt hot and close before Marie stepped out onto the dance floor with Cuthbert Grant. Since then it had bumped up several degrees higher. It was as if there were a circle drawn around him, and anyone who stepped inside it became—like him—the focus of all eyes. She wondered if he'd become oblivious of it over the years. The few glances she sneaked up at his face showed only a workmanlike concentration on the task at hand or a triumphant grin when he thought he'd gotten part of it right.

The tune came to an end. He bowed to kiss her hand. She muttered something unintelligible, and he glided away.

Marie's mother decided it was time to collect the family and head home. Marie climbed up to the sleeping loft and extricated her littlest brother and sister from the entwined pile of snoring children, handing

Margeret down to her mother and keeping Cuthbert for herself. The rain had stopped. It was a short walk down the river path to the house that Angus McGillis had built when he decided to cash in his chips and retire to Red River. It was a remarkable, whitewashed, gabled affair with two full stories and an attic—one of the few buildings outside the walls of Fort Garry that was anything but a shed or a one-room log cabin. The room Marie shared with her sisters was on the second floor, where they could look out over the crowns of the oak and elm trees lining the riverbank.

Marie opened the window to let in the moonlight. Her father was determined to have all the windows in the house paned with glass someday, but glass had to be imported—in hand-size squares packed in barrels of molasses or flour—across the ocean and seven hundred miles upstream from Hudson's Bay. So for now they had to make do with scraped-thin leather parchment stretched across the window frames.

When her sisters were all settled in, Marie went to the trunk at the foot of her bed and fished out her diary and one of her rawhide envelopes filled with beads. Although she could read and write tolerably well, her diary was a knotted ball of string with beads and berries threaded on for special days. It was a tradition she'd learned from her grandmother, Unpredictable Loon of the Assiniboine Nation—the fiercely independent Sioux offshoot that owned the plains between Cree territory and Blackfoot. Assiniboine women had always kept a diary, tying in a new knot every evening for another day of life, attaching a feather of goose down or a painted pebble to mark the birth of a child or their man's safe return from a war. With the coming of the white fur traders, they'd adapted to tying a larger knot for Sundays and to using thread or string instead of buffalo sinew.

Marie threaded on a bright green bead and tied a knot. But instead of putting her diary away and going to bed, she stayed sitting by the window, watching the constellations wheel across the black mirror of the sky until it softened to gray and the stars faded into it.

CHAPTER 3

Grant borrowed a canoe to cross over to Fort Garry. Although the sun wasn't high enough to cook off the last wisps of morning mist, the river was alive with inhabitants taking advantage of the short summer. A Hudson's Bay Company York boat was curling around into the mouth of the Assiniboine, its eight oarsmen standing and sitting in unison as they plied the boat's ten-foot-long sweeps. Swallows skimmed along the surface snatching flies. A pair of redheaded boys angled for catfish from a dugout pirogue. Several Saulteaux canoes were coming upstream from Chief Peguis's village at the delta where the Red flowed into Lake Winnipeg. In the willow bushes crowding the shoreline, red-winged blackbirds exchanged opinions on how many days were left before the leaves began to turn.

Grant beached the canoe on the wide swath of cleared shore fronting the fort and climbed up one of the network of paths worn into the clay. Three Crees were having words with the gatekeeper. As Grant went by, one of them called: *"Wakiye,* Wappeston." Wappeston meant White Ermine, the name Grant had been given when he and his sisters were orphan children living in their uncle's tipi.

Grant called, *"Wakiye,"* back over his shoulder and kept on walking. The gates opened onto a wide square of hard-packed earth with patches of stubborn grass—not nearly as wide, though, as Grant would have recommended if Mister Garry had asked his opinion. It would get awfully crowded at peak trading times or when the annual supply brigade came in from Hudson's Bay. There wasn't room to expand the square, though, since the area enclosed by the palisades also had to accommodate three sprawling warehouses for furs and trade goods, a barracks building with two separate messes (for the gentlemen who worked with their brains and the servants who worked with their backs), a three-storied edifice housing the headquarters of the Company's Northern Department, two isolated stone sheds for the blacksmith's forge and the powder magazine, and sundry wooden structures for the icehouse, cooperage, carpentry, stables, outhouses, etcetera.

Six people were standing yelling at each other in the middle of the square: a middle-aged couple in much-scrubbed homespuns and four men in motley splicings of trade cloth with scraps of military uniforms.

The farm couple were yelling in Gaelic salted with bits of English; the other four were yelling back in thick Swiss accents that seemed to be badly slurred. When it came to imbibing spiritous liquors, Grant was the last man to call anyone else's kettle black, but incoherency at eight o'clock in the morning seemed a bit much. The Swiss motley drunkards were from the Des Meurons regiment of mercenaries that had originally been brought to Red River and given free land to defend the Scots colonists from Cuthbert Grant.

All six stopped shouting at each other when they saw Grant. One of them spat on the ground. Grant kept on walking and stepped up to the door of the whitewashed headquarters building. Inside was a white-walled room with three young clerks perched on long-legged stools, scribbling away at high, narrow, slant-topped desks. One of them looked up from his ledger at Grant and snapped: "The store's in the next building on your left. Do you understand English?"

"Tolerably well. I haven't come to trade, I've come to see Mister Simpson. My information has it that he's actually in residence for a change, instead of charging off across the country on one of his inspection tours."

"Is Mister Simpson expecting you?"

"We didn't arrange a formal appointment for a specific time and place; I only just arrived last night."

"Mister Simpson's time is at a premium. If you leave your name, I'll speak to him when it's convenient. Come back tomorrow and I'll tell you if and when he'll grant you an appointment."

"Perhaps you misheard me. I didn't say I'd come to beg an appointment with Mister Simpson, I said I'd come to see Mister Simpson."

One of the other two clerks bounced down off his stool, interjecting: "I'm quite sure Mister Simpson is as eager to see Mister Grant as Mister Grant is to see him. It is Grant, isn't it? My name's Hargrave. James."

"How do you do, Hargrave James."

"I'll just duck in and let Mister Simpson know you're here."

"Thank you."

James Hargrave scuttled out through a door in the back of the room, knocking on it on the way through. The remaining pair of clerks went back to assiduously scratching the points of their goose quills across their ledgers, sneaking looks at Grant while he pretended to be looking out the window.

James Hargrave came back through the door in the back and held it open, announcing: "Mister Simpson will see you now." Grant negotiated his way around the desks and through the doorway. The door closed behind him.

He was in another white room, but this one was long and narrow and had only one narrow little excuse for a window. There was a serviceable oak desk and two straight-backed pine chairs. The chair behind the desk was occupied by a tiny man with orange hair, ice blue eyes, and a plain black broadcloth suit.

George Simpson had been the right man in the right place when the two companies amalgamated. He'd been in the service of the Hudson's Bay Company long enough to have impressed the London Committee with his abilities, but not long enough to have taken an active part in any of the unpleasant incidents of the trade war. Consequently he'd been appointed governor of the Northern Department, which stretched from Lake Superior to the Pacific Ocean and from the North Pole to the border of the American Republic. Within its territories, the Hudson's Bay Company was lord of all, and the governors of the Northern and Southern departments were its representatives here on earth. Governor of the Northern Department was a long way to go for the illegitimate son of a Scots chambermaid, but Grant suspected it wasn't near long enough for Simpson.

The governor rose from his chair—or perhaps just leaned forward; it was difficult to tell—and extended his hand. "Good to see you back, Grant. Take a pew. How was London?"

"It stinks. Literally. The air tastes like it was breathed by Julius Caesar and several generations of Druids before him."

"I hadn't expected to see you until the brigade came in. I'd assumed you'd come across with the supply ship."

"I did. When the brigade reached the foot of the lake I bought a horse from Chief Peguis instead of waiting for the brigade to line its way up the rapids. I expect they'll be here the day after tomorrow."

"Ah—so you got the message I'd left for you at Norway House?"

"Yes. It's a very generous offer—or it may be. I'm not sure precisely what you meant by 'an annual salary to a maximum of one hundred and twenty pounds.' "

"A formality to give the committee the impression we did some hard dickering. What say one hundred and nineteen? You'll earn it. Every shilling of the Northern Department's hundreds of thousands of pounds in transactions gets toted up here. And I warn you, I don't like columns of figures that don't balance."

"Nor do I. When do I start?"

"There's no need to rush into it."

"Not for you, perhaps. I'm broke."

"You misunderstand me. You can start drawing your salary as chief clerk immediately. I'll have Hargrave open an account for you with one hundred and nineteen pounds' credit. I meant there's no need to rush into your duties. There won't be nearly enough work to keep the other three clerks busy until the buffalo hunters start coming back from the plains. Take a few weeks to get reacquainted with the country and clear the soot from your lungs."

The governor of the Northern Department paused to study his immaculately filed fingernails and added offhandedly: "I imagine you have a lot of old friends and family gathering at Pembina for the hunt."

Grant threw back his head and laughed, then realized he was laughing alone. Any of the old hands from the old days would have joined in from their side of the desk, but George Simpson just sat there with a fixed, polite expression. The fact was that Pembina was the real reason Grant was being brought back into the fold. The surveyors laying down the American border along the forty-ninth parallel of latitude had discovered that the Company's trading fort at the juncture of the Pembina River and the Red was just south of the line. It wasn't common knowledge yet, but the métis nomads who put up wintering cabins around Pembina were bound to find out sooner or later. The Company hadn't a shred of legal right to enforce its Royal Charter trade monopoly against inhabitants of the American Republic. Sooner or later the Pembina métis were bound to realize that there was nothing to prevent them from going into business for themselves, funneling their Indian cousins' furs and the Company's profits down the Missouri to St. Louis.

George Simpson was hoping Cuthbert Grant could solve that little problem for him. If he could, the London Committee would be very pleased with George Simpson.

Grant coughed away his laughter and said soberly: "That's very good of you—I'd been hoping I could get down to Pembina to renew old acquaintances. Unfortunately, there is another matter I have to find some way to attend to. As you may have surmised from my confession of pecuniary embarrassment, I still haven't managed to settle the matter of my inheritance."

"Why ever not? No offense, Grant, but it looks to me as though you'd passed the age of majority some years back."

"Eight and some—nine come December. But for most of them I was somewhat preoccupied dodging musket balls and blizzards and such in the *pays d'en haut*—that is, in Rupert's Land, as we call it now. And now that I've finally got around to attend to the matter, I'm encountering some difficulty prying my father's money loose from the MacGillivrays."

"Are you, now? Why don't you leave it with me."

"That's very good of you."

"Not at all." The little ice blue eyes glittered. "I'd be delighted."

CHAPTER 4

Marie McGillis was teaching her mother how to make bread. Her mother had been cooking for her family and for fortfuls of New Year's feasters for twenty years, but yeast bread wasn't in her repertoire. Flatbreads like bannock were. Father Picard at the mission school had been showing Marie how to bake loaves of bread that rose and melted in the mouth like clouds. It would have been entirely academic in the days when the McGillises had to do all their cooking in a crude clay fireplace. But the kitchen hearth in the house her father had built at Red River was an elaborate fieldstone affair with an iron drawer slotted into one side for an oven.

Marie's mother was working the dough for its second rise, slapping it over from one side to the other and punching it. Marie said: "You have to punch it harder. Punch it as hard as you can."

Her mother looked up with a dawning gleam of wonder and delight. "I get to punch something as hard as I can?"

"Father Picard said you should punch it till your arms hurt."

Her mother grinned down at the fat slab of dough, then hauled off and laced into it. Between the damp smacking sounds and punctuating grunts, a tapping sound came through from the front of the house. Someone was knocking at the door, which was unusually formal. In the Red River Settlement, the latchstring was always on the outside of the door.

Marie left her mother happily punching away and went out through the front parlor, dusting flour off her hands and wiping her eyes. The front door had a tendency to stick in the summer, so she butted it hard with both hands to spring it open. Unfortunately the visitor on the other side chose that exact moment to try knocking again. There was a thump and a *"Merde!"* and the door bounced back toward her. A male hand closed around its edge and swung it wide open.

The hand belonged to Cuthbert Grant. His other hand was cupped over his nose. Marie said: "Oh! Mister Grant! I didn't! I—oh . . ."

"I have been hit harder in the past without permanent injury." His voice came out nasally through the muffling hand. "Although just at present no specific occasions come to mind."

"I'm sorry, I—oh . . ." She started to lift the corner of her apron toward his nose, then realized it wouldn't reach that high, that the apron was caked with flour, and that it wouldn't have had much medicinal effect anyway.

He peeled his hand off his nose and said: "See? No blood. And I believe it's still as relatively undeformed a nose as ever it was."

"It's a beautiful nose. I mean—"

"No need to modify that on my account. And I'm the one that should be apologizing; I've obviously interrupted you."

"We were baking bread—" which reminded her that her face was dappled with flour. She still had the corner of her apron half-raised. She considered wiping her face with it, to give the impression that that's what she'd been intending to do all along, but all that would accomplish would be to smear on more flour from the apron.

"Well, I won't keep you. Is your father about? I've been told he has a buffalo runner for sale."

"He's out in the barn."

"Ah. Thank you."

She went back into the kitchen. Her mother had pounded the dough into submission. They cut it and shaped it and laid it in the bread pans that her father had gotten the fort blacksmith to piece together. Marie couldn't quite remember whether Father Picard had said the second rise should swell to twice its size or thrice, so she settled on a rough guess at two and a half and set the pans on the edge of the hearth with a cloth covering them. Her mother stoked up the fire to start the oven warming. Marie went to the window that looked out toward the barn and swung it open.

She stood at the window, fanning herself with her hand. The sun was having a baking day of its own, but at least there was a bit of a breeze and it was too late in the year for mosquitoes. In the paddock beside the barn, Cuthbert Grant was studiously running his hands over the hocks of a rangy pinto while her father leaned on a fence post puffing his pipe.

Marie's mother brewed up a pot of tea and said: "Why don't you take a couple of cups out to them? They'll need to wet their throats after all that hemming and hawing."

Marie filled a couple of their best enameled tin cups, added in a dash of her father's rum, and carried them outside. As she approached the paddock, Mister Grant was saying: "If you can't see your way clear to come down any lower than that . . . Not that I blame you, after all the time it took to train her. But I have to practice economy until I get some concrete notion of what my living expenses are likely to be. If I lay out twenty pounds on a buffalo runner, I won't have enough left to fill out the rest of my outfit."

Her father said: "What else do you need?"

"Well, I stored my saddle and so on at Fort Garry when I went east, but I'll still need to purchase powder and shot, tea and flour, and some moccasins. English riding boots may be all well and good for rein-trained English hunters, but when it comes to running buffalo . . ."

Marie said: "Mama thought maybe you'd want a cup of tea."

Her father said: "Matter of fact, my throat is getting kind of dry."

Mister Grant said, "Thank you, Marie," and took a sip. He took a second look into the cup after his first swallow and smiled broadly: "Thank you!"

Her father smacked his lips and said: "How much is that little skinflint Simpson paying you, if you don't mind me asking?"

"Not at all," although it looked to Marie that he was a bit embarrassed by the question. "One hundred and nineteen pounds to start."

"To *start*? You must be hell on wheels with an account book."

"Well, I do have a certain amount of experience."

Her father squinted at him and muttered: "You watch out for that little bastard—he'd sell his mother to the Sioux if he thought it'd give him a leg up." Then he suddenly turned to Marie: "Say, Marie—do you think you could whip up a couple pairs of moccasins for our friend here by tomorrow morning?" Marie nodded automatically. "How's that, Grant? We'll throw in the moccasins with the price of the horse. I can't do better'n that, and—take my word for it—neither can you. You won't find a woman with a better pair of hands in the whole *pays damned haut*, if I do say so myself. Well?"

"Done."

The two men spat in their palms and shook hands. Marie's father turned back to her and said: "Well, aren't you going to take his measure?"

"Huh?"

"His feet. Or can you guess just by looking?"

"No, I'll"—fluttering her hand over her shoulder—"I just got to get—" she turned and walked toward the house. As soon as she was through the door she broke into a run through the kitchen and the parlor, ignoring her mother's squawks about the bread, up the stairs and to the trunk at the foot of her bed. She rummaged out a piece of chalk and a stiff hank of scraped buffalo hide. She charged back downstairs, telling her mother on the run that the dough should rise a while longer. Then she bounded out the door and pulled herself up short to saunter back across the yard toward the paddock.

Mister Grant fingered the boardlike bull's hide in her hand and said: "I do hope that's not what you plan to make them from."

"No—this is just for the pattern." Then she realized he knew that as well as she did.

He plunked himself down on the ground with his back against a fence post and wrestled off his riding boots. She laid the bull's hide flat and drew chalk outlines around his feet as he stood on it. He rested one hand on her shoulder to keep his balance. His feet were surprisingly pale, but it was said that was one of the reasons the Crees had christened him Wappeston, because his skin went as white as an ermine's when there was no summer sun to bake it brown. His toes twitched as the chalk went around them, although she tried not to tickle.

She carried the hide back inside, gave a perfunctory yes to her mother's questions about whether the loaves were ready to go into the oven—although she wasn't sure herself—and commandeered the kitchen table to carve out the patterns. It was hard and delicate work. The old bull's hide was as tough as burl oak, and one slip of the knife would leave the pattern short a few ticklish toes. She got it done without any amputations, took the patterns upstairs, dug out a roll of smoked moose hide she'd been saving, and went to work.

The moccasins themselves were easy enough to whip up. Assiniboines made their moccasins with a one-piece upper sewn around the edge of the sole, rather than the sole folded up to join a toepiece as the other Plains tribes did. It was the decoration that took time. She would have preferred to do them in quillwork, but that would take days, so she decided to do one pair in beadwork and the other in embroidery. The beadwork pair would follow a geometric Assiniboine pattern, the embroidered pair the floral style of the métis.

She had just finished the sky blue parts of the beadwork and was reaching for her pouch of purple beads when her mother shouted up the stairs: "Marie! Is it supposed to smell like this?" Marie pricked her finger with the needle, dropped the pouch to scatter purple beads across the floor, and ran downstairs.

The bread was only slightly singed on top. Her mother came at the loaves with a knife. Marie told her to wait a few minutes and then scrape off the black bits, the second instruction shouted as an after-thought from halfway up the stairs.

When the call to dinner came, she had finished the first upper of the beaded pair but still had to add the black border around the other one. Over a few slurps of venison stew she gave in to the fact that she wasn't going to have time to bead the ankle flaps as well. She excused herself while the rest of the family were still exclaiming over the bread.

When her sisters came up to bed, she lugged her things downstairs and finished the embroidery by the light of the kitchen fire. Toward the end she wasn't entirely sure whether she was sewing in orange thread or red. She gratefully switched to a heavy needle and a coil of buffalo sinew to do the coarse work of fixing the uppers to the soles. Long after she'd tied a new knot in her diary and flopped into her bed, she was kept awake by skeins of northern lights sewing themselves across the lining of her eyelids.

An instant later, the squawling stampede of her little brothers and sisters dragged her into the morning. She snatched up the moccasins and carried them to the window. They were gruesome. The orange band on one of the geometric patterns varied from three beads wide to two. The wild roses on the embroidered pair looked more like pink starfish.

She brushed her hair and washed her face and pulled her dress on over her head with resignation. After forcing down a couple of mouth-fuls of maple syrup–flavored oatmeal, she went and sat in the parlor with the horrible moccasins crumpled together in her hands. There was a soft clop of an unshod horse approaching the front of the house. Her father stuck his head in the door and said: "He's here."

She dragged herself to her feet and plodded toward the doorway with her eyes down at her feet. The floor planking became the border of fieldstones in front of the door, then the path trampled through scythed grass. The front hooves of a horse appeared. She stopped and offered up the moccasins without raising her eyes. A hand took the moccasins from her hands. There was an intake of breath, and then a baritone voice exclaimed: "Good Lord! If I'd known this was the kind of work you do, I'd never have taken these as a side trade with a horse—it should've been the other way around."

She raised her eyes. Everything they encountered on the way up was a work of art—the hand-carved wooden stirrups, the braided-leather girth and reins, the resplendently quillworked saddle pad, the fringed and beaded rifle sheath, the embroidered antelope-hide pistol holsters slung across his horse's shoulders . . .

Her mouth gaped open and she said, "They'll feel tight till the skin stretches to fit you."

He kicked his feet free of the stirrups and cocked one leg across his horse's neck, trying to pull his boot off with one hand while the other held his rifle. She reached up and said: "Let me—just put your foot down. . . ." It took some twisting and wrenching to get his boot off. She went around to the other side of his horse and wrangled the other one off.

He tugged on the embroidered pair, flexed his feet in the stirrups, and sighed. "Ah! I feel as though my feet've been encased in plaster of paris for the last year." He stuffed the beaded pair into one of the rawhide panniers slung behind his saddle pad, took the boots she proffered up to him, and looked around for where to put them.

She said: "If you got no room, we could keep them here until you come back."

He smiled. "I was hoping you'd give me some excuse," and he leaned down to hand the boots back to her.

Her father came around the corner of the house leading the spotted buffalo runner on a *shagganappi* halter. *Shagganappi* was the Cree word for thongs of green buffalo hide, used by the fur traders and their métis descendants to mean anything that was crude, rough, and reliable. He handed the lead to Mister Grant, who nodded good-bye and reined his saddle horse around toward the south and Fort Pembina.

Marie's father called: "You watch your topknot down there! The Sioux've been acting up lately." The only response was an over-the-shoulder grin as the saddle horse broke into a trot with the buffalo runner loping along beside.

Marie's father shook his head and grumbled: "He can grin till his face cracks, still don't make him bulletproof."

CHAPTER 5

Grant rode south from the McGillises' along the riverside trail, passed the wooden church of St. Boniface, forded the little creek grandiosely named La Rivière Seine, then left the riverside tree belt to cut straight across the prairie. The sky and earth mirrored each other—a blue plain dotted with little plump clouds and a green one dotted with clumps of poplars and scrub oak. A meadowlark was trilling a solo over a chorale of bobolinks. Pink-and-purple asters poked up among the billowing waves of multicolored grasses. A congregation of six-foot sunflowers stood following their god across the sky. For the first time since he'd climbed into an eastbound canoe sixteen months ago, Grant felt at home.

It hadn't always been that way. When he'd first come back to the *pays d'en haut* after twelve years in Scotland and Montreal, the prairie and its immense sky had seemed like a featureless, boundless void that would suck the air out of his lungs. Now he found it hard to believe that he'd even considered staying on in London, trying to make a life where he couldn't climb onto a horse and ride forever between the earth and sky in any direction the fancy took him.

It was possible to ride the fifty miles from the Forks to Fort Pembina at one go. Grant had done it on several occasions in the past. But there was no urgency this time, and his body had grown unused to spending long hours on the back of a horse. When the light began to turn rose-colored, angling straight in across the prairie, he swerved his horses into the face of the sun and made for the fringe of woods along the riverbank. Making camp wasn't complex. He hobbled the horses, stripped the harness and gear off the saddle horse, and rolled out his traveling bed—a buffalo robe for the earth and a blanket for the night air. Before turning his attention to building a fire and making a meal out of flour and jerked buffalo, he baited a couple of hooks with lumps of tallow and dropped them in the river, fixing the ends of the lines to an overhanging branch.

In the middle of the night he was jerked awake by a thrashing sound in the bush. His first panicked thought was that he'd overestimated the domesticity of the Cree and Saulteaux in the neighborhood, then he realized it only meant catfish for breakfast. He rolled over and went back to sleep.

The raucous dawn riot of water birds, prairie birds, and woods birds was just settling down when Grant tossed the remnants of the catfish to the horses—a *shagganappi* pony could and would eat anything—and pissed out the embers of the fire. He slapped his saddle on the buffalo runner, to get acquainted, but shifted it back onto the saddle horse as soon as they stopped for lunch. Received wisdom had it that there was no surer way to ruin a good buffalo runner than by using it for anything but running buffalo. The morning's ride had taught him that she had a bit of a tendency to respond more quickly to directions from his right knee than his left, but once he'd learned to compensate they'd gotten along fine.

Fort Pembina was on the opposite shore of the Red, just downstream from where the Pembina River flowed in from the west. One of the reasons for Fort Pembina's existence was a ford across the Red, although there were gaps that still had to be swum across in the spring. At this time of year, though, the water was low. The buffalo runner was reluctant to take Grant's word for it and dug in her heels on the shore. Grant wrapped the end of her halter around his forearm and dragged her into the river. Once she was wet she didn't seem to mind.

They came out on the west bank into a haphazard village of brightly painted tipis and green log shanties on the broad swath of cleared ground that surrounded all trading forts, what the traders called the plantation. Mahogany-colored faces looked up from card games and cooking fires. Some of them split into grins, some stayed shyly impassive, some called out Grant's name and came forward. He nodded and waved back at them, called out the names he could remember, and shook the hands extended to him as he trotted by.

The fort gates were wide open. The palisade enclosed an area less than a quarter of Fort Garry's, and some of the uprights were leaning out of line. Grant slowed his horses to a walk and wove his way through a swirl of beaded, feathered, and top-hatted hunters toward the store and the likely location of the chief trader. As he climbed down off the saddle, a whiskey-warm tenor trumpeted: "Wappeston!"

He turned around to see a tallish, bony, nut brown man with a wispy beard and hound-dog eyes dodging through the crowd at a pace just short of a run. Grant shouted, "Pierriche!" and leaped forward to meet him. They collided, threw their arms around each other, pounded each other's backs, and stepped back to get a look at each other.

Pierre Falcon was more than Grant's favorite brother-in-law. Although most people credited Cuthbert Grant with inventing the New Nation, Grant knew the idea had started with the songs Pierre Falcon made up about the métis and the country they lived in, songs that were being sung around campfires all across the *pays d'en haut* while Cuthbert Grant was still sweating his way through Inverness College.

Falcon said: "Look at you—you got all pale-faced while you was off across the Stinking Water. If you ain't careful you're going to end up with a blistered nose just like some Englishman."

"And you appear to've got all lazy. What are you doing lounging around Pembina with all these slow starters?"

"It ain't got nothing to do with lazy. We headed out ten days ago, but then we went and lost a cart fording the Souris. Just happened to be the cart with the powder keg in it. Mary and the rest of them are camped there waiting for me. Josephte and Maria Theresa are with them, too."

"When do we start?"

"Whenever you're ready."

"I had been planning to pay a call on the chief trader, but to hell with formality. We still have a good five hours of daylight left today. . . ."

"Come on, then—I was just finishing loading my horses."

Falcon had already lashed the new powder keg onto one side of a packhorse. There was another, smaller keg waiting to balance the load, branded "HBC—JAMAICA." Grant raised his eyebrows at it. Falcon shrugged. "Serves me right for packing both kegs in the same cart. I chased it along the shore for a mile or three, but it was smack dab in midcurrent. There's going to be some folks suddenly start believing in miracles where it finally washes up."

They camped for the night beside a creek on the fringe of the Pembina Hills. Among his other accomplishments, Falcon could work miracles with dried meat and wild onions and sage. They bunged the "Jamaica" keg and leaned back to digest in the red-and-blue light of campfire, pipe bowls, moon, and stars. Grant sighed away his first sip of rum-and-creek and said: "You're wintering around Pembina now?"

Falcon grunted. "It's good country, but the Sioux won't leave us alone. Last winter they killed a couple of hunters that wandered too far."

"I hear the Sioux say it's good country but the métis won't leave them alone."

"We got no wish to start a war."

"All it takes to start a war is a few foolish young men—as though there were any other kind."

"Oh, I known a few foolish old ones, too," said Falcon.

"And even those wise Sioux who wish to avoid a war—a batch of métis living on their doorsteps must be like a pebble in their shoe."

"They better get used to it. We got to hunt buffalo to live, and nowadays the herds stick pretty much inside Sioux territory—or Assiniboine or Blackfoot. None of them much care for trespassers, but . . ." He trailed off with a shrug.

"Poaching is one thing," said Grant, "permanent homes are quite another. Why spend your whole life wondering if the Sioux have come calling on your family while you were out ice fishing? There's plenty of land around the Forks where you could put up a wintering cabin, and no tribe goes raiding there anymore." Although there were hundreds of places throughout the *pays d'en haut* where one river ran into another, "The Forks" meant the place where the Assiniboine joined the Red.

Falcon snorted. "The Company and them Red River colonists don't care for us any more than the Sioux do."

"Perhaps in the past. Circumstances change."

"People don't."

"The Company's hired me on as chief clerk at Fort Garry."

"No!"

"Yes."

Falcon puffed up his sparsely mustached upper lip like a bullfrog's throat, then let the air out with a contemplative pop. "The North West Company did its best to use you and then hang you out to dry. You figure it's going to feel better from the Hudson's Bay Company?"

"If you insist on dealing with the present on the terms of the past, you might just as well throw away your horse and gun and go running after the buffalo with a stone axe."

"Mind if I write that down?"

"Not at all—I'll call for a stenographer." Grant took a strategic pause to puff his pipe and refill his cup, letting the crickets and a distant loon fill the silence. "For their own separate reasons," he said, "everyone in the *pays d'en haut*—the métis, the new Company, all the tribes, even the farmers at Red River—all want the same thing: to keep the country from being trampled under by 'civilization' for as long as possible."

Falcon crinkled his hound-dog eyes across the campfire and said: "What're you up to?"

"The same as always—merely expressing my opinion."

"Huh. You always express it, but you don't always express it all."

"I don't always know it all."

"I been waiting ten years to hear you say that."

They bickered jovially until Orion climbed up over the hills. In the morning they rode on westward, past the gap between the Pembina Hills and Turtle Mountain. Around midafternoon they caught up with another party of hunters crawling along at cart pace. They heard the other party long before they saw them. The wooden hubs and axles of Red River carts were never greased, because the dust coming off the prairie would coagulate the grease into a lump of cement before the cart had gone two miles. Consequently, a Red River cart in motion gave out an unearthly, constant shriek. It was said you got used to it after a while, but Grant had seen gray-bearded carters stop to kill a prairie dog and smear its innards onto the axle just for the sake of a few minutes' peace.

There were four carts in the party, trailed by a string of buffalo runners and spare saddle horses flanked by a pair of outriders. As Grant and Falcon came up on them, the carts came to a halt, the horses turned their attention to the grass at their feet, and everyone climbed down off their carts and saddles to pass the time of day.

The little caravan consisted of five métis hunters with their seven wives and assorted children. There wasn't much point in going on an extended buffalo hunt without women and children to make pemmican—the virtually indestructible compound of pounded buffalo meat and tallow that fed the fur traders' boat brigades and kept many a lonely outpost from starving to death in the depths of February. Men could and did make pemmican on occasion, but the returns weren't much when the same people who did the hunting and patrolling also had to do the butchering and rendering.

Grant knew two of the hunters from the old days of the fur trade war. Among the ones he didn't know was the one who appeared to be the leader of the party—at least to the extent that any group of self-willed, self-sufficient nomads was ever likely to allow. He was a big, scarred swaggerer named Sikahow, He Combs His Hair. Combs Hair was unusual in that he was among the very few men Grant had to look up at. Also, though métis wardrobes were an individualistic and inventive hodgepodge, it was damned rare to come across a métis who favored a breechclout and leggings over trousers.

It turned out that the buffalo weren't as far out on the plains as Grant had expected at this time of year. Combs Hair's party had been harrying an offshoot of the main herd and were casting about to cut their trail again. Combs Hair figured on catching up with them by sundown or tomorrow morning at the latest. Falcon said to Grant: "Why don't we stick along with these folks and get in a day's hunting along the way? Mary won't mind me showing up a day or two late if I bring in fresh meat. I can maybe borrow a buffalo runner. . . ."

Combs Hair said: "I got three; you can take your choose."

At sunset they still hadn't struck the herd but were definitely in the right vicinity. For the latter part of the afternoon they'd been traveling through a trampled swath of close-cropped grass, dust wallows, and plates of buffalo dung that were too fresh to use in the campfire. They formed the carts into a half-moon barricade for the night and set up a rotation to guard the horses.

Grant was awakened by a hand over his mouth. Falcon brought his head down close and whispered: "Something's wrong." He jerked his head toward the horses.

Grant threw off his blanket, took a pistol in each hand, and went with him out onto the prairie, crouching low so that any object in front of him would silhouette itself against the upturned bowl of stars. The night air was crisp and savory with the tastes of crushed sage and buffalo. The crackling sound of his moccasins settling softly on the cropped grass seemed to echo like starched lace in an empty ballroom. The shapes of horses appeared among the lower stars. They were shaking their heads restlessly and puttering their lips.

A segment of the prairie at Grant's feet suddenly leaped up to meet him. He pulled a trigger and then leaped aside as the gun crack and fire flash showed his position. Something whizzed through the air beside him. He dropped the spent pistol and shifted the other to his right hand.

Another gun banged and flared a funnel of sparks off to his left, and then another to his right. There was a sound of retreating hoofbeats. Grant flung himself prone. With his field of vision skimming straight across the plate of the prairie, he could just make out a handful of horsemen galloping away. He fired the pistol at their backs, although at that distance it wasn't likely to hit anything.

He rose back up to his feet. There were shouts and pounding moccasins in the darkness all around him. Combs Hair hollered: "Build up the fire!"

Grant called: "Pierriche?"

Falcon's voice came out of the night: "I got no holes in me. How about you?"

"None that I've noticed."

The campfire's embers blossomed into a bonfire. The other hunters were calming the horses while their wives calmed the children. Combs Hair came forward with a torch, wearing nothing but his breechclout. A quick inventory showed that no horses were missing. The Sioux had been interrupted before they could cut any hobbles.

A howling broke out on the other side of the horse herd. The wives of the hunter who'd been standing guard had found their man with his throat slit.

The Sioux who had come up off the ground at Grant was still lying there, coiled tightly around the bullet in his belly and hissing through his teeth. Combs Hair looked down at him and then shoved the torch in his face. There was a scream and the smell of burning hair. Grant started forward toward Combs Hair, but Falcon stepped between them. Combs Hair stood grinning at him over Falcon's shoulder. Grant said: "While you're amusing yourself pulling the wings off flies, we could be catching the rest of them."

Falcon shook his head and said: "By the time there's enough light to track them they'll be back at their village. We can't fight the whole Dakotah Nation."

Combs Hair grunted: "Mighty Wappeston could—if they didn't all run away when they heard him coming."

In the morning they buried the unlucky sentry, piling rocks over the grave to keep the wolves from digging him up. The wounded Sioux had crawled off somewhere to die or—Grant hoped—to live long enough to serve as an example. The cart ponies were hitched back between the shafts, and the hunting party lurched into motion on the trail of the herd.

Combs Hair scouted ahead with Alex Kennedy, a young métis who'd been barely Marie McGillis's age when he'd ridden with Grant from the Qu'Appelle to Seven Oaks. As the sun reached its height, a horseman broke over a distant ridge and came galloping back toward the carts. Falcon said: "It's Alex."

Grant squinted at the dust-blurred, fingernail-size stick figure and said: "How can you tell?"

Falcon shrugged. "It's Alex." Once again Grant gave in to the fact that no amount of years in the country where he'd been born would ever replace the formative decade he'd wasted in foreign schools.

Alex Kennedy leaped off his horse, shouting: "The herd's there! Just over that ridge!" Grant jumped off his saddle horse, tore off his saddle pad, and went running for his buffalo runner. The other hunters were all doing the same thing.

As Grant knotted the cinch strap around his buffalo runner, she began to snort and skip. He peeled the sleeve off his rifle, tossed it into one of the carts, and checked to make sure his shot pouch was full. When it came time to charge into the herd, he would fill his mouth with musket balls because his hands would be occupied with his rifle and powder flask. He was just climbing into the saddle when he heard a distant popping sound, followed immediately by a wave of rolling thunder. The thunder didn't stop but became less ear-shaking as it moved farther away. Falcon spat: "Son of a bitch!" Grant kicked his horse into a gallop toward the ridge with the other four chasing along to catch up.

He knew exactly what he was going to see when he crested the ridge, but he refused to believe until he saw it. Below him was a smashed plain of hammered-flat grasses and brush, punctuated by three twitching dark brown hummocks. The horizon was a churning swath of black and brown with a dust cloud hovering over it.

As the cloud disappeared over the horizon, Combs Hair came trotting back to the nearest dead buffalo. By the time Grant reached him, Combs Hair had already cut out the steaming liver and was happily slicing off bites with his skinning knife as the blood ran down his chin. Grant clamped both his knees hard into his buffalo runner's ribs and jumped down as she reared to a halt. He was only two steps away from Combs Hair when Falcon rode his horse in between them, saying: "Wappeston—don't . . ."

Combs Hair smiled and swallowed. "If you want to kill some meat of your own—they went that way."

Grant said: "They won't stop running now until dark!"

Combs Hair shrugged. "Ain't my fault if you can't catch them." He came around the rump of Falcon's horse, chewing up the last mouthful of liver and licking his knife. "I been wondering, Wappeston . . . did the Crees give you that name 'cause you got the heart of a white weasel? Or was it because you disappear when you hear the footsteps of a man? Or was it maybe because"—he lined the blade of the skinning knife along Grant's nose to let him smell the blood—"you like to sneak along sucking the blood from what real hunters have killed?"

There was a curious sensation that Grant experienced from time to time. All the colors within his field of vision became deeper and richer. His heart kicked into a pace that pumped twice as much blood as his body was built to accommodate. Just at the point when it felt as though his veins were about to burst, there was a snapping sound in his mind.

His left arm shot up, slapping against the tender underside of Combs Hair's knife wrist. At the same time, his right hand grabbed the front tail of Combs Hair's breechclout and twisted it upward. The mighty hunter's eyes bugged out and his empty hands fluttered to keep his balance.

Falcon drawled down from his horse: "Yeah, it mighta been for all those reasons that they named him after an animal as fast as a rattlesnake, and maybe a couple of other reasons more. Hey, Wappeston—" He nudged Grant with the toe of his moccasin. "This here Combs Hair might look big enough, but it's still just trash fish. Throw it back and let's go on about our business."

Grant released his hold on Combs Hair's breechclout and turned to get back on his horse. From behind him he heard a thump such as might be made by a wooden stirrup kicked against flesh, and Falcon said: "Don't be stupid. I just saved your life—or the lives of your unborn children."

Grant and Falcon rode back to the carts and switched their saddle pads from the buffalo runners to their saddle horses. They left the hunting party behind and rode northwest, angling around the wooded folds of Turtle Mountain toward the upper reaches of the Souris River. Halfway through the morning of the next day, Falcon whipped his horse toward a plume of smoke. Two tipis and half a dozen awninged carts were perched in a grove of poplars beside the ford that had proved treacherous.

After the cacophony of "What the hell took you so long?" "Look who I brought back!" and "Where the hell's my wife?" one of the occupants of the camp managed to get in: "Mary and Josephte went picking berries—should be back soon. But in the meantime, here's someone you might want to say hello to."

Grant followed the gesturing hand down to a knee-high, caramel-colored butterball blinking up at him with big black eyes. He crouched down to put his eyes on her level and said: "Maria Theresa? . . ."

"Papa!" She hit him midthroat like a pudding shot from a cannon and knocked him slantwise to Sunday, laughing.

CHAPTER 6

The straggling little settlement at the forks of the Red and Assiniboine rivers was entering into its golden days. The poplars rippled bright gold, the oaks red gold, and the elms a garish yellow gold. The Scots colonists and a few of the more ambitious retired fur traders were sickling through fields of gold.

Marie McGillis rowed across to Fort Garry with her mother, to help carry back the blanket cloth she was going to use to make new winter coats for Daniel and Donald, who were growing out of their clothes even faster than they could wear them out. As the prow of the boat touched the landing place, one of the young men lounging around the fort gates came bounding down to help draw it ashore and offered to carry whatever needed carrying.

Marie said: "We can manage just fine, thank you." It was amazing how interchangeable and callow the young men of Red River had become in the course of the last few weeks.

His eagerness flagged only for an instant. "Well, when you're ready to go home I'll row your boat for you."

"Then how would you get back across?" That stumped him. Marie left him puzzling it over and followed her mother up the bank.

The fort was in a moderate bustle. A few of the hunters had brought in their cartloads of pemmican and buffalo robes to trade, but most of them would stay out on the plains until the first snow. As Marie and her mother came up to the steps of the trading store, Cuthbert Grant stepped out the door. He looked more tanned and fit than when she'd seen him last, and he was carrying a hefty little brown-skinned girl who looked to be about three years old. He was flanked by a stringy young boy and an elegantly thin, if somewhat pinch-faced, métis woman. "Ah, good morning, Mrs. McGillis, Miss McGillis."

Marie's mother said: "Good morning, Mister Grant."

"This lump of underdone buffalo suet"—tickling the little girl's belly as she chortled happily—"is my daughter, Maria Theresa. Say 'how d'you do,' Maria Theresa."

"Won't!"

Mrs. McGillis said: "Ain't you the pretty little thing? And ain't you glad to have your papa home?"

"No!"

Marie just stood rooted behind her mother, forcing a polite smile that she hoped looked natural.

Mister Grant indicated the woman and the boy and said: "This is my sister Mrs. Josephte Wills and her son, John. Mrs. McGillis and her daughter, Marie." They said their hellos. "Well, I'd love to stay and chat, but we're trying to set up housekeeping before I have to start earning my salary. There are a couple of abandoned hunters' cabins on the east bank we're going to shore up for the winter."

Mrs. McGillis said: "If there's anything we can do to help . . ."

"Thank you, we just might take you up on that. Oh, and tell Angus that his buffalo runner was almost worth the price—and the moccasins were worth a good deal more. Good day."

Marie was desperate to ask her mother a question, but she managed to contain herself through the extended bartering in the company store and the blanket-burdened walk back to the boat. Then she had to get the boat launched and turned around and work the oars while her mother gave directions from the stern. But once they were halfway across, and there was no one to overhear, she said as idly as she could manage: "I couldn't help but wonder, Mama—but I thought maybe it'd be rude to ask him—who her mother is."

"Whose mother?"

"Maria Theresa—Mister Grant's little daughter."

"It wouldn't've been rude, but it likely would've been embarrassing for him. She's long gone."

"Dead?"

"Not likely. With her kind, bad things only happen to the people around them."

"You know her?"

"As much as I'd ever want to. Madelaine Desmarais. Her family used to come in to trade when your father was working the Qu'Appelle posts. The way I heard the story, she fastened on to Mister Grant when he was looking for someone to help dance away his troubles. When the dancing stopped and the troubles stayed, she lit out and left him with the baby."

"Where is she now?"

"God knows. Going from one hunter to another, depending on who's had a lucky season or a good run at cards. You better lean harder on your right oar."

In the afternoon Marie was helping her mother dig out the potatoes, listening to her father spitting Gaelic curses at the building materials he was busying himself with, when Cuthbert Grant came out of the path through the woods, balancing his daughter on his head. She was screaming with delight and terror and kept wrapping her legs around his eyes. He stopped beside the garden and said: "Here I thought I was being so wise in clearing out of my sister's way, and it appears I'll only get in yours."

"Not at all!" Marie's father barked from the direction of the barn, stomping forward. "Gives me an excuse to stop for a cup of tea before I burn that *bheannachd* rope or hang myself with it."

"Rope?"

"Or so it calls itself. *Rinneadh* bloody serpent, more like. I have to add a byre onto the side of the barn before winter to house the new heifer. Wouldn't have to if I'd built a big enough bloody barn to begin with, but—So clever me figures better to build something that'll last. I hacked me down a couple of oak trees and adzed them into post beams that'll last out the last days. I dug me a couple of good deep postholes to set them into, and all I got to do is hoist 'em up with a block and tackle and drop them into the holes. Damned clever, eh? Only thing I didn't figure is, the only place to fix the block and tackle is the barn roof and the angle means the *bheannachd* rope just swings them *rinneadh* beams away from the holes."

Mister Grant scratched his rounded, cleft prow of a chin and said: "Mind if I have a look?"

"Help yourself. It'll make for a good story when the subject of what an idiot McGillis is comes up."

Marie went back to poking her fingers into dank mounds of earth and feeling around for living lumps among the root tendrils. She had already seen what Mister Grant was going to have a look at. The two beams were each about a foot square and almost as long as the height of the house. They were stretched out on the horse-cropped grass with their ends pointed roughly toward the holes that had been dug to receive them.

After a moment the two men came back toward the potato patch with Mister Grant horsey-ing Maria Theresa on the crook of his arm and Marie's father grumbling: "You'll break your back."

"One way to find out. Don't worry, Angus—if I feel anything start to crack, I'll just drop it on your foot. Miss McGillis, would you mind, just for a moment . . . ?" And he slung Maria Theresa down in front of her.

Marie leaned up onto her knees, dusting off her hands on her skirt, and looked into the oversize black eyes, as opaque and fathomless as their father's. Marie reached out her right hand with the forefinger extended, and both little brown hands came up to wrap themselves around it. Marie's and Maria Theresa's fathers were heading back toward the barn. Mister Grant untucked his shirt, looked back over his shoulder, muttered, "Excuse me," and pulled it off over his head.

Marie squatted down cross-legged to watch and pulled Maria Theresa into her lap, shushing her apprehensive mewlings. Mr. McGillis picked up a long-handled maul leaning against the barn and took up a position by the beam end that was nearest to one of the postholes. Mister Grant slung his shirt over the paddock fence and crouched down at the other end of the beam with his forearms between his knees. "Ready, Angus?"

"Ready to watch you break your back."

The back in question erupted into a relief map of the Highlands, and the arms bent outward and then inward. Mister Grant shot straight up with the beam end balanced on the heels of his hands, straightening his legs as soon as his arms reached their fullest extension, all in one smooth motion. One instant the end of the beam was on the ground, the next it was seven feet in the air, supported by a pillar of long arms swelling into massive shoulders and tapering down to the waist and trouser-straining thighs.

Marie heard a funny, muffled gasp from beside her and looked over to see her mother gawking in a decidedly unmatronly manner. Mrs. McGillis winked and whispered: "Well, there's no law against looking."

Marie looked back toward the barn. Mister Grant had started shuffling his feet forward, walking his hands along the beam to sharpen its angle. He stopped and braced himself and nodded down at her father, who bunted his end of the beam with the maul and then hauled off and whacked it hard. The earthbound end of the beam jumped forward. Mister Grant jumped forward with it, maintaining the upward angle, and barked: "Again!" They went through the same performance twice more. On the third whack the beam gave a smaller jolt forward and shot downward into the hole. Mister Grant ran along underneath, bouncing his hands under the beam until it swiveled straight up into the hole. He leaped to catch it and hold it before it overbalanced.

Mr. McGillis exchanged the maul for a spade and hurried to shovel in the earth while Mr. Grant stood hugging the post beam in place. When the hole was filled with earth, Mr. McGillis stamped it down, then threw the shovel aside and packed it tighter with the maul. After one last whack with the maul, he cricked his back straight, using the maul for a cane, and said: "It's done!"

Mister Grant pushed himself away from the planted beam and slumped forward with one hand still leaned against it and his rib cage swelling out and in. Mr. McGillis shook his head and said: "I think perhaps we should pause for a pot of tea before tackling the next one."

Mister Grant managed to gasp out, "If you say so," and they both laughed.

Marie's mother got up and went into the house to put the kettle on. The men stumbled back toward the garden, Mister Grant wiping his face and chest with his shirt, and flung themselves down on the grass beside Marie. By the time Mrs. McGillis came out with the tea and Mister Grant's boots, which Marie had spent an evening cleaning and polishing, Mister Grant's swollen muscles had smoothed down to near normal configurations and the red mottling on his skin had begun to fade. Some of the red patches wouldn't fade so easily, though—the scratches along the base of his neck and shoulder where he'd hugged the rough-adzed beam in place. Marie wanted to tell him that she had some bethroot and willow bark inside the house to make a poultice the way Unpredictable Loon had taught her. But when she rehearsed in her mind the right way to make the offer, she could hear him replying that they were only little scratches and he didn't put much stock in Indian superstitions anyway. Mister Grant might be Chief of the Métis Nation, but in some ways he seemed more of an educated white man than any of the white men she'd met, and the whites couldn't seem to tell the difference between medicine women like Unpredictable Loon and the mystic men and women with their rattles and visions.

By the time he was halfway through his second cup of tea, his breathing had settled down enough for him to say conversationally: "It's going to take me a while to sort out the geography of this place—the human geography, that is."

Marie's father said: "This place?"

"The Red River Settlement, or Colony, or whatever it chooses to call itself. You see, until Mister Simpson took it in mind to stamp me with the Company's seal of approval, it didn't seem politic to spend a great deal of time here. And the place has grown up since the days I knew it."

Mr. McGillis shrugged. "Ain't much to get familiar with. It all breaks down to the churches."

"The churches?"

"Like this—" Her father leaned forward and drew a wobbly line in the dirt, then another line running into its side. "This here's the Forks, with Fort Garry *there*. Now, over on *our* side of the river is the Catholic church—there. Nobody in his right mind wants to have to be going back and forth across the Red to go to church, and around freeze-up and breakup you can't cross at all without taking your life in your hands, so most of the Catholics live on the east bank. This is a few old-time Canadian freemen like Jean Baptiste Lajimodierre that didn't want to go back to Lower Canada, some métis hunters whose wives got tired of living their whole lives in tents, and a few retired Highland fur traders who were fortunate enough to have ancestors who didn't betray the true religion of the Stuarts."

"Spare me the Papist sophistry, Angus."

"The true religion is also why—" he drew a scratchy little line running into the Red from the east— "the Des Meurons got given land along the Seine, or German Creek, as they're calling it now. German-Swiss or not, the most of them are children of Mother Church, so the land they were given was on this side of the river.

"Now over on the west bank is mostly the Protestant side. Except for Fort Garry, which is dedicated to the Company's religion, that we all know is 'Profitant.' Heh heh, 'Profitant.' At any rate . . .

"For a couple miles north from Fort Garry you got nothing on the west side until you get to Point Douglas and Fort Douglas. From there north for a few miles is the Kildonan colony—what we used to call the Selkirk colony before the earl of Selkirk renamed it in honor of . . ." He trailed off with a sudden fit of throat clearing.

Mister Grant said dryly, "In honor of the Highland refugees from Kildonan parish, who clung stubbornly to their new homes even after

I'd burned them out twice and massacred a sizable segment of the male population."

"And *here*, right about the midpoint of Kildonan, is their Church of St. John's."

" 'St. John's'? That sounds a bit idolatrous for a Gaelic Presbyterian kirk. . . ."

"It isn't—it's Anglican. You see, the gentleman the Colony appointed to go out and fetch back a minister just happened to be Anglican, and he decided . . . The Presbyterians didn't *quite* lynch him, and they've worked out a compromise. The Anglican minister will soft-pedal the doxology and the Presbyterians will attend. However . . ." Marie's father began to chortle. "The Anglicans always stand to sing and sit to pray, while the Presbyterians sit to sing and stand to pray, so at any given point in the service . . ." Mr. McGillis started laughing so hard, he could only flap his hands up and down by way of illustration until he found enough breath to wheeze out: "I wonder sometimes that the poor reverend don't get seasick."

Out of all the facets Marie had seen so far of Cuthbert Grant, the current one was the most surprising: laughing at her father's jokes, leaning forward to study the dirt map as though it were intensely interesting to him.

"Going north along the river from Kildonan," her father carried on, "are a few more retired traders like yours truly—except they happen to be of the Protestant heresy.

"Well, that's about all there is to the place. Oh—except for Chief Peguis's Saulteaux north of the rapids. Some of the missionaries are trying to turn them into Christian farmers, but I don't know if they stand much chance."

Mister Grant smiled. "Old Peguis was always a recalcitrant old heathen."

Mr. McGillis shrugged. "It ain't so much the religion, it's the farming. And the other tribes. The Crees are still talking about driving the Saulteaux back east where they came from."

"That wouldn't bode well for the Red River Settlement farmers caught in between."

Her father cackled. "Hell, that's the least of their worries! If the Sioux or the Assiniboine was ever to take a good look at all these here rich-looking farms stretched out naked along the banks of the Red—" He choked himself off with another series of false throat clearings and dropped his head to shoot a surreptitious glance at his wife and daughter. "Not that there's any danger of that, of course—the Indians need the Company too much to . . ."

Mister Grant looked again at the fractured mosaic her father had scratched in the dirt and said: "The more you tell me about this little pastoral haven, the more it appears to be a collection of powder kegs rubbing against each other."

"No, no, no—not at all. All the different groups keep pretty much to themselves. So long as no one tosses in a match to set them off . . ."

Mister Grant's eyes shot up toward her father's. The black eyes and the gray riveted together for an instant, then the black eyes drifted away in Marie's direction and suddenly disappeared into laugh lines.

"Good God!" Mister Grant pointed at Maria Theresa sleeping in her lap. "She won't even do that for my sister, after a year of Josephte being 'Mama.' I do hope, Marie, that when the time comes, a certain unknown young man—or perhaps he's known already?—will appreciate how lucky he is.

"Well, Angus, I think I've caught my breath sufficiently to plant another tree."

CHAPTER 7

"Good morning, Mister Grant," said the junior clerk.

"Good morning, Mister Hargrave."

"Did you have good hunting out on the plains?"

"Fair to middling. Is Mister Simpson in his office?"

"I believe so. Just let me announce you." James Hargrave slid off his stool and went to the door to the inner office. He rapped on it with the knuckles of his left hand and simultaneously poked his head in to say: "Mister Grant is—"

He was cut off by an enraged bellow from beyond the door. He yanked his head back out like a man discovering a wolverine in his woodshed, snatched the door shut, and stood red-faced, looking down at the floor.

It looked as though he had just worked up the courage to try knocking again when George Simpson's voice cut through the woodwork: "All right, send him in." Without raising his eyes off the floor, Hargrave held the door open for Grant and then closed it behind him.

As Grant was stepping into the long white room, someone else was skipping out through the side door behind Mister Simpson's desk, someone in a brightly beadworked dress. "Ah, Grant. You must excuse me—my bit of circulating copper is presuming to act like a wife, and that always puts me in a temper. High time I had her put off at York Factory or some other out-of-the-way place. But enough. Did you have a successful journey?"

Grant couldn't help replying ingenuously: "Twelve bags of pemmican and eight buffalo robes." If George Simpson wanted to play it coy about the real reason he wanted Grant to go rambling around Pembina, Grant could play, too.

"Ah. Well, that should help augment your meager salary. And I suppose you took the opportunity to reacquaint yourself with old friends and various relatives?"

"Yes, there were several campfire conversations that went on into the depths of the evening. We'll see what the results of them are in a month or so when the hunters come back from the plains."

"Well, I suppose you'll want to get settled in to work. Come along and I'll get you started. I'll have the fort carpenter knock up a desk and stool of your own, but in the meanwhile you can take over McDermott's desk." McDermott didn't look too pleased about it but kept his mouth shut. "Now, you'll see here that we keep a separate ledger for each district. . . ."

Grant followed him through the general breakdown of the Company's accounting practices, saving questions about details for the other clerks. Simpson was in the process of showing him an example of the annual account submitted to the London Committee by the Northern Department, when a pair of heavy boots stomped through the front doorway and a gritty voice grated: "I didn't believe it when they told me, so I had to come see for myself."

Grant turned around to see a portly man with a florid face framed by a bristling jaw beard. They had met before. Alex MacDonell had been sheriff of the Selkirk colony and the man who'd put his name to the terms of surrender for Fort Douglas, because all his superiors in the colony hierarchy lay in the tangle of corpses at Seven Oaks.

George Simpson said to him: "And now that you've seen whatever it was you came to see, you can go on about your business and allow us to carry on with ours."

"I don't know what the hell you think you're about, Simpson— whether you're just plain daft or too high and mighty for your own good—but I'm here to tell you that we'll not have *that* man at Red River."

The governor of the Northern Department's watery blue eyes began to glitter like sunlight bouncing off a glacier. "To whom exactly are you referring by 'we,' MacDonell? Your own wee self? Or perhaps your wee caucus of like-minded drunkards on the wee council of your wee little colony? If the latter is the case, allow me to remind you that the colony has no say whatever in how I choose to administer the Northern Department of the Company of Adventurers Trading into Hudson's Bay."

"You can go on all you like, my wee mannie," said MacDonell, "about administering this and that. It won't mean a pinch of snuff to the people who saw their brothers and neighbors butchered by *that man there.*"

"Mister MacDonell," Grant interjected, "if you have anything to say regarding what you will or will not stand for from 'that man there'—he's standing right here."

"Aye, you'd like that, wouldn't you—you bullying bastard. If you're fool enough to stay where you're not wanted, on your own head be it." He turned on his boot heel and stomped out.

The governor of the Northern Department said: "Now you'll notice here, Grant, if you follow along this list of exports versus imports . . ."

When Simpson had sealed himself back into his private office, Grant said to McDermott: "Be a good fellow and take your desk back, would you? It's going to take me a couple of days at least of circulating among the three of you, looking over your shoulders and asking harebrained questions, before I'm ready to put pen to paper."

On the third morning the fort carpenter proudly presented a new-minted desk and stool. Grant jumped back into a river of numbers and was pleasantly surprised to discover that he hadn't forgotten how to swim. There was something immediately gratifying about adding up three columns of figures in his head and then discovering when he went through the painstaking process of toting them up that the totals matched exactly.

It took him a while to get accustomed to the Hudson's Bay Company's method of balancing the books, which the old North West Company traders never would have stood for. When the annual ship pulled into York Factory with the trade goods for the coming year, part of its return cargo was to be a full accounting for the outfit of the preceding year. It meant that the London Committee got to gaze proudly at a growing shelf of ledgers labeled "Outfit of 1820," "Outfit of 1821," etcetera, and the traders scattered across Rupert's Land got to choose between overordering and incurring the wrath of the committee or underordering and disappointing those trappers who brought their furs in after the outfit for that year had all been traded away. It wasn't the way Grant would have run things, but until he rose to the rank of chief trader or chief factor and began to share in the profits, it was none of his business—literally.

In the evenings he carried on with the job of winterproofing the pair of swaybacked old cabins he'd commandeered for his flotsam-and-jetsam excuse for a family. When pellets of sod filtered down into his eyes from the aged roofs, he reminded himself that two side-by-side cabins were a godsend, even if they were as decrepit as the Ancient Mariner. Josephte and John could have their own home, and he and Maria Theresa could have theirs, and if, by chance, Maria Theresa were to find a new stepmother . . .

Sunday found him at loose ends. The roofs of both cabins had been shored up and patched; he had refilled all the gaps in the walls where the old clay and moss chinking had been flaking away; the cracks in the clay-and-latticework chimneys had been mended and the flues cleaned out with a bundle of spruce branches on a *shagganappi* rope. The endless cosmetic fussing and puttering with the interiors was Josephte's bailiwick.

Mister Simpson preferred that his employees attend divine services on Sundays. Whether it was due to any strong religious leanings on Mister Simpson's part or simply a matter of appearances and Company policy, Grant hadn't asked, and he doubted whether Simpson knew the difference. But he also suspected that Mister Simpson would be glad to make an exception in his case, for the sake of keeping the peace. Grant had been baptized Presbyterian, but if Alex MacDonell was anything to go by, it would probably be politic to give the Kildonan people a few months to get used to his presence in the vicinity before thrusting himself into their church.

Josephte was getting Maria Theresa and John gussied up to make the walk to St. Boniface Church. When the first missionaries had appeared in the *pays d'en haut*, Josephte had already spent several years as a widowed mother living in the households of relatives, including her sister, Mary Falcon, and had fallen in with the general current of the Falcons flowing toward the Catholic mission. Grant wasn't sure he much cared for the notion of Maria Theresa having all this genuflection and pope worship seeping into her when she was too young to think, but it didn't disturb him enough to create a disturbance about it. When the children were sufficiently primped, he swung Maria Theresa up onto his shoulder and said to Josephte: "I'll walk you over to the church and then come back and chop some wood."

"It would do your soul more good to spend an hour in the house of God."

"Our souls won't do us much good if the house of Grant runs out of firewood halfway through February."

The trail to the church led them past Angus McGillis's place. The McGillises came trooping out of the house in their Sunday best and in descending order of size, except for Marie, who brought up the rear to herd the little ones along, carrying her baby brother in a mossbag and cradleboard slung over her shoulder. She was wearing a blue-black dress that contrasted with the black locks of hair poking out from under her shawl. Her hair wasn't the blue-black kind like Grant's, but rather the black that showed chestnut-red highlights when the sun hit it. He didn't have to peel her shawl off to know that there was a flowing mass of soft dark waves underneath it, just as he didn't have to peel her dress off to guess at her shape. In his younger days he might have thought her blocky or pudgy. But he'd had enough general experience since then to suspect that she was one of those shortish women whose shoulders, breasts, and hips happened to be large for her height, so that clothes tended to bag and disguise the in-curved waist inside.

The McGillis and Grant parties fell in together, Angus gibing Grant with: "I thought you were a plain kirk man."

"I am. But if I can't manage to save my sister and her son from idolatry, the least I can do in Christian charity is walk them to the gate."

The churchyard was vibrant with beribboned carts and saddle horses and clans of métis in beadworked vests and rainbow-colored sashes and shawls. Everyone was kissing each other hello. Josephte paused on the church steps to take Maria Theresa from her father. Maria Theresa set up a howl as he peeled her off his shoulder. He cradled her on the crook of his elbow as an interim measure, and she wrapped her arms around his neck in a strangling grip, her howls softening into snufflings. He muttered, "What the hell—when in Rome . . ." and followed the McGillises inside.

He ended up squeezed into a pew next to Marie McGillis, both of them cooing to their respective little fusspots. The fact that the one Marie was trying to shush happened to be named Cuthbert made for a certain amount of confusion and bemusement. The warmth of her thigh traveled through the wool folds of her skirt and the worn-thin buckskin of his trousers. He looked around at the gypsy-bright parishioners crowding onto benches and filling the standing room in the corners. Even the Des Meurons had managed to rustle up relatively white shirts, or at least trim their beards. Grant muttered sideways at Marie McGillis: "I feel like a bit of a wart on the nose of things, with everyone else in their finery and me looking like a farmhand in my Sunday worst."

"You could never look like . . . I mean . . ."

She trailed off into the general hush as the priest stepped to the altar. The momentary silence allowed Grant's memory to replay the sound of Marie McGillis's voice. It was an unusual voice, melodious, but with a permanent light rasp. It was the voice, for all her dewy shyness and sudden bursts of laughter, of an old soul. As soon as that thought passed through his mind, Grant mocked himself for putting such a metaphysical coloring on what was probably the result of a childhood bout of croup.

The priest launched into the mass. Church Latin wasn't quite the same kind taught at Inverness College, but once Grant got his ear attuned he found he could generally understand what the rest of the congregation was only responding to by rote. And it was easy enough to follow them when it came to kneeling or standing or sitting down again in unison. When it came time for communion, he stepped out into the aisle to let the McGillises file past and then sat back down out of the way.

A strange alchemy had been wrought by the mingled elements of the last half hour: the joyful gathering in the churchyard, the choral call-and-response of the mass, the melting warmth of Maria Theresa nodding off in his arms and of Marie McGillis's leg against his. It had created a soothing, soft thrill inside his rib cage that was setting off clangs of alarm in the back of his skull. He'd felt that melting thrill before, back in the days when he was too young to be wary of it. To an orphan who'd come back to a home he'd forgotten, there couldn't have been anything more seductive than to find himself enfolded by the clans of the North West Company and the New Nation. But the only reason he was still alive to recognize the feeling was that he'd bolted back out into the cold at the last instant.

As the celebrants filtered back from the altar, Grant stood up again and stepped aside to clear the way into the pew. From his height he could see over the fringe-yoked shoulders and shawled heads to the mist-sheened black eyes of Marie McGillis coming toward him.

Although he chopped and sawed a goodly pile of firewood over the course of the afternoon, and wolfed down at least a bucketful of

Josephte's venison-and-turnip stew, when he fell into bed he didn't sleep. With a mattress three buffalo robes thick between him and the floor, his wrung-out muscles should have settled in like a sea otter rocked on the waves. Finally he gave in and got up to fetch his pipe and a cup of rum and to toss a couple of quarter rounds of firewood onto the embers in the hearth. He puttered about as quietly as possible so as not to wake Maria Theresa.

He settled back into his bed with his pipe and cup and watched the flame ghosts dance across the pole-and-sod ceiling. Some of the patterns bore an uncanny resemblance to the face of Marie McGillis. She had a heart-shaped face, with a cleft in the chin that looked like an upside-down heart within the larger one.

Some of the other fire patterns looked like the whorls of embroidery or quillwork on the congregation of St. Boniface's little church in the wilderness and on the surplice of the priest. Grant didn't suppose himself any more or less religious than the next man. But there was something undeniably compelling in that communion of shyly reverent, hatchet-faced buffalo hunters and warriors. The alarm bells chimed again.

Grant thought of a wolf pup that Falcon had adopted once. It had run off when it grew old enough to hunt for itself. Falcon swore he'd seen it again on a winter evening years later, standing on a ridge looking down on the snow-capped cabin with its square of warm orange parchment window. He said he'd called to the wolf, but it wouldn't come in.

CHAPTER 8

After helping her mother clean up the breakfast dishes, Marie slung a rawhide bag over her shoulder and walked out onto the prairie to gather rosehips. In the churchyard the day before, some of the neighboring girls had invited her along on an expedition to pick labrador tea today, but she'd told them there was something else she had to do. Marie had never been one to prefer her own company, but she knew that she'd feel more alone among a gaggle of girls her own age. They would be giggling and trading salacious jokes and strategies about their young men. And she couldn't mention the only subject she thought about these days.

Although there was already a breath of winter in the wind buffeting the grass, there was still enough heat left in the sun to make her strip off her shawl once she'd left the river and the trees behind. She drifted from one stand of wild roses to the next, remembering the places where the meadow had been splashed with pink in June. As she plucked the plump, bloodred fruits from among the thorns, she found herself humming a sweetly melancholy song. She'd never been able to understand other people's romantic attachment to the spring. Although she was certainly as delighted as anyone else when the ice began to melt and the black-and-white world of winter blossomed into green, the spring didn't have that quickening undercurrent of all the feathered creatures singing their good-bye songs and all the furry creatures hurrying to get themselves denned and stocked up and mated while there was still time.

She managed to fill up the bag without scratching her fingers deep enough to draw blood, then turned to head homeward. She baked the rosehips dry in the other innovation her father had built into the kitchen fireplace—a thin, broad metal drawer slotted under the hearth—then scooped half of them into a bag to hang in the larder and the other half into another bag. Like all good Indian or métis women, her mother had an ever-replenished collection of beaded rawhide bags, pouches, and envelope-shaped panniers in all sizes.

"Mama," she said, "I'm just going to take these over to the holy fathers. Papa can't stomach rosehip tea anyways."

"Well, he likes rosehip jelly."

"There's plenty left to make jelly."

Except for the weather-grayed cross nailed to the roof peak, the rectory of St. Boniface was indistinguishable from the clay-plastered, squared-log servants' barracks at Fort Garry. Marie came into the churchyard just as the boys not out on the plains with the buffalo hunters were being set free from school. Father Picard stood on the doorstep watching his scholars scamper off in all directions. He pulled open the drawstring to peer in at the rosehips and said: "Bless you, Marie—what a kind thought. The bishop and I were just talking about you."

"About *me*?" The "me" came out as a mouselike squeak, but it was too late to go back and change it.

"Yes. We both agree that it would be a shame that someone with such a quick mind should have to stop her education. It may take years before the bishop can persuade any of the convents in Quebec to start a real girls' school here. And we can't put you in with the boys, of course. But there's no reason why I couldn't take an hour a day alone with you to— Good afternoon, Monseigneur."

Marie turned around to see the bishop of Juliopolis sailing across the churchyard with the hem of his cassock flapping in the wind and his hands clasped behind his back. He was beaming and grinning at the world and slapping the back of his right hand into the palm of the left in time to some jig tune playing in his mind. Although he didn't look markedly different from the plain Father Provencher Marie had first met when her father retired to Red River, the fact that the Pope himself had decided to create a bishopric for him made her duck her head and murmur, "Your Reverence."

The bishop nodded abstractedly in her general direction and sailed on, still beaming. Father Picard winked at her and said: "He's always in a good mood when he's had good fishing. He's just netted a big one."

"A big one?"

"About as big as they get in these waters. Cuthbert Grant."

The next six nights and five days crawled by. Marie dug through her collection of bull-hide moccasin lasts and started working on a pair of real Assiniboine moccasins. The Cree and métis and the other Plains tribes made repeating patterns in a mass of beadwork or isolated images on a background of open leather. The Assiniboines would cover an entire moccasin or shirt yoke with tight-packed beadwork that might have a green triangle in one corner, an orange square in another, and a comet of blue and yellow crossing the middle. Her father referred to it as "tartan designed by a committee of poets," but he was proud enough to wear the ones her mother made for him. She hoped no one would ask her whom these ones were for. She knew she was being the silliest of little fools, but she couldn't help herself. It would take her weeks to finish them.

On Sunday morning the blue shadows under her eyes in the buffed-steel looking glass above the washstand made her slap her face repeatedly with icy water, much to the amusement of her younger sisters. During the parade to the church, she kept looking back over her shoulder or craning her neck to see around her parents on the path ahead of her, but she saw no sign of the Grants. They weren't in the churchyard, either. But as she was settling in on the end of a pew, she saw a close-cropped head of thick black hair several rows ahead, sticking up over the floral shawls and uncovered, shoulder-length manes around him.

After mass she dragged her heels on the way out the door. She had just stepped out into the sunlight when the baritone came down over her shoulder: "Good afternoon, Miss McGillis."

She looked back. Maria Theresa, cradled in his arms, goggled her eyes and stuck out her tongue. Marie poked the end of the velvety pug nose with the tip of a finger. Maria Theresa snorfled and sneezed and giggled.

Unsure whether she was leading or following, Marie stepped sideways out of the flow of parishioners bottlenecked at the doorway. He did the same. She slung her baby brother's cradleboard around in front of her to take the weight off her shoulder and cradled it in both arms. Mister Grant said: "I was thinking of taking a walk out on the prairie while the weather still allows. Might I persuade you to walk out with me?"

They were suddenly surrounded by both their families. She muttered something inarticulate in response. It must have had an agreeable sound to it, because he turned and handed Maria Theresa over to his sister. Marie slipped her arm out of the shoulder strap and extended the cradleboard toward her mother, who seemed strangely reluctant to take it. She did eventually, though, and Marie turned and allowed her legs to carry her along automatically.

The next thing she knew, the buzz of the churchyard had faded behind her and her skirt was swishing through the knee-high grass beside Cuthbert Grant's broadcloth trousers and embroidered moccasins. She could hear the sighing of the wind and the faint cry of one of the last hawks of the year circling overhead. Any other sounds were drowned out by the drumming of her heart and the wind-cave roaring of the air going in and out through her nose.

Mister Grant seemed quite content to stride along in silence, making her hustle to keep up. When he finally did speak, it was to say: "I'm beginning to suspect that my brain has calcified over the years. What with transubstantiations and immaculate conceptions and God knows what else . . . The bishop must be wondering if I'm ever going to get it right. You did know I'm planning to convert? . . ."

"Yes. Father Picard told me." She clamped her mouth shut again.

"The bishop told me you're one of the stars in the firmament of the mission's efforts to educate the female half of the population. I found it rather an embarrassing comparison, actually, to my own feeble study thus far."

She didn't quite know what to say to that and suspected he must be teasing her. Besides, she needed all her breath to keep up with him.

"The bishop also told me you've been besieged with suitors." Now she knew he was teasing her. "Have you come to an arrangement with any of them?"

"Arrangement?"

"To be married."

"No one's asked me."

"More fools they." He came to an abrupt halt. Her momentum carried her on another step or two before she could pull herself up short and turn back. He was looking down at her with an abashed expression on his face. "Oh, dear, look at you—I'm running you into the ground, aren't I? How thoughtless. . . ."

"I'm all right."

He pointed at a copse of poplars off to the right. "We can sit down in the shade and catch our breaths." He started off at an amble and let her set the pace. The rattle of dried grass against her skirt gave way to the crunch of dead leaves underfoot. A few feet inside the border of the poplar grove there was a thigh-high boulder crowned with amber moss. Mister Grant patted the boulder, said, "How's this?" and hunkered down beside it with his back against a tree.

She settled her bottom onto the cushion of moss. The little piece of the world enclosed within the clump of trees seemed soft and dank after coming in off a meadow naked to the noon sun. The air tasted of leaf mold and balsam and the still damp clay that held a pond through most of the summer.

Mister Grant looked at her legs, clucked, "Now look what I've done," and leaned forward to pick the burrs off her Sunday skirt.

"I'll just get more on the way back."

"Not necessarily. Perhaps I'll be more careful of what I'm walking you through." Through the fabric of her skirt, the fingers plucking out the burrs touched against her ankles, her calves, her knees. His head was bent forward over the task at hand. She found it very difficult not to reach up her hand and finger-comb the thick, blue-black, sleek-looking mane. Just as she was about to give in to the impulse, he leaned back against the tree again, slapping his hands together, and shrugged. "Well, I got the most of them, at any rate."

"Thank you."

"My pleasure. Mind if I smoke?" He produced an amber-stemmed meerschaum pipe from a pocket of his coat.

"Of course—I mean, no . . . I mean, go ahead." But it seemed like a lot of trouble to go to for a few puffs of tobacco, since the fastest method Marie had ever seen for getting a flame was to dribble a pinch of gunpowder onto a fistful of dry grass and strike a spark from flint and steel.

He packed his pipe and then reached into another pocket to tug out a flat tin box and flip the lid, exposing a double row of orange beads. He plucked out one of the beads. It was fixed onto the end of a splinter of wood. He closed the lid again and scratched the bead across the base of the box. There was an instantaneous flare of smoke and flame and a choking smell that set her gagging and coughing. He shook out the flame and lurched forward, clasping her knee, saying: "I'm sorry—forgive me. I didn't mean to—are you . . . ?"

"I'm all right."

"I should've thought . . . they do warn on the package that the fumes might . . ."

"What *is* it?"

"Something I brought back from England. I expect they'll become quite common. Just a compound of phosphorous and sulfur on—"

A fit of laughter snapped out of her—one of those embarrassingly childish bursts that she kept trying to curtail. She covered her mouth and recovered her composure enough to try to explain. "Sorry, it just struck me that . . . The bishop and Father Picard and all of them, they always talk about the sulfurous fires of . . . of hell, you see. And I kept asking them what it meant and they tried to tell me, but I couldn't get it. And now, just one little whiff, and now I sure know what they were talking about."

"It's actually even more amusing than you might think. They call these Lucifers."

"You're joking."

"Not at all. They also call them Promethean matches. Prometheus was an ancient Greek Titan who stole fire from the gods and gave it to the human race. The gods chained him to a rock and sent eagles to claw out his liver in punishment. And as you know, Lucifer means 'the bringer of light,' so—"

"No, I didn't know that."

"Oh. Well, it does. Damned strange, don't you think? Essentially the same figure and the same story in two different mythologies—but the pagan Greeks saw Prometheus as a heroic Titan who suffers eternally for making their lives better, while we Christians see Lucifer as . . . ." He trailed off with a dark chuckle and sucked on the stem of his unlit pipe.

She said: "If you want to light another one, I can hold my nose."

"Thank you, that's very good of you. Here goes. . . ." Once he got his pipe going he really started talking, of London and Montreal and Inverness, of the Blackfoot and the Sioux and the Cree, of Pierre Falcon and Robert Burns.

She reveled in the river of his words like an otter. When the current slowed she would ask him a question such as "How'd your buffalo hunting go?" and get a waterfall of tumbling plans to weld the scattered family groups of métis hunters into one immense caravan that could defy anyone.

Finally he cocked his eyes toward the sky and said: "Good God— I've kept you out till sunset." He stood and reached down a hand to help her up. As she straightened her knees he moved forward and bowed down. His mouth met hers. His forearms locked around the small of her back and he wafted her up off the ground, still kissing her. The front of his body melded against hers.

He put her feet back on the ground and broke away abruptly, muttering hoarsely: "I'd best get you home before your father loads his gun." But his hand snaked out to hold hers for the long walk home.

At the edge of the barnyard, he stopped and turned to face her. He said: "I'm afraid I've gone and talked away the day without hearing more than a word from you. Were I to come by again tomorrow evening, would you be willing to walk out with me again?"

She nodded, and he lowered his head to kiss the webs of skin between her knuckles where the back of her hand was curled around his fingers. He let go and disappeared into the darkness.

He didn't come back the next evening. After dinner—telling her mother she was pecking at her whitefish only to be careful of the bones—she went outside and commandeered her father's rocking chair. When the red in the western sky gave way to purple, and the silhouettes of swallows were replaced by scythe-winged nighthawks, she jolted up out of the chair, stomped inside, and scooped a double handful of dried rosehips into a pouch. Her mother said: "What are you doing?"

"I was trying to think of who else we could give some of these to. So I'm going to take them to Mister Grant and his sister." Her mother sighed through her front teeth and turned away.

There was just enough light left to see the pathway winding between the woods and the river. The faces of the two side-by-side cabins were angled just enough toward the west to catch the last cobalt glow. Marie marched to the nearest of the two cabins, snatched hold of the latchstring, and jerked the door open, calling: "Hello!"

The interior was bathed in rosy waves of firelight. The only occupant was a raven-haired woman kneeling on the hearth rug with her back to the door. Her head revolved to look over her shoulder at Marie. The firelight gleamed on a swanlike throat and half-lidded black eyes. A velvety alto voice said: "And who are you?"

"Marie McGillis. I . . . I thought Mister Grant—and his sister were . . . I brought some rosehips. . . ."

The woman uncoiled her long legs, rose up—a good half foot taller than Marie—and moved languidly toward the door. "That's a nice thought, Marie McGillis. We don't want any scurvy in the family. I'm Madelaine Desmarais—Madelaine Grant, that is. I'll tell my husband you came by."

A tight-throated baritone above and behind Marie said: "No need. I can see for myself."

Marie whirled and held up her pouch. "I brought some rosehips. I thought . . ."

The varnished wooden mask hung in the night said: "Thank you."

Madelaine Desmarais said: "Here, child—I'll take them." Marie turned again and released the pouch into Madelaine Desmarais's hand.

Mister Grant said: "Come along, Marie, I'll walk you home."

Madelaine Desmarais smiled. "I doubt she's in any danger of being jumped by a gang of rowdy bucks hereabouts—more's the pity, for her sake."

"I said I'd walk her home. Come along, Marie."

Marie plodded back along the pathway with her head down and her right arm scalded by the hand clasped around it. When they reached the point where the amber light shone clearly through the windows of her father's house, Mister Grant stopped and said: "Believe me, Marie, if I had thought for one instant that she might . . . Our marriage was only à la façon du pays. But I can't change the fact that she is the mother of my child."

"Of course. I understand. Good-bye." She shook her arm free and headed toward the light.

In the morning she went straight to confession while the rest of the family was busy with breakfast. The silhouette through the grill was Father Picard's. The screen of confessional anonymity was only a formality in a community with three priests. "Forgive me, Father, for I have sinned."

"What sins have you committed, my daughter?"

"I prayed for somebody to die."

CHAPTER 9

Grant was pleasantly surprised to wake up to the sensation of a woman's body curled against his. Then he remembered who it was. He disentangled himself without waking her, stood up, and pulled on his trousers. Maria Theresa's little bed in the corner—a doubled buffalo robe with a shawl-size rabbit blanket—was empty. She must have toddled across to Josephte's cabin for breakfast. He picked up his shirt off the floor and stood looking down at Madelaine Desmarais.

Even in sleep, there was a look to her of barely suppressed animation. It was amazing, given the way she lived her life, that there was nothing haggard about her. Her skin had that shimmering rose-and-ivory blush that came out in some métis women, like the skin of a ripe crab apple. He reminded himself that she was, after all, only a few years older than Marie McGillis. Women tended to grow up quickly in the *pays d'en haut.*

He shucked on his shirt and went over to the cabin next door. Josephte and John and Maria Theresa were attacking bowls of porridge and maple syrup. Josephte got up to fill another bowl and slapped it down on his place at the table. Maria Theresa strained mightily to swallow her current mouthful, dribbling only a little onto her chin, and said: "Papa—do I got to call her 'Mama'?"

"That's who she is, Maria Theresa."

"She going to stay with us?"

"Yes."

Josephte said: "For how long this time?"

"For good."

"I wouldn't call that 'for good.' What was 'for good,' up until last night, was that it looked like you'd finally grown enough sense to get yourself a real wife."

"I see no reason why Madelaine and I can't formalize our marriage, as soon as the bishop is satisfied that I know what I'm converting to." She opened her mouth, but he said, "Josephte—one can't simply discard people for the sake of convenience."

"That one does."

"You've had your say." The rest of breakfast passed in silence, except for slurping sounds and the glutinous clatter of porridge bowls and spoons. Grant scraped the bottom of his bowl and stood up.

"Thank you. Now I'd best get myself shaved and dressed and be off to earn our livings." He filled a cup with hot water from Josephte's kettle and carried it back toward his own cabin and the razor waiting on the mantelpiece, where Maria Theresa couldn't get her hands on it.

Madelaine was awake and dressed and on her knees scouring out the fireplace. She grinned at him over her shoulder. "Good morning! If I'm going to be able to cook you anything that don't taste like old soot and ashes, I figured I'd better—" She was cut off by a sudden fit of coughing that racked and twisted her. Rocking back and forth on her knees, she clutched her ribs with her arms. It didn't stop. Grant ran to the mantelpiece, slapped down the cup, and snatched up the little brass key from its place beside his razor. He crouched beside the black wooden trunk he'd brought back from England and fumbled with the lock. Inside were two cantilevered racks housing glass jars of powders and liquids, with other articles jammed into the space beneath.

The coughing behind him was growing thicker and deeper, the gasps of breath more desperate. He finally managed to get the lid open, snatched out the laudanum bottle, and jerked out the stopper as he whirled around to grab Madelaine. While his right hand pressed her head against his chest and forced it back, his left hand tilted the bottle over her mouth. She choked and gasped and fought, and then the coughing stopped.

He let her go. She hauled in half a dozen deep breaths, gazing at him with eyes of wonder. Her chin and the bodice of her dress were dappled with tarry droplets of laudanum and flecks of bloody sputum. She wiped her lips and chin with her hand and said: "How . . . ? How did you do that?"

"I apprenticed myself to a doctor while I was in London. Laudanum isn't a cure, but it will stop the coughing. Tincture of opium. Take too much and it will stop your breathing. It was dangerous as hell for me to feed it to you that way, but I had to take the chance that only a little would get down." While he'd been talking, he'd uncased a segmented wooden tube from the bottom of his medicine trunk and fitted it together. "Lift up your blouse."

"Didn't you get enough of that last night?"

"Lift up your blouse." He pressed the end of the stethoscope against her ribs and listened, trying to recollect the exact sound he'd been taught to listen for. The amplified booming of her heart was almost drowned out by a crackling, rattling wheezing. He took the stethoscope apart and fitted its pieces back inside each other. "How long have you had tuberculosis?"

"Had what?"

"The coughing sickness."

"It isn't—"

"It is. We've both seen enough of it to know."

She began to cry. "I don't know how long. At first it was just once in a while. I thought it was just from too much smoke in a tent or . . . It's just the last year or so that . . ."

"It isn't irrevocable. If you don't put any strain on yourself, if you settle into a slow and steady life for long enough to give your body a chance to replenish itself, there's every chance your lungs will heal themselves. The air is clean and dry here." He found where the stopper had rolled and set the laudanum bottle on the mantel beside the razor. He added, in a flat, professional tone without looking at her: "If it starts again, just take a tiny sip, no more. The safest method is three drops in a cup of water, if your hands aren't too convulsed to pour."

He locked the medicine casket again, propped his shaving mirror on the mantel, and lathered up. The cup of hot water was no better than lukewarm, and his hands were shaking, so he took it one careful stroke at a time. His hands gradually steadied to the point where he figured he could trust his voice to say matter-of-factly: "That's why you came back, isn't it?"

"No!"

"Madelaine—I'm not some boy you met last night."

"Well, if it was because of that, a little bit, it was only so much as . . . I *wanted* to come back, so many times, but I was afraid you hated me for running off. But when this started to get so bad, I finally got more scared of dying alone than I was of you hating me."

"Well . . . we'll win out over it, you'll see." He toweled off the remaining ridges of lather, shrugged on his coat, and headed for the door. She began to laugh. He stopped and turned back.

She managed to suppress her laughter long enough to sputter out: "They ain't going to believe you."

"Who won't? What?"

"No one's going to believe you if you tell them you had to force a bottle between my lips."

Gauging by the height of the sun when he launched his canoe into the Red, he was late for work; by the chill still hanging over the water, he was early. He plied his paddle automatically and set his mind to accepting the fact that his best-laid schemes had ganged just about as a-gley as they possibly could. He didn't believe for a moment that Madelaine had come running back because of any deep wellspring of feeling for him or Maria Theresa. Madelaine would never be more than vaguely aware of anyone or anything beyond herself and what she wanted at the moment. But now that a settled home life was her best chance to keep alive the only living thing she'd ever loved, she could be relied upon to play the part of wife and mother with energy and élan.

He beached the canoe on the western shore and climbed up the bank to Fort Garry. The gatekeeper called out a cheery "Good morning." Grant nodded and walked on toward the countinghouse. The other clerks pried their noses out of their ledgers as he came through the door. James Hargrave said: "Good morning, Grant— Good God! Late night last night?"

"Something like that. My wife came home."

"Your—?"

"Have we got back the figures from the meeting at Norway House yet?"

The southwest quadrant of the sky was red and orange by the time Grant pushed his canoe back into the water. Usually, if he were heading home this late, he'd go straight to Josephte's cabin to apologize and to make a show of enthusiastically gobbling up whatever she'd left warming in the pot for him before collecting Maria Theresa and putting her to bed. Tonight he went directly to his own place and pulled open the door.

Madelaine was humming to herself and rigging up a curtain made of blanket cloth across the corner where their bed lay. Maria Theresa was lying stiffly in her own bed, pretending to be trying to go to sleep. Madelaine said: "I made some fish soup! Maria Theresa ate up a whole bowl all by herself, didn't you, Maria Theresa?"

Maria Theresa murmured: "Yes, Mama."

Grant sat down to eat his soup and to listen to Madelaine chatter melodiously about the various plates and skillets and pantry supplies she was going to have to get from the Company store. In the middle of the list she paused to give a couple of delicate little coughs—more like throat clearings than anything to do with her chest—and reached for the laudanum bottle.

Grant said: "You'd best be spartan with that stuff. When that bottle's gone there won't be any more. I can order more in my personal outfit when the spring brigade goes out to York Factory, but it'll be another year and more after that while the supply ship goes back and forth across the ocean and the brigade brings the outfit upstream from the bay."

"They must have laudonull—"

"Laudanum."

"—in Montreal. The Montreal brigade could bring you back another bottle quicker'n that."

"There aren't going to be any more Montreal brigades, just a single express canoe for Company dispatches."

"The express canoe couldn't carry one little bottle? . . ."

"No doubt they could—in exchange for a month of my salary."

"Since when did you worry about the cost of anything?"

"Since I spent three years trying to live without an income."

She wrinkled her nose into a pretty pout, lisped, "Yeth, Papa," and set the bottle back on the mantelpiece. He laughed and shook his head and went back to his soup.

By Sunday he'd grown so accustomed to the presence of Madelaine that he was caught off guard when they encountered the McGillis family in the churchyard. Madelaine was visibly miffed when Maria Theresa toddled over to Marie McGillis and demanded to be picked up. Angus did his best to make jovial conversation, but it didn't hold up. Grant asked Marie how she was today.

"Fine, thank you, Mister Grant."

Madelaine said, "We better be getting on in before all the benches get filled up," and took Maria Theresa back.

On the way home, Madelaine said airily: "It'll sure make things awkward for you if you've gone and got her pregnant like you did me."

"There's no danger of that."

She blinked at him and then laughed. "My, my—you're turning into quite the monk in your old age, aren't you?"

"Madelaine—I am willing to accept the fact that things are as they are. Were I you, I wouldn't try to spoil them."

The following afternoon he was jolted out of inking in the accounts for the Athabaska District by nearby gunfire and bellowing and the hoofbeats of galloping horses. He looked out the window to see a riot of feathered and beribboned horsemen whooping in through the fort gates. The hunters were starting to come back from the plains.

He went out onto the front step to watch them gallop around in circles, leaping off their saddles and back on—sometimes backwards— and wheeling their horses around on their hind legs. From behind him

James Hargrave said somewhat tautly: "They could be quite hair-raising, couldn't they—if one didn't know they were generally good fellows at heart."

"Generally. And then there's some who'd bite your throat out for showing up in a vest with the same bead pattern as theirs."

The wild hunt grew even wilder when they saw that Grant was watching. He knew most of them by name. There was Jean Baptiste Dumont and his three tree-tall sons, Jean and Isidor and crazy Gabriel. There was Urbain Delorme, demonstrating how he could load and fire three times in the time it took most men to reload once. There were the Sinclair brothers trading horses in midgallop. And bringing up the rear, trotting carelessly along as though the thundering swirl around him were just so many summer dust devils, was Pierre Falcon.

Falcon climbed down off his horse by the countinghouse steps, held up his hand palm forward, and said in English: "How and ugh, heap big Mister Trader. We come to get swindled."

"Then you've come to the right place, laddy-buck," said Grant. "Drop your trousers and bend over."

The galloping and whooping settled down enough to reveal a high-pitched shrieking approaching from the west: the women and children following along with the carts. Falcon said with an exaggerated show of diffidence: "You're going to have a busy afternoon. Every man of us brought in a full cartload of pemmican and robes. Some of us two." The thick-wooled skins from the autumn hunt were always called robes, regardless of whether they ended up as cloaks, coats, or bedding. The spring hides were only good for *shagganappi*, tent coverings, or shoe leather.

Grant said: "You'd each have half a dozen cartloads if the hunt was conducted properly."

"Properly?"

"We'll have the entire winter to chew it over. That is, if you're planning to winter in the general vicinity."

"Matter of fact, me and a lot of others have been talking over the fact that there's a lot of good, wooded riverbank around the Forks that don't belong to nobody—except the Company. And somebody told me the Company don't much care where we pitch our tents or knock together a wintering cabin, so long as it ain't inside the fort or in some farmer's garden."

The head of the line of carts snaked through the gates. Driving the lead cart was Madame Pierre Falcon, née Mary Grant. It was hard to believe that the same tree could produce both a lime and an apricot, but Josephte and Mary were the proof.

Grant lifted his little sister off the cart and kissed her hello. She smirked at him, with her eyes sparkling even more than usual, and said: "How's Marie McGillis?" He blinked at her. She reached up to slap his shoulder. "Don't play innocent with me! The moccasin telegraph still works."

"I believe Marie McGillis is well. As is my wife, Madelaine."

"Madelaine?"

"Madelaine Desmarais—or Madelaine Grant, rather, as soon as the bishop agrees to formalize it."

Mary's starry-night eyes clouded over and her smirk drooped into a straight line. She looked sideways at her husband, who looked at the sky. Grant said: "Well, I have work to do. . . ."

He left the Falcons and crossed the quadrangle toward the trader's store, where the ledger of individual hunters' accounts was kept. Mister Simpson had suggested that Grant should second himself to the chief trader when large parties of hunters or trappers came in. "Not that I don't value your contribution in the countinghouse, Grant, but you do have a way with those people."

Grant had refrained from replying: "Perhaps because I'm one of them."

Grant spent the afternoon shuttling between the store and the line of carts, working his way from cart to cart toting up bags of pemmican and bales of buffalo robes, marking them as Prime or Utility, dispatching relays of fort servants to ferry them into the warehouse. Whether rightly or wrongly, both sides of the trading counter seemed to trust him, so he did his best to live up to their expectations.

As the afternoon wore on, the sounds of music and boisterous voices began to drift in over the stockade. Out on the plantation, the hunters and their families were setting up their tents and settling in to celebrate. Grant was back in the countinghouse, cleaning the ink clots off the day's goose quills, when Madelaine came in. She said: "Josephte wanted to come over to see her sister, so I thought I'd come along. There's so many people paddling across for the kick-up, it wasn't hard to get a ride."

"Where's Maria Theresa?"

"Josephte's got her. Well? We going to go and say hello?"

He rolled down his shirtsleeves, took his coat off the wall peg, and walked out with her. The plantation had sprouted a dozen pipe-clayed, vermilioned tipis, surrounded by empty carts slanted forward on their shafts and a grazing herd of hobbled horses. Several quarters of buffalo were sizzling over a firepit. Falcon and a number of other fiddlers were rosining up their elbows and loosening their throats around a barrel of high wine—the old fur trade staple made from the cheapest wine going, heightened with port or rum or gin or whatever else happened to be at hand. It was still a cut above the firewater that used to be concocted for the Indian trade, which was likely to be flavored with anything from cayenne pepper to gunpowder or turpentine, with a liberal dash of red ink for coloring.

Madelaine was right about the number of people from the east bank who'd crossed over for the celebration. Even a few of the Des Meurons had come along on the off chance of cadging a drink. The entire McGillis family was there. Grant downed a cup with Angus and tried not to watch Marie dancing with a succession of young men. Madelaine had disappeared somewhere into the melee. He left Angus at the barrel and circulated among the hunters, listening to their stories of close escapes and slipping in a few hints about his half-formed idea to unite all the separate hunting parties into one hunt, but his heart wasn't in it.

By sundown he was ready to go home, and so was Josephte. Maria Theresa had fallen asleep under a cart, wrapped up in her mother's shawl. He settled her into the crook of his arm and went to find Madelaine.

She was dipping a cup into the latest barrel to have its head knocked in. She said: "Don't be silly, things are just getting started. We're going to build a bonfire and dance all night."

"You forget I have to work in the morning."

"Well, I don't. Go home and get your sleep, I can get back across in someone else's boat."

He considered reminding her that dancing all night wasn't necessarily the best thing for her health, nor for her supposed intentions of being a wife and mother. But when it came down to it, he didn't care a great deal. Josephte dragged John away from the horse races that were an invariable element of all métis gatherings, and the four of them went back across the river, Josephte holding Maria Theresa while Grant and his nephew paddled.

Grant was thoroughly asleep when he heard the creak and scrape of the door jerking open. Falcon's voice whispered: "Wappeston!"

Grant called back softly, so as not wake Maria Theresa, "I'm here."

"It's . . . it's Madelaine . . ."

Grant yanked on his trousers, tossed a handful of spruce twigs on the hearth embers, and said: "Has she had an attack?" In the light from the flare of spruce resin and crackling needles, Falcon's hound-dog features wrinkled further in confusion. "Of the coughing sickness!"

Falcon shook his head. "She's been shot."

"What?"

"There was a card game. One of the Des Meurons was cheating. Against crazy Gabriel Dumont. Gabriel went for him with a knife. The De Meuron had a pistol. Gabriel jumped out of the way as it went off. Madelaine had been standing behind Gabriel, for luck. She was still alive when I left, but it don't look good."

Grant cupped his right hand over his eyes and rubbed, hard. Falcon added: "I got a boat waiting."

"Take Maria Theresa to Josephte's. I'll meet you outside."

As Falcon attended to Maria Theresa with, "Ssh—it's just me, your uncle Pierriche," Grant threw on his coat and moccasins, tossed another spruce knot on the fire, and unlocked the medicine chest. He filled his pockets with a lancet, forceps, a wad of dressing cotton and a bandage roll, a spool of surgical thread, and his case of needles. As an afterthought he snatched the laudanum bottle off the mantel, then went out the door and down to the boat with its crew of shocked-sober oarsmen.

The bonfire on the plantation was bursting and crackling, hurling red light across the white walls of the tents and on the murmuring silhouettes shuffling back and forth between them. Madelaine Desmarais was stretched out on a buffalo robe with her head pillowed in Mary Falcon's lap. The left half of her blouse was black with blood. A hank of cloth wadded under her left breast was soaked through as well.

Grant crouched down beside her. She didn't appear to see him; her eyes were bright and staring at the stars. With every shallow exhalation of her breath came a soft whimpering sound. The sounds, and the riveted clarity in her eyes, were less of pain than of surprise.

Mary whispered: "I would've tried to get the bullet out, and put a proper bandage on, but Pierriche said . . ."

Grant nodded at her, then leaned forward to peel away the sopping wad of cloth and cut open Madelaine's blouse. The firelight ran its fingers over the beautifully molded, rose-nippled artwork of her left breast. The buoyant curve of its underside was gashed. Underneath it was a jagged hole he could have stuck his thumb into. White teeth of rib splinters shone inside its lips. Little red bubbles, with the same gloss as bubbles from a toy pipe, popped out of the ooze with every shuddering breath.

One look and he knew he didn't have a hope in hell of digging out the bullet without digging half her insides out along with it. Maybe a real doctor could have done something for her, but he was only an amateur with professional tools.

He looked up at Madelaine's face. Her eyes had stretched even wider. Her head was shaking from side to side and her little pink mouth was opening and closing, with the same glistening red bubbles popping out through her teeth as the ones that were frothing in the new mouth under her left breast.

He worked his right hand between the nape of her neck and Mary's lap, propped up her head, and reached into his pocket for the laudanum bottle. He pulled the stopper with his teeth, kissed the glass lip against hers, and tilted the bottle. Her eyes goggled. She choked and gulped and sputtered and swallowed. He held it there. The bright black sheen across her eyes softened. Her breathing slowed and the whimpering sounds stopped, and then her breathing stopped.

He lowered her head back into Mary's lap, put the stopper back in the bottle and the bottle back into his pocket, then stood up slowly. Mary crossed herself and murmured a prayer. Unseen hands shyly patted his shoulders and muttered consoling sounds.

A hunkered boulder beside the bonfire uncoiled itself and shambled forward. Crazy Gabriel Dumont's slablike face was scoured with glistening tracks of tears. One bear-paw hand unsheathed the immense knife in his waist sash and extended the pommel toward Grant. There was a snuffled "I'm sorry."

"It was an accident, Gabriel."

Two other monoliths appeared on either side of the first one and put their paws on their brother's shoulders. Gabriel Dumont sheathed his knife, wiped his nose and cheeks with the back of his hand, and said brightly: "All of them Des Meurons lit out as soon as it happened, but I know which one of them it was. We got enough good men here to go over to German Creek and root him out."

"I *said* . . . it was an accident."

The bishop showed some reluctance about burying Madelaine Desmarais in the churchyard. "After all, my son, she did die unshriven. And she never showed more than a passing interest in the Church during her life."

"That's true, Monseigneur. It's also true that she, like most people in the *pays d'en haut,* never laid eyes on a church or a man of the cloth until a very few years ago. Perhaps in this country you have to stretch your hand out a little farther, if you expect the people to take it."

A lot of people came to see the bishop officiate at the funeral. Most of them were friends of the bereaved rather than the deceased. The friendships Madelaine Desmarais had struck up tended to be the kind that didn't extend to funerals. The McGillises came, as Grant saw when he looked up from throwing in the first handful of earth. Marie McGillis looked stricken, and her eyes sheared away from his the instant they touched.

Chapter 10

Marie McGillis climbed up onto a Red River cart half-loaded with camping gear; Daniel and Donald climbed into the second cart. Her father climbed onto his saddle horse, and they all waved good-bye to the rest of the family for the next few days. It was time for the autumn goose hunt. They traveled north to the foot of Lake Winnipeg, where the Red fanned out into a vast delta world of floating reed islands, gnarled tentacles of water lily roots, bush-choked mud bars, and disappearing channels. It was also a world of water birds, particularly at this time of year—Canada geese, snow geese, widgeons, teals, mallards, mergansers, buffleheads—all squawking away at each other while they stocked up on minnows and wild rice for the next leg of their long flight south.

Hunters with guns were prowling the edges of the marsh or paddling canoes through the frost-brittled reeds. Those who didn't own guns, or who preferred their roast duck without lead pellet stuffing, were plying a variety of old Indian tricks. Some were using dogs trained to run back and forth along the shoreline and lure the curious within range of a bow or throwing stick or net. Some had planted wickerwork decoys and were lurking in the undergrowth practicing their quacking. Some had used home taxidermy to make a hat out of one of last year's luckless ducks and were prowling nostril deep through the icy water to grab the webbed feet of the shortsighted and drag them under to drown. Canoefuls of Saulteaux and métis were harvesting wild rice and cattails. Out on the lake, boats and canoes were hauling in whitefish and goldeye with nets or trolling lines. The sky was a haze of smoke from drying racks of fish and birds and wild rice. Every gunshot darkened the sky further with a cloud of beating wings wheeling away to settle within range of another hunter's gun.

Marie's father led the McGillis expedition in a wide circuit around the border of the marsh so they could set up camp by the lakeshore. Marie jumped off the cart and got a fire going while her father and brothers wrestled down the big, three-legged iron kettle from the second cart. Once it was filled with lake water and the fire between its legs was crackling away nicely, she and Daniel went into the bush to cut green willow saplings while her father and Donald headed into the marsh with their guns.

By the time she'd built a rack of willow wands lashed together with *shagganappi,* her father and Donald were emerging with their moccasins and pant legs soaked in swamp water and a brace of geese in each hand. They dropped the birds in the kettle, warmed their hands over the fire, reloaded their guns, and trooped back to the marsh while Marie hauled out her knife and went to work. Once the hot bath had loosened the oil matting the feathers together, the feathers had to be singed off and the soft down scraped into a bag, to save for pillows and mattresses and quilts. Her undersize hands were an advantage when it came to reaching up the birds' vents and hauling out their innards. She saved the giblets to fry up for dinner and tossed the offal to the hordes of scruffy dogs that were as inevitable to any wandering band of Indians or métis as clouds of deerflies to a summer moose.

Daniel attended to building and feeding the smudge fire under the drying rack and making sure the flames didn't start eating the struts. She handed him each bird as she was done with it, and he strung it up by the neck inside the smoke. The smoke stung her eyes. Her hands were alternately soaked soft and pricked by crisped feather shafts. The really nasty part wouldn't start until they got back home and hauled out the pickling tubs, but then her mother would be there to join in.

It didn't cross Marie's mind to grumble or feel hard done by. The goose hunt was as much a part of the autumn as the turning of the leaves, and even the squirrels had to work to live. Besides, as long as she was occupied with singeing and scraping and eviscerating, she could forget the vortex that had been steadily consuming more of her since the night she'd knotted the green bead into her diary.

Her father and Donald came squelching back with five more birds before she'd finished with their first bag. They squatted down beside the fire to lend her a hand and thaw theirs. Daniel came over from the smoking rack, wheedling, "If you're going to help Marie, could I shoot some ducks?"

Her father grunted: "Shooting *at* 'em's one thing, shooting 'em's another. Oh, all right—go try your luck."

Daniel bounded over to the carts to fetch his hand-me-down old rusty popgun and then disappeared into the reeds. Mr. McGillis winked into the eye of the duck he was plucking. "Fear not, little *canard*, you won't be lonely much longer. Not once yon mighty Nimrod gets to decimating the duckling race."

As Marie was stringing up the last brace from the second bag, and her father and Donald were recharging their guns to go for a third, shouting voices erupted from beyond the curtain of reeds. One of them was unmistakably mighty Nimrod's. They went to have a look.

Daniel was standing waist deep in marsh water, holding his aged little gun in one hand and a duck's feet in the other. One of the Kildonan farmers clasped the duck's neck, stretching it out like pulled taffy. He was squatted in a dugout canoe. Daniel was squalling: "It's *mine*!"

The Kildonan man was shaking his head and bellowing: "It is *not*!" The duck, who was saying nothing, was a pintail, which was almost as good eating as a wood duck or green-winged teal but a good deal larger than either.

Mr. McGillis called out: "What's the trouble here?"

"It's my duck, Papa! I shot it, but he—"

"It is *not*." The Kildonan man bristled. "*I* shot it. It's mine!"

"For God's sake," Mr. McGillis said disgustedly, "it's the boy's first kill."

"It is *not*! *I* shot it!"

There was a soft thump of hoofbeats, and a crisp-edged baritone said: "Who's being scalped alive here?" Marie looked over her shoulder to see Mister Grant and another of the clerks from Fort Garry, both of them on horseback with fowling pieces propped across their ponies' necks.

Mr. McGillis said: "How do, Grant. Nothing serious—just a grown man trying to steal a boy's first duck."

"It is *not*! *I* shot it."

Mister Grant said: "Oh, for God's sake—there must be three hundred thousand sitting ducks within easy range. There's plenty to go around without stealing from boys."

"Plenty for *you*, maybe," the Kildonan man barked back, keeping the duck stretched taut while the boat bobbed up and down. "You half Indians have all the time in the world to laze around potting ducks, but some of us have wheat to thresh and hay to get in. So that you'll have someone to beg from come winter."

Mister Grant handed his fowling piece to the other clerk and reached into the pannier behind his saddle to draw out a knife that was more like a cutlass. He slid off his horse and marched methodically through the reeds into the marsh. The farmer in the boat didn't relinquish his hold on the duck, but his other hand sloped the muzzle of his fowling piece toward the broad chest wading out toward him. "Keep back, I'm warning you, I'll blow your guts out!"

"I have no more intention of using this knife on you than you have of pulling the trigger on a fowling piece you discharged at this duck and haven't reloaded." There was an arc of white light as the knife whistled through the air, then a burst of blood and feathers. Daniel fell backward, brandishing the back half of the duck, as the dugout jolted away in the opposite direction. "There—that's what the kirk calls 'Auld Testament justice.'"

With the sudden release of tension, the boat bobbed bow to stern and almost swamped. As the farmer was splashing and thrashing to keep from losing his balance and his half a duck, Mister Grant helped Daniel to his feet and they both waded back to the shore, trailing marsh bubbles as each step smacked free of the sucking mud.

The Kildonan man snatched up his paddle, turned his boat around, and propelled himself away. Just before he disappeared in the maze of reed-walled channels, he shouted back: "You should be happy—you got the Pope's nose!"

Mr. McGillis hissed: "Loan me your gun, Grant, mine's but half-loaded."

"Let him have his joke, Angus—that's about all he's got. Hello, Marie."

"Hello."

"Angus—can't you tell when your daughter's half-immolated with smoke and overwork? You give even your horse a chance to breathe itself out. Marie—if you're willing, I'd be more than glad to walk out with you for a moment where the air is fresher."

"Papa?"

"Grant might have a point there, for a change. Don't forget your way back."

"I won't, Papa."

"By the by," Mister Grant added over his shoulder, "this is James Hargrave. Do show him a thing or two about the goose business while we're gone."

Once they had left the marsh behind for the clean breezes of the lakeshore, she said, "I was sorry about Madelaine Desmarais," then wished she hadn't. It sounded like empty-headed politeness at best.

He simply said, "Thank you," and continued ambling along. Sand

and rounded pebbles crunched under their feet. The sunset had turned the surface of the lake into a rippled mirror of molten metal.

He stopped and stood staring out over the lake with his arms crossed, shaking his head slowly. He said: "There aren't a luckier batch of human beings on the face of the planet." He stooped to tap his knuckles against a handy stump of driftwood. "We—and our children, with luck—have this whole vast and beautiful country to ourselves. Oh, I know—the *pays d'en haut* can kill you with cold or fire or flash floods or a thousand other ways, and some of the people in it can be just as cruel. But if we can learn to live with her—the *pays d'en haut*—we can live an enviable life. Would you be willing to live yours with me?"

She blinked several dozen times at the rippling light on the lake and said: "Willing to . . . ? Pardon me? . . ."

He swiveled to stand in front of her and take hold of her right hand—the one she'd been shoving into goose guts all afternoon. "No—pardon *me*. I'm not making myself clear. I'm asking you, Marie, to marry me."

She blinked stupidly up at the monumental, beautifully molded piece of statuary and blurted: "Yes!"

"Thank you." He smiled and caressed her cheek. "Now I suppose we'd best go ask your parents if they'll consent to give their blessing."

"My mother isn't here, she's back at home."

"Ah. Well, I suppose we'll have to wait until you're back from the goose hunt. A few days more or less . . ."

"But I'm sure they won't mind. I mean, I'm sure they'll be happy about it."

"Not near so much as I."

It might have been two or three more days that the McGillis goose hunt stayed at Delta Marsh; Marie was in too much of a daze to tell. It was very late at night when the carts shrieked into the barnyard at the Forks. Once the geese and ducks were hung up in the smokehouse and the horses stabled, Marie stumbled up to bed but couldn't sleep. She finally decided to take the half-beaded Assiniboine moccasins downstairs and work herself to sleep where she wouldn't disturb her snoring sisters. There was light coming up from the parlor and a sound of murmuring voices. She crouched down in the shadows at the top of the stairs.

Her father was saying: "I thought you liked the boy—"

"Boy!" Her mother's voice broke in. "He's thirty years old!"

"Ssh, you'll wake the whole menagerie. Anyway, he isn't thirty, not till December."

"Don't split rabbits."

"Hairs."

"Hares, rabbits, what's the difference." It was always easy for Marie to tell when her mother was agitated; she'd start to lose her grasp of English. "He's a grown man, and then some. What does he want with a girl like Marie?"

"At a guess—I'd say he wants a wife that'll make him a happier man than he is now."

"Then let him go find a woman his own age."

"Seems to me you're forgetting, Margeret, that I wasn't any spring chicken when I lucked across a pretty girl doing kitchen work at Fort Carlton. Or are you saying you don't want Marie to make the same mistake you did?"

"Don't be an ash, Angus—"

"Ass."

"Well, don't be one. This ain't the same as it was with you and me."

"And just exactly how the hell's it different?"

"He ain't a simple man like you."

"Well, thank you."

"You know what I mean. While you were working away doing your job for the Company and making a good home and family, he was—"

"Oh, for God's sake—you're not going to dredge up all that old business about the fur trade war? He didn't want that any more'n anybody else did, he just got himself stuck in a position where all hell was coming down and he had to take it by the throat or go under."

"But you were here the same time and you didn't get stuck there, did you? And neither did anybody else. It was *him*. Because . . ." Marie could hear her mother fumbling for the words, and her father waiting. "I think he's a fine, strong, good-looking man with a kind heart. But . . ."

"But what?"

"He was born with the mark on him."

"Oh, for God's sake, Margeret, you should have been born in the Highlands with white hair and eyes that were two different colors."

"I ain't talking about witchcraft, Angus. It's just a fact. There's some people that can't just be people, they got something else inside them. He'll burn her up. You know what my mother's people say: 'Beware the orphan. . . .'"

"They also say Ta-Tanka leads all the dead buffalo into a cave in the ground and brings them back alive come spring."

"I—"

"I ain't done talking. You got less faith in your daughter than I do. She might seem like a little girl now, but I can see she's going to be a match for anybody. Including you and me. When it comes down to it, it doesn't matter a good goddamn what either one of us thinks, because we only got two choices. We can either give 'em our blessing and hope it works out for the best, or tell 'em no and make them do it in spite of us. I'd like to stay on friendly terms with our daughter and our new son-in-law. How about you?"

CHAPTER 11

Falcon made a great show of fumbling through his pockets for the ring, to the great delight of the congregation. Grant slipped it onto Marie's sweat-slick, trembling finger. He wondered if it hadn't slid on a bit too easily. The fort blacksmith had fashioned it out of one of the store's stock of brass earrings, but he hadn't had much experience at sizing rings. Grant had already added "one gold wedding ring, 1⅞-inch circumference" to the list for his personal outfit.

The bishop blessed their union. Grant got off his knees, raised Marie to her feet, and bent to kiss his bride. She had a good mouth for kissing—just wide enough to have something to pucker, with firm, rounded lips that gave way enticingly. She was still a bit self-conscious as to how to go about it, but that was part of the charm.

Outside the church there was much whooping and firing of guns into the air. Everyone was decked out in everything from aged tailcoats covered in beadwork to antelope-skin dresses fringed with satin ribbons. They all fell in behind the bride and groom and paraded to the McGillis place, where a row of trestle tables had been laid out in the yard, covered with platters of moose nose, buffalo tongue, roast duck, smoked goldeye, fresh-baked bread, wild and domestic vegetables, blueberry puddings, and several kegs of high wine. There was a breath of frost in the air, but not enough to inhibit dancing around a bonfire.

Grant watched Marie jigging with her father. Her wedding dress was white cotton decked with white silk embroidery and white lace. Her skin had a glow to it today like burnished copper held to a candle flame, and her black eyes twinkled with stars. All in all, he couldn't have made a wiser choice.

He went over to the knot of fiddlers and engineered a four-hand reel, with some help from Angus McGillis and a few of the other old hands who could remember it from their youths in Stromness or Inverlochy. There were a number of collisions before the dancers got it right, and a great deal of hilarity.

George Simpson crossed over from Fort Garry to extend his congratulations and present the happy couple with a black-striped, white, three-point Hudson's Bay blanket. The Company gauged its blankets according to weight and size, and a three-point was the kind people made winter coats out of.

Marie was gratifyingly tongue-tied on being introduced to the governor of the Northern Department as Mrs. Grant. Simpson said: "Your husband is a remarkable man, Mrs. Grant—but I suppose you know that. One of my first encounters with him was when one of my boatmen absconded from Fort Garry to Pembina. It gets damned difficult when a servant can take an advance on his wages one day and disappear into the wilderness the next. I happened to mention my problem to your husband, and three days later he was back from Pembina with the deserter in tow." He added with a wink, "Let that be a lesson to you. Well, it was at that moment I said to myself: 'Cuthbert Grant will be back on the lists by next year or I'll know the reason why.'"

Grant stood on the crest of the riverbank with his arm around Marie, watching the governor's elite new crew of imported Iroquois boatmen paddle him back to Fort Garry. Three weeks earlier it wouldn't have been possible to see the river or the fort from where they were standing, but the impenetrable curtain of riverside woods was now just a sparse web of bare branches.

Marie said: "He seems like a nice man."

" 'Nice'?" Grant laughed. "George Simpson? Now, now, I'm not making mock of you. He can certainly be affable enough when it suits his purpose. But 'nice'? Oh, dear. . . ."

By seven in the evening the sky was pitch black, and Grant was glad to have the excuse to call it a night. Not that he was opposed to being the center of attention, but he knew that when he was, he tended to drink too much. With enough drink in him, any evening would slide by in a jovial river of affectionate faces and brilliant witticisms. But in the morning his every word and gesture from the night before would echo back with a hollowness that made him cringe.

He found Marie at the end of the plundered row of tables, in conference with her mother. He said: "Perhaps it's time we were wending our weary way home."

Marie glanced confusedly at the doorway to the big house not five steps away from her, then blushed and lowered her eyes.

The torchlit procession down the riverside path to the Grant cabins was rife with requisite rude jokes. The newlyweds affected not to hear them. Josephte opened the door of his cabin. She'd scrubbed the place from floor to ceiling and set out a cold supper. Grant turned to Mrs. McGillis and said: "Good night, Mother." He hadn't called anyone by that name since he was six years old.

"Good night, son." Then he and Marie were alone, with the sounds of the revelers fading beyond the closed door.

He went to the spread of cold duck on the table and said: "Are you hungry?" She shook her head. "Perhaps later, then."

She was standing with her elbows pressed against her waist, staring down at the floor. He threw a couple of logs on the fire and came back to the table to blow out the wick floating in a bowl of fish oil. The firelight flickered on her softly, painting the white dress amber. He moved toward her, reaching up to unbutton her dress. But she looked so trembly that, instead, he stepped in closer, picked her up in his arms, and carried her fully clothed to the bed behind the curtain Madelaine Desmarais had strung up. He laid her down as gently as possible on the buffalo robes and blankets and said: "I think I'd like a sip of wine. Would you?"

She nodded her head jerkily, with her lips compressed together. He stood back up, saying: "I'll be only a moment." He had a fleeting impulse to turn that into a joke but decided against it.

Under the gurgle and splash of the cups filling up, he thought he heard rustling sounds behind him. When he came back she was lying rigidly with the blankets pulled up to her chin and her dress folded on the trunk beside the bed. He extended one of the cups to her. She crept one hand out from the blanket to take it. He raised his cup in a toasting gesture and downed a healthy quaff. She propped the side of the cup against her chin and tilted it to take a tentative taste.

He considered telling her that he was at least as nervous as she, since he was a virgin when it came to virgins, then decided against that as well. He set his cup on the floor, then peeled off his coat and draped it on the trunk beside her dress. He leaned forward to tug off his new moccasins with their retina-burning Assiniboine beadwork, saying: "These really are quite resplendent, you know."

"Thank you."

"Thank *you.*" He proceeded with disrobing, making a point of focusing his attention entirely on the task of removing each article of clothing so she wouldn't feel constrained to look away. Once he was naked, he raised the hem of the blankets and slipped in beside her.

For someone who was lying stiff as a plank, she'd done a creditable job of warming the bed. He pried the cup loose from her fingers, laid it aside, and cocked his torso across hers so he could kiss her. Her mouth tasted of wine and smoked fish. Her breasts pressed pliantly against his chest, with the nipples poking out like little pink tongues. He kissed his way down to the hollow of her throat. She let out a soft, gravelly sigh, and her hands came up to flutter nervously against his shoulders.

When it seemed that she'd gentled down to the feel of his hands roaming over her legs and his lips on her breasts, he skated one hand across her taut little belly into the curls of crinkly down and insinuated a fingertip into the moistening lips, scalding it. As he shifted his body on top of hers, she sucked in a deep gulp of air. It came out in a strangled whimper as he butted his way through the membrane. He grunted through his teeth: "Believe me, it hurt me as much as it did you." One of those full-throated bursts of giddy laughter catapulted out of her, and she wrapped her legs around his waist.

When the hearth fire died to a feeble glow, he got up to feed it from the stack of split poplar. The sudden flare of light showed him the supper still waiting on the table and reminded him that he was standing naked. At least he wasn't even partially erect anymore, so he didn't feel too ridiculous. He turned toward the bed and said: "Could I seduce you into a bite of duck?"

She nodded her head and went to work manipulating her way out of the bed while keeping a blanket wrapped around her. He took two strides to her, ripped the blanket away, and looked her pointedly up and down, making a show of drinking in the lathe-turned breasts, delicate waist, and opulent outcurve of hips. "From this moment on, Mrs. Grant, the only reason I'll allow you to deprive me of this splendor is if someone else is present or there's snow drifting in under the door."

She looked down at the floor and giggled, then flared her eyes up at his and flung herself against him with a wet, sweaty smack. He managed to regain his equilibrium, and they sat down to tear into what Josephte had provided. When he was beginning to feel well and truly gorged, Marie sucked the last bone out through her duck-fat-slicked lips and chirped brightly: "Must be getting time for bed, eh?"

CHAPTER 12

Within a week of Marie becoming Mrs. Grant, the winter started to set its teeth in. There was a light snowfall that came and went, and then another one that stayed. Marie's father lent her husband his rowboat to go back and forth to work, as the canoe was too fragile to butt through the skin of ice growing out from the shoreline.

The change in the seasons didn't make that much immediate difference to Marie, since she was spending most of her time indoors. The interior of the cabin had to be completely rearranged to fit in her own things and all the wedding presents, ranging from pots and skillets to a bearskin rug. Little Maria Theresa had to be fed and watched over and taught to sing her uncle Pierre's song about the puppy and the porcupine.

The afternoons were largely taken up with manufacturing her husband's dinner. He seemed to like her cooking, although he didn't much care for whitefish because there were more bones than fish. Evenings were the time for tea and tobacco and talk of plans. He'd decided they should have a big house like her father's, with plenty of room for the children who would come along. There were more than enough unoccupied locations along the riverbank to make for a winter's worth of conversations about the advantages of one spot over another.

During waking hours there was a constant coming and going between the two cabins. The Falcons had moved in with Josephte and John for the winter. It had quadrupled the population of Josephte's little cabin, but it was the life they were all accustomed to: clan tipis were filled with infant cousins rolling around the floor. The crowding wasn't insupportable, since in any weather short of a blizzard, most métis could be found roaming about outside when they weren't sleeping or eating or visiting. Marie got the best of both sides—plenty of company when she wanted it and privacy at night. But it was a lot of new family to get used to all at once, most particularly her sisters-in-law—butterball Mary Falcon, who always seemed to be laughing, and string-bean Josephte, who never did.

Marie was kneeling by the hearth one evening waiting for her husband to come home, taking tentative tastes of the simmering pot of rabbit stew to determine whether it needed more salt and rehearsing various ways to slip something into the impending "And what did you do today?" Despite all the intimacies of the last few weeks, she still didn't know what to call him. Her natural inclination was to keep on calling him "Mister Grant," but that wouldn't do, except on those occasions when he nudgingly referred to her as "Mrs. Grant." She'd been noticing, though, that Pierriche always called him Wappeston, never "Grant," as James Hargrave and the other Company gentlemen did. And no one ever called him—heaven forfend—"Cuthbert," except his dry-tongued sister. Marie was willing to take it on faith that "Cuthbert" was a grand old Scottish name he'd inherited from his father, but she still couldn't say it with a straight face.

She heard footsteps crunching through the snow and frozen grass and leaned forward as though focusing her attention on the stew. She heard the door jerk open and felt the puff of cold air from across the room. As offhandedly as possible, she tossed over her shoulder: "Is that you, Wappeston?"

"I trust that doesn't mean you were expecting some other man. I commandeered a chunk of moose rump from one of the fort hunters' bags. It should thaw by tomorrow."

"Oh, thank you, Wappeston. I'll just set it in this pot to thaw. Stew's almost ready, Wappeston. Sit down and I'll get you a cup of tea."

He sat down and helped Maria Theresa scale the slope up to his lap. As Marie was pouring out the tea, he said: "I'm afraid we're going to have to do without each other for a few days, perhaps as long as a week. The river's reached the stage where there's too much ice for a boat, but not yet enough to walk across. There's a room in the clerks' quarters I can put up in until the river freezes solid. I'm sorry, but I'm afraid it's somewhat beyond my powers to slow or hurry the advance of winter." He sipped his tea and added with a wink, "Perhaps you'll be just as glad to have a few days to yourself."

In the morning she stood on the bank with Maria Theresa in her arms, watching him work his way across the river. He started out walking across the ice, hunched forward with his arms stretched out to push the boat in front of him. When the ice started to give way he dove into the boat, sending up a splash of spray and ice shards. Alternately hammering and poling with one oar, he broke his way out into the open channel, then unshipped the other oar and rowed hard to build up as much momentum as possible.

The sound of the boat biting into the ice on the western shore carried across the river. He inched his way farther in, smashing a way through the ice with the pile driver of an oar butt sending up showers of sparkling splinters. When a downstroke produced nothing but a muffled thud, he cocked one leg over the gunwale to set his weight down on the ice, balanced half-in and half-out.

She heard the crack of the ice giving way and saw his leg plunge down into the water. The hull buoyed up as he swung himself sideways and back. There was a thump and a curse when his shoulder hit the gunwale. The hull splashed back down, almost tipped the other way, wobbled, and finally settled.

Maria Theresa was squalling, either because she'd caught a whiff of her stepmother's fear or because Marie had squeezed her too hard. Marie nuzzled and rocked her and told her her papa was safe. When Marie looked up again, he was dragging the boat out onto the shore. He flipped it over, turned to wave his arm at her, and hustled up the bank before she could wave back.

As he disappeared through the fort gates, Marie told herself that the only reason he was being so brusque was to get inside before his moccasins and pant legs froze solid. She carried Maria Theresa back into the house and busied herself with the waistcoat she was embroidering for him for Christmas. As she sewed she carried on a mental conversation wherein she consistently adressed him as "Wappeston," to train her mind out of the "Mister Grant" habit.

The first heavy snowfall of the year got under way—big, fat white flakes drifting down from a soft gray sky. Marie bundled up Maria Theresa and took her out for a romp in the snow with her cousins. By the time they went inside, the descending curtain of white had grown so thick that she couldn't see the clouds it was falling from, and the big black oak tree beside Joesphte's cabin was only a blur.

After a functional supper of bannock and warmed-over rabbit stew, she put Maria Theresa to bed and sat up plying her needle by the light of the fire, still talking to "Wappeston" as though she were a convert drilling herself on the correct responses to the mass. She made a point of keeping herself awake much later than usual, crawled into bed yawning, and then lay awake for half the night. She couldn't seem to get warm or comfortable, although she piled on every spare blanket in the house and tried every position from lying sprawled on her belly to curling up tightly on her side.

When the orange glow of the parchment windowpane told her the night was over, she dragged herself out of bed, built up the fire, and made tea for herself and breakfast for Maria Theresa. She sat dully slurping cups of tea, telling herself that she was acting like a feather-weight little girl. Every married couple in the *pays d'en haut* had to live through enforced separations, sometimes for months on end, and they all managed to do it without turning into blithering ghosts of themselves.

When it was about the time Wappeston would usually be shrugging on his coat to cross over to the fort, she bundled up Maria Theresa again, wrapped her blanket shawl around the both of them, and went outside. The snow was up over the ankles of her high-topped winter moccasins, except in the places where Maria Theresa's cousins had trampled fox-and-geese runs. The sky and the earth were both white, with nothing between them but the black claw shapes of trees and the black-and-white squares of cabins. The only hint of color was the blue green of the occasional black spruce.

She carried Maria Theresa to the crest of the riverbank, breaking a new path through the snow. The black ribbon of open water between the jaws of ice looked a little narrower than yesterday, or perhaps she was just willing it to be. On the opposite shore, she could just make out the stick figures of people moving in and out of the fort gates. She half expected that he would at least come out onto the bank to wave to her. She waited until Maria Theresa started protesting against the wind and then went back inside.

The day crawled by. She told herself that if she let herself lie down for just a moment, she'd never get to sleep that night. Several times she caught herself getting furious at Maria Theresa over minor mischiefs. At sunset she went out to peer across the river again, but there was still no sign of him.

After washing up the supper dishes, she lugged the bucket to the doorway, pushed the door open with her shoulder, and flung out the dirty water. Just as she let fly, the starlight off the snow showed her a tall human figure approaching the house, directly in the line of fire. She yanked the bucket back too late. There was a splash and a sputtering curse. She squealed: "Oh! I'm sorry! I didn't— Oh!"

"I've had some charming welcome-homes in my time, but I must admit . . ." She dragged him into the house, squeaking apologies. "Not to worry, I was actually finding it a bit disorienting to have the bottom half of me soaked through with river water and the top half dry."

She got him out of his clothes, wrapped him in a blanket, sat him down in front of the fire with a cup of rum-laced tea in his hands, and went to work rubbing the blue out of his feet. He said: "During the course of the day it became clear that I wouldn't exactly be doing the Company a favor by staying in the fort. I couldn't see straight because I'd had no sleep the night before. It'll be a bit of an inconvenience going back and forth until the river freezes solid, but the worst that can happen is a pair of wet moccasins."

"No! You have to stay there till it's safe."

"Ah—so I was right in guessing you might be ready for a holiday from marriage."

"I hate it! I mean, not having you here. But better I spend a few nights missing you, Wappeston, than forever."

He reached down to caress behind her ear and said: "Don't fret yourself about me, *Waposis*, Little Rabbit, I didn't live this long without learning when not to push my luck." He drained his cup, then stretched and yawned theatrically. "I'd say it's getting past our bedtimes, wouldn't you?"

For the next week she stood on the riverbank every morning and evening with her heart in her throat, watching him slog and row and splash his way to Fort Garry and back. There came an evening when he pushed the boat all the way across without once having to jump into it. He came up the bank panting, "I think that's just about enough of that," and the next morning he walked across without the boat. Two days later he roped his saddle horse out of the herd in the meadow behind the two cabins, and from then on he rode.

On the last Saturday before Christmas, he pushed aside his scraped-clean dinner plate and said: "Thank you, that was delicious. Oh, by the by—after mass tomorrow, do you think I might persuade you to come over to the fort and give me a hand with a bit of work? The other clerks have an ice-fishing appointment."

"They're making you work on Sunday?"

"It isn't the kind of work the Company pays me for—rather a bit of a Christmas present. Hargrave and the others have been complaining lately about the strain on their eyes and their brains, working in a white room squinting at black numbers on white paper. So, if I might persuade you to lend me a hand . . ."

"A hand with what?"

"I'm sure Mary and Josephte won't mind keeping an eye on Maria Theresa while we're busy at the fort."

"Busy doing what?"

"Oh, and we'll have to come back here after mass before going across, to change into old clothes—the kind we might wear for butchering buffalo."

He refused to tell her anything more, although he appeared to enjoy her efforts to pry it out of him. So she played along, to the point of nudging him with her elbow during the benediction. After they'd come back to the house and changed, he saddled up his horse and gave her a hand up. As he reined in in front of the countinghouse, she began to smell an unpleasant odor. It was much thicker inside the clerks' office. The fort carpenter was stirring a bubbling pot over the hearth fire. There were three tin pails in a line beside him and a stack of coarse-bristled paintbrushes. He looked back over his shoulder as they came in and said: "Afternoon, Mister Grant."

"Good afternoon, Andrew. This is Mrs. Grant."

"Pleasure to meet you, ma'am."

"Thank you," she said.

"Well, it looks as though you're all ready for us, Andrew."

"Nigh about. I just need you to give me a hand pouring the glue. Takes a big pot for three colors at once. If you'll but take hold of the handle there . . ."

Now that Marie was close enough to look down into the three pails, she could see that they were all about three-quarters full of liquid color—vibrant orange, scarlet, and royal blue. The two men went from pail to pail, pouring out the bubbling hoof glue and stirring it in. When the glue pot was empty, the carpenter set it down by the hearth and said: "Now all that's left to do is set it."

"How long will that take?"

"Not but a moment, but—ahem—um, not while Mrs. Grant is here."

"Why ever not?"

"Well, you see, it's . . . I don't think you or her would like it if . . . There's only one way to do it, and . . . If you wouldn't mind, ma'am, just stepping out the door for just a minute or two?"

Her husband looked at her and shrugged. She said, "I don't mind," and went out to wait on the front step. After a moment she heard her husband's laughter from inside, and a moment later he opened the door and beckoned her back inside, still laughing.

The fort carpenter was stirring the paint pails, blushing redder than the scarlet one and muttering: "I didn't make it up, it's the way it's always done."

"I don't doubt your word for a moment, Andrew. I suppose it's some sort of chemical reaction with urea, or ammonia. . . ."

"I don't know about that, Mister Grant, I just know it don't fix worth piss without—I mean . . . Begging your pardon, Mrs. Grant."

When the carpenter was gone, Wappeston fished a piece of yellow chalk out of his desk and went around all four walls drawing a line at his eye level and then another about three feet from the floor. He said over his shoulder: "I was rummaging through the back of the warehouse and came across a shelf full of the most garish powdered colors an opium dreamer ever saw. Seems the last chief factor was under the impression that the natives are mad for bright colors—which is true, but he didn't think through to the fact that they manufacture their *own* colors out of berries and such. Well, I suppose the lines are straight enough for our purposes. What say we start with the top band first? You have your choice of stools to stand on. I'd say our best chance for covering spillage is to put the red on top, orange in the middle, and the blue on the bottom; what do you say?"

By the time they finished they were working by hearth light and candlelight, and their clothes, hair, hands, and faces were spattered with rainbows. He threw his paintbrush into the pot, threw her blanket at her, and charged for the door, shouting: "Damned fine job. Thank you. They'll be back any moment. Don't worry about the cleaning up—least they can do is . . ."

They came within a hair of getting away clean. But as the horse was carrying them out the gate, three other horses were coming in, carrying three frostbitten-looking clerks. James Hargrave held up a string of fish and said: "Look what we— Good God, Grant, what've you been up to? Practicing your war paint?"

"Uggh."

CHAPTER 13

On New Year's Day, the only man working at Fort Garry was Cuthbert Grant. The gatekeeper was on duty as well, but his work consisted of feeding a fire to keep his rum flask warm. Grant had packed off Hargrave and the other bachelors to their celebrations while the old married man filled in, updating the accounts that had fallen behind during the festive season. The accounts would have survived one more day without attention, but then there was the matter of the governor's New Year's regale.

The Highland Scots who'd constituted most of the officer class of the old fur companies had imported the tradition of Hogmanay—the New Year's feast that was more important on the Scottish calendar than Christmas. In the days when every Hudson's Bay Company fort had had a North West Company fort planted across the river from it, the traders had developed a tradition of taking turns hosting the Hogmanay rites, the only day in the year when competition was put aside. The two governors at Red River had adopted that tradition, and this year it was the colony governor's turn. Grant had a strong suspicion that his presence at Colony House would have cast a pall upon the proceedings.

Consequently he was spending his Hogmanay scratching black squiggles onto white paper in a multicolored room. The governor of the Northern Department hadn't been pleased at first that a place of business had been transformed into a playroom, but when the reasons had been explained he'd come around. Hargrave had spent the next night painting the ceiling purple.

It was going dark outside the window. At this time of year that meant it was barely four o'clock, but Grant was beginning to think it was time he hung it up for the day regardless. The candles he'd set on the top corners of his desk didn't seem to be doing the job.

He paused to cut yet another new point on his flabby excuse for a quill. One more point and he'd be up into the feather and could throw the damned thing away without being accused of wastage. He decided to finish inking in the last few lines on the current page and then go home to Marie and Maria Theresa. He was dipping the pen in the inkwell when he heard the front door open and several sets of boots stomping toward him. He started to turn in that direction, saying: "I would've thought you young fellows had more stamina than—"

Something heavy and hard hit him across the side of his head, knocking him off the stool. The floor gave him a wallop. Before he could start to rise he got kicked in the stomach. He doubled himself around the booted leg to pull its owner down, but a blow in the back sprung his grip loose. He was surrounded by boots coming at him sideways and cudgels coming down. He saw a pick handle coming at his eyes and threw up his forearm to block it. There was a crack and a white starburst of pain, and his hand went numb.

He flailed back at them feebly, trying to fight his way up to his knees. But every time he squirmed in one direction he got hit from another. Something hammered him square between the eyebrows. The drum of the boots and clubs grew muffled. The thumps and grunts and "How do you like it, you black bastard?" faded away.

He woke up choking. His right cheek was pressed against a splintery seam in the floorboards, and his left eye wouldn't open. All he could see was the firelit foot of a desk leg a few inches in front of his face.

He took a stab at turning his head. Several other portions of his body stabbed back at him, springing out a high-pitched whimper through the membranes behind his nose. Someone above and behind him laughed.

He held his breath and lolled his head around slowly. Far away there was a colonnade of blunt-toed boots.

He would have been perfectly content to stay right where he was until they'd gone, if it hadn't been for that whimper. He told his body that it was going to have to move. The arm he'd blocked the pick handle with felt broken, so he used the other one to push himself up onto one hip. One patch of his rib cage protested loudly. He made a grab for the desk leg and managed to haul himself up its length without pulling it over. As his knees straightened and his head hit the higher altitudes, he got dizzy again. He clutched the corner of the desk and held himself upright.

Several miles away in front of the door, there were four men wearing heavy coats and cudgels. They were all flushed with the effects of alcohol and physical exertion in winter clothing in a warm room. Grant didn't know the names of the two younger ones, but he'd seen them at the fort before, coming in to trade the potatoes they'd grown at Kildonan. One of them looked as though he were about to lose his Hogmanay dinner.

The other two were the colony blacksmith and a corporal of the Des Meurons. Alex MacDonell wasn't there in body, but Grant could see his spirit hovering behind them. It was embarrassing that they were only four, but then they'd caught him by surprise.

He hauled in as deep a breath as his cracked ribs would allow and said: "Congratulations. . . ." But all that came out was a mumbled cough. He spat out something red onto the floor and tried again—this time using only the right side of his mouth. "Congratulations. All four of you have achieved a state of perfection. Because you've just made the last mistake you'll ever make."

Three of them obliged him by leaping forward swinging their clubs, so that he could turn his forward-falling faint into an impression of launching himself to meet them and fight back.

The next thing he was aware of was a red-and-white glow flickering through his eyelids. He pried his right eye open and found himself staring into the bed of coals that had filtered down from the hearth grate. He listened for a moment and heard nothing but the whisper of the dying fire and the rasp of his own breathing. He flopped himself over onto his back. Once the resulting concussion of red fog faded, he swiveled his head to look across the floor. The only feet and legs between him and the door were those of desks and stools.

Without giving himself warning, he sprung his stomach muscles taut and hinged into a sitting position. He hung there for a while, breathing through his teeth, then he swung over onto his knees and straight up to his feet. He spotted a nearby stool and swiveled on his heel, so that he sat down on the stool instead of the floor again.

"There now, that wasn't so hard.

"Easy for you to say.

"Now walk over to your coat.

"Just as soon as you turn off the bells and fireworks and light some lamps."

He pushed off from the stool and staggered step by step toward the black cloud of his buffalo coat hanging against the red-and-orange sunset. He got there just in time to pitch forward, with his forehead holding him up against the fur. He caught his breath again and lifted down the coat. There was no point trying to get his cracked arm into the sleeve, so he just caped the left shoulder of the coat over his, manipulated his right arm through its sleeve, and fastened as many buttons as would close.

The shock of crystal cold outside the door helped to sharpen his one good eye, but it also sharpened the pain. He propped himself against the shaggy flank of his *shagganappi* pony and tightened the cinch one-handed. It took three tries to get up on the saddle. He turned the horse toward the gate and held it to a walk. He hunched his head down into his coat so the gatekeeper couldn't see his face.

"Are you all right, Mister Grant?" the man said. "Just a bit too much Hogmanay, eh?"

Everything grew clearer as Fort Garry dropped away behind him— the sharp crackle of snow under his horse's hooves, the spangled black sky, and what he was going to do.

There were at least a hundred warriors of the New Nation wintering around the Forks. In the week or two that it would take for his body to heal, another fifty or so could be brought in from the Pembina Hills. He'd done his damnedest to play by the civilized rules of the new order. It was time to see how they liked playing by what the old hands called Hudson's Bay rules—which consisted entirely of "whoever's left standing wins."

PART TWO

WHITE HORSE
PLAINS

Beware the orphan, who has grown up on the outfringes of the camp without a mother's or father's influence to guide him.

CHAPTER 14

The Point Douglas Sutherlands were making their way home from the governor's Hogmanay, crunching briskly along a footpath tramped between the drifts. It was the kind of night where the snow squeaked underfoot, when it seemed as though anybody raising his arms too high over his head would gash his fingers against the star-splintered, obsidian sky.

There were three Point Douglas Sutherlands, so bundled up in coats and plaids and mufflers that the only discernible details were that one of them was a sleeping child cradled in its mother's arms, that the mother was somewhat taller and broader-shouldered than the man walking in front of them, and that the man walked with a limp and was carrying a blanket-wrapped bundle of his own. They were called the Point Douglas Sutherlands to distinguish them from the various other Sutherlands among the strip farms dotted along the west bank of the Red. The nickname was used only for the family as a whole, though. After ten years of marriage, Alexander Sutherland's wife was still usually referred to as Kate MacPherson.

As they reached the doorway of the squared-log cabin, which they'd rebuilt three times after Cuthbert Grant's warriors had burned or torn it down, Sandy thrust his bundled fiddle at her. "I just have to go out back to the necessary," he hissed, and scuttled around the corner of the house. Kate managed successfully to juggle fiddle, child, and latch-string with only two hands, muttering inventive Gaelic phrases. She pulled the door shut behind her, set John and the fiddle down on the table, and threw a few pieces of spruce on the coals in the hearth. As the room sputtered alive with the crackle and hiss and perfume of burning resin, she peeled off her outer layer of woven and knitted wool.

John was waking up and protesting against finding himself trussed up on the tabletop. She got him undressed and put to bed in the cradle his father had built when he'd grown too big for his first one. He was growing too big for this one, too, but not quite big enough to be trusted not to fall out of the half loft if they made a bed for him up there. Perhaps she wouldn't have been so inclined to leap to such ideas if he'd been one of eight or ten children, as in the households of most Kildonan women her age. But the midwife had told her he was the only child she'd ever be likely to have—and a miracle she'd had the one.

The fire had built up enough strength to take on a couple of poplar logs. Sandy should have finished his business and been back by now. Well, she'd warned him about washing down pickled goose with brandy. She lit a greasy buffalo-tallow candle and changed into her bedtime garb of nightgown, shawl, and rabbit-fur-lined moccasins. Then she knelt on the buffalo robe in front of the hearth to let down and brush out her waist-length copper hair, which was rapidly becoming alloyed with silver.

There was still no sign of him. Perhaps he'd got himself froze to the seat and she'd have to heat up a kettle of water to melt him loose. By the time she'd untangled her last braid, she was beginning to get genuinely worried. The wind was picking up, doing its damnedest to chew through the thatch. She was just about to throw her plaid on and stick her head out the door when she heard several sets of heavy footsteps crunching along the path by the side of the house.

She went to the door and pushed it partway open. Sandy was straining to lift down a large, dark object draped over the back of a horse. He grunted over his shoulder: "Lend a hand—he's too big to carry on my own." She opened the door wide and helped him wrestle with the limp body of a man whose only signs of life were the occasional unconscious grunt of pain or bewilderment. He would have been enough of a load without the buffalo coat. By the time they got him to the bed, both she and Sandy were gasping for breath. Sandy limped back to close the door.

When Kate'd got her wind back enough to raise her head and look at what her husband had dragged home, she gasped: "Oh, my God!" The face of the man on the bed was a swollen, oozing, black-and-purple ruin. But the dried blood and puffed-shut eye couldn't disguise the fact that he was Cuthbert Grant.

Sandy came panting back, saying between breaths: "I saw a dark shape out on the river. Went to look. Found him lying on the ice. With his horse waiting for him to get up. I cannot guess how long he was lying there, but he's bound to have some frostbite along with all the rest."

She reached down her ragbag and snatched up the water bucket she'd set on the hearth to melt the ice off the top. "You must go fetch the doctor from Colony House! And the sheriff—"

"No!"

"He needs a doctor!"

"*Think* for a moment. I had plenty of time to think it over while I was loading him on his horse and leading it here."

"Think of what?"

"Of who it was did this to him."

"Who?"

"I cannot say exactly, but—"

"Well, if you cannot say, then—"

"*Listen* to me, just for a moment, if you can. Whoever it was, it was certainly not any of his own people from the other side of the river. Nor was it likely to have been any of the Company men he works with. If it had been Indians, they would have killed him outright. And however this happened, it was no stand-up fight. I can think of a few men hereabouts might go toe to toe with Cuthbert Grant, but not to do *this* to him. So what does that leave? I will tell you what it leaves. It leaves a bunch of brave Kildonan men jumping out of the dark with clubs against a man they would none of them dare to face in daylight."

"You have no proof of that."

"Do you think his friends will wait for proof? The moment they hear of this they will be loading up their guns and saddling their horses to come for revenge. And who will stop them? That raggedy batch of ex-mercenaries over at German Creek? The Hudson's Bay Company clerks? The only man that could stop them is lying on our bed unable to speak a word."

"Well, get out of my way and let me do what I can for him. But I am telling you—if I find anything worse than bruises and scrapes and a bit of frostbite, I will go fetch the doctor myself."

"Have you not heard a word I—"

"Have you not thought what all your careful thinking will come to if he *dies*? Lend me a hand with his coat."

Working off the big buffalo coat was made easier by the fact that only one arm was through its sleeve. Grant grunted and hissed as they maneuvered him from side to side and dragged his coat from under him. Sandy set it down on the floor and said: "I must go across and tell his wife before she starts a search for him. I hope to God I can make her understand."

"Well, you cannot do it standing here." He was almost out the door when she called: "Alexander!" He stopped and turned. "I know you only thought of what we must do for our own sakes *after* you had put him on his horse to bring him here. Oh, go on about your business and let me get on with mine."

She moved the candle over by the bed, fetching her sewing shears along the way, and snipped the frozen thongs on Grant's moccasins. His feet and hands had the same pale blue tinge as the unswollen portion of his lips. But the only patches of black appeared to be bruises. She draped a blanket over his torso and legs and went to work soaking his hands and feet with cold water, dipping a rag in the bucket and then compressing it gingerly around toes and fingers and ankles. He winced when she started on the left hand. She dropped the rag back in the bucket and sheared open that shirtsleeve.

There was a puffy, black-and-lime-green ridge along the blade of his forearm. Although his eyes stayed closed, he gasped and thrashed his head from side to side as she felt her way along the ridge, but she found no cracks in the bone.

The cuff of the shirtsleeve she'd cut open was crusted with melting ice crystals. The blue tinge in the unswollen corner of his mouth was creeping outward into his cheek. She threw the blanket back. His trouser legs and portions of his shirt were soaked through. Here and there a few die-hard crystals of snow and ice twinkled in the candle-light.

She sheared his trousers apart, carving a line up beside both outside seams and chopping through the waistband. She threw the front half aside, quickly tugged the blanket over to cover him from the waist down, and then carved his shirt in half along both sleeves and through the neck. His skin was surprisingly pale between the splotches of red and black and purple. There was one particularly ugly black swelling on his rib cage that was weeping through the webbing of skin. She dabbed at it carefully with the damp rag and then leaned toward the candle to get a look at the rag. There was no hint of yellow or green, just a few crystal droplets with a glint of bright red.

She tugged the back half of his shirt out from under him, pulled the top hem of the blanket under his chin, folded the bottom hem over his knees, worked the remnants of his trousers free, and covered his feet again. The fire was sinking low. She wedged a few more logs on top of the stumps of the old ones, stirred the coals, and came back to the bed.

The splotch of blue seeping into his cheek had grown larger. One blanket wasn't much to keep him warm, but getting the bedclothes out from under him would entail wrestling his battered body back and forth cruelly. Her foot encountered his buffalo coat where her husband had dropped it on the floor. She hefted it up, shook out the melt-off trapped among the woolly curls, and laid it down gently on top of the blanket.

His breathing rattled and wheezed, but his eyes stayed closed. One of them was so puffed up that she doubted it would open even when he came back to his senses. She wrung out her rag again and started dabbing at the dried blood on his face. Through the bruises and swellings and scrapes, she could still see the features of amber marble she'd first laid eyes on ten years ago. Despite the distorted lips she could still see the surprisingly delicate, straight-lined mouth that had kissed hers twice.

She didn't want to believe her husband's guess that it had to have been Kildonan men who'd done it, but there was no denying the scorn she would hear in several of her neighbors' voices if they could see her weeping over Cuthbert Grant. She knew he'd killed more than a few men, as Sandy had during his years of wearing the King's red coat. She'd seen both of them go as cold and hard as a knife when it came down to need. But neither of them would do this to a dog for spite.

The corner of Grant's mouth that wasn't a purple mushroom snarled open. His hands and legs began to gyrate under the covers. She flipped back the top corners of the coat and blanket and found his right hand fisting and unfisting furiously, scraping the fingernails across the palm as his blood needled its way back into the patches of frostbite.

She grabbed his hand in both of hers and pried open the fist. "Mister Grant, you mustn't. I know it hurts you, but you will scrape off the skin." He couldn't hear her. His other hand was still trying to dig itself apart, and his feet were rubbing frantically against each other.

She let go of his hand and ran over to the doorway, where her mittens were hanging beside her coat. When she came back his hands had come together, scrubbing each other palm to palm. She separated them and maneuvered her mittens onto his hands, glad for a change that her hands were as indelicately oversize as the rest of her. She let his hands go back to work on each other; they could scratch away all night long without wearing through the layers of moose hide and rabbit fur. That still left his feet, which were rubbing away more frantically than before.

She dumped out her ragbag on the floor, fished a couple of long strips from the pile, knotted one around each of his ankles, and secured the other ends to opposite corners of the foot of the bed. But while she'd been busying herself with his feet, the wringing of his hands had worked one of the mittens off. She put it back on, picked out two more longish rags, and tied his wrists to the bedposts.

Now that he could do nothing about the pain, he began to make soft whimpering noises. They appeared to be echoed at a higher pitch from somewhere behind her. John. She left her invalid securely spread-eagled and went to see to her son.

He was only half-awake as yet but was reaching a dawning awareness that something inside the house wasn't what it should be. She crouched down beside the cradle and smoothed his hair off his forehead, crooning: "Ssh . . . nothing to fret about, Johnny. It is only a poor, hurt man your father found lying in the snow. Go back to sleep now." She waited until his breathing settled back into a slow, deep, even rhythm, then stood up and fed the fire before going to see how Grant was doing.

In the flare of firelight as she approached the bed, it appeared that his hands and feet had stopped fighting the frostbite, although his good eye remained closed. She was halfway through the last step that would take her to the side of the bed, when the black buffalo coat and the big body beneath it erupted, rearing upright at an angle, snapping the rag binding one wrist as the mittened fist shot toward her. She started to throw her arms up and turn aside, but it slammed the side of her head, spinning the house around and tilting the floor.

She managed to hold on to the thought that she mustn't cry out or knock anything over on the way down, so as not to wake John. She jolted hard against the packed-earth floor and found herself sprawled in front of the hearth, with a cushion of numbness implanted across her left cheekbone and temple and extending itself into her eye.

She turned her head and focused on the bed. He had thrown the mitten off and was yanking at the rag binding his other hand. She snatched up a stick of firewood and pushed herself up onto her knees. "If you do not leave that and lie back peaceful, Mister Grant, I will by God *bash* you peaceful."

His head swiveled from the rag knot to her, and his good eye squinted hard. "Mrs. Sutherland? . . ."

"My husband found you lying on the ice and brought you back here. I had to tie your hands and feet to keep you from hurting yourself with the frostbite. If you are in your right mind now, I will cut you free. Ssh—John is sleeping."

His cyclops gaze remained fixed on her for an instant, then he nodded his head. She got up and found her shears to snip off his rag manacles, whispering: "My husband always keeps a dram about the place, for company. Would you care for a little in a cup of water?" He nodded again and settled his shoulders back onto the bed with an involuntary grunt.

When she came back with his whiskey and water, he'd come to himself enough to have gritted his teeth and features into a mangled approximation of a stoic mask. He took the cup from her, hissed, "Thank you," and tilted the rim to the half of his mouth that could open. He coughed and choked, dribbling a little down his chin, then drained the rest and handed the cup back to her.

"Mister Sutherland has gone to tell your wife. I wanted him to fetch the doctor as well, but he thought that . . . I could feel no broken bones, but if there are, or if you feel there is anything wrong inside you, we will bring the doctor in regardless."

"I believe . . ." She had to strain to make out the words in the puff-lipped slurring. "I believe I have a few cracked ribs and bruised bones, but nothing broken."

"Who did this to you?"

His eye slid away from her and hooded into a black mirror.

"I should think you would know by now, Mister Grant, that we are not about to throw you back out in the snow if it turns out that—" She was cut off by the sound of approaching horses. He heaved himself up on one elbow, and his eye flicked quickly around the room, settling on Sandy's hunting gun hanging above the mantelpiece.

"You should also know that no one crosses the threshold of this house without our leave." She started for the door, flicking the left side of her hair from behind her ear to hide the bruise that she could feel forming where Grant's fist had hit her. She was still a few steps from the door when it burst open of its own accord and someone shot across the threshold without asking leave—a black-haired, black-eyed girl about the height of Kate's shoulder. The girl paused just long enough to jerk her head from one corner to another, then the black eyes fastened on the bed and she charged past Kate without a "How do you do."

Sandy stumped in behind her, followed by a bony man lugging a black wooden box. His hound-dog eyes caught Kate's, and there was a mutual flicker of recognition. It was the Mister Falcon that Mister Grant had delegated to help her search the killing ground for Sandy after Seven Oaks. She had never imagined that rumpled, kindly scarecrow could ever look like he was about to kill somebody.

CHAPTER 15

Except for the splash of candle flame showing Marie where her husband lay, everything in the cabin was just a blurred obstruction. As she flew toward the bed, his arm came up to shield his face. She skidded to a halt at the side of the bed, fought down the impulse to fling herself onto him, and instead knelt down. She reached up both her hands to take hold of his and tug it toward her. As his arm and its shadow came away from his face, a gasp like a half-formed shriek wrenched out of her. She'd prepared herself to see a black eye or a split lip, but the sudden revelation of a distorted shaman's mask where her husband's face should be was like being kicked in the heart.

He slurred thickly out of the corner of his mouth: "That bad, hm? Don't worry, Waposis—it looks worse than it is. I was too pretty to begin with. Ah—Mrs. Sutherland, my wife, Marie."

Marie looked up at a tall woman in a nightgown. One wing of her long copper hair was pushed back behind her ear, the other draped loose, curtaining the left side of her face. The woman said something Marie couldn't understand. Wappeston said: "My wife does not have the Gaelic."

"Oh, I am sorry, Mrs. Grant. I had thought, with a name like McGillis . . . I am afraid I had to destroy your husband's shirt and trousers. They were covered in snow and ice, you see, and he was so cold . . ."

Marie looked down at the pile of chopped-up clothes beside her and realized he was naked in the bed. She looked up at Mrs. Sutherland and said: "He's got other shirts and pants at home, and I can make him more."

Pierriche set down the medicine chest. Marie unlocked it and hinged back the lid. Wappeston grunted hoarsely, "First, the laudanum," waggling a finger toward one corner of the box. "Black. In a bottle. Three drops—cup of water."

Marie pulled out and glanced at three bottles in that corner before she found what looked to be the right one. She held it to the candle to read the label. By that time Mrs. Sutherland had fetched a cup of water. Marie measured in three of what she hoped were the right-size drops—which would have been difficult enough without her hands shaking and her vision blurred with tears. She raised the cup toward his lips, but his hand came out and took charge of it. He drank it all down, swallowing with some difficulty, then lolled the empty cup toward her and dropped his head back onto the pillow.

After a moment his strained expression softened and he raised his head again, whispering: "I believe . . . the only place needs binding . . . ribs. Roll of dressing cotton . . ." He waggled his finger at the box again.

She swiveled out the shelf of bottles. Among the cased lancets and other implements in the space below were several rolls of gauze and bandages. She plucked out one roll of each, saying: "I can make a poultice later. My mother has the herbs."

Pierriche said: "Mary and Josephte both got lots of medicine plants."

Wappeston grunted and kept pointing at the box. "Salve. White, in a jar . . ."

There was a glass jar nestled in among the bandages. Marie was reaching for it when a snarl of pain snatched her attention back to the bed. He was trying to push himself upright. She started to spring up to help him, but Pierriche and Mrs. Sutherland were already there, holding his shoulders and easing him into a sitting position. As the blanket and his coat slipped down to his waist, showing the welts and bruises mottling his body, Marie managed to cut off her gasp this time. He raised one elbow to show the weeping, black swelling on his side and waved her forward.

She fished out the jar and uncorked it. A sharp, camphorous odor stung her eyes and the lining of her nostrils. She said: "This is the wrong one. It'll burn the—"

"I *know,*" he barked through his teeth. "That's what it's *meant* to . . . Smear it on, then gauze and bind it."

She did as she was told. His breath hissed in and his spine snapped straight as the white gel touched his scraped skin, but he nodded at her fiercely to smear it on. She furled the gauze into a wad big enough to cover it, pressed this dressing and the end of the bandage roll against his side, and unwound the bandage with Pierriche taking it from her for the circuit around his back.

Wappeston grunted, "Tighter!" then gasped and jerked his chin up and down when she pulled it tight. It went around him four times. When she came to the end of the roll and looked to tie it off, she realized that she'd buried the other end in with the dressing.

Mrs. Sutherland said, "I have some pins," and secured it neatly without once pricking his skin.

Pierriche eased him back on the bed and pulled up the blanket and coat to cover him. Mrs. Sutherland said: "Would you like another dram of whiskey?"

Mister Sutherland's voice came from behind Marie: "I think we could all do with one." He busied himself around the table.

Pierriche said softly: "Who was it, Wappeston?"

Wappeston's open eye blazed at the ceiling, and he said in a stone cold voice Marie had never heard before: "Four. One De Meuron and three colony men. The ones I don't know the names of I'll know by sight. Few days I'll be back on my feet. Send word out to the plains and the hills. Tell them to gather on the east side of the Forks. By the time they get here . . ."

Pierriche grunted affirmatively. Marie said: "Tell who?"

Her husband's coal hard eye swiveled toward her as though she'd just asked why the sky was blue. Pierriche said: "The *bois brûlé.* The warriors of the New Nation."

Marie whimpered: "No . . ."

Wappeston winked his good eye at her and patted her hand. "No fear, Waposis. This time they won't be sneaking up on me."

Mister Sutherland appeared with a cup in each hand, saying: "I do apologize for profaning good whiskey, Mister Grant, but my wife tells me you should take it with water." He held one cup over the candle for a moment, then handed it to Wappeston and cocked the other one over the flame. "Would you care for a dram, Mrs. Grant?"

"Thank you." When he handed it down to her, she could feel the heat through the handle. As she raised it toward her mouth, the fumes burst inside her nose. She knew she had no right to tell Wappeston what he should do after what had been done to him, but she was still searching for a way to make him listen.

As Mister Sutherland brought two more cups forward, Pierriche said: "Do you want, Marie, for Wappeston to turn his other cheek so they can smash that one, too? It'll be a beautiful day when Jesus rules the world, but till then . . ."

Mrs. Sutherland said: "So, Mister Grant, you will turn Red River into a slaughterhouse once again because four men bruised your pretty face? That's fine justice."

The head on the pillow turned stiffly toward Mrs. Sutherland, and the mangled mouth rasped out: "Ah—so now we see where the lines are drawn."

"Oh, aye—they are drawn where my husband picked you up off the ice and carried you back here instead of leaving you to die. And for that you will make another massacre."

"You must know by now, Mrs. Sutherland . . . that I am not in the habit of butchering the innocent. It is only those four . . ."

"Once it starts, no one will be able to tell who is innocent or not until it comes time to sift through the ashes. Do you think our people here, or the Des Meurons, will stand aside and whistle while you and your bully boys ride in to drag out those four? Is that what you want?"

"What would you have me do, Mrs. Sutherland? Wait until they do the job properly next time—on me or my wife or my daughter or . . . ? Is that what you want?"

"You should know better than to ask me that. I want the men who did this to you to be punished, but no one else. Give the governors a chance—to see if we can have some justice here beyond claymores and hatchets. If it turns out we cannot, then you can do a proper job on us and get it over with. But first *try* to see if there is another way. After all these years, you owe us that much."

"You are . . ." His voice grew more thick-tongued, and his head lolled sideways as the forced clarity of the last few minutes took its toll. "You are quite . . . right, Mrs. Sutherland, I owe you at least . . ."

Marie looked back and forth between her husband and the woman he'd been willing to listen to after dismissing his Little Rabbit with a wink and a pat on the hand. Mrs. Sutherland's husband said: "But if your people, Mister Grant . . . Mister Grant?"

"Hm?"

"If your people were to get word of what some of our people have done to you, before you are well enough to tell them to wait . . ."

"Unh . . ." His good eye fluttered open and shut. "Pierreesh . . . Fort Garry . . . ekshplain Hargrave . . . mop up blood . . . tell Shimshon . . . but all elsh ssh for now . . . ssh . . ." The eyelid closed and his breathing settled into a slow, deep, even rhythm.

Mrs. Sutherland said: "Mister Falcon? . . ."

Pierriche nodded. "All right. We can keep it quiet for a day or two, maybe. It'll take that long to get the word out and bring the hunters in—"

"But he said—"

"He *said* we wait a few day till he got time to think it out, and till he see what Simpson and the colony governor do." He looked down at his drugged-to-sleep brother-in-law. "I should've brung along the carriole to take him home in, but I didn't know how bad . . . You wait and I go back, hutch up the dogs and—"

"No!" Mister Sutherland shook his head. "You have to go keep the clerks from raising the alarm—if they have not already done so—and put it in the hands of Governor Simpson. By the time you do that and then go fetch your dog sled, other people will be up and about. Leave him here and fetch him tomorrow night. There is enough of a wind to wipe out the tracks you made tonight if you go now."

Mrs. Sutherland said to Marie: "You are welcome to stay here until tomorrow night, but I am afraid we do not have much spare floor or bedclothes, not once my husband and I have rigged up a bed for ourselves. And your husband is far too broken up for you to sleep on the bed. . . ."

"I'll go across with Pierriche and we'll come back to get Wappeston once it's safe tomorrow night. If it ain't asking too much for you to keep him here till . . ."

"No—no trouble. Well, I suppose, then . . ."

Marie kissed Wappeston's hand good night and got up on her feet to join the migration to the doorway. As Pierriche tugged his cap on and pushed the door open, Marie turned to say something—she wasn't sure exactly what—to Mister and Mrs. Sutherland. She happened to turn just at the instant when a flare-up of the firelight coincided with a wafting back of the wing of Mrs. Sutherland's hair that was hanging loose. It was just enough to catch a glimpse of a purple bruise before the silvered copper curtain closed over it again.

Suddenly this towering, imposing white woman with the mysterious influence over Marie's husband became an object of sympathy. Marie had heard of men who beat their wives, but she'd never imagined such a mild-seeming, lame little man as Mister Sutherland could be one of them, or that a woman as big and powerful as Mrs. Sutherland would allow it. As Mister Sutherland stood waiting to pull the door shut, Marie grabbed one of Mrs. Sutherland's broad hands in both of hers and said fervently: "Thank you!"

CHAPTER 16

With the assistance of laudanum and the occasional spoonful of hot broth, Grant slept through most of the following day and was still dazed when Marie and Falcon came to fetch him in the dead of night. Marie brought along a change of clothes that he struggled into in stages. It seemed that every bone and muscle in his body had a bruise or a scrape on it.

Once they'd buttoned him into his coat, he put one hand on Falcon's shoulder and the other on Marie's and limped lopsidedly to the door. He stopped there and turned back to the Point Douglas Sutherlands, who were standing by the table waiting to take possession of their bed again. He knew he should say something, and opened his mouth to do so, but for once in his life there weren't words waiting to slide off the end of his tongue. Before he could formulate any, Mrs. Sutherland said brusquely: "You would have done the same if it had been one of us."

Mister Sutherland said: "Get along with you before the wind comes up again."

Falcon's carriole was waiting outside. A carriole was a pointy-nosed toboggan with a housing of rawhide parchment stretched over a willow frame. In shallow, wind-packed snow or on frozen rivers, dashing young men liked to harness their carrioles behind their swiftest saddle horses and go whipping along like a canoe in white water. But for workaday usage, a carriole was usually pulled by three or four of the scruffy little wolf dogs that spent the summers getting underfoot.

With Marie and Falcon helping, Grant managed to get himself wedged into the cockpit, although a large shoehorn would have helped. Falcon took up a position beside the team and uncoiled his dog whip. Marie trotted along behind. What with the jolt of outside air and the bumpy ride across the river, Grant was more than ready to close his good eye again the instant his back hit the bed. But Maria Theresa woke up when they came through the door and refused to go back to sleep before she'd seen her papa. He sat up to receive her and edged into a corner where his face would be in shadow. She still cried when she saw him and tentatively reached out one pudgy hand toward his puffed-shut eye, asking: "Does it hurt?"

"Not so much, butternose. If we both go to sleep, it'll be better in the morning."

Over the next few days, Marie and Mary Falcon and Joesphte kept up a steady rotation. It seemed that every time Grant opened his good eye, there was one of them kneeling by the bed with a cup of soup or a fresh herbal poultice to draw the poison out of the welt on his ribs or a cold compress for his swollen eye or a wad of willow bark to chew against the pain. He wasn't sure if any of their concoctions had much medicinal effect, but they did serve to keep him and the bed aromatic.

When his nurses decreed that he was well enough to receive visitors, he discovered what it would feel like to be in an open coffin with a file of mourners shuffling by. Except that a corpse didn't have to summon up the energy to calm down shambling hard-cases with murder in their eyes.

The houseful of muttering tea drinkers cleared itself out on the afternoon when both governors came by. The colony governor was decidedly nervous, and there was even a ripple or two under the icy surface of the governor of the Northern Department. Simpson said: "We mean to schedule a council hearing to deal with this the instant you are up and about. Do you think in a week, or perhaps two, you'll be . . . ?"

"A week. The longer we leave this, the greater the chance that some . . . other unfortunate occurrence may take place in the meanwhile."

"It's liable to be a stormy session," Simpson cautioned him. "Most of the colony people are just as appalled as we are at what's happened. But . . ."

"But Alex MacDonell is still a member of the council."

"There is no proof," the colony governor put in, "that Alex Mac-Donell had any part in—"

Simpson waved that away and continued addressing himself to Grant. "We know who all four of them were. It might've been damned awkward if it was just your word against theirs, but the fools stopped for a pull on the gatekeeper's flask to work up their courage."

"You have my word, Mister Grant," said the colony governor, "that justice will be done. You have my word."

"Oh, by the by, Grant—I thought you might be interested to know about the dispatch from the London Comittee. The winter packet came in while you were . . . indisposed. The committee informs me that William MacGillivray has been given to understand that they expect to see the matter of your father's estate settled by the time the committee convenes again. No doubt slippery Simon will find a way to stall a little longer, but the writing is on the wall. So, if you're amenable to the Company acting as your banker, I see no reason why you shouldn't start drawing against an open-ended account immediately."

"That's serendipitous. I've found myself reflecting lately that perhaps I wasn't made to make my living clerking for the Company after all."

"Perhaps not. . . . We'd regret losing your talents, of course, but not all men were meant to spend their lives harnessed to a desk. So . . . might I ask what you've been considering as an alternative?"

"I haven't had much time to consider it. Only half-formed notions as yet. I expect they'll coalesce in time."

"Well, that is the one advantage to being invalided—gives a man time to stop and take stock. When they do—coalesce, that is—you must come by and tell me what your plans are, once this unpleasantness is over with.

"Oh—and perhaps you might lend me a hand with another matter once you're up and about. The buffalo hunters who chose to winter here rather than at Pembina seem to think that the Company is under some obligation to provide them with provisions through the winter—"

"Perhaps they somehow got the notion," Grant said, "that the Company preferred they winter here rather than at Pembina. At Pembina they could take a crisp day's jaunt into the buffalo's wintering grounds and come back with enough meat to feed their families for a month. At the Forks it can get to be lean pickings."

"Of course the Company doesn't wish to see anyone starve, but neither are we a charitable organization. I've tried my damnedest to explain it to them, but it might penetrate more easily coming from one of their own. It's an awkward situation for all concerned."

"It is that."

When the governors had gone, Grant dropped his head back on the pillow and breathed deeply. Visitors were one thing, but he wasn't quite up to extended bouts of fencing.

Marie said brightly: "Well, there's some good news, at least."

"What—that both our esteemed governors are scared to death? They have good reason to be."

Two days later Grant went for his first walk outside since New Year's. There had been a couple of heavy snowfalls while he was flat on his back, so he stuck to the trampled trails. It was a gray day, which were always noticeably warmer than the sparkling clear days. The ravens were taking advantage of the comparatively balmy air to practice their midair falls, dropping out of the sky like crumpled black rags and then swooping away with a croaking laugh just before they hit the snow.

He walked halfway to Marie's father's place and came back relatively pleased with his progress. His ribs and the bruised bone in his forearm were still giving him a fair bit of pain, but it appeared that he was going to live. The question now was what to do while he was living.

By the time the council meeting came up, he was well enough to ride, at least as far as Kildonan. His buffalo coat had two deep hand-warmer pockets, long enough to accommodate his pistols. Marie looked at him askance as he checked the loads. He winked at her. "Don't fret, Waposis, I'm sure it will all be perfectly civilized. But a wise traveler always takes out adequate insurance."

"If it's going to be so civilized, why can't I come along?"

"Because while I'm closeted in the council meeting there will be nothing for you to do but stand around in the snow twiddling your thumbs until they freeze and fall off. The meeting might go on all day. But I will most assuredly be home in time for supper."

He kissed her good-bye and went out to where Falcon was waiting with the horses.

As they trotted through the gates of Fort Douglas—a dilapidated palisade housing the colony stores, servants' barracks, and Colony House—Grant was aware of heads turning to follow their progress across the snow-packed square, but he kept his eyes trained straight ahead. He and Falcon added their horses to the line hitched in front of Colony House and climbed the stairs.

Inside the front door was a wide anteroom with benches along the walls. Among the benches' occupants were the Fort Garry servant who'd drawn gate duty on New Year's Day and the Point Douglas Sutherlands. Grant nodded at the Sutherlands. Mister Sutherland said: "You look a good deal better than the last time I laid eyes on you."

"I feel a good deal better, believe me."

The functionary who'd scuttled out through the double doors at the back of the anteroom when Grant and Falcon came in emerged to say: "Mister Grant, the council will see you now. Might I take your coat? . . ."

"No, thank you."

As Grant stepped into the council room, the doors closed behind him. It was a big room with a long table across the middle. George Simpson occupied the head of the table, with the colony governor at his right hand. Although the colony council was ostensibly autonomous, the rule was that the colony governor gave up his chair if the governor of either the Northern or Southern Department of the Hudson's Bay Company happened to be in attendance.

The six councillors were ranged up and down both sides of the table. Grant knew them all, to varying degrees. The fair-haired, brittle-looking one was John Pritchard, whom Grant had clerked for in the North West Company before Pritchard switched sides. Pritchard was also the staunch Anglican who had been responsible for fulfilling the earl of Selkirk's promise to provide his colonists with a minister.

Across the table from Pritchard sat Alex MacDonell, who looked to be in the process of chewing his teeth into powder. Behind Mac-Donell's chair stood four red-faced men in various postures of defiance. Grant glanced at them once and recognized them even without their cudgels.

Simpson said to the clerk scribbling notes at the foot of the table: "Fetch a chair for Mister Grant."

"*That* man," Alex MacDonell exploded, "has no place at this table," slapping his hand on said table by way of illustration.

The pale blue eyes at the head of the table tracked like swivel guns to Councillor MacDonell. "I think the question of who should or shouldn't have a place at this table is not one you would be wise to raise at present." The governor of the Northern Department was enjoying himself immensely.

The clerk came forward with a rough-lathed wooden armchair. Grant settled onto it and gingerly worked his arms out of the sleeves of his coat. Perhaps he exaggerated just a little, to encourage the impression that the only reason he'd kept his coat was to provide a bit of padding between hard surfaces and his battered body.

Simpson said: "Now, Mister Grant—would you agree with the gate-keeper's identification of these four men as the very ones who came to attack you at Fort Garry on New Year's Day?"

Alex MacDonell exploded again: "They've never denied it! Why should they? We should be giving them a parade instead of—"

"*Mister* MacDonell—I believe I'd asked a question of Mister *Grant*. If you have recently taken it in mind to change your name to Grant, I would appreciate it if you would inform me of the fact so we might avoid future confusion. Now, Mister Grant—Mister *Cuthbert* Grant, that is—are these the men?"

Grant hadn't been prepared for the humiliation. He was accustomed to solving his own contretemps, and now he was being asked to point out the bad boys to Papa so Papa could spank. But he managed to swallow it and said: "They are."

"And would it be fair to say that this was an unprovoked attack that descended on you with no warning?"

"It would be fair to say that if it weren't, there would not be four of them standing there."

One of the four snorted: "You did not talk so fierce when you were down on the floor."

Grant leaned back in his chair, slid his hands in his coat pockets, and smiled: "I'm not down on the floor now, am I?"

"The only question remaining," Simpson interjected, "is whether there were only these four or whether they were encouraged by any other persons behind the scenes."

MacDonell couldn't contain himself any further. "They were encouraged by the shocked feelings of several hundred good people who could not bear to see the murderer of their husbands and fathers and neighbors strutting about here scot-free! Anyone in Kildonan would have encouraged these four good men to do the right thing."

"Anyone," the governor of the Northern Department asked blandly, "such as yourself?"

"I don't deny it, and why should I? They showed a lot more Christian forbearance to that butcher than he ever showed to us. And you can put *that* in your pipe and smoke it, my wee mannie."

The wee mannie's glacial expression didn't even twitch. "As there appears to be no more questions about the matter, I believe the council will agree with me that a fine of two pounds per man—"

One of the four expelled: "Two pounds!"

"—is relatively lenient under the circumstances. Shall we put it to a vote?" Five hands came up. "The fine will be remitted posthaste to Mister Grant's account. And if it is true that there were hands even more cunning and cowardly manipulating these four men from behind, I trust that their puppets can convince them to show enough decency to help pay the cost of their actions. I believe that's the end of it."

"It is *not!*" Alex MacDonell bellowed. "You'll wish it was, but it is not. I have had all I can stomach of this backwater colony, but you can take my word for it—I will represent this matter as it should be when I get back home."

"I have no doubt," Simpson said, "that your sad story will cause much lamentation in Britain, among all the dockside tavern scum you stand the gin for. Gentlemen—I suggest we adjourn for a quarter hour before moving on to the next item on the adgenda."

Grant was grunting up off his chair and heaving on his coat to follow the flow of councillors out the door when George Simpson materialized in front of him. "By the by, Grant—how's your deliberations going?"

"Deliberations?"

"Yes—on what you plan to do instead of clerking at Fort Garry."

"I'm afraid they're still as half-formed as when I saw you last. I suppose I was waiting to see how this resolved itself."

"Well, now that it's resolved—do come see me, even if you just want to chat."

"Thank you. I certainly shall."

George Simpson was replaced by John Pritchard, saying: "Congratulations!"

"Congratulations?"

"On your inheritance. I've had my own dealings with the MacGillivrays, and I know how much it means to have the London Committee weighing in on your side. You might consider investing in the Buffalo Wool Company."

"I hadn't thought of it. I must confess I'm a little unsure of how—"

"No, we can! Lady Selkirk is introducing buffalo wool shawls in all the fashionable salons in London and Edinburgh! Just one look at the figures and you'll see—"

"Perhaps some other time. I'm afraid, at the moment, I'm a bit . . ."

"Of course, of course—how thoughtless of me, you're still recovering. Perhaps if I stopped by tomorrow, or the next day . . ."

"I imagine I'll be home. Now, if you'll excuse me . . ."

In the anteroom, Alex MacDonell was ranting at anyone who would listen. His apoplectic gaze happened to light on Alexander Sutherland. "And *you*, Sutherland! You're a traitor to your own people—harboring the butcher of Seven Oaks!"

Grant considered going over to defend them, but he should've known better. Mrs. Sutherland bounced up off the bench and stooped to put her face into that of the man who'd been colony sheriff at the time. "We will take no lectures on Seven Oaks from *you*, Alex MacDonell. My husband was *there*, while you were barred up safe inside Fort Douglas.

"And the only reason you're still here to rave about it is that Cuthbert Grant pitched his tent in front of the fort gates to stop the métis and the North West Company from finishing the job. So you can put *that* in your pipe and smoke it, my wee mannie."

On the ride home Falcon said: "Well, that's that for that."

"It appears to be."

"This here Simpson, he's a man that thinks ahead of all the governors we had before."

"He appears to be."

They passed by a ragged collection of snowed-in tents on the east bank, where some of the hunters from Pembina were huddling their way through the winter. One of the blanket-coated group hunkered over an ice-fishing hole stood up and beckoned. Grant and Falcon swerved their horses in that direction.

The ice fishers wanted to know how things had gone at the council meeting. Grant was beginning to feel the effects of his first full day out of bed, so he let Falcon tell the story and looked around at the buffalo-hide tents and thrown-together shanties. The only child in evidence was a sunken-cheeked boy warding the dogs off from the lone catfish the fishermen had managed to catch. Grant suspected that the rest of the children were being kept inside around the fires, so as not to burn off their one meal of the day by running about in the snow.

Some of the men around the fishing hole cheered and laughed when Falcon came to the end of the story, and some of them just shook their heads in amazement that the white governors would punish white men for battering someone who wasn't white.

Grant said, "I'm ashamed to say I can't stay upright much longer," and they let him and Falcon go on their way.

Once they were out of earshot, Grant said: "It seems such a pity, when all they'd have to do is shove a few potatoes in the ground every spring and they'd have plenty of food to tide them over the winter."

"What—turn *jardinier*? Spend their lives grubbing in the ground with a pointed stick like them Kildonan farmers?"

"A little plot of root vegetables or an acre of barley hardly makes for full-time slavery. Especially with the kind of soil you find along the riverbanks here. Once the seed is in, the people who are too old to hunt can spend a lazy summer playing scarecrow, and everyone else is still as free as ever to go roaming. Except that they'd return in the winter to a secure and well-stocked home base. They could have the best of both parents of the New Nation—our mothers' people's freedom to enjoy the whole wide *pays d'en haut*, and the freedom from want that the white farmers enjoy."

"So where're you planning to put it?"

"Put what?"

"This here 'secure home base'?"

"I'm not planning anything, I was just—"

"I know—it was just the sound of your little brain going tick tick tick all the time your body's been chained to a bed."

Once Marie had settled Grant back in bed with a cup of revitalizing brandy, he told her what had happened in the council meeting, ending with: "Wergild. It's supposedly the first step on the road from barbarism to a civilized society. I can still hear Mister MacAndrew in ancient history class: 'Wergild, d'ye ken? Bluid money, not bluid feuds.'

"I suppose it is more civilized, but when it comes to personal satisfaction, wergild doesn't have a patch on the old-fashioned way." He looked up from his cup at his wife and had to laugh at himself. Of course she didn't have the vaguest notion what he was talking about.

CHAPTER 17

Something kept gnawing at Marie. She knew she had every reason to be happy, and she was quite sure she had been during the giddy first weeks of being Mrs. Grant. But now she had an increasing feeling of something jagged and empty growing beside her heart.

Since Wappeston had got back on his feet, he was gone during most of the daylight hours—off talking to the hunters he'd persuaded to winter at Red River, or to the bishop or her father or God knew who else, perhaps that Mrs. Sutherland for one.

When she asked him what he'd spent his day talking about, he'd say something like "Oh, this and that, Waposis—the state of the weather, whether it's been a good year for snaring rabbits . . . Are there any more potatoes?"

One evening, as he was finishing his supper, she blurted out: "What are we going to do?"

"Do?"

"Yes. That's what you've been talking about to all those people, ain't it—everyone but me—about what you're going to do instead of clerking for the Company and building a big house here like we planned."

"In point of fact, I'm sure I could continue working for the Company, at one of the Athabaska posts or in Blackfoot country, as long as it was far away from Red River. But I don't think that holds much appeal for either of us.

"What I've been doing with all this galloping about from one tea party to another—and what I'll have to continue doing for some time yet—is trying to follow a formula I learned in a rather brutal school. To get what you want, you start with finding out what the people around you want. For instance, the bishop wishes the bulk of his parishioners didn't scatter across the prairie for months or years at a time and wander back just as pagan as before he baptized them. The Kildonan people want to raise their crops and their families without fear that the Sioux or the Assiniboine will fight a war against the Saulteaux in their backyards. Most métis just want to continue going out to hunt the buffalo without fear of the Sioux or winter famine. The Company wants to keep on doing business without any disturbances to the orderly flow of profits."

"What do *you* want?" Marie insisted.

"What do *you* want?" he asked.

"I want . . ." She paused to moisten her lips and to accept that she wouldn't know until she'd said it. "I just want us to be happy. To have a good home, with our family and friends around us, and not be afraid that it could all crash apart any moment."

"Well, that's a damned fair definition of what I want. That's what I'm working on. Any notion where my tobacco pouch has got to?"

He spent the evening as usual, sucking on his pipe and staring through the wall, replying to her and Maria Theresa with abstracted grunts. After he was asleep she realized she'd left off the most important thing that she wanted.

The next afternoon Pierriche stuck his head in the doorway and said: "Wappeston about?"

"No, but he should be back in not too long. I just made a pot of tea, and there's some brandy to go with it. . . ."

"You wouldn't mind if I was to sit down and wait for him?"

"Would you like some maple sugar in your tea?"

"Not if there's brandy."

She fetched a cup and they sat for a moment in silence, except for the slurping sounds of sipping too hot tea and the intent gurgles of Maria Theresa scaling her uncle's knee. Once the child was triumphantly ensconced in his lap, Marie said: "Does Wappeston talk to you?"

Pierriche laughed. "Ask Mary when I come stumbling home at dawn."

"Why is it he won't talk to me? Oh, he says 'Good morning' and asks if the winter's getting to me, but it seems like there's a fence back there I just can't climb over. What am I doing wrong?"

Pierriche looked at the table, puffed out his upper lip like a bagpipe bellows, and let the air out with a thoughtful farting sound. "No, Marie, you ain't doing nothing different than you should—or could. She's bound to take a while. It ain't no easy thing fighting a ghost."

"Madelaine," she said.

"Madelaine?"

"The ghost of Madelaine Desmarais."

"Huh? Madelaine Desmarais never meant a fried goddamn to him. Don't get me wrong—he liked her. And she was Maria Theresa's mother, so . . . But the ghost I meant is Bethsy McKay's."

"Bethsy McKay?"

"He never told you about Bethsy and James?"

"James?"

"Hoo boy." He wiped his hand down his face and sighed. "Yeah, that'd be just like him, wouldn't it?

"The story goes like this when it's told short. When Wappeston first came to the *pays d'en haut*—I mean, when he came *back* here after they took him out to Scotland and Montreal for his school—he met this woman, this girl, name of Bethsy McKay. Sister to John Richards McKay. Wappeston and Bethsy got married, just *à la façon du pays,* but that's the only way you could in those days, and it's still been good enough for me and Mary.

"Wappeston was no older than you are now, and him and Bethsy were crazy in love. And when I say crazy I mean crazy. Bethsy was . . . well, she was something. They had a little son. James. But all that was in the time of the war between the two companies. Wappeston went to Montreal for the murder trials, and Bethsy and James stayed at Fort Esperance on the Qu'Appelle. When he came back they were gone, nobody knows where. It's been more'n five years and still no one's heard a word of them, not even her brother.

"And there's another part of it. Back in the first days of the New Nation there was the three of us—Wappeston and me and Bostonais Pangman. About the same time Bethsy and James disappeared, so did Bostonais. No one took much notice at the time—Bostonais was always lighting out on his own when he got fed up with having too many people around him. But this time he's been disappeared five years.

"Maybe it was just coincidence. Maybe Bostonais got caught by some Blackfoot war party—but it does seem funny they'd all three vanish at the same time.

"In the end, it's been a lucky thing for Wappeston. If Bethsy hadn't run off, he wouldn't be married to you now, and in just these few months you've already been a better wife to him than Bethsy McKay was ever going to be. He knows that, too—back in there somewhere.

"There's a lot of twisted paths back there. Since the time Wappeston was born, just about all the people he's loved have been dying on him or running out on him or turning on him. Eventually he gets around to figuring out when he's happy, but it takes him a crucifying long while.

"Goddamn—I must've talked a lot. Not only did I dry my throat out, but someone snuck in here and drank my tea and brandy while I was doing it."

CHAPTER 18

On the day appointed for Grant's interview with the governor of the Northern Department, Maria Theresa decided that it would be a particularly effective morning for getting underfoot and clutching at his leg while he was trying to shave. Marie finally took her in hand so he could proceed to meticulously remove every last whisker bud without replacing them with bleeding nicks. Then he shook out and pulled on a freshly laundered linen shirt, gave his best broadcloth coat a good brushing, and combed his hair until the teeth slid like shot through a goose.

As he reached down his buffalo coat and otter fur cap, he chirped as jauntily as he could manage: "Well, Waposis, when next you see me we will either have a brave new world opened up in front of us or . . . or we won't."

With a fervency that took him by surprise, she said: "If you don't get what you're hoping for from George Simpson, I know we'll get by just fine anyways."

He leaned forward to cup her heart-shaped little chin in his hand and winked. "No fear—with twelve or thirteen thousand pounds on account, we won't starve." Then he kissed both his girls good-bye and went out to saddle his horse.

The gatekeeper at Fort Garry called out: "Good morning, Mister Grant. Good to see you back." Grant waved back and trotted on toward the countinghouse.

Hargrave and the other clerks pumped his hand and slapped his back, gingerly. Hargrave said: "I hear you're going to be leaving us."

"It was the purple ceiling that finished me."

"What are you planning to do instead?"

"That rather depends on my conversation with Mister Simpson."

George Simpson appeared in the doorway to his sanctum sanctorum. "There you are, Grant! You look a hundred percent again. How are you feeling?"

"Perhaps seventy-five to eighty."

"Percent or years?"

"Take your pick."

"Well, at this time of year it's about the same for all of us. Hargrave—tell one of the kitchen sluts to fetch us in a pot of tea. Other than that, we're not to be disturbed. Come in, Grant. Sit yourself. It's just about time for my morning pipe. Here, try some of mine."

Once they were ensconced and puffing away—Grant on his meerschaum and the governor of the Northern Department on a shilling-the-dozen clay churchwarden—Simpson leaped directly to "So, Grant, I'm fascinated to hear your plans for the future."

Grant faked another couple of puffs to make his pipeload catch, in order to remind himself to keep his voice evenly businesslike and to take it slow—but not too slow.

"It isn't only *my* future, actually. No man's an island. I've been considering a number of facets which at first glance might not seem to be directly connected."

"Such as?"

"For one thing—the fact that our mutual efforts to convince the Pembina métis to winter at the Forks don't appear to have been a raging success."

"How not?"

Grant bit his tongue before it could come out with "Why don't *you* try living on frozen fish heads?" Instead he said: "Well, some of them, of course, thought far enough ahead to settle in here with a good stock of provisions. Those who didn't though, are hardly likely to want to repeat the experiment of wintering at the Forks. Or to encourage their cousins who stayed at Pembina to give it a try.

"Another facet has to do with the Sioux and the Assiniboine. Among the Plains tribes, in spring a young man's fancy turns to thoughts of war. The Kildonan farmers might not seem rich by European standards, but they're an awfully tempting target. Even if the Chiefs don't want any trouble with the Company, a few young men on an illicit raid can cause a lot of damage.

"There is another problem that the Company finds itself faced with every winter. Even in the most amenable of wintering grounds, a week-long blizzard or a slump in the game population means the Company must either supply free provisions to the métis or lose its buffalo hunters. But if the buffalo hunters were settled on farms of their own—"

"I don't believe the Company would be enthusiastic about seeing the buffalo hunters it depends upon for pemmican turned into farmers."

"Neither would the hunters, believe me. The kinds of farms I'm speaking of are more like permanent wintering cabins with rather offhanded gardens. Even a very modestly stocked cellar can make a great deal of difference come February."

The tea arrived, giving Grant a welcome opportunity to catch his breath and moisten his throat. He glanced across the rim of his cup at the icy little man waiting on the other side of the desk and decided it was time to drop the preliminaries.

He counted a slow three in his mind and said: "There are other facets, but they all direct me to the same conclusion. For all practical purposes, the Company is sole owner of a piece of land several times the size of Europe. Forty or fifty square miles more or less wouldn't make a great deal of difference to the Company. If the Company—" Something dry lodged itself in his throat. He washed it down, excused himself, and tried again. "If the Company were to grant me a sufficient piece of land somewhere to the west or south of the Forks—within a few hours' ride, at most—I would undertake to settle the Pembina hunters there, along with a number of other métis.

"Any raiding party of Sioux or Assiniboine with designs on the Forks would then have to contend with a few hundred proven warriors."

"A few *hundred?*"

"Well, there wouldn't be that many to begin with, of course. It would probably take a few years to convince some of the die-hard nomads. But I can guarantee a substantial core to start with. My father-in-law, for one."

"McGillis? But he's . . . ." Grant waited for Simpson to complete "he's white," but instead he amended it: "He's only just finished building his place here."

"Quite true. But he seems to believe he can make a good profit selling it—given the increasing number of Company traders choosing to retire to the Forks. What with McGillis and Falcon and myself and a few others who've already committed themselves, I think we can call up the most powerful force there is for convincing other human beings to follow a given course of action."

"And what force is that, pray tell?"

"To make it fashionable."

That managed to spring out a brittle chuckle that was George Simpson's closest approximation to a laugh. "Along with that, we would have God on our side. The bishop has evinced a great deal of interest in establishing a mission at any permanent métis settlement. And that would certainly please certain pious members of the London Committee who feel the Company should be doing more to convert the natives from paganism."

Simpson said stiffly: "Wherever did you get that notion?"

"Well, one clerk or another has to make a fair copy of the minutes from the Northern Department's annual council. I suppose a good clerk would only pay attention to forming his letters artfully and keeping his margins straight, but we've both agreed I wasn't born to be a clerk.

"And then there is the problem of the buffalo hunt itself. The annual returns should be much higher—in terms of both pemmican and hunters. The establishment of a permanent community would help make that possible.

"But I'm not certain whether it's within your power to even consider my modest proposal, or whether it's something that would have to be put to the London Committee."

The governor of the Northern Department actually smiled. "If it isn't in my power at present, I suspect it will be soon." He lined one stubby little forefinger along his snubby little nose and winked. Grant was almost willing to swear he could see canary feathers poking out from the pursed little grin. "Between you and me and the bedpost— the governor of the Southern Department is being retired. And I have reason to believe that the committee is coming to the conclusion that two governors' salaries constitutes an unnecessary expense."

"Good God!" If what Simpson was hinting at came to pass, little Georgie would be the ruler of all North America north of the forty-ninth parallel—excluding Russian Alaska and the odd corner of Lower Canada.

George Simpson's features melded back into their customary bland imitation of a Scottish leprechaun. "So, Grant—what you're proposing, in essence, is that the Company give you your own private principality."

Grant laughed. "You can't have an emperor without a prince or two."

Instead of laughing back, the putative emperor said crisply: "Do you have a specific locality in mind?"

"Several places have suggested themselves. Either west along the Assiniboine or south along the Red—not too far south, of course."

"Um-hm. I shall have to reflect upon it, of course, but on the face of it your proposal does have several factors to recommend it. Once you've settled on a specific locale, come see me again. Barring unforeseen circumstances, I'd be surprised if we don't have a done deal."

Grant had to tell himself several times that that was it, he'd done it. When it finally sank in, it took a Herculean effort to nod his head calmly instead of whooping and jumping for the ceiling. On the way to the door, he turned back to say: "By the by, I noticed that Fort Garry has a number of mothballed pieces of artillery—including a brass field gun. Two-pounder, I believe. I'd be interested in buying it, if—as I suspect—it's of no use to the Company."

"So long as you don't plan to use it on the Company."

"With any luck I won't have to use it on anyone."

CHAPTER 19

Marie had just hung up her blanket and was about to start skinning out the day's bag from the rabbit snares when she heard hollering and a horse galloping toward the house.

Pierriche's voice shouted out next door: "What's all the damned whooping about?"

Wappeston's voice boomed back: "Dig out that bottle of brandy you've been saving and come next door and I'll tell you."

The door jerked wide open, letting in a cloud of blown snow with her fur-clad husband in the middle of it. He yanked off his cap and announced while tugging off his mittens: "Well, Waposis, it looks as though you're about to become a queen—in a small sort of way."

She meant to bite her tongue but was too late. "I'm going to be something bigger'n that." He froze in his tracks with his coat half-unbuttoned, and his grin melted. She said, "I'd thought so for a while, but I wanted to be sure before . . . But now my mother and Mary and Josephte all say it's for sure."

Pierriche appeared in the doorway, cradling a square-shouldered bottle in the crook of his arm. He took one look at Wappeston gawking at her and said: "So she finally got around to telling you."

Wappeston grumbled, "Did *every*one know except me?" and then leaped across the room to her, picking her up by the armpits and enveloping her in the folds of his buffalo coat. He kissed her mouth and the side of her neck and then suddenly grew more tentative and set her back down. "I'm sorry, I should've considered . . . I shouldn't be bouncing you around. . . ."

She blushed and giggled at him. "I ain't *that* far gone yet. My mother says it won't even start to show until the spring."

"Well, it looks like we have two reasons to drink your brandy, Pierriche. My news pales by comparison, but nonetheless . . ." He shrugged out of his coat and hung it on the peg by the door while Pierriche squatted on the overlapping buffalo robes and bearskin in front of the hearth and went to work getting the cork extracted intact. Marie half filled three cups with tea, and Pierriche added in a dash of flavor from the thick-walled, green glass bottle. Wappeston took a deep slurp, smacked his lips, and launched into the story of his parley with George Simpson.

Partway through it, Mary and Josephte came in, leaving the older children watching over the young ones, and he had to run over the first part again while Marie fetched two more cups. When he came to the triumphant conclusion, she still didn't understand what he was so excited about. She understood that it meant they would have a place to build a house, but they were surrounded by endless open country where generations of métis had been putting up cabins wherever the fancy struck them.

Pierriche and Wappeston launched immediately into debating whether this or that location was too deep into the territory of this or that tribe or too susceptible to spring floods or too far from the Forks or too close.

Marie suspected this conversation was going to go on for days—salting in the opinions of other men such as her father and the hunters wintering at the Forks and the bishop and Chief Peguis and Jean Baptiste Lajimodierre and . . . She got up to start working on dinner.

When she and her husband were snug in their bed with the fire banked up for the night, he was still vibrating with excitement, although at a slightly slower rate. He said: "It can't last forever, you see. I mean, the country—the *pays d'en haut.* Oh, as long as our lifetimes, I should think. Perhaps even a bit longer, with luck. But eventually, all those people crammed into the cities in the east—you can't imagine it if you haven't seen it, human beings squirming together like maggots—someday they're going to burst in here like Noah's flood, and the life we take for granted will be gone forever.

"But when that day comes"—he reached over to pat her belly—"the deal I just struck with George Simpson means that our children will still have a little piece of the *pays d'en haut,* a place that no one will be able to take away from them or from their children."

A teary "Oh!" sighed out of Marie, and she was suddenly moist all over. Now that she understood, she was astounded that she could've been so dull as to not see immediately why he'd been so elated about his plans coming true. It was for their children.

As she rolled over to melt herself against him, he said: "And I know already what we're going to call it."

"We don't know yet whether to pick a boy's name or a girl's."

"Hm? Oh, absolutely—no point naming babies till you see them. . . . We'll call it Grantown. Between terms at Inverness College I was boarded with some Highland cousins of my father's at Grantown-on-Spey, on the edge of *sliobh grantia,* which was where Clan Grant got its name—the Plain of the Sun."

O ver the next few weeks, the floating geography conference came and went. Marie overheard enough of the conversations to gather that the general consensus seemed to be resolving in favor of a place called White Horse Plains—the place Wappeston had come out with in his first conversation with Pierriche.

It was decided that Marie's husband and father and brother-in-law would go out to White Horse Plains to have a closer look. Marie surprised herself by declaring that she would go along with them. Wappeston shook his head. "Not at this time of year, Little Rabbit. We'll have to do it in a jumper along the Assiniboine, and all the twists and windings will stretch it out into a full day's traveling. We'll have to camp there overnight."

"I've camped out in the snow before. Somebody's going to have to take care of you three. My father ain't cooked for himself in twenty years, and you and Pierriche have got spoiled over the winter."

That seemed to settle it, especially when she insisted, "I'd like to have one look at where we're going to end up living the rest of our lives."

It was still dark when they set out, traveling in two jumpers. A jumper was a Red River cart with its wheels replaced by runners for the winter. All four travelers and their camp gear would have fit in one jumper, but taking two meant they wouldn't have to walk home if one of the horses froze its lungs.

The jumpers' wooden runners skidded and hissed. The horses' hooves clopped sharply where the wind had scoured the ice clean and thudded hollowly where the wind had packed down a muffling cushion of snow. It was a soft winter night with the moonlight diffusing through the clouds. A cloudlike white owl wafted by.

The sun had come up to make a slightly brighter twilight when they stopped at a place Marie recognized—the Passage of the Assiniboine, where the combination of low-scooped banks and silted-up gravel bars made a reliable crossing place for carts. Wappeston called across to Mr.

McGillis and Pierriche in the other jumper: "You see? This is half-way—so at White Horse Plains we'd find the Passage just as convenient as it is from the Forks." Pierriche and her father shrugged skeptically at each other, playing up the part of wary customers.

They all climbed down, hobbled their horses, and built a quick fire on the bank to make some tea, running in circles and jumping up and down in the snow while the water was boiling, to work the blood back into their feet and legs. They washed down a few leathery strips of jerked venison with hot rum tea, pried the ponies away from the green frozen grass they'd pawed their way down to, and climbed back into the jumpers.

The cloud-masked, cottony white sun had climbed as high as it was going to get when the winding of the river started to go even more erratic with loops and switchbacks and meanders. "You see?" Wappeston shouted to Marie over the hissing and drumming of the jumpers. "When the river folds up on itself like this, it means that the belt of trees lining the shore joins up into something resembling a genuine forest."

She looked at the banks to try to see what he was seeing. Even though most of the trees were just leafless skeletons, there were enough of them to provide a shelter against the house-rattling winds of the plains. For no good reason, she began to feel a funny buzzing sensation under her breastbone.

The farther they snaked along the coiling maze of horseshoe bends, the stronger the buzzing grew. The flashing of Wappeston's eyes and teeth said that he was feeling the same thrum in his chest. From the onrushing sound of the jumper behind theirs, and Wappeston's straining to hold their pony to a trot, her father and Pierriche and the horses were feeling it, too. She shouted at her husband: "My condition ain't all that delicate yet."

Then the jumper bearing her father and Pierriche surged up beside theirs, with Pierriche snapping his whip and shouting obscene endearments at his horse's head. Wappeston barked at her, "Hold on!" and laid into their pony.

The horse race tore around turns with the jumpers skidding sideways and treatening to overturn. Marie gritted her teeth and dug her mittens into the cart rail. Sometimes one jumper surged a few feet ahead, then the other, but neither one could break into a clear lead. Wappeston started bellowing at their horse in a language Marie didn't understand, but it seemed to bear a resemblance to a demented version of a mass.

As they rounded a bend that seemed no more or less suicidal than the last few dozen, both drivers hauled back hard on the ribbons and brought their horses to a halt. Pierriche shouted across: "I'll do you a favor and call it too close to call! What were you doing back there, praying?"

"What's a chariot race without a little Latin? If you think we were whipping these horses, you should've seen how they whipped the first stanzas of the *Aeneid* into me at Inverness."

Where the jumpers had ground to a stop, there was a sheltered bowl in the north bank of the river. Wappeston jumped down and held up his arms to help Marie over the railing. Pierriche, already down and strapping on his snowshoes, called to Wappeston: "If I remember, there's a stand of spruce just over that hump in the ground."

"I believe you remember correctly."

Pierriche fished his axe out through the lattice of cart rails and disappeared over the snow ridge rimming the bowl. Mr. McGillis commenced wrestling the tent poles out of their jumper. Marie fished out her snowshoes and her husband's, and the two of them went to work stamping down a circle of snow in the middle of the bowl.

The men did a lot of grumbling that if they'd come without her they would have just dug burrows in the snow instead of all this unnecessary fussing. They got the tent up and hung the inner curtain that would channel the cold air through the smoke hole and lay down a mat of spruce boughs and buffalo robes around a fire—a fire, they pointed out, that was either going to drown in the snow it melted or set the spruce floor alight or perhaps, at best, gradually melt the snow out from under their beds until the slant rolled them down into the flames in their sleep. Their grumbling miraculously evaporated, though, once they were all lolling back and opening their coats in a snug conical home surrounding a bubbling pot of buffalo-and-barley soup.

After the pot had been scraped clean and the dregs of teacups and pipe bowls dumped into the snow, Wappeston said, "Come on, while there's still some daylight," and stooped out through the door flap.

By the time Marie got her snowshoes fastened on, he was already disappearing over the ridge. She and the others hustled after him, like following a bear dog that's caught a whiff of grizzly. They only managed to catch up with him because he was breaking trail and had to double back out of a few thickets that proved too dense to push through. He tossed back over his shoulder: "When I was camped with the brigade here once, I took a notion to take a walk through the woods. . . ."

"Because," Pierriche panted, "you was so crazy with old memories you weren't fit company even for voyageurs."

The clawing network of tangled branches came to an abrupt end. Marie stopped beside Wappeston. There was a pristine white gully with the marring black scrawls of trees starting up again on the other side. He pointed ahead and said: "You see? We're camped on an island. On the shore there, those tall skeletons are elms that fill out into a canopy in the summer. Elms and burl oaks and poplars and maples—"

She interjected: "Sugar maples?"

Pierriche said: "Not so much. But there's a lot of 'em just a short ride south."

Wappeston kept on pointing ahead. "And just beyond those trees is the point of a low ridge—you can't even see it under the snow—that is the start of"—sweeping his arm back in an arc—"White Horse Plains.

"If there were a two-storied house straight across from us—two stories and an attic—you could stand on the widow's walk and see into the council lodges of the Sioux a hundred miles south, or the Assiniboines to the west. The house would be sheltered by trees, but just a few paces past the barn there's an open prairie that could be cleared for plowing by simply burning off the grass."

He said a good deal more that she didn't hear. She was occupied in watching the snow across the channel forming into a mountainous white house, leaving green fields where the drifts had been.

Back in the tent, Pierriche said: "That little soft ridge you was talking about—that's Coteau des Festins. I bet that's where the camp was when the story happened that gave White Horse Plains its name, or its *names.* Some people call it Phantom White Horse Plains, some call it Ghost Horse Plains. The true name is just plain the Place Where the Ghost Horse Runs, but white men got no patience for the truth.

"There's a lot of different ways of telling the story, but I know the true one. It was back in the days—not so long ago—when the tribes around here was just starting to get horses from the tribes in the south. There was an Assiniboine Chief. He had a daughter and she was . . . well, almost as beautiful as Marie or my Mary.

"There was two young men come courting her, a Cree boy and the son of a Sioux Chief. The Cree were enemies with both the Assiniboines and the Sioux. But the Cree boy had this horse—a white stallion that shone and ran like the wind on the snow. What the mestizos way down south call a *diablo blanco,* a white devil. The Cree boy said he'd give the white horse to the Assiniboine Chief for his daughter.

"So the Assiniboine Chief did what he thought was a smart thing.

He didn't want to make the Sioux feel insulted, so he waited until midsummer when the Sioux would all be way south on the prairie hunting buffalo, and then he had a marriage between his daughter and the Cree boy. But on the day when the Cree boy came with the white horse and held his hand out for the Assiniboine girl, here comes a cloud of dust galloping up from the south—the whole goddamned Sioux Nation mad as hell.

"Now the Cree boy throws his bride up onto the white horse and he jumps on his own gray pony and they take off with the Sioux chasing after them. There wasn't any Sioux horse had a hope in hell of catching that white devil. But the gray horse was just a horse like any other. As the Cree boy saw he couldn't get away, he shouted at his bride to keep on going and he turned to make his stand. But she turned back, to try to get him onto the white horse that no one could catch. It seems the Assiniboine girl thought the Cree boy was . . . well, something almost like Wappeston or me.

"The Sioux arrows killed her and him and the gray pony, but the white horse got away. And now, after a hundred years and more, you'll still hear people tell you they was riding across Ghost Horse Plains on a moonless summer night, when they'd had nothing to drink worth mentioning, and they'd seen something silvery white moving like a gust of snow and heard a drumming like wild hooves of the devil searing the earth."

He took another sip of his rummed tea and shrugged. "Well, that's what they say, anyways."

CHAPTER 20

Grant grew impatient waiting for the ice to break, although he had plenty enough to keep him busy. There were arrangements to be made with the fort carpenter and boat master, a mountain of seasoned lumber to be inspected and purchased, endless ordering from the Company stores. When he'd managed to get every accomplished woodworker on the east side of the Red beavering away on a bedstead or a cart or a kitchen table, he rode over to the Point Douglas Sutherlands' to make inquiries about Kildonan carpenters. Mister Sutherland climbed onto their Indian pony turned plow horse and escorted him north along the trail connecting the clumps of thatched houses and barns along the riverbank.

Mister Sutherland turned in toward one homestead with a long, low shed beside the barn. Inside the shed, a grim-faced little Highlander was planing the pieces of an embryonic washstand, or perhaps a writing desk. It was a writing desk Grant was interested in at the moment. There was a bit of tension at first, until Grant spoke to him in Gaelic and made it clear he wanted to pay him money to do a job of work. As with most transactions at Red River, no money actually changed hands. When the work was done, Grant would simply write a note instructing the Company clerks to credit the workman's account from his.

Then there was the main task of populating Grantown. Some reluctant individuals had to be convinced that he wasn't trying to turn them into *jardiniers*; some overeager ones had to be given the impression that that was exactly what he was trying to do. If he let in too many flighty ones at the start, the place was never going to grow into more than another semipermanent winter camp. But if he couldn't get people who weren't his immediate relations, Grantown would never be more than an overgrown family farm.

He got the distinct feeling it was going to work the day Urbain Delorme said to him: "Me and the wife've been talking, and we wondered if it'd be all right if we was to throw in with you." Urbain was generally regarded as the best hunter in the Red River Valley—next to Jean Baptist Lajimodierre. It would have been an even greater coup to get Lajimodierre to throw his weight in with the Grantown scheme, but he and his family were too well fixed at the Forks.

When Grant told Marie about Urbain Delorme, she clapped her hands and squealed with delight. Sometimes she surprised him with the things she understood without having them explained. Although her concave little belly had only infinitesimally edged toward convex, her skin had already taken on that eerie, earthy, ethereal glow, and her melon breasts were impossibly ripening further. She was eating like a carnivorous Clydesdale.

Every morning after breakfast he would go out to look at the expanding network of black capillaries on the white skin of the river. When the capillaries grew into veins and the floes began to grind against each other, he told Marie: "We'll leave in three days."

"But there's still snow on the ground."

"I know. But if we wait until all the snow's gone and the ground starts to thaw, we'll have to haul a train of carts through knee-deep gumbo and flooded creeks."

Most of the carts and cart ponies and cargo were already stockpiled on the west side of the Red, moved over when the ice was still solid.

The few carts and household necessities still on the east side were ferried across. The wheels were knocked off and given a ride, the awning that usually rode on top was wrapped around the bottom, and the instant raft was unceremoniously launched in a race for the other shore. The race part came from trying to reach land before the bull's-hide awning started letting in too much water. Fortunately on this occasion, instead of having to paddle against the spring current they were towed across by a couple of the fort's York boats.

They managed to make it across with no casualties beyond a few soggy moccasins. When the carts were all reassembled and hitched up, Grant swung up onto his saddle horse and nodded at Marie, who was standing at the front rail of the lead cart. She snapped the reins against the cart pony's rump, and the caravan lurched into motion.

Grant stayed where he was, to make sure the mob of carts behind fell into line without getting themselves entangled. There were almost a hundred of them, bearing fifty families and their possessions, along with loads of lumber and tools and the Company servants temporarily assigned to help build Grantown. When the last cart was in motion, Grant trotted ahead to take the lead.

They followed the puddled ruts of the cart trail running west toward Portage la Prairie. The last time Grant had led a line of carts along that trail, they'd been traveling in the opposite direction, and the trail had ended in the bloody nightmare of Seven Oaks. Sometimes Grant got the feeling that his whole life was just a motion toward or away from that one day.

They forded Catfish and Sturgeon creeks, passed by the Passage of the Assiniboine, and came to Ghost Horse Plains just as the sunset started to turn the western half of the sky into a fountain of blood. By the time night came down, Coteau des Festins was once again a firelit village of pipe-clayed tipis.

The next morning, without waiting for breakfast, Grant paced out the perimeters of his house and showed the fort carpenter and his crew where to start. Then he worked his way eastward along the north bank of the Assiniboine, pacing out the rough frontage of each lot. Directly to the east of his own double-width lot would be Angus McGillis's, then another lot each for Marie's brothers Donald and Daniel, who would soon be old enough to build homes of their own. The next lot was for François Morin, who had come from the Qu'Appelle to build a home at Grantown for his many children and his wife, Grant's sister Marguerite. Then came Falcon's lot and a dozen others.

When Grant came back to his own house site, the carpenters were already setting in the first corner post and Marie was standing incandescent with her fist in her mouth. He paused just long enough to give her a kiss and a wink and carried on westward. He paced out the double lot for the Catholic mission, which would be his and Marie's other next-door neighbor, then Urbain Delorme's lot and the others beyond. At a later date they would haul out the chain and lay out the boundaries precisely, but the immediate concern was to get a rough idea so everyone could start building.

The next month and a half was a spring festival danced to the drumming of axes and mallets and the fiddling of whipsaws. On one of the rare nights Grant didn't fall asleep the instant his back hit the bed, he sneaked the blankets off Marie and marveled at all the different kinds of growing going on at Ghost Horse Plains this spring.

The tent village on Coteau des Festins gradually melted along with the last holdout splotches of snow. The tents of those who were content with sod-roofed shanties of unpeeled green logs were the first to go, followed by those who wanted dovetail-cornered squared-log walls but were good enough with a splitting axe to do the job in half the time it would take with an adze. Finally the only tents left were the ones housing Grant's family and Angus McGillis's. Falcon delighted in ambling past the sites and remarking to Grant and Angus on what a pleasant, warm, dry night's sleep he'd just had in his snug new cabin.

Like Falcon and a number of the others, Grant and Angus were building their houses in what had come to be known as the "Red River style." The first stage was essentially the same as the first step of building a fence, except the fence posts were squared logs as high as the outside walls of the proposed house. The posts were footed securely in ground that froze two feet deep in a moderate winter. The posts had grooves cut down their lengths on two sides. Once the posts were up, the spaces between were filled in with beams, each with its ends tongued to fit the grooves. The walls of most Red River houses were no more than seven feet high, so two men working together could simply lift up the tongued beams one by one, slot their ends into the grooves, and drop them down until the stack reached the height of the posts. A few days of lifting and stacking produced an interlocked structure with solid hardwood walls eight inches thick.

But the outside walls of Angus's house were fifteen feet high, and Grant's were twenty, so their beams had to be hoisted by pulleys rigged to the roof trees. And the fort carpenter had taken his crew and gone back to his Company duties after putting up the frames and giving Grant a hands-on rudimentary course in house building.

There was no shortage of volunteer labor, but even less of a shortage of work. While some men were swarming over the house frames fitting wall beams into place, others were hasping cedar into roof shakes. Another crew was working in the saw pit. There were no sawmills west of Upper Canada, so the only way the people of the *pays d'en haut* could turn logs into floor planks was to dig a log-long, man-deep pit and stand one man inside it working one end of a whipsaw while another man standing on the rim plied the other end.

In among all the hubbub of working men, Marie and the other women and older children were constructing massive communal banquets or hoeing burned-off swatches of prairie into gardens.

When the first wild rose proved it was past time to start on the summer buffalo hunt, the McGillis house was finished, but the Grant house wasn't. Grant wasn't too surprised or distressed. His house was bound from the start to be more of an undertaking, since it would have to house not only him and Marie and their children, but also Josephte and John and Father Picard until there was time to build a chapel and a rectory. And the main floor of the house had to be big enough to serve as a meeting hall until an alternative was available.

Grant was ready to leap to the next exhilarating bit of madness—his scheme for the buffalo hunt.

On the last day before the people of Grantown embarked on the hunt, Father Picard held mass in the unfinished house. The entire citizenry managed to squeeze in, standing heel to toe. The sunlight through the framework of open rafters cast elongated shadows of bars and crucifixes.

The next morning Grant and Marie broke down the tent they'd been living in and loaded it onto the cart carrying their camp gear and provisions. There were six other Grant carts. Father Picard stood at the rail of the second one, holding the reins, and Josephte and John the next two. The other three had been turned into a train by the simple expedient of tying each horse's halter to the back rail of the cart ahead. Behind them, a knotted, milling line stretched the whole length of Grantown—the Falcon carts, the McGillis carts, and then those of the Delormes, the Lussiers, the MacDougalls, the Zastres . . . Grant had advised them to bring every cart they could lay their hands on, because this year they were going to fill them all.

The carts were a jumble of styles. While the basic frameworks were all essentially the same—two long shafts fixed to an axle between two high, dished-in wheels—some carters built a long, narrow box of willow latticework on top while others preferred a square, oak-railed one; some fixed a plank across the front to sit on while others preferred to stand or to perch on the cargo. The living things milling around the carts were even more of a jumble. Saddle horses reared, dogs ran yapping in circles, cart drovers argued about their place in the line or wandered off to see if they could get up a card game before it came time to roll out. Grant wondered if he'd utterly lost his mind to imagine anyone could ever convince such a collection of rabidly independent, offhanded individuals to act together as a unit.

He helped Marie boost her barrel-bellied body over the rails of the lead cart. He didn't at all fancy the idea of her giving birth out on the prairie, but her mother and all the other wise women had assured him that the baby wouldn't come until a few weeks after the hunt was home again—provided the Sioux left any hunt to come home.

With Marie safely ensconced and holding the reins, Grant reached inside his shirt and pulled out a length of cloth that had been lying folded at the bottom of a trunk for seven years. He clucked at his horse to keep still, gingerly stood up on the saddle pad, and tied the ends of the cloth to the tall poplar pole fixed to the front of Marie's cart. It was a bisected blue blanket with a white infinity symbol that Bethsy McKay had sewn for the flag of the New Nation. As the wind unfurled it, some of the hunters who'd ridden behind it before set up a cheer.

Grant dropped back onto the saddle and trotted ahead to take the proffered halter of the pony hitched to the stubby little brass field gun on its preposterously high-wheeled carriage. He raised his arm over his shoulder and called out the words that had started every canoe brigade of the North West Fur Trading Company and every foray of the army of the New Nation: *"En avant!"*

I t took them five days to cover the seventy-odd miles southeast to Pembina, hooking through the gap between the Pembina Hills and Turtle Mountain. Grant was just as glad that the going was slow. It gave them and him some time to get used to managing a caravan of several hundred unruly cart horses and even more unruly drovers. He'd worked out a number of details in his head while he was recovering from his New Year's greetings, but half the time he was making it up as he went along.

As he led the way up the last hill before Fort Pembina, Grant close-reefed the knots in his stomach against what he was going to see when his horse crested the ridge. A few dozen waiting carts and hunters would be a reasonable success; a handful would be worse than none at all. The one possibility he hadn't prepared himself for was what he found spread out below him. Virtually the entire plantation around the fort was covered with vermilion- and ocher-daubed white tents and cart awnings. Packs of children and dogs chased each other up and down the avenues of the tent city. Cooking fires sent a forest of smoke trees reaching for the sun. It appeared that every hunter who'd wintered at Red River or Pembina or farther west along the Assiniboine or Qu'Appelle had heard the word and elected to come to the appointed rendezvous with the hunters of Ghost Horse Plains.

There were puffs of smoke followed by popping sounds as some of the men below saw the blue-and-white flag coming over the hill. As the downward angle of his saddle pad leveled out and his horse carried him forward onto the flats, Grant saw a number of hunters and their wives coming out of the massed camp with their palms held up to greet him. But he didn't stop or swerve to meet them; he trotted straight on, with the axles of the Grantown carts squealing along behind him, toward the one corner of the meadow that wasn't occupied by carts or tents or grazing horses. At the edge of the open ground, he threw up his left arm and let it drop again as he trotted on. At about the midpoint he twitched the halter to turn his horse and clamped his knees in to bring it to a halt.

At the spot where he'd flung up his arm, Marie had turned the cart horse to the left and was coaxing it with whip and reins into a wide circle around him. The rest of the long line followed her lead and swerved at the same point, like a coiling snake. When Marie's cart had come full circle and her horse was about to ram into the side of one of Urbain Delorme's carts at the turning point—the nose of the snake bumping up against its own belly—she turned the pony sharply to face inward at her husband. Father Picard did the same with the cart directly behind, lining up his wheel against hers. Josephte and John did the same, John jumping down quickly to loose the slipknots on the leads of the entrained carts and drag them into line.

Grant had to restrain himself from trotting forward to help when Marie heaved her swollen body over the cart rail and waddled about unhitching and hobbling the cart horse. Before the sun had moved half its width across the sky, he was an equestrian statue at the center of a palisade of carts bisected by a rope stretched down the middle to separate the grazing horses from the tents and campfires.

He could have cheerfully kissed the lot, right down to the grizzledest tobacco-chewing beard scratcher. Instead he kept his eyes front and his spine straight and clucked his horse into a trot to where Marie and Josephte were unloading their gear. He swung off the saddle and handed the halter to John. Marie was holding the coat Bethsy McKay had made for him—cut on a pattern Beau Brummel would have recognized immediately, although the antelope-hide fabric might have given him pause in the few places it showed between the color-wheeled beadwork, quillwork, and embroidery.

The carts that made up the circle were all angled inward, with their harness poles grounded and their butts tilted to the sky. Grant wasn't quite sure whether that was the best arrangement—the poles took up a lot of camping and grazing space—but it suited his purpose for the moment. He shrugged on the coat of many colors, whipping his chin with trailing fringes, and vaulted over the front rail of the nearest empty cart. He paused there for an instant as that old, familiar feeling came over him again—the sick-making thrill of knowing that the next few minutes would either prove him a tactical genius or a dead fool.

He started to walk up the slope of the cartbed toward the ready-made pulpit at the other end and came within an ace of literally falling on his face. As his weight passed by the balance point of the axle, the cart started to tilt. He clutched for the rail. The cart shifted and shivered dangerously, then thudded and shuddered and stayed stable on its original angle. He looked back over his shoulder. Marie and Mary had each plunked their ample bottoms down on the ends of the cart poles.

Grant silently promised a candle to whichever saints were responsible for Marie's fecundity and Mary Falcon's taste for slabs of bannock fried in buffalo fat, then levered himself up toward the high end of the cart box. It appeared that the entire population of the tent city grown up around Fort Pembina had drifted out to whorl against the wooden walls of the White Horse Plains hunt. Through the back of his neck, he could feel the eyes and ears of the people of Grantown forming the other slab of the vise. He took a firm grip of the top rail, sucked in his cheeks to squeeze some juice into his mouth, and announced: "I don't know how many of you came intentionally for the rendezvous and how many happened to be here by coincidence. But we will welcome any of you who wish to join us. Tomorrow we set off on the hunt, and we don't intend to turn back homeward until every last one of our carts is filled to bursting—if it means following the herd into the Black Hills."

That got their attention. The Black Hills were the sacred heart of the Dakotah Nation. Grant waited for the murmurs to die down and then went on, "But anyone who wishes to accompany us must be prepared to abide by our laws."

Someone bellowed: *"Laws?"*

"There are only eight simple rules. One: No buffalo are to be run on the Sabbath day. Father Picard will give mass and communion every Sunday." That called up grumbles mingled with mumbles of approbation.

"Two: No party is to fork off from the main party, nor lag behind, nor go before.

"Three: No one will run buffalo before the general order is given."

"Who'll give the order?"

"The Captain of the hunt."

"Who the hell is that?"

"In future hunts, it will be up to you to determine in open election. But for this hunt—you are looking at him. Four: Every Captain, with his soldiers, shall patrol the camp in turn and keep guard. In this case, 'Captain' means Captain of Ten. We've already selected our own Captains of Ten, by the same method that anyone who chooses to join us is free to follow. Any group of hunters that wishes to join together and nominate a Captain, and to ask enough other hunters to join with them to make up a company of ten, is free to do so.

"Five: Anyone who breaks any one of these laws once shall have his saddle and bridle cut to pieces." There were no mumbles this time, only acidic grumbles.

"Six: Anyone who trespasses against these laws a second time shall have the coat stripped off his back and sliced to pieces."

The grumbles grew louder. Grant opened up his throat and chest to crank his voice a notch louder. "Seven! For a third offense against these laws, the offender who has already had his harness and his coat cut up shall have his back cut up—with a whip."

There was a roar of anger, not only from in front of him but behind him as well. From out of the wave, a saw-toothed tenor penetrated, "I'd like to see the man who thinks he can take a whip to me!"

Grant tracked the voice to a pock-faced young man with shoulders the width of most barns. Several thoughts chased themselves nose to tail through the back of his mind. One of them was an observation that all his uncertainties always disappeared the instant someone else poked a finger into his chest; another was a fervent thank-you to the pockmarked young man. Grant smiled at him and said: "Do you suffer from myopia?

"Eight: Anyone committing a theft, even down to the value of a sinew, shall be paraded through the camp, with the camp crier calling out that person's name three times, adding the word *thief* each time."

The murmurs at the eighth and final law were universal and under the breath, taking the wind out of the sails massing against the previous three laws. Grant congratulated himself. He was old enough to know there was an infinite number of things he didn't know, but he did know that the people of the New Nation would rather have the skin flayed off their backs and all their hunting gear chopped up than be paraded in shame.

He sucked in one last deep breath. "Well, those are the laws that anyone coming with us will have to live by. A great many other facets still have to be worked out, but we'll leave those aside until we find out how many of you—if any—choose to fall in with us tomorrow morning."

And to his great surprise and consternation, every last blessed one of them did.

CHAPTER 21

Every morning a blank load fired from the cannon signaled the six hundred carts of the buffalo hunt to start rolling farther into Sioux territory. Maria Theresa loved the boom and buck of the gun, so Marie would take her by the hand and follow Wappeston when the Captain of the day announced that the tents were all packed up and the cart ponies harnessed. Maria Theresa's walking was still a chancy proposition at best, but it matched pace with Marie's pregnant waddle. Marie was finding it increasingly hard to believe that she wasn't about to give birth to triplets any minute. The muscles at the base of her back ached from heaving the extra weight around, and she was constantly searching for something to do with her hands other than scratching the itchy skin off her breasts and belly.

On the fifth morning after they'd left Pembina, Wappeston got impatient waiting for the Captain of the day and decided to go load the cannon so he could fire it as soon as he got the word. Marie and Maria Theresa trailed along in his wake. Marie wanted to tell him not to expect too much. Just yesterday he'd invented a new order of march, traveling in four parallel lines instead of one long one. It was bound to take people a while to get used to curving the lines into four arcs of a circle for the night and straightening them back out in the morning. But she couldn't catch up with him to say so.

Half a dozen hunters were gathered around the cannon, peering down the barrel and toying with the ramrod. She could see Wappeston waving them off and heard one of them say: "I'd like to take a try at firing this thing."

"No. No one touches this but me. Hand me that and move back."

The one holding the ramrod handed it over and they moved back, grumbling. Marie handed Maria Theresa into their charge and waddled on to where Wappeston stood measuring out the powder, so she could talk to him without being overheard. She murmured: "If you showed them how to do it, you wouldn't have to come out to the cannon every morning."

"No."

"You can't do everything yourself."

"I have no intentions of trying to. But I will do *this* myself."

"It seems to me—"

"There was a man named John Warren. He was the only casualty the first time we rooted out the colony and sent them packing—the summer before Seven Oaks. We were doing a very effective job of scaring them off—hiding in the bushes around Colony House and firing potshots into the roof and window frames. We were under the impression that we'd confiscated all their artillery, but it turned out they still had one little swivel gun tucked away. John Warren poked it out the window at us and touched it off. It blew apart and took his hand off. He bled to death in a hurry. That's the sort of thing that can happen if you load a cannon incorrectly."

"And you know how to do it right?"

"If I knew that, I could teach them. If I make a mistake, I'll have only myself to blame." He glanced up from the powder keg to her, and what he saw made him laugh. "Don't fret, Waposis—if anything, I'm inclined to be so parsimonious with the powder that it wouldn't blow a wad of feathers out the barrel. Besides, I had need of two hands even before you got pregnant. Now move back a few steps."

She went back to Maria Theresa. He finished loading the cannon, primed one of his pistols to spark the touchhole, and stood waiting. Pierriche came galloping out from the still-circled carts and hauled his pony to a halt halfway between the cannon and its audience. Marie called to him: "I thought you were Captain of the day yesterday."

"I was. Urbain's today. But Honoré MacDougall was taking his own sweet time getting his carts hitched, and Urbain started yelling at him that he was holding up the start, and Honoré started yelling back and—"

"Loan me your horse," Wappeston cut in, and was up in the saddle almost before Pierriche was off it. He wheeled the horse around and whipped it back toward where it had just come from. Pierriche started ambling after him. Marie scooped up Maria Theresa to follow along. Pierriche stopped and took Maria Theresa away from her, saying: "I think one child at a time's enough to carry."

As they crossed back inside the circle of carts, Marie began to hear the angry voices raised above the general morning hubbub. The sound put her in mind of something her father used to grumble about when he was a fur trader, that if he shouted an order to one of his indentured white employees and a métis contracted for the season, the Scot or Canadian would say, "Yes, sir!" and jump to it, while the métis was just as likely to take his offended sensibilities off fishing for a year or two.

Some of the people who'd been waiting on their loaded carts were now climbing down again to see what the fuss was about. Marie and Pierriche wove their way forward through the curious. In the middle of the horseshoe of onlookers, one of Honoré MacDougall's three carts stood waiting with its pony hitched in place and ready to go. The other two were still resting at an angle, with their empty shafts slanted to the ground. Urbain Delorme's ten soldiers were sitting on their horses, one of them holding the halter of Urbain's abandoned horse. Urbain and Honoré MacDougall were squared off in front of each other. Both were red-faced and flare-eyed, but at least they weren't yelling at each other anymore. Instead, Honoré was pointing at Urbain with one arm and gesturing with the other as he yelled up at Wappeston on Pierriche's horse: "I don't know who Delorme thinks he is, to give me orders! I been loading up my own carts and catching up with herds since he was running bare-assed around his mother's tipi!"

Urbain opened his mouth to reply, but Wappeston cut him off with a slicing motion of his hand. Wappeston swung his off leg over the saddle, slid off Pierriche's horse, and advanced toward Honoré, beckoning at Urbain's soldiers: "Come lend a hand." Honoré dropped into a defensive stance, and several other MacDougalls pushed their way forward through the crowd to even the odds.

Marie wasn't at all afraid that Honoré or any other MacDougall would inflict any serious damage on her husband face to face, but she had a sickening feeling that this was the moment where his whole grand plan was going to fracture into brawling and bile. She was as surprised as Honoré appeared to be when Wappeston walked right past him to the first of Honoré's horseless carts and stooped down to take hold of one of the harness poles. A couple of Urbain's soldiers followed his lead with the other pole. They hefted up the poles to straighten the cartbed, swung the cart around, and dragged it out of the circle.

Before Honoré could quite make up his mind how to react, Wappeston was coming back, dusting his hands and gesturing at Urbain's other soldiers to do the same with Honoré's other carts. He stopped in front of Honoré and said: "You'll have to fall in at the end of the line and eat everybody else's dust." His voice kicked up a few notches louder as he turned outward to the crowd. "The same goes for everyone, including myself. Anyone who's still dawdling when the rest of the camp is packed up and ready to move loses his place in line. Urbain—you'll hear the signal as soon as I've walked back to the gun."

When he came to bed that night, she said: "How do you know what to do?"

"What to do?"

"With all these people. There's so many ways it could turn into a fight, or for everybody to get up on their high horses and go off on their own. But you always know what to do to keep that from happening."

He laughed. "It's kind of you to put it all to my account, Little Rabbit, but I'm afraid it has more to do with circumstances beyond my control."

"But you must know that nobody else but you could—"

"Leave it alone!" he barked. The voice was one she'd never heard before—cutting and hard, with a serrated edge. It jolted her heart out of its soft-edged cocoon of blanketed body warmth and sighing grasslands night breezes and the feel of the child growing beneath it.

When she was a child, her father had had a big old wolf dog that would grin and loll its tongue out as she crawled all over him and pulled his ears. One day when she was four or five, she'd plopped her hand on his head as she had a thousand times before, and he'd jerked away, snarling and snapping.

After a moment, the stranger in her bed growled softly: "I think it would be better, Waposis, if we were to save our congratulations until we're all home safe with bulging carts. We haven't even faced the first real test yet."

"When's that come?"

"When we catch up with the herd."

That happened two days later. He had set up a rotating system of guides, some of whom were Captains as well, with each guide in charge of piloting the hunt for one day in the direction where he judged they'd find the herd. The first guide to get lucky was Pierre Falcon. He came pelting back toward the cart train, pointing his arm behind his shoulder and trumpeting: "Medicine Child Creek—I knew it!" He didn't get much chance to bask in congratulations; the hunters were already yanking their guns and saddles off their carts or saddle horses and charging for the remuda of buffalo runners.

Wappeston bellowed after them: "Remember—no one runs the herd before the general order!" He galloped past Marie to the cart behind Josephte's and flung the halter of his saddle horse at John as he slid off the saddle, shaking the scabbard off his rifle. "Saddle up my buffalo runner!" As John jumped onto the saddle and headed back down the line toward the horse herd, Wappeston turned and walked past Marie's cart onto the prairie, checking the priming on his gun. About a hundred yards in front of the lead rank of carts he stopped and turned and stood waiting with his rifle cradled in the crook of his arm. Marie felt the hairs at the nape of her neck prickling.

Two hunters whose place in the cart line happened to be closest to the horse herd galloped past her, whipping their buffalo runners with the barrels of their guns. Wappeston threw up his arm and bellowed: "Wait!" One of them reined in his horse; the other didn't. As the whooping horseman galloped past him, Wappeston swiveled and raised his rifle, tracked and led him, and shot the horse out from under him. The buffalo runner somersaulted, and the hunter on its back flew forward about fifteen feet before colliding against the prairie with a dusty thud.

On either side of Marie's cart, the wave of hunters galloping forward from the horse herd hauled their buffalo runners to a squealing, aghast halt. Out on the prairie, Wappeston was walking calmly toward the screaming, thrashing horse, reloading. Its downed rider crawled back up to his feet and then came running at Wappeston with his knife blade flashing in the sun. Wappeston laid him out with the butt of his rifle—Marie could hear the crack over the snorting and muttering around her—and carried on toward the horse. There was another gunshot, and the screaming and thrashing stopped.

The stalled wave of hunters on either side of her clucked their horses to a walk and washed up around the point where Wappeston was stripping the saddle and halter off the dead horse. John Wills went galloping past Marie on the speckled buffalo runner her husband had bought from her father. He reached the crowd of horsemen standing back from his uncle and promptly came galloping back. "Aunt Marie—Uncle Cuthbert says he's got another buffalo runner. Do you know it to see it?"

"Yes, but I can't hardly . . ." She looked around for someone whose body was in a more appropriate condition for jumping up behind a rider and galloping about to cut another horse out of the herd. Her eyes lit on Pierriche and Mary's oldest son. "Jean Baptiste—do you know the horse? The gray one your father trained? . . ."

"You bet." He was up behind the saddle and kicking at the speckled pony's ribs before John had time to twitch the halter.

The women and children and the men too old to hunt had all climbed off their carts and drifted forward to get a look at what was happening out on the prairie. Two of the hunters had got the downed one back on his feet and were walking him around. John and Jean Baptiste came galloping back from the horse herd, Jean Baptiste riding bareback on the gray, and carried on toward the milling army of buffalo hunters.

There was a hissing voice beside Marie's cart. She looked down to see Josephte and Mary Falcon straining their eyes to get a fix on what the men were up to. Josephte was hissing: "Your brother's gone insane."

Mary Falcon twinkled back: "Oh, I bet he knows what he's doing."

Marie knew exactly what he was doing. The laws he'd made up for the buffalo hunt said that anyone who broke them once would have his saddle and bridle cut up, not have his horse shot. So Wappeston was giving him his horse.

The hunters mounted up again and moved off at a trot, leaving a writhing mound of black and yellow dogs covering the carcass of the horse and Jean Baptiste and John walking back to the carts. A cloud of dust rose up to mask the hunters, but from her vantage point in the cart Marie could see over it to where a seeming mirage of a black lake eclipsed the rim of the world.

When the hunters stopped kicking up dust so she could see them again, they were almost out of her range of vision, although still only halfway to the horizon and not yet at the shore of the black lake. In the haze of distance, the tree islands and waves of sun-blanched grass swam up and down around the black stick figures of horsemen. The massed column spread itself out into a broad, thin line stretched parallel to the distant dark shore. They began to move forward at a walk, shrinking to a black thread that blended against the mirage and disappeared. There was a sound like fingers snapping under water, followed immediately by muted thunder.

Josephte said, "Well, I guess we better be catching up with them," and headed back toward her cart. Marie wasn't sure whether it was the right thing to do. He hadn't given instructions one way or another.

But they certainly didn't have to worry anymore about frightening off the herd with the shrieks of cartwheels. She snapped the reins to start the pony moving.

As they came up to the spot where the hunters had stopped to spread out in a line, she could see that the trampled plain ahead was dotted with black-brown mounds, like monster molehills. She had come up on something resembling the same scene many times before, but not on this scale. The dead and dying buffalo were spread out over a milewide swath that stretched ahead as far as she could see.

John jumped off his cart and ran ahead of hers, scampering from carcass to carcass. At the third one he waved his arm over his head, shouted, "It's Uncle Cuthbert's," then ran on to the next.

Marie swerved her cart in that direction, reined in, and hauled her body over the rail, lowering herself to the ground in stages. There was a moccasin lying among the blood-spattered, crushed grass stalks beside the dead cow. She stooped to pick it up. It was the worn-out remnant of one of the pair she'd beaded for him last fall.

All the men, before they climbed onto their buffalo hunters, tucked several old moccasins or gloves or spare tobacco pouches into their shirts or *ceinture flèches*—the woven sashes that served to hold their coats closed in the winter and their pants up in the summer and could be pressed into service for anything from a towrope to a splint binding. The tokens were needed only to identify the first few kills, so the women and children could get started while the men were still running the herd or making their way back. Any hunter who couldn't remember and identify every beast he'd shot was likely too inexperienced or panicked to have shot any.

Marie tucked the moccasin into a pannier hanging on the cart to save for next time, drew out her skinning knife, and went to work, heaving up the left foreleg so she could start her first cut from the chin down to the tail. Buffalo could be skinned from front to back or back to front or even across the middle, depending on which way they'd fallen. No one wanted to be wrestling a third of a ton of dead weight for the sake of uniformity.

Marie had to keep swallowing saliva. There were some parts of a buffalo—the liver in particular—that were astoundingly tender and delicious when wolfed down still steaming with the warmth of life. She had thought she'd liked the taste before, but now she was ravenous for it. Her mother's voice cut over from a hundred yards away, where she was butchering her father's first kill of the day: "Marie! Raw meat's bad for the baby!"

Marie sighed, "Yes, Mama," scooped out the guts to throw to the dogs, and went on flensing the hide off the carcass.

The men and buffalo runners came hobbling back, wrung out like used-up dishrags from riding the storm of hooves and horns. Wappeston unloaded his medical box to attend to a Dumont with a gored leg.

The hunt camped there for three days, stuffing themselves with buffalo brains and buffalo tongue and buffalo hump in between scraping hides and making pemmican—pounding sun-dried meat into flakes to mix with melted tallow in bags made from green hides.

Wappeston helped a little with the butchering, but he had lots of other things to do and the fact was he wasn't very good at it. Marie found it hard to keep up with the other pemmican makers, but at least she had Josephte and John to help. It didn't help that her husband had accounted for nine buffalo, while the next-highest kill—Urbain Delorme's—was seven.

Pierriche's comment to her was: "Yeah, he ain't the best shot in the world—Wappeston—but when it comes to galloping point-blank through a stampeding herd, good shooting don't count near as much as being crazy."

When there was nothing left but bones and the skinned corpses of a few incautious wolves, the Captain of the hunt announced that they would move on the next morning. When he came to bed he said: "I know the last few days have hardly been a picnic for you, but you'll be able to rest when we next catch up with the herd."

"Why's that?"

"I'm going to make a free run for the widows and orphans who have no one to hunt for them."

In the morning he tied the flag onto the flagpole of her cart and fired off the cannon. Although in any given season the horizon-stretching herd of buffalo was like a needle in the haystack of the plains, once the herd was lucked on to the first time or its trail was struck, any child could follow it. As the hunt pushed farther in past the border of Sioux territory, the tall-grass prairie gave way to dusty clumps of sagebrush and yellow tufts of buffalo grass. The islands of poplar and scrub oak grew fewer and then disappeared altogether, so the campfires and pemmican furnaces were made entirely of buffalo chips kindled with twitchgrass. They came into country that none of them had ever seen before, except for a handful of the more adventurous or suicidal old hunters, and even they had never come this far with carts and families.

· · ·

On a dry, bright afternoon when the few clouds in the sky seemed to want to drift everywhere except across the face of the sun, the guide for the day came galloping off a ridge up ahead and wheeled his horse to a rearing halt beside the Captain of the hunt. "The Sioux! About three hundred warriors. Headed this way."

Wappeston said something to the hunter who had the day's charge of leading the horse pulling the cannon, then turned his horse around and beckoned to Marie. She clucked the cart pony forward as the word went back through the lines of carts behind her. When her cart came up beside him, he held up his hand for her to stop and then stood in his stirrups and made a circling motion over his head. Within a few minutes the four files of carts had arced themselves into a circle around the flag, with the cannon outside it pointing toward the distant ridge. The men jumped off their carts and saddle horses and ran out onto the prairie, each with his rifle in one hand and a spade or mattock in the other. The women and children unhitched the cart ponies and herded them into the roped-off area where the buffalo runners were already settling in to graze, then went to work locking the cartwheels together with tent poles thrust through the spokes and filling in the gaps between with sacks of pemmican. All except Marie, because Wappeston slid off his horse and said: "Get a fire going." He lifted the powder keg and the cannon's ramrod off the back of the cart and headed out toward the cannon with the powder keg under one arm and the ramrod slung over his shoulder.

It didn't seem to her that he'd been brusque or rude, just that he had no time at the moment for "please" and "thank you." She'd grown accustomed to seeing him wield authority, as Captain of the hunt or the planter of the town at White Horse Plains, but this was different. This was the Cuthbert Grant the veterans of the army of the New Nation traded campfire stories of, who'd stood alone on a rock in the middle of the Qu'Appelle ordering the Hudson's Bay Company brigade to stand and deliver.

She climbed off the cart, dug out her fire bag and sack of buffalo chips, and knelt down to go to work scraping her flint and steel against each other—his Lucifers had run out partway through February. She managed to produce several showers of sparks that came nowhere near the little mound of tinder: her hands were shaking too much. She stopped and focused her mind on what she'd seen in her husband a moment ago—a perfect assurance that if they all went ahead with the tasks he'd set for them, they could weather any storm. When she tried the flint and steel again, her hands were still shaking, but not nearly so much. She couldn't explain it, but she was certain he had something of the same effect on everyone who was as uncertain of themselves as she was.

By the time she'd blown the sparked tinder into enough of a flame to ignite a crumpled wad of buffalo chips, he was back from the cannon. She fed some larger pieces to the fire and glanced over her shoulder to see him plunge his arms into the caisson box filled with things for the cannon. He came out with several articles she'd never seen before. One of them was a flat little cigar box, the others were three lumpy, canvas-skinned sausages about as long as her forearm and twice as big around. He plucked a handful of cheroots out of the cigar box, tucked one between his lips and the others in a pocket of his coat, and put the cigar box back. As he came toward her, with the canvas sausages draped heavily over one cradling forearm, she saw that the black beams that his eyes had turned into at the first word of the Sioux were now sparkling. One corner of his mouth kept twitching upward. She remembered the other part of the story told by those who'd seen him standing on that boulder in the Qu'Appelle with a pistol in each hand—they'd said he was laughing.

"Good fire, Waposis. Keep it going." He crouched down and angled his head to light the cheroot in his mouth without lighting his hair. When he stood up again, his eyes caught hers staring quizzically at the canvas sausages. He winked at her. "Odds on that none of our Sioux visitors have ever seen grapeshot before, either."

He headed back toward the cannon, bouncing along as though there were springs in his moccasins. Something resembling hatred or horror stabbed into her and twisted. She and the baby inside her, and everyone else she knew and loved, had followed him out here to a place where three hundred of the fiercest warriors of the plains were about to descend upon them. And he was dancing with death.

She went back to building up the fire, telling herself that his jaunty intoxication was just another facet of that calm she'd found so reassuring. Someone shouted: "There they are!" She stood up to get a look but couldn't see over the rampart of carts. Wappeston came running, snagged his brass spyglass out of one of the panniers on his saddle horse, vaulted over the cart rail, and stood up on the mound of pemmican and camp gear.

Pierriche appeared and climbed up beside him, shading his eyes with one hand. Wappeston handed him the telescope. Marie bent down to feed the fire some more and heard Pierriche say: "So what do you think? Figure they got all gaudied up like that 'cause they'd heard

Father Picard was here to give communion?" Then she heard her husband laugh back with an eerie delight. "That one in the fur hat with the red-painted antelope horns, that'd be La Terre Qui Brûle—figures he's hell on wheels."

"How's your Dakotahan?"

"Not so good. Urbain Delorme probably speaks better Sioux than anyone else here."

The Captain of the hunt bellowed: "Urbain! What say you and I take a ride out to have a word with Monsieur Qui Brûle? . . . Urbain?"

Jean Baptiste Falcon called back: "He's out digging his hole, just like we practiced."

"Ah. Would you be so good as to fetch him, Jean Baptiste?"

Through the crackle of buffalo chips burning into flakes and the trill of meadowlarks, Marie began to hear a soft thrumming of three hundred unshod horses. Or perhaps she was feeling it through the drumskin of the earth.

Jean Baptiste came jogging back, trailing a dust-streaked, grumpy-looking Urbain Delorme. "Jean Baptiste says you wanted to ask me something."

"Quite right. I'm told you have a remarkable facility with the Sioux language."

"As good as anybody else's, I guess."

"Would you care to take a little ride with me, to ask La Terre Qui Brûle and friends to what we owe the pleasure?"

"Just the two of us?"

"If you'd rather not, I suppose I could stumble by with sign talk, though I'm a trifle rusty. . . ."

Urbain sucked in a deep breath, scratched the back of his neck, emptied his lungs with a chesty growl, and muttered hopefully: "Wouldn't it be smarter to make them come to us?"

Before she'd had time to think about it, Marie chirped to her husband: "Assiniboine's close enough to Sioux. If you'll lift me on a horse, I'll come and translate for you."

Urbain's face lit up red and he bellowed for one of his sons to fetch his horse for him.

Wappeston bounced off the cart and up onto the saddle, winked at Marie. "Won't be but a moment. Keep a candle in the window," he said, and kicked his horse with his heels.

She banked up a few more plates of dried buffalo shit around the fire, planted the heels of her hands on her thighs to crack her knees straight, waddled over to the cart, and started to climb the ladder of rails. Pierriche bent down to give her a hand up. Once she was standing on the summit she could see that the Sioux had stopped halfway between the ridge and the cart circle when they saw two riders coming out to meet them. She could also see the backs and hats and gun barrels of the hunters crouched in the hastily scooped-out depressions they'd dug in a circle about a hundred yards wider than the circle of carts, but she guessed that the Sioux couldn't see them.

Pierriche handed her the spyglass, but she didn't open it. She said: "When you told me he was crazy, I thought you was joking."

"Huh?"

"He's having the time of his life, ain't he?"

"Well . . . well . . . well . . . When someone's got a knife at your throat, ain't much you can do but smile. I won't lie to you—by the time the sun goes down, this piece of ground might look like what we left at the last place we made pemmican. But me, I think us *bois brûlé* can take any tribe or any army there is, so long as we got a War Chief that knows his business like your man does.

"What's going on out there? If it looks fuzzy, just give the big tube at the end a bit of a twist in and out till it comes clear."

She wouldn't have thought it would be difficult to see three hundred mounted Sioux a quarter mile away, but once her field of vision was reduced to the little circle at the end of the tube, she found herself treated to a close-up view of a rock, a cloud, an old bleached buffalo skull, anything but what the glass was supposedly helping her to see. After raising and lowering the telescope several times to coordinate the spyglass with what she could see with both eyes, she managed to get a fix on the line of warriors and moved along it looking for her husband. While she'd been range finding, two of the Sioux had ridden forward to meet the two métis riding out from the circle of carts. Both pairs of riders were sitting on their horses face to face, waving their arms about in that parley habit of speaking in words and sign talk at the same time. Wappeston had offered La Terre Qui Brûle and his herald a cigar, and the three of them were puffing away while Urbain did the translating.

Pierriche muttered: "That La Terre Qui Brûle, he's a gassy one." It was strange to hear his voice next to her ear when her eye told her she was a quarter mile out on the prairie. "All he's got to say is 'Those are our buffalo you been killing; give us the meat and clear out,' but it'll take him half the day to get around to it."

It was only a moment later, though, that Wappeston and Urbain turned their horses around and came trotting back toward the carts,

Wappeston lighting a fresh cheroot from the stub of the first. Pierriche clucked: "Guess he told him to stop gassing and get to the point. La Terre Qui Brûle won't like that. Well, guess I better be getting out to my gopher hole. You want a hand down?" She shook her head. "Well, you make sure you get down from here when they start coming. I think our holes are far enough out to keep 'em back out of range of the carts, but I've more'n once seen a strong bowman shoot an arrow clean through a buffalo."

Father Picard's voice went up from somewhere behind her: "St. Joseph and the Blessed Virgin, hear us and pray for us now and at the hour of our deaths, protect us in this hour of danger . . ." Marie crossed herself and crouched down, partly because her knees were shaking and partly so Wappeston would be less likely to notice where she was perched. As he and Urbain reached the cannon, they reined in. Wappeston slid down, taking his rifle with him. He propped the rifle against one of the cannon wheels, reached up to take his pistols out of the saddle holsters, and handed the halter to Urbain. Urbain trotted on, circling around to the back of the palisade of carts.

There was the sound of a galloping horse and an ululating howl. Marie looked ahead and saw that one of the Sioux had broken out from the fanned-out line and was galloping straight toward the cannon. Marie threw up the telescope and managed to catch him. He looked to be no older than she was, although it was difficult to be sure with half of his face and body painted red and the other half black. His black horse was decorated with red handprints and circles. He had a brass-studded trade gun slung over his back, but the only weapon in his hands was a coup stick, which he whirled over his head. The sunlight flashed on his arms, covered in brass bracelets from wrists to elbows. He sat his churning pony like a hawk riding the wind, his unbraided black mane pluming out behind him like the horse's mane and tail.

Marie lowered the telescope and looked to her husband. He was standing beside the cannon with his arms crossed, calmly puffing his cigar as the young Sioux bore down on him. Maybe he was expressing his complete lack of concern over whether the Sioux counted coup on him or not, but this coup stick had a decorative stone knob fixed to the end of it. She opened her mouth to shout to him, but she was too late. The Sioux was almost upon him, already leaning out from the saddle. Wappeston's arms uncrossed and straightened in front of him, both of them extended farther by the length of a pistol barrel. There was a double crack with flares of smoke and sparks. The Sioux flew off his saddle pad as though he'd run into a tree. But one of his feet caught in the stirrup. The painted horse galloped on past the circle of carts, with the painted warrior bouncing up dust alongside. Marie hoped he was dead.

His three hundred friends erupted in a wave of war cries and came on in two wings, with a gap in the middle to let the cannonball pass harmlessly between. Wappeston had dropped his pistols and crossed his arms again, still puffing calmly on his cheroot. Marie looked from him to the charging warriors. With the hooves of their ponies thundering and churning the parched prairie into dust and powdered grass tufts, they seemed to her the three hundred horsemen of the Apocolypse riding a storm cloud. A few of them were brandishing scalp-decorated muskets, but most of them had spears or bows or war clubs.

The sound of gunshots cracked through the roar of the wave—not from the buffalo hunters crouched in their holes, but from the Sioux. Wappeston's body spun sideways and fell against one of the cannon wheels. She screamed, then saw he wasn't hit—he was wrenching the wheel around to angle the cannon slightly sideways. He snatched the cigar out of his mouth and thrust the lit end at the touchhole. The cannon went off with a boom and a jump backward and a cloud of smoke and flame. It was echoed by a sharp chorus of bangs and smaller smoke puffs from behind every sagebrush or clump of tumbleweed or prairie-embedded boulder.

When the smoke cleared, a swath of the prairie had been transformed into a heaving mass of shattered horsemen. Behind them, the backs of their brothers were receding over the ridge. An explosion of cheers and laughter went up from the two concentric circles surrounding Marie and the blue-and-white flag. Hats and guns were thrown in the air. The jubilation faded to the point where she could hear Father Picard leading a prayer of thanks. But the chanting of the congregation wasn't loud enough to drown out the other sounds—the screams of horses writhing their lives out into the yellow grass and the teeth-gritted singing of death songs in Sioux.

"What are you doing up there, Little Rabbit—trying to draw their fire?" She looked down. He had somehow contrived to make his way back from the cannon to her cart without her noticing. He held up his arms to help her down.

Once her feet were on the ground, she wrapped her arms around him, squeezing her swollen body against his, and choked out: "Why did you have to wait so long?"

"Wait?"

"When the Sioux with the coup stick was coming at you. There was a knob of rock on the end of that stick!"

"Yes, I couldn't help but notice."

"Then why did you have to wait so damn long before—"

"The truth is"—he lowered his voice and glanced from side to side—"I'm not exactly the best shot in the *pays d'en haut.* John!"

"Yes, Uncle Cuthbert?"

"Would you be so good as to fetch my medicine chest—I believe it's on the back of your mother's cart. Perhaps Jean Baptiste will lend you a hand."

Marie said: "Who's hurt?"

"None of us. They didn't get close enough in. But it might be that a few of them need only a tourniquet, or a bit of metal dug out, to put them right again."

"I'll come help."

"I think not."

"I couldn't bring all of my medicine plants, but I brought some. I can help."

"I have no doubt you could. But some of the dead ones out there might be not quite so dead as they seem." He patted her shoulder and went off, calling for the Captain of the day to collect his ten soldiers and follow along.

The night's celebrations were winding down when a pair of hunters happened to stumble past Marie while one of them was shaking his head and muttering: "Did you see him out there, just standing and puffing his cigar as calm as Sunday? He ain't human."

An elbow nudged her ribs from the other side. Pierriche winked at her and murmured: "It's good for them to think so, but you and I know different, don't we?"

Except for the occasional distant columns of camp smoke, they saw no further sign of the Sioux. The gumweed and toadflax were gilding the green hills by the time the hunt from White Horse Plains forded the Pembina again. It was lucky that the river was a good deal lower than it had been in early summer, because this time the cartbeds were all sagging under the weight of sacks of pemmican, bladders of tallow, slabs of smoked meat, and rolls of rough-cured hides—the adult ones scraped clean for *shagganappi* or parchment leather or tent coverings; the yearling ones with the hair left on to sell as quickly as possible to the Buffalo Wool Company before it went bust.

They were nearing Rivière aux Îlots de Bois and only two days from the big white house waiting at White Horse Plains when the base of Marie's abdomen suddenly snapped taut like a drumskin laced too tight. Her knees hit the cartbed. The horse neighed angrily as the reins wound around her hands yanked his head back to his shoulder.

She'd had a few false alarms like this already. Mary Falcon had said it was just her body giving her a bit of practice. There was at least another month to go before the baby was due.

She got her breath back, pried her teeth out of the cart rail, and climbed to her feet. Then another one hit her, this one hard enough to double her over as it knocked her down again.

A fist-size black cloud was thudding above her eyes. She realized she must have whacked her forehead against the cart rail on the way down. Wappeston was yelling from far away: "What's wrong? Is it time?" Mary Falcon and Josephte were scrambling aboard and taking hold of her.

Marie hollered back in a whisper: "It's too early . . . it's just—" She was cut off by another wallop under her belly.

Mary Falcon said: "No, it ain't, this is it. Help me lift her out off—" There was a hacking and ripping sound. Marie managed to open her eyes long enough to see that Wappeston was chopping his knife against the thongs binding the front quarter of the railing to the sideposts and tearing it open.

The rippling explosion inside her faded. She gasped out, "I can walk," and managed to get one leg out of the cart before the next one hit her. When it passed, she had both feet on the ground. Mary Falcon and Josephte were holding her arms and helping her around toward the back of the cart. Wappeston was cutting the horse free of the shafts and bellowing: "We'll make camp here!" Marie was opening her mouth to tell him not to make everyone stop on her account when the hands playing with the toggles on the drumskin twisted again—this time past the snapping point. There was a bursting sensation, and hot water gushed down her legs.

The next thing she knew, she was squatted naked in a firelit cave. They'd rigged a skirt of tent awnings around the rim of the forward-tilted cart and lighted a wick in a bowl of buffalo tallow. Given the springy, itchy feeling under the soles of her feet, and the curls of coarse wool that her toes were winding themselves into, they'd laid a buffalo robe on the ground under the axle-treed wooden roof. Her mother and Josephte were on either side of her, holding her up. Mary was dabbing at her face with a damp cloth. There was a vague memory of hands peeling her clothes off. Her mother was saying: "Oh, my dear, I'm sorry—I was so sure it wouldn't come till . . . I'm so sorry. . . ."

Marie shook her head and panted out: "I got no birthroot." She'd ceased using its alternate name, "bethroot," ever since Pierriche had told her of Wappeston's first wife. When Marie had winnowed through her stock of pouches and panniers to bring along a selection of medicine plants that wouldn't fill up half a cart, it had come down to a choice between birthroot and tansy leaves. Bruises and sprains seemed likely on the buffalo hunt, so she'd taken her bag of tansy leaves for poultices and left the birthroot behind.

Mary Falcon stuck her head out the curtain and yelled to someone: "Go see if anyone's got birthroot!" Marie felt a rending sensation deep inside her—like a pair of hands thrusting up and ripping outward. She heard and felt herself screaming and tried to choke it off—there were so many other people camped just beyond that leather curtain. Mary Falcon was back in front of her, saying: "You go right ahead and scream your fucking lungs out if you want, dear—God knows I did—and to hell with them. But if you want something to bite down on . . ."

Marie grunted and jerked her head up and down. Mary Falcon's hand came toward her. Marie opened her mouth and bit down on an unpeeled green stick a couple of finger widths' thick. It was there just in time for the next pair of hands that thrust up her and pried. As her teeth ground through the bark, she tasted willow, so it would help to dull the pain as well as to keep her from screaming too loudly or cracking chips off her teeth.

Another face popped into the cave—Marguerite, Wappeston's other sister. Marguerite shook her head and said: "No one's got bethroot."

Josephte snapped: "Did you ask everyone?"

"Well, most—"

"Well, ask them all, damn it!" Marguerite disappeared.

It went on forever. Once—or many times, Marie wasn't sure—hands pried the willow stick out of her mouth for long enough to slop in a splash of rum. It helped to dull the pain a little more, but not enough. The hands holding her up kept slipping off and slapping back against her sweat-soaked skin.

Marie spat out the chewing stick with a pop like a cork. It whapped Mary Falcon across the nominal bridge of her pudgy pug nose and bounced off. Marie tried to yell: "I can't! Kill it! Or kill me—get it over with!" But all that came out was another wordless scream. There was an oozing, wrenching, sliding sensation, and then she was empty and they were laying her down on her back.

A warm snake was dangling out of her. There was a stab of pain from outside her body, then a wet smacking sound, and a new voice took over her own squalling. A river of something warm and clotted poured out of her. Hands were elevating her legs and hips and tugging the buffalo robe out from under her. When they let her down again she discovered there'd been another one layered under it.

Josephte's voice whispered: "I'll bury it."

A wet howl tore out through Marie's throat. A pudgy hand caressed the side of her cheek, and Mary Falcon's voice came out soft and close, the breath in the words puffing against her ear: "She meant the buffalo robe, dear. Your daughter's going to live to bury us all." And a tiny, warm, mewling, damp, squirming thing was laid between her breasts.

Mary Falcon leaned away and said: "If Jean Baptiste had come that easy, I wouldn't've kept chasing Pierriche out of my bed for so long after."

They swabbed the sweat and blood off her and her daughter, covered them with a blanket, and then parted the curtains to let her husband in. He folded back the rim of the blanket to have a look and rasped out: "What I've accomplished this summer isn't a patch on what you've just done. We'll call her Elizabeth."

Marie didn't argue, but she'd be damned if it ever got abbreviated to "Bethsy."

CHAPTER 22

As the long train of carts splashed its way across the Passage of the Assiniboine, most of them turned right, toward the Forks. Grant turned left, leading a pair of carts crammed with Marie, Elizabeth, Maria Theresa, Josephte, John, and Father Picard and all their gear. He wanted to get a look at the job the carpenters had done on the house and get Marie and their frail new daughter settled in as soon as possible. Falcon had taken charge of his seven cartloads of pemmican and hides, to be toted up with all the others at Fort Garry and added to his account.

The shifting green meadows were sprinkled with rosy purple blazing stars and white evening primroses. In the dank woods by the river

there were ghostly clumps of waxy silver Indian pipes, or corpse flowers. Grant was quite proud of himself for being able to identify the
flowers. It was only in the last few years that he'd begun to take the
time to learn such little details of the country he'd killed more than
a few men for.

There were a number of very tall plants with cloud clusters of tiny
white flowers, something like Queen Anne's lace, but not much. He
remarked to Marie by way of conversation: "I must ask someone
sometime what those are called."

"What what are called?"

"Those white-capped flowers along the border of the marsh. The tall
ones."

"Water hemlock. They look a lot like water parsnips, but they ain't,
they're poison. They say that's what Jean Baptiste Lajimodierre's Cree
wife tried to feed to the white wife he brought back from Canada, but
someone warned her."

"You do amaze me sometimes."

"Because I know something you don't?"

He put it down to the side effects of childbirth and let it drop. She
was recovering remarkably quickly, all things considered.

As the trail wound past the new-built cabins sprinkled among the
woods at White Horse Plains, the few old people and woodworkers
who'd stayed behind came trickling out waving and calling. Grant
curtailed the welcome-homes and carried on toward the shingled roof
peak poking up over the crowns of the trees.

The house was completed—on the outside, at least—except that the
walls were still raw wood. He would have to get some whitewash on
them before the weather turned nasty. He slid off his horse and helped
Marie out of the cart. The operation was complicated by the fact that
she had to cradle Elizabeth in her arms in an improvised mossbag,
instead of the beaded cradleboard that was waiting somewhere among
the piles of household goods they'd left behind.

They paused on the way to the door to have a look at Marie's
garden. Several rows of potatoes and carrots had contrived to come
up without human assistance, although from the raggedy look of their
foliage there were several fat rabbits and gophers in the neighborhood.
Josephte and John and Father Picard stood waiting relatively patiently
for the householders to cross the threshold first, but Maria Theresa
made a toddling beeline for the front door and snagged the latchstring.
The door was a snug fit, though; even throwing all her weight against
the latchstring, she couldn't tug it open.

Grant took Marie by the arm and walked her up the step. He shooed Maria Theresa aside and jerked the door open. The hinges turned smoothly. Then he turned and scooped Marie up in both arms and carried her inside. She whooped and squealed. Elizabeth woke up and joined in with her own caterwauling. He set Marie back on her feet as the others followed them in, and they all set off exploring and exclaiming.

There was still a silt of sawdust on the floor and on the household furnishings stacked up in various corners. The air inside was thick with the taste of fresh-cut wood. The orange-white wood grains were buffed by the amber light coming in through the parchment windows. He had panes of glass on order, but it would be another year before they were brought across the ocean and upstream from Hudson's Bay, provided any of them survived the trip.

There was a huge fieldstone fireplace in the kitchen and a slightly smaller one in the immense open parlor that took up all the rest of the main floor. Grant left the others celebrating the wonders of the kitchen and parlor and climbed the stairs, leaning his weight against the banister to make sure they'd anchored it securely. He walked along the corridor, poking his nose through doorways. Bedsteads had been set up in three of the eight upstairs rooms—a large one for him and Marie and narrower ones for Josephte and Father Picard. Among the piles of flotsam and jetsam downstairs there should be three rolled-up feather mattresses that Marie and her mother and Josephte had spent part of the winter sewing and stuffing. John and Maria Theresa could make do with buffalo robes on the floor for the nonce, and it would be some years yet before Elizabeth graduated to a bed.

His inspection of the second story was rather quick and cursory. He was drawn toward the end of the corridor and another set of stairs, more like a fixed stepladder, leading up to a trapdoor. As he climbed the steps he wondered whether he shouldn't hire the fort carpenter to construct a long, counterweighted trap with a built-on sliding ladder, to keep the hallway unobstructed and to keep the access out of reach of little hands. Ruminating on hinging mechanisms and pulley systems, he threw the trap back, stood up in the inky attic, and promptly whonked the crown of his head against a rafter. He should've thought to get a window put in.

After a moment the flare of light behind his eyes died down and they adjusted to the twilight seeping up through the trap. The roofline angled in sharply from all four walls, but instead of the usual single roof tree where the four planes met, there was a rectangle of beams with a rough-runged ladder standing straight up and down. He gave the ladder a shake to make sure it was solid, then climbed up high enough to get his forearm against the ceiling and give it a push. As the trap swung open he was blinded a second time, this time by blazing sunlight rather than darkness. He blinked away his blindness, climbed out onto the rim, and dropped the trap back down to make a floor.

He found himself standing on the summit of a wooden mountain, the highest point within the circumference of the horizon—if one excluded the thread-thin top twigs of the burl oaks, where even the squirrels didn't venture. The fort carpenter had complained vociferously about the impossibility of putting a widow's walk on a hip roof, but he'd done it nonetheless. The wooden railing he'd put up around it, though, was definitely bordering on the wobbly, perhaps in hopes of revenge for all the extra time and trouble. A proper iron railing could be wrought by the fort blacksmith over the course of the winter.

The wind stroking the grass into wave crests down below positively howled up here. He planted his feet wide and shuffled around in a cautious circle. After spending a goodly part of his adolescence rambling about the Highlands between school terms, heights didn't bother him, by and large—as long as they weren't sheer. It was that rickety railing that was throwing him off. He'd always had an unreasonable fear of getting himself into a high place where there was nothing to grab on to if he lost his balance.

It was amazing how far he could see from up here, even without his telescope. To the west, the green-gold tabletop of White Horse Plains stretched out until it faded into a distance that could have swallowed a hundred *sliobh grantias* without burping. To the north, Coteau des Festins spread out toward the blue-black ridges of Stony Mountain and the spruce lake country beyond. To the east, the awning of trees bending over the Assiniboine wound its way toward the Forks, until the wooded creeks fanning out from either side blended together and hedged off any bets he might have of seeing as far as Fort Garry. He was willing to bet, though, that if the cannons in the fort bastions were to fire, he'd be able to see the smoke puffs rising over the trees. To the south, he was just about willing to swear that those hazy purple mushrooms hovering between the earth and sky were the start of the Pembina Hills.

As ridiculous as it seemed, a certain half-breed orphan was now the lord of all he surveyed—and from up here he could survey a sizable chunk of the planet. There was a thumping underneath his moccasins. He moved off the trap and levered it open. Marie's head poked out into the sunlight. He lowered his hand to help her up. When she was safely ensconced on the rim, he lowered the trap again, saying: "Don't lean against the rail. It appears to be the only piece of shoddy workmanship in the whole place. Well, how do you like your seigneury?"

"My what?"

"Ah—I should've realized that'd be the one French word that didn't make its way here from Quebec. I suppose 'county' or 'fiefdom' or any other feudal term wouldn't mean much, either, to anyone who grew up in the *pays d'en haut*. But, for better or worse, those are the terms that now define what you're looking at. And you and I are now the lord and lady of the manor."

She said fervently: "It's a beautiful house."

"Hm? Oh, yes—by and large they've done a serviceable job, given a bit of tightening here and there. Once we've got the furniture and so on in place, I'll take a ride over to Fort Garry to buy some lime for whitewash—the Kildonan people have developed a bit of an industry of going down to the lake to burn limestone for tanning solutions and mortar and so on. You look a mite chalky. Do heights disturb you? I should've realized that growing up on the prairies didn't give you much opportunity to accustom yourself to—"

"Eliza needs feeding."

"Not to mention the rest of us. First fire in a virgin hearth, hm?"

After two days of unpacking crates and sacks and moving furniture, the house began to take on the aspects of a home. A bit sparsely furnished, perhaps, but it would fill up in time, as would the unoccupied rooms on the second floor. Marie appeared to have just about completely recovered her strength and coloring—spurred on by the delight of setting up her kitchen, one wall of which was now decked out with her collection of decorated pouches and panniers filled with dried wild herbs and medicine plants and the first fruits of her garden.

On their second night in the new house, Grant woke up alone. He sat up to see if Marie was crouched down tending to Eliza. In only a few short days, Marie had definitely established the fact that "Eliza" was the short form they were going to use.

The moonlight through the open window showed him that Eliza's corner was empty. During daylight hours, Eliza's cradleboard was hung from a peg on the wall in the kitchen or whatever other room Marie was occupying herself in. But when her parents went to bed, her cradleboard was set down on the floor. It was an old custom of the Plains tribes, because ghosts can climb in through the smoke hole at night and down the tent poles. Marie had been apologetic about being so superstitious, but Grant didn't mind in the least. He'd done the same thing with Maria Theresa's cradleboard when he was her only parent. It was the custom, and he liked customs.

He sat in the bed for a moment, trying to come up with some logical reason why Marie and Eliza weren't there. Perhaps she'd taken her downstairs to change her mossbag on the kitchen table. But if Eliza had let it be known that her quarters had grown too damp, the announcement would have awakened him as well.

He threw the covers off, tugged on his trousers, and stepped out into the hallway. The only sounds were the wood-muffled snoring of Josephte and Father Picard. He padded down the corridor, brushing one hand along the wall to keep him on a straight course and slowing to a tentative shuffle for the last few steps. It would be a while yet before his feet were absolutely sure they could find the top of the stairs in pitch blackness.

He made his way downstairs with one hand trailing along on the banister. There was no light coming from the kitchen. A bit of moonlight filtered through the parlor windows, but not much. He called softly: "Marie?"

There was no answer. He fumbled his way to the kitchen doorway, barking his shin on a chair. The moonlight through the kitchen windows fell on no one. He called again, "Marie?" but no one answered.

He found the back door and pushed it open. A full moon stood over the trees. With his pupils swollen to soak in every scrap of light inside the house, the light outside seemed glaring. There was no sign of life beyond the horses shaking their heads inside the roped-off temporary paddock. Perhaps she'd taken it in mind to make a midnight trip to the necessary—pregnancy and childbirth did play hell with a woman's bladder. But why would she take Eliza with her?

He made his way along the darkened pathway their comings and goings had already started to wear down beside the garden. He knocked on the outhouse door and then pulled it open. There was no one there.

He turned around in a circle, unsure what to do next. If he shouted for her, he'd wake the whole house. The apparent clarity of the moonlight was a bit of an illusion. It tended to flatten out the objects it touched on, and the shadows behind them were broad and deep enough to hide a hundred Maries. And then, out of the sighing tapestry of night breezes ruffling the leaves, the peeping of frogs and crickets, and the murmur of the river, he heard another sound. It was too faint to be certain, but it sounded like a human voice singing.

He tracked it through the woods, stepping carefully and inventing several new names for himself for not having taken an extra five seconds to tug on his moccasins as well as his trousers. He stopped when he came to the point where the tree belt gave way to the moonlit expanse of Coteau des Festins growing out of White Horse Plains. Although the voice was still far from distinct, there was no mistaking that ever-musical alto with true notes and a rasp in the throat. It appeared to be coming from the point of the wedge of Coteau des Festins, where the runoff flowing in along both planes met and pooled into enough moisture to feed a thicket of poplar and wolf willow through the driest summer.

As he drew closer, he began to hear words in the song. He didn't understand them, but he recognized the sound as Sioux, possibly Assiniboine. It was definitely coming from somewhere inside the thicket. Rather than crashing his way through, he lowered himself prone in the grass and wormed his way forward under the tangled branches. In the middle of the thicket there was an open circle of ground that was a pond in spring but at this time of year was a dished-in floor of dried plates of clay, with mud in the cracks between the plates. Within that circle, Mrs. Grant was singing and dancing naked in the moonlight.

The steps of the dance seemed to be somewhat arbitrary. Sometimes she whirled and sometimes she shuffled from side to side, milk-heavy breasts bouncing and black waves of hair swirling like a cape. There was one gesture she kept repeating, though—pincering her hands out in front of her and then flicking them back over her shoulder, as though plucking fireflies out of the air and tossing them behind her. Every time she turned or whirled, she always returned to face the same point, where Eliza in her cradleboard was hanging from the branch of a tree.

Grant started to stand up, saying: "What are you doing?" Marie shrieked and whirled to face him, backing away and trying to cover herself with her hands. He repeated it louder, so she could hear him over the crackling of the twigs breaking against his shoulders: "What are you doing, Waposis?"

She came at him with both hands out to push him away, sputtering: "Please—you mustn't see and I mustn't stop. Go back to bed. It'll be all right."

Her onslaught actually managed to drive him back a couple of steps, before the branches behind him tangled into a thick enough mat to stop him and stab him. He grabbed hold of her wrists and said: "You mustn't stop what? What are you doing?"

"Please—it's the first full moon after she was born. I have to dance and sing to her all night, and grab all the troubles that might come to her and throw them away. Please—I'll bring her back when the sun comes up."

He held her wrists a moment longer, then let them go and turned and bulled his way back into the open, talking to himself. If Marie wanted to indulge herself in superstitions, it wasn't going to do their daughter any harm—at least not that particular superstition. It was a chilly night for dancing naked, though, as his shirtless, goosefleshed torso could attest. There were no Cree or Saulteaux currently wandering in the neighborhood, and at this time of year the wolves and bears were too well fed even to consider human prey.

Nevertheless, when he got back to the house he didn't go to bed. He felt his way to the corner of the parlor where his rifle and shot pouch and powder flask stood waiting for the resolution of the debate regarding the safety of display pegs above the mantle, snagged his summer coat off the wall peg by the back door, and went out into the night again. He settled down with his back against a convenient tree and listened to the distant singing until the eastern sky turned gray.

He managed to get back into bed before the house started stirring. He waited until he'd heard the rest of his polyglot household rouse and make their way downstairs. When he came into the kitchen, Josephte was laying out breakfast for Father Picard and John and Maria Theresa, and Marie was feeding breakfast to Eliza. There were blue shadows under the soft black eyes. Josephte said: "You've taken to sleeping late now you're lord of the manor."

"I'd thought my wife would wake me."

Marie said: "I thought if you were tired you should sleep." Her voice was even whispier and raspier than usual. He settled down to his buffalo steak and potatoes and told himself he would exchange some winkingly conspiratorial words with her when they were alone. He didn't get the chance. Falcon and the rest of the hunt came rolling back from Fort Garry, a bit green from celebrating. Several more of the winterers from Pembina and the Forks had decided that it might not be such a bad idea to throw in their lot with the homesteaders of White Horse Plains, so by midday Grantown was once again echoing with the happy racket of axes and mallets.

When Marie crawled into bed, Grant crooked his arm under her neck to make a warm pillow for her and whispered: "You seem weary, Waposis."

"Um-hm."

"Then go to sleep."

She did.

The next morning, before they set off for Fort Garry, he rigged a plank across the front of one of his carts to make a seat and loaded his girls onto it, Eliza in her cradleboard slung over Marie's shoulder and Maria Theresa squeezed in between her stepmother and father. As the cart squealed into motion, Eliza woke up and started squalling. Marie unlaced the quillworked rawhide covering of the cradleboard—rather like an oversize moccasin with a wooden sole—extracted Eliza in her beaded moose-hide mossbag, and flapped open her dress to nurse. During their last few weeks in the cabin at Red River, Marie had prepared herself for motherhood by making several dresses on an old pattern of the Plains tribes that had gone out of fashion once there were white women's clothes to copy. Grant was willing to accept that there must have been some pragmatic reason for the Cree and Saulteaux women to start modeling their clothes after the dresses or blouses and skirts of the Kildonan women, but the old Indian dresses made a lot of sense for nursing mothers. They were structured in two pieces—a high-waisted skirt held up by shoulder straps and a sleeved yoke that hung down just under the breasts. When it was feeding time, all the mother had to do was flip the yoke cape over her shoulder. On days of blistering sun or stormy weather, the yoke was an awning to shield the baby's head.

It was a calm sky that morning, and the sun wasn't high enough to burn yet, so Grant got to watch. It was a curious sensation, partly arousing and partly melting. Maria Theresa gawked at her stepmother's gold-and-purple, bursting breast and shyly reached her hand up to touch the dark halo of down on her gurgling half sister's head. Grant found himself suddenly transported back to a snowed-in cabin on the Qu'Appelle, watching his son suck the soft breast of Bethsy McKay. He yanked his eyes away from Marie to the trail ahead and popped the whip over the pony's head.

By the time the cart rolled through the gates of Fort Garry, Eliza was trussed back in her cradleboard and comatose again. The fort was bustling with the usual summer stew of sun-browned or -reddened faces, beaded leather, striped blanket cloth, and tartan plaids. The one odd touch in today's pallet was the unusually high percentage of Des Meurons lounging about and puffing clay pipes and making lewd suggestions to the Kildonan women scurrying by.

Grant reined the cart horse to a halt in front of the countinghouse, gave Marie and Maria Theresa a hand down, and then reached back for the cradleboard hanging inside the cage of cart rails. Marie said: "No—don't wake her."

"I do believe in letting sleeping babies lie, as a general principle, but Hargrave and the others would never forgive me if we didn't let them have an ogle of her."

The cloud that flitted across her face quite clearly said: "*You're* not the one who'll have to coax her back to sleep again." Maternity had definitely had a prickling effect on her.

"I suppose you're right. If they're that desperate to have a look, they can come out here and do it without disturbing her."

Hargrave bounded off his stool and around his desk as they came through the door. "Grant! I was wondering when you were going to get around to sticking your nose back in. Mrs. Grant, Miss Grant, a pleasure to see you again. And where is this *new* Miss Grant we've heard about?"

"Outside, snoring like a bandsaw."

The clerks trooped out to gawk, peering at Eliza through the grid of cart rails and making the obligatory oohing and ahing sounds of young males who couldn't tell one baby from another. Hargrave said: "Congratulations."

"Thank you."

"I didn't mean you, Grant. Your wife's the one did all the work. Congratulations, Mrs. Grant."

"Thank you."

"Not at all. Well, you certainly picked the right day to come calling. If you stick around the fort another hour or so, you'll be able to watch the boats coming in. We got word yesterday they'd reached the foot of St. Andrew's Rapids."

Grant said: "Boats? It's too early in the season for the brigade."

"Not the brigade—the immigrants."

The vertebrae in Grant's neck snapped stiff. He snapped his mouth shut and waited for a breath before opening it again, so he could say in a relatively controlled voice: "I had been under the impression that the Company wasn't encouraging immigration."

"Yes, by and large . . ." Hargrave appeared to be having some trouble of his own maintaining a matter-of-fact tone of voice. "But in this case . . . a very carefully selected few, you see . . . from Switzerland. Well, no rest for the wicked. Do look in again before you head back to Grantown. I'd be very interested to hear your impressions of . . . the immigrants."

When the clerks had gone, Marie said: "What was that all about?"

"Damned if I know. Would you like me to take Maria Theresa?"

"I can manage."

"Fine—I'll meet you over at the store." But before he'd gone three steps a pudgy projectile hit the back of his knee. He caught his balance and looked down to find Maria Theresa wrapped around his leg. He scooped her up, shrugged at Marie, and carried on toward the blacksmith shop.

The smith looked up from his forge—blue eyes blazing through the storm of smoke and sparks—and bellowed between hammer clangs: "It's not here! I did my part and handed it over to the carpenter!"

Grant pried a bit of slack into the vise of Maria Theresa's arms around his neck and shouted back: "Fair enough—but there's another job I want done! A four-foot-high railing to enclose an area four feet by five! The corner posts have to have long enough stems to anchor through a roof beam!"

"I won't have time to start on such a thing until December!"

"Fair enough! Could you have it done by spring?"

"If the damned charcoal burners get busy soon! If the damned brigade brings down the strapping iron I ordered in last year's outfit! If the damned Company hires me a new apprentice with enough brains in his butt to not sit down on the horn of an anvil I've just been shaping red-hot horseshoes over!"

"Fair enough!" Grant toted Maria back out into the relative quietude of the market square and across it to the carpentry. Another citizen of Grantown was there already, one of the pair of young métis who'd discovered while working on Grant's house that they both had more of a flair for wood than gunpowder and were actually considering giving up the buffalo hunt to set themselves up as partners in carpentry. The would-be woodworker was standing in a corner, salivating and staring at the fort carpenter, turning an oak branch on a foot-treadle lathe.

The carpenter pulled back and let the lathe wind down. "Good afternoon, Mister Grant. It's done and waiting for you. If you'd care to follow me into the stockroom . . ."

"Certainly. But first—any idea if they'd happen to have another lathe like that in the depot stock at York Factory? And the tools to go with it?"

"Hard to say. I'll have to check with Hargrave. But if they don't, I could put it on order with the next outfit if you're seriously interested."

"I am. I'm sure you have a much better idea of what to order than I will ever have. If the Company doesn't offer you a commission as middleman, come to talk to me." Maria Theresa's head was jammed so tightly against the side of his neck that he had to turn around to address the budding Grantown woodworker. "I have no doubt that you and your partner will be so inundated with lathework orders that you'll be able to pay me back before I even miss the initial outlay."

"Yes, Mister Grant! I'm sure! It won't take more'n—oh, a month or two after we got it. Thank you!"

"If anyone deserves thanks, it's Maria Theresa. She's the one who's forced the issue. At the rate she's growing she's going to need a full-size bed with lathe-turned posts before you can turn around twice. And now . . ." He turned back to the fort carpenter.

"This way, Mister Grant. . . ."

With Maria-monkey clinging around his throat, Grant followed the fort carpenter into a cavern of sun shafts and wood. In a far corner, set aside from the stacks of lathed table legs and pegged desk drawers, there was an object rather like a monstrous wooden wishbone with an iron nose. The fort carpenter said: "Well, there it is. Farm implements ain't exactly the back of my hand, but I asked around in Kildonan—for what that's worth. I'm told the Company and the Selkirks are going to bring out an expert next year, to build an experimental farm. But he ain't here yet, is he? And you said you wanted it now, so . . ."

"I'm hardly an expert myself, but it looks splendid. If any flaws appear in the course of usage, I'll let you know." He shifted his arms so as to cradle Maria Theresa's bottom in the crook of his left arm while his right hand took hold of the plow and dragged it out across the quadrangle to the cart. Marie was standing by the doorway of the store, watching anxiously to make sure that the fort servants loading sacks of flour, kegs of gunpowder and rum, and bolts of cloth didn't crush Eliza.

A mob chorus of cheering and shouting blew up in the vicinity of the fort gates. Grant let go of the plow handle and turned to look. A spout of Company boatmen—leathery brown métis and blond, boiled-lobster Orkneymen—burst in dragging baggage trunks and herding a flock of gawking immigrants.

Grant's first thought was that the London Committee and George Simpson had all lost their collective mind. The immigrants were pasty-faced, mushroomy, middle-aged men and women with a plethora of pale-haired daughters. All were rolling their eyes and shrieking in some Teutonic dialect.

James Hargrave appeared beside Marie, stifling chortles to the point of suffocation. Grant looked again at the milling mob of soft old couples and their softer-looking daughters, and then he saw.

The hovering Des Meurons descended like a wolf on the fold. Any girl between the ages of twelve and twenty, and several who stretched the boundaries, found her hand snatched by a raggedy ex-mercenary kneeling in front of her. More Des Meurons began to pour through the gates, some of them muddy-footed from jumping for the shore before their boats had quite completed the crossing from the east bank. Bishop Provencher followed on their heels, along with every priest he could scoop up on short notice. In a moment there were lines of couples in front of each of the priests, some of the girls primping and blushing while some of them were dragged along, with their pastry-cook fathers ineffectually trying to beat off their soon-to-be sons-in-law. The Anglican missionaries came pelting in from Kildonan, hoping to make a few converts from the ones stuck at the tail end of the line.

Grant was laughing so hard that he had to take hold of the plow handle again to keep from falling down. Marie had tears rolling down her cheeks, but not from laughter. She said: "Those poor girls . . ."

That started him going again. He managed to get enough breath to gasp out, "Oh, don't . . . don't weep for them, Waposis. . . . In another few days they'll be boxing their husbands' ears to get out and plow the fields. 'And he who once putting his hand to the plow and looking back . . .'"

CHAPTER 23

Marie was shaking the bearskin hearth rug out the front door when a cart went by carrying four girls her own age. All had bags or buckets slung over their shoulders to go berry picking. One of them waved at her, but the others were too busy giggling behind their hands and exchanging words with the pair of gaudy young horsemen trotting alongside. For an instant Marie felt like a caged deer watching the rest of the herd scamper by. She told herself not to be ridiculous, there wasn't one of them wouldn't change places with her in an instant, and went back inside her big white house.

Eliza was crying from her cradleboard in the kitchen. Marie heaved the bearskin down in front of the parlor hearth and went into the kitchen. Eliza was squalling herself red-faced and squirming. Marie lifted the cradleboard off the wall peg and set it down flat on the kitchen table, ashamed of herself for thinking of her little miracle as an annoying inconvenience. She unlaced the sheath of the cradle-board, extracted Eliza and her mossbag, then unlaced the mossbag and extracted Eliza from the soaked moss. Cradling the infant in one arm, she fished a rag out of the ragbag on the wall, dried her off, dropped the rag in the washing basket, and set Eliza down on the braided rug in front of the hearth to wriggle and giggle as Maria Theresa scuttled forward for tickling duty.

Marie took up the mossbag again and headed out the back door, detouring en route to give the stew pot on the hearth a stir. She emptied the soiled moss beside the back step onto the growing pile that she intended to rake out over the garden after the first hard frost. Josephte was busy with a scrub board and tub, hanging the wet clothes on a *shagganappi* rope strung between two trees. Marie had actually begun to feel a certain amount of affection for her purse-mouthed, fleshless sister-in-law, after asking herself just how cheery *she* would be if she'd been condemned to a life of helping out in another woman's home.

After turning the mossbag inside out to shake off the last clinging crumbs of damp moss, she was about to go back inside when she saw her husband coming back from his first day of plowing furrows onto the prairie out beyond the woods. He was streaked with soot from the burned-off grass and he was walking awkwardly, with his arms bent at the elbow and his half-curled hands bobbing limply in front of his chest like a prairie dog standing sentry. She said: "What's the matter?"

"Matter? Nothing of any import, just a damned nuisance."

She stepped forward to meet him and reached up to unfurl one of his hands. Along the midpart of the palm and the fronts of all four fingers there was a mushroom farm of blisters, some of them broken and oozing. He shrugged at her and grumbled: "And here I'd been under the impression I'd spent a good part of my life doing rough work with my hands."

"Come inside, I'll fix something for it. It'll just take me a minute to finish up with Eliza first."

"I can do that. Wouldn't be the first time I'd changed a mossbag. In fact, when Maria Theresa was Eliza's age, there was no one else to do it. Isn't that right, Maria Theresa?"

"I don't remember."

Marie said, "Not with your hands like that, you won't. Sit down, it'll only take . . ." by which time she had already relined the bag with fresh moss and was ladling Eliza in among it. She kissed her daughter's yawning little mouth and hung the cradleboard back up, then swung out the iron hook holding the stew pot over the fire, hefted the pot onto the hearthstone, covered it with a cloth and covered the bottom of a smaller pot with water from the bucket, hung the small pot on the hook, and swiveled it back in over the fire. She went over to the wall that was covered with her collection of pouches and panniers and reached for the smaller of the two that were decorated with magenta beads in a pattern resembling blooming fireweed. The bigger one was stuffed with fireweed leaves, the smaller one with shredded roots. She pulled open the drawstring of the pouch and sifted a handful into the already steaming water in the pot.

While she was clattering and rattling about, and he was sitting with his elbows propped on the table rim to lessen the flow of blood into his hands, she said: "You don't have to keep doing this to yourself. You got lots of other things you want to be doing around here besides plowing, and it wouldn't cost much to pay some other man to push the plow around."

"It's a good thought, Waposis, but I'm afraid it wouldn't do the trick. Even after just one day, Urbain Delorme's already out hacking away with a mattock behind his own place—once he saw that I was willing to be a part-time *jardinier* myself. So even if I only manage to get a few acres plowed before we leave—"

"Leave?"

"On the autumn buffalo hunt."

"You never said anything about—"

"It never occurred to me that I'd have to say anything. What we managed to accomplish on the summer hunt will go for nothing if we don't follow it up in the fall. If you prefer to stay behind and tend the house, I'll understand. Eliza might not be quite ready for—"

"No! I mean, no, I don't see no reason I should stay behind. There'll be plenty of other women going along, with babies even younger'n Eliza. I just hadn't thought of it till you said it, that's all."

The fireweed concoction in the pot had boiled down to a kind of sludgy tea. She poured it into a bowl to cool and hefted the stew pot back onto the hook. He said musingly: "I do wonder whether the bucking and jouncing of the plow handles is partly because the cart pony wasn't made for that kind of work. I think I'll put the word out at Red River that I'm interested in buying two or three male calves to grow into oxen." Something started him laughing. "I don't know if you noticed, Little Rabbit, but there are a great many more cattle on the farms around the Forks than there were when we left for the hunt in the spring. The American drovers who brought a herd up to Red River last summer pretty much skinned the sporrans off all the Kildonan people desperate for milk and beef. So this summer they drove up an even bigger herd, expecting to repeat the performance. What they hadn't thought of was that the farmers who'd been willing to pay any price last year to get a cow in their barn now had one, or two or three. So the skinners got skinned. It was either sell them at a loss or herd them all the way back to Ohio. Things do have a habit of balancing out."

She carried the bowl over to the table, tested the temperature with a finger, then dunked his right hand into it. As the fireweed hit the blisters, he hissed in a gasp and tried to snatch his hand back out, but she held it in. After a moment the sharp black sparks in his eyes softened and the lids settled to half-mast. She let go of his wrist and said: "Now give me your other hand."

"One wasn't enough?"

When Eliza's cradleboard was propped in the corner of the bedroom and there was only a ghost of moonlight filtering in through the parchment windowpanes, he drifted one half-cupped, herb-leathered hand over her left breast, brushed a kiss across her left temple, and murmured: "Good night, my love."

As he started to roll over, she said: "I think a month is long enough."

He stopped in midroll and turned back. She knew her body wasn't as taut as it had been before Eliza, and never would be again, but he didn't seem to mind.

A few days before the date he'd fixed on to set off on the fall hunt, word came from the Forks that the York boat brigade had come in from Hudson's Bay. Wappeston saddled up his horse, saying: "They won't have unpacked and sorted out the personal outfits yet, but the mail packet may contain some news of my father's estate. I should be back by midafternoon."

Marie spent most of the morning working with a hoe, widening her garden patch for next year. It was goldenrod time. When she'd looked out the bedroom window that morning to see how the day was going to be, the meadow beyond the trees had been a blaze of sunlit gold. She leaned on her hoe for a moment and considered taking a couple of empty sacks out onto Coteau des Festins and filling them, so she could fill some winter afternoon making yellow dye. She told herself to get back to her hoeing. If she managed to break enough ground for two more rows of beans, she would reward herself tomorrow with a long walk picking goldenrod in the last summer breezes.

Pierriche came by in a cart. He draped his gangly forearms over the top rail and said: "Wappeston shoulda broke that for you with his plow."

"He offered. I told him it was too big a tool for too small a job. Besides, there's a lot of tree roots and things in around here that the hoe can skip over and the plow couldn't."

"I guess you know best about your own garden. I saw Wappeston on his way out and asked if he'd mind me borrowing his plow to see if I could make it work on my own piece of ground, since he won't be using it today."

"You might as well take the red mare, too. She seems to be getting used to pulling it. Have you got much broke by hand already?"

"A little. I don't exactly sweat at it like he does. Ain't none of us going to get much more done this year. I saw a yellow leaf this morning. By the time we get back from the fall hunt, there won't be nothing between our houses and the wind off Hudson's Bay except a rattling of bare twigs."

"I was thinking of maybe finding a few baby spruces and planting them in a line along the edge there. Do you think they'd grow?"

He arched his eyebrows, stretched his eyelids, puffed up his upper lip, and let the air out with a soft pop, then shrugged and said: "Spruce trees seem to grow where they want to. Mary said to tell you she went and picked more cattails than she knows what to do with, if you want some."

"Yes, thanks."

"I'll bring 'em over when I bring back the plow. Don't go hoeing too long in the hot sun, now."

As the cart ambled on to circle around the woods out to where the plow was sitting in the field, Marie set down her hoe for a moment to check that Eliza was still sleeping peacefully in her cradleboard slung from the branch of an oak tree. A chipmunk was twitching on the next branch over, arrested by this strange new creature dangling in his tree. He squeaked and skittered away as Marie approached. Eliza was still in deep hibernation, bobbing gently in the breeze like a cocooned caterpillar busy growing wings.

By the time the sun kissed the tops of the trees on the other side of the river, she had finished her two rows and Wappeston hadn't come home. There was still no sign of him when supper was ready. Josephte had tried an experiment with the hearth oven and a *tortierre*, the meat-and-vegetable pies that the voyageurs had brought with them in memory from Quebec. Marie fed Eliza and then sat down with Josephte, John, Maria Therese, and Father Picard to tuck into the *tortierre*. For someone that skinny, Josephte was a remarkably good cook.

After the dishes had been cleared away, Marie went to work on the two old pemmican sacks of uprooted cattails that Pierriche had brought over. The roots had to be peeled and set on the hearth to dry. When it came time to use them, they could be cooked as a vegetable or pounded into fibers that made a kind of flour. The downy top spikes were shredded into a bag to use for caulking walls or stuffing winter moccasins or for tinder. Everyone else went off to bed, but she kept on working. An occasional horse went by on the trail in front of the house, but none of them turned in. When the candle guttered out she gave in and carried Eliza upstairs.

She lay awake and alone a long time, imagining all sorts of things that could have happened to him. The four men from New Year's and a bunch of their friends had taken their revenge for the fines they'd had to pay. His horse had stepped in a badger hole and he was lying out on the prairie bleeding. Some Sioux warriors had sneaked up to the Forks on a horse raid and had come across him riding alone.

She was listening to a distant whippoorwill when she heard the soft clop of a walking horse approaching along the trail. This one turned in. As it passed under her window, she heard a low voice humming a slow version of a tune that put her back into her room at Fort Montagne à la Bosse on a New Year's night with the voices of drunken fur traders filtering through the walls, chorusing: "Such a parcel of rogues in a nation."

The hoof thuds and humming were replaced by a puttering of horse lips, a baritone mumble, and the creak of a saddle girth. After a moment she heard the back door open and close, then a creaking of stairs and banister rail and the muffled thumps of moccasined feet planted heavily and unsteadily along the hallway.

The bedroom door opened and closed, and a large shadow moved across the vague parchment glow of the window. The shadow didn't stumble or bump into any of the furniture, but it emanated a distinct odor of rum and moved with the tightrope-walking grace of a man who might appear comatose until a bottle tips off the table and he snatches it by the neck in midair. She opened her mouth to tell him to be careful not to step on Eliza, then decided not to insult him.

He popped the pin out of the wood-and-leather window latch and swung the window open, propped his hands on the edge, and leaned out as the night air and the moon- and starlight poured in. The leaves of the trembling aspen beside the house whispered sibilantly in harmony with the rhythms of the river and the hunting hoot of an owl.

Marie swallowed to moisten her throat and said: "You've had a long day's riding back and forth."

He glanced back over his shoulder. "I didn't mean to wake you. Go back to sleep."

"I wasn't sleeping. Come to bed."

He grunted affirmatively and nodded his head but stayed leaning out the window with the moonlight turning his features into a grim, blue-white marble statue. Eliza sighed loudly, and then her breathing settled back into the rhythms of sleep. Marie whispered: "Did they have news?"

"News? Ah—yes, they had news. The estate has been settled."

"That's wonderful!"

"Wonderful? Yes, I suppose it is to be wondered at. Matters were expedited by the removal of a major impediment to both sides' wishes."

"Pardon me?"

"William MacGillivray is dead."

She didn't know whether to say "I'm sorry" or "Congratulations." But he was definitely unhappy about something, so she chose the former. "I'm sorry."

"Are you? I'm not sure I am. While I was growing up, he was the closest thing I had to a father. But then he did try to hand me over to the hangman for political expedience, and he did his damnedest to rob me of my father's money. In fact, the two might have run together quite conveniently.

"The final figure is eight thousand four hundred and twenty-two pounds, nine shillings and fourpence."

She was about to break into whoops of congratulations, sleeping babies be damned, when she realized that the lowest figure he'd ever mentioned before had been twelve thousand pounds. He went on with a brittle laugh: "It seems I was a rather expensive child, doesn't it? Either that or good old Simon has meticulously calculated just exactly how much he can steal from me without it being quite worth my while to take a year to travel across the ocean and hire a solicitor to recover all that's owed me." He paused to drag in and let out a rasping breath. "I'm sorry."

"Sorry? We're the richest people in the country! And I wouldn't want you going away for a year even if it was another *ten* thousand pounds. Come to bed."

Sometime later he murmured: "Perhaps you should think carefully about this notion of coming along on the fall hunt."

"I have."

"Have you? Have you considered the possibility that—I think it's unlikely, but it's possible—that La Terre Qui Brûle might be able to use what happened on the spring hunt as a tool to weld together the whole Dakotah Nation? They could be waiting for us. I don't want to lose you."

"I don't want to lose you. If you got killed by the Sioux, I'd just as soon me and Eliza and Maria Theresa did, too—eight thousand pounds or not. Now go to sleep." Amazingly, the massive head weighing down her shoulder and her left breast did exactly that.

The fall hunt was even more successful than the summer hunt had been. The cart train was almost twice as long, partly because some of the hunters who'd been part of the inaugural hunt had discovered they could have filled more carts if they'd had them and partly because most of the hunters who'd stayed aloof from the first mass hunt had changed their minds. The only Sioux the hunt encountered were a few horse-raiding parties of young men eager to prove themselves. Proving them mistaken was like swatting flies.

By the time the loaded carts wallowed back across the Passage of the Assiniboine, there was a membrane of ice along the shore. By New Year's Grantown was a collection of fluffy white roofs and smoking chimneys, with a network of trampled paths from door to door. Before sunrise on New Year's Day, a torchlight procession of jumpers and carrioles and outriders set out along the frozen Assiniboine. Wrapped up in buffalo robes and blankets, with Maria Theresa snuggled under one arm and Eliza cradled in the other, Marie dozed in and out of a rushing parade of hissing sleigh runners, chorused songs calling up wolf echoes, leather bottles of body-warmed rum kissing her mouth, and the sparkle of stars and ice crystals in the snow and the sky and the air in between.

Hogmanay at Fort Garry was so hot with candles and Yule logs, fiddles and bagpipes, roast beaver tail and mulled wine, that Marie was hard-pressed not to strip off more than her blanket and mittens. Replacing her winter moccasins with summer ones for dancing helped a little, although the dancing didn't. She danced with owl-eyed James

Hargrave, wolf-eyed George Simpson, hound-dog-eyed Pierriche, and God knew who else in the menagerie. She also danced with her husband, whose eyes put her in mind of no others.

When she couldn't dance anymore, she settled down on a bench in the corner to feed Eliza and watch the milling crowd through her half-lidded trance. A wave seemed to be passing through the crowd. At the crest of it was a black-maned head overtopping most others— Eliza's father wending his way from one side of the room to the other. Although a few of the Kildonan people or Des Meurons pointedly turned their backs as he passed by, everyone else turned toward him with a grin or a raised glass or a slap on the shoulder or a bellowed joke or a shy smile. As before, when she'd watched him enter that wedding celebration back when she was still Marie McGillis, he kept flicking his eyes away from the ones trying to meet his, deflecting them with quick words or winking nods that appeared so smoothly affable to everyone else but seemed so painfully forced to her.

And now she saw how much he wanted this, yet was like a desperately thirsty man who privately knows he doesn't deserve a proffered cup of water.

She noticed another wave passing through the crowd from the opposite direction. She couldn't see what was causing it, but she could see that it consisted of faces frozen into ghastly approximations of a grin, of stiff-edged greetings and almost forelock-tugging bows. As the two currents met, the tide in front of her parted just long enough for her to see her husband nodding cheerily at George Simpson and getting a curt nod in reply and then a flicker of the little man's pale blue eyes stabbing icicles into the broad back passing by. It was only a glimpse, and then the crowd closed in front of her again. But it was enough to chill the warmth she'd been melting into a moment before.

On the way home she said: "That man hates you."

"Which man? I could think of several."

"George Simpson."

He laughed. "I think 'hate' is somewhat too strong a word for any emotion Georgie Simpson might have—were he to have any."

"Listen to me just this one time. He *hates* you."

"I'm not a fool, Little Rabbit, despite some evidence. It's good of you to try to warn me, but I'm already well aware of the fact that little George is no fonder of me than he is of any other living thing— including himself, I suspect. But as long as I am useful to him—and believe me, he needs me as much as we need him—it doesn't make a damned bit of difference."

CHAPTER 24

Grant sat digesting his breakfast, ruminating on whether he'd made all the preparations necessary for the trading expedition he was about to set out on, focusing his meditative gaze on his new winter coat hanging on a peg by the back door.

A buffalo coat was a fine thing for keeping a horseman warm, but a tad heavy for snowshoeing. So Grant had acquired a white, hooded, thigh-length, woolen capote, courtesy of his wife's dexterity with shears and sewing needles and three-and-a-half-point Hudson's Bay blankets. The door jerked open and Falcon poked in his snowflake-haloed head to say: "We're ready."

Grant shrugged on his new coat, belted it shut with the multi-colored assumption sash Josephte had woven for him, then turned to kiss his family good-bye. Marie's eyes were moist. She said: "I'll miss you."

"And I you—particularly when I crawl into my solitary bed in a snowbank. I don't imagine we'll be longer than three weeks, but if the weather turns nasty, we'll just dig in and wait it out. So don't be alarmed if I'm not home on the dot of February."

Falcon was waiting out in the snow, along with four sturdy-looking young métis, twelve scruffy-looking dogs, and two shaggy ponies. The dogs were harnessed to three carrioles, the horses to two jumpers. Grant doubted they would need the carrying capacity of both jumpers, but when it came to business he believed in being optimistic.

Falcon climbed onto the lead jumper and took the reins. One of the young men—Marie's younger brother Daniel—gestured Grant toward the one carriole that wasn't packed with freight. Grant shook his head and took down his snowshoes from the second jumper, saying: "My racquet legs need breaking in. You ride until the first stop."

Daniel somewhat sheepishly climbed in and settled himself among the buffalo robes and blankets lining the carriole. The other three young men—one of whom was Daniel's brother, Donald—commented loudly on the way his big sister's husband was spoiling him. Grant took it as a good sign. If they were already making mock of each other, they'd get along fine.

Grant stood up from strapping on his racquets, unfurled the braided dog whip coiled around his shoulder, waved good-bye to his family shivering on the doorstep, and snapped his whip over the lead dog's head. It was more of an anemic pop than the gunshot crack it was supposed to be—he was definitely out of practice in more ways than one—but it did the job. As the carriole lurched into motion, Grant set his legs into a trot, not quite tripping over his snowshoes, and the rest of the expedition fell in behind.

It was an odd set of circumstances that had put Grant back in the fur trade business. Several bumptious American traders had set up a camp where the Souris crooked out from between Turtle Mountain and the Pembina Hills, nibbling at the underbelly of the Company's vast private preserves. The location was convenient for those Cree or Assiniboine or métis whose stomping grounds happened to fall between the Company's posts at Brandon House and Fort Qu'Appelle. Added to the convenience was the rumor that the Americans were bringing back the good old days when alcohol was a standard article of trade.

The London Committee believed in avoiding direct confrontation whenever possible. So George Simpson had come up with a plan to cut off the Americans by licensing a private trader to bring a traveling store to every tipi door, which was about as convenient as any trapper or hunter could ask. The licensed trader would then sell the furs and buffalo robes to the Company. Simpson seemed to be under the impression that the plan would be particularly effective if said licensed trader was Cuthbert Grant.

Marie had pointed out ad infinitum that the house of Grant was hardly in need of more money at this point. He had tried to make her understand that there was no such thing as too much money, and that there wouldn't be many opportunities offered to go trading with the Company's backing but without the Company telling him how to go about it. It had taken so much conversation to get her to accept those simple facts of life that he hadn't even tried to get across the real reason why it was worth his while to spend the worst part of the winter snowshoeing across the prairie. The more little problems that Cuthbert Grant solved for George Simpson, the more secure Grantown would be.

It was a crisp morning. Excluding the voice of the wind, the only sounds were the squelch of snowshoes, the crunch of hooves, the patter of paws, the sibilant rush of toboggan beds and jumper runners, the cloud-puffing panting of the snowshoers, lopers, and trotters, and the occasional distant crack of a tree limb snapping in the cold. Sun dogs bounced off the white horizon as they left Grantown behind for

the bald sweep of White Horse Plains. Grant made a mental note to
smear a bit of soot under his eyes when they stopped for their midday
tea and bannock, against going snowblind from the glare.

When the sun got as high as it was going to get, they were halfway
to Portage la Prairie and Grant was halfway to an early grave. His lungs
and heart and the muscles in his legs were having birth contractions.
He left it to Falcon to build the fire, freed himself from the instruments
of torture strapped to his feet, and slumped down with his back
propped against a carriole. Falcon looked up from scooping snow into
the kettle and said cheerily: "Long time since you last had to work for
a living, ain't it?" Grant mittened up a wedge of broken drift crust and
heaved it at him.

When they reached Brandon House, they'd gone a hundred miles
in three days and Grant was beginning to feel as if he might live after
all. Despite his parting words to Marie, he could sleep surprisingly
cozily curled up in a snowbank like a sled dog. A quibbler might point
out that the dogs slept in their own pelts instead of buffalo robes, that
they didn't have the option of hitching a ride on a carriole or a jumper,
and that they curled up with bellyfuls of frozen fish instead of hot
pot-luck stew. But the effective principle was the same.

The expedition laid up for a day at Brandon House and then set off
on a circuitous course westward toward Fort Qu'Appelle—looping
southwest or northeast from one wintering camp to another. The
weather held steady—cold as the Vikings' Hel, with a weasel-toothed
wind that always managed to veer into the quarter their course was
about to turn toward. But the few snowfalls that came down weren't
enough to mire the horses or whip up into a blizzard.

The first five camps they visited made it apparent to Grant that he'd
made a mistake. In every tipi or cabin he was presented with an
abundance of fine furs and virtually nothing in the way of buffalo robes
or deerskins. Some winters were like that—good for the small animals
and bad for the big ones. A black fox pelt might be worth a lot in trade,
but its skinned-out body didn't do much toward feeding a trapper's
family. Consequently Grant's trading outfit of axe heads, knife blades,
beads, and blankets stayed baled while the expedition's stock of provisions—pemmican, flour, smoked goose, even the dogs' frozen fish—
was steadily winnowed down in trade.

The horses were perfectly content to carry on scraping holes in the
snow and stuffing themselves with crisp-frozen grass, but the human
and canine contingents were another matter. When there was only one
day's rations left, Grant decided to make a straight run for the place

in the Qu'Appelle Valley where the Dumont clan always wintered. The Dumonts might be wild and improvident by some people's lights, but they hadn't raised up generations of six-and-a-half-foot sons by neglecting to lay in enough provisions for the winter.

Grant's belly constricted as the carriole slid around the last bend in the Qu'Appelle below the Dumonts' winter home. There was the cluster of cabins right where they should be, but they were drifted over with pristine white snow hills, and there was no smoke coming out of the chimneys. It appeared the Dumonts had divined that this would be a good year to winter in another part of the country.

Grant and Daniel McGillis snowshoe-shoveled their way into the door of the cabin handiest to the river while Falcon led the other three junior members of the expedition up the slope of the valley to cut firewood. When all six of them were leaned back in the toasty cabin, burping out their last supper, Grant said: "Well, whether I like it or not, and I don't particularly, there are facts to be considered. We could make it back to Yellow Shirt's camp in a long day's run. But, given the fact that we managed to get twelve marten pelts out of him for one sack of pemmican, I highly doubt he's in any position to—"

"Ssh!" Falcon cut him off. "Listen!"

Grant obediently cocked his head back and opened his ears. Strain as he might, he could hear nothing but the endless sighing of the wind. He opened his mouth, intending to say, "Listen to what?" but instead snapped it shut again and sat bolt upright. The voice of the wind had changed character. The whistling owl hoot that had been scouring his cheeks since he waved good-bye to Marie had become a *ban sidh* howl.

He jumped up and flung open the door. Flying snow crystals bit into his eyelids. He jerked his head back, blinking and squinting, and then looked again. The ragged horizon line of the valley rim was barely discernible through the gathering white dust storm. The dogs and horses were nowhere in sight. He slammed the door and said to Falcon, "How long is it going to last?" forgetting himself and asking in English.

Falcon replied in the same language: "Your guess, she's probably about so good as mine."

It went on all through the night and was still going on in the morning, battering the walls and driving powder trains of snow in through the door frame and the chinks in the shutters. After a breakfast of tea and tobacco, Grant threw the last stick of wood on the fire and said: "Which one's the better horse?"

Falcon looked up from knotting two *shagganappi* ropes together. "Matilda, the black one. Maurice kicks and nips when he gets tired."

Grant shrugged on his coat and loaded his pistols while the other five squirmed into their coats and mittens and fur caps. "Daniel, you'll come along with me. Bring your knife and your dog whip. Well, gentlemen, this is where we pay for all those lazy days coasting along the trail." He put his shoulder to the door, managed to plow back enough of the snow banked up against it to open it halfway, and stepped out into a whirling white maelstrom. He slitted his eyes before the wind-driven crystals pitted them to pieces and stepped aside to let the others follow him out.

They strapped on their snowshoes hurriedly and in silence; unmittened hands weren't a wise idea for an instant longer than absolutely necessary, and it was hard enough to snatch in breath out of the wind without yelling superfluous pleasantries over it. Falcon tied the end of his double-length rope around one of the log ends projecting from the corner of the cabin, pried his axe out of another log end where he'd imbedded it the night before, and set off for the wooded slope behind the cabins, playing out the coiled rope behind him. Donald McGillis and the other two young men followed close behind him, trailing their hands along the rope and leaning into the wind. Their silhouettes quickly grew hazy and then disappeared altogether in the swirling fog of milky glass chips.

Grant shouted across the arm's-length gap between him and Daniel McGillis, "Come on!" and set off exploring the haphazard compound that had grown up through various generations of Dumonts adding on new cabins or sheds or horse corrals. Maurice and Matilda had found a spot between two close-together cabins where the bite of the wind was a shade less sharp and were patiently waiting out the storm, passing the time by pawing up patches of last year's clover. Grant grabbed a mittful of brown mane and dragged Maurice around to the front of the cabin the trading expedition had expropriated. Maurice complained and reared and tried to bite him.

Daniel drew his knife to start the butchering. As the blood steamed out into the snow, the drift beside the wall with the chimney on it erupted with dogs. Daniel beat them off with his whip. Grant threw them horse guts for breakfast.

The blizzard blew itself out the next day. They rearranged the cargo of furs and gear and horse meat to fit on one jumper and three carrioles and started for home. Maurice fed them halfway to Brandon House, then it was time to start killing the dogs. Their brothers and sisters wolfed them down happily. The expedition was reduced to two carrioles and a jumper and was cutting across the prairie in a straight line toward Brandon House when the sky started dumping down snow again and the wind began to howl. Grant said: "I say we make a run for it."

Falcon nodded. "Down on the river—longer but safer."

They managed to get into the Assiniboine Valley before the storm grew quite thick enough to blind them. Once they were on the river, it didn't matter whether they couldn't see ten feet in front of them. As long as their snowshoes or vehicles didn't start slanting upward they were keeping a true, if winding, course east. After a time, Grant didn't know if it was day or night. He was reduced to one need and one interesting question. The need was not to lose sight of the hazy shape of the lead dog churning along beside him. The interesting question was whether his leg muscles would be able to raise the snowshoe for the next step.

The snow and wind died down and the earth and sky separated themselves once again. Grant called a halt and collapsed against the snow-padded riverbank. The pounding of his blood finally slowed enough to begin to feel the cold again. Falcon gasped out, "I better get some firewood," and struggled up the bank. When he got to the top he stopped and just stood there.

Grant sat with his head craned back over his shoulder, waiting for Falcon to do or say something. When he didn't, Grant croaked at him: "What?"

"We're in the sand hills."

"No! We couldn't've—"

"We did. You can take my word for it or come up and look for yourself."

Grant took his word for it. At some point during the blizzard, they'd run right past Brandon House and kept on going. Depending on where in the sand hills they were, Brandon House might be five miles behind them or fifty. Grant scooped up a mittenful of snow, scrubbed it down his face, and said: "Which dog's closest to dead?"

On a mid-February midnight, or perhaps it was March, with the northern lights painting the snow red and green, Grant threw open the door of his house and bellowed: "I'm home, dears!"

He wasn't there long. As soon as the ice broke and the sap started running, he led the entire population of Grantown south to Rivière aux Îlots de Bois. Families of Red River métis had been making the same pilgrimage for years, although not this far east. There were more than enough maple trees for each family to stake out their own stand, camping in the snow for the firelit festival of rendering maple blood into sugar and syrup, flicking steaming dipperfuls across the snow for the children to gobble up as candy.

When they got back to Grantown it was time for sowing—tromping up and down the muddy furrows broadcasting handfuls of Kildonan wheat or barley or oats, then rushing to plow or hoe them under before the blackbirds gobbled them up. By the time Grant had sewn his fields and Marie had planted her garden, it was time for the summer buffalo hunt to set out. But neither he nor she nor anyone else from the big white house went with it, except Father Picard. The blue-and-white flag went out at the head of the hunt again, but the cannon stayed behind.

Grant had decided that the laws of the hunt had become firmly enough established to function under another Captain of the hunt. If they couldn't, if the mass hunt only existed as an extension of his personal ability to bully people into line, then he'd have to rethink the whole business. But he suspected that the organization would get along just fine without him, particularly if the new Captain the hunters elected was Pierre Falcon. Perhaps Grant would've been inclined to man the mechanism a little longer before throwing it on its own resources if it weren't that he'd been asked to turn admiral instead of captain.

The Company was having problems with its boat brigades. The ending of the North West Company canoe brigades meant there was an overpopulation of experienced boatmen already resident in the *pays d'en haut,* so it was obviously an unnecessary expense to keep on importing boat crews from the Orkney Isles. Unfortunately the local boatmen were fractious and were having difficulty making the adjustment from canoes to York boats, while the Company's officers were having difficulty adjusting to crews accustomed to the rather rough-edged disciplines of the old nor'westers. George Simpson had come up with a notion that the transition might be smoothed if Cuthbert Grant was to command this year's boat brigade to York Factory. Grant would have been the first to concede that he didn't know a damned thing about York boats or inland navigation that the boatmen didn't already know. But he'd learned a long time ago that a figurehead performed its function admirably with just an authoritative wooden smile and a finger pointed past the bowsprit.

Consequently, as the hunters were heading off to the plains, Grant kissed his wife good-bye and spent the summer herding a flotilla of thirty-foot rowboats down the Red to the vast sweep of Lake Winnipeg pouring itself into the churning bottleneck of the Hayes River running down to York Factory on Hudson's Bay. At York Factory they traded their cargo of furs and country provisions for the outfits and indents of the inland forts, including the stock of trade goods for the licensed trader Cuthbert Grant, then turned around and headed back again. The difference was that the return trip was against the current.

He was back home in Grantown before the autumn hunt set out, but he and his family and his cannon didn't go with them. By all accounts, Falcon had done an admirable job as Captain of the summer hunt, and there had been no untoward difficulties with the Sioux or with the fiercely independent cogs and gears that made up the watch-works of the hunt.

Besides, the American traders had responded to the tactics of last winter by moving even farther into the Company's territories and building a fort even farther north along the Souris. George Simpson was of the opinion that there was enough time left before winter to slap up another fort across the river from it, as the North West and Hudson's Bay companies used to do to each other, and was willing to provide cut-rate labor and materials.

So Grant kissed his family good-bye and set off with six carts, four Company servants, and eight Grantown men who'd decided for various reasons to forgo the autumn hunt. The American fort was on the west bank of a ford. Grant set up camp on the east bank and didn't ride across to say hello. The American traders didn't poke their noses out of their fort to see what all the chopping and hammering was about. Within a week the east bank was graced with a moderately serviceable palisade of green poplar logs—more of an overgrown picket fence than a palisade—enclosing a sod-roofed trading store cum barracks. Before Grant could get around to coining an appropriate name for it, the crew had already christened it Fort Mister Grant.

As soon as the gates were hung, Grant filled in the blanks on a form printed in London over the seal of the Governor and Committee of the Company of Adventurers Trading into Hudson's Bay, saddled his horse, and splashed across the ford to the neighbors'. As his horse paused on the bank to shake off the water, several slouch hats and gun barrels appeared between the points on the palisade. Grant trotted closer, reined in his horse in front of the gates, and held up the folded, filled-in form. "I have something for you gentlemen to read—that is, if any among you happen to be of the literate persuasion. . . ."

One of the slouch hats growled: "I don't need readin' and writin' to pull a trigger, nigger."

"Ah. In that case, I'd be more than delighted to read it for you."
He flapped open the sheet of paper, cleared his throat, and commenced: "'Be it known to all those occupying this establishment located at the north bend of the Souris River in Rupert's Land, that you are trespassing upon property granted exclusively to the Governor and Company of Adventurers Trading into Hudson's Bay, as defined by Royal Charter in the year of our Lord sixteen hundred and seventy, and reaffirmed by Parliament in the year of our Lord eighteen hundred and twenty-one—"

"Be it known to *you*, nigger, that I got a double load of buckshot pointed right at your guts, and your royal goddamned parley-mint and your piece of ass-wipe ain't going to stop me from blowing you in half if you ain't back across that river before I can spit."

A still, small voice at the back of Grant's head said: *Oh, damn— didn't think of that possibility, did you?* At the same time he felt a surge through every vein in his body of that old electric feeling. The curls of bark peeling off the palisade logs, the furry warmth of the horse's ribs between his knees, the taste of autumn in the air, all shocked into a rich-hued clarity. He cleared his throat and said: "You're quite right—there's nothing anyone can do to stop you from pulling that trigger. But if you do—before the bang of your gun has quite faded, that river is going to be boiling with a bunch of very annoyed 'niggers' who will burn your fort around your ears and slow-roast you over the coals. Do try to be wise and let a word be sufficient. If you can't rise to that, I do sincerely hope that all of you are bachelors."

He leaned forward to poke the piece of paper in between the gateposts, then turned his horse and trotted back toward the Souris. Remarkably, he made it across the ford and inside Fort Mister Grant with his back intact.

The Grantown faction of his crew were in favor of slipping across the river at night and passing sentence on the trespassers. Part of Grant was inclined to agree with them, but his verdict was to wait and see what developed. What developed was that every incoming party of Indians or métis with furs or meat to trade swerved around or past the American fort and went for Fort Mister Grant like iron filings to a magnet. The Americans hung on, though. They were still there in December. Grant left a skeleton crew behind and headed home for the festive season.

Eliza had learned to toddle a few steps while he'd been gone. Marie was still nursing her, which would have shocked a European woman, but métis and Indian children lived on breast milk until they were ready to eat what their parents ate. It was the colony governor's turn to host the New Year's regale, so Grant held his own Hogmanay in the big white house. Once he'd recovered, he began to pack his traps together once more. Marie said: "Can't they run the fort without you?"

"I'm sure they could, if it weren't for the other fort across the river. As long as the Americans are there, I have to be." He kissed his family good-bye and whipped his dogs into a lope.

The winter dragged on at Fort Mister Grant. At least they didn't have to live on pemmican; every Indian or métis who brought in furs to trade also brought along a deer haunch or a brace of grouse. Grant couldn't imagine what the Americans were living on. The area around both forts had been thoroughly hunted out.

Come March, the Americans were still there. Grant saddled up his horse and rode across the river. "Hello the fort!"

"I warned you to stay away from here!" But the voice it came out in was cracked and wispy.

"And I warned you not to stay here. You made a mistake. God knows we all do—the trick is to live to learn from them. If you want to pack it in and head back home where you belong, we'll provide you with traveling provisions."

"Wouldn't do us no good."

Grant tried to figure out why not, then realized and added: "And horses."

As the ragged party of trespassers disappeared over the southern horizon, Grant hitched up his dogs, strapped on his snowshoes, and hit the trail for home, leaving instructions to saw up the fort on the west bank of the Souris for firewood.

The Marie who levered herself up from behind the kitchen table wasn't the same one he'd left behind. This one was swollen like a summer pumpkin and glowing like a harvest moon. He laughed. "So much for the old wives' tale that nursing women can't conceive."

"Old wives have to come up with something to pass the time."

CHAPTER 25

Marie jolted awake with a sudden awareness that there was a large, growling creature in her bed and that Maria Theresa and Eliza weren't. She finally put it together that the growling creature was her snoring husband and that the reason Eliza and Maria Theresa weren't sleeping with her as usual was because he was.

She sat up—no mean feat in a feather bed, even without a pregnant belly—and gazed down for a moment at the big, tousled head and the long black eyelashes that were placidly sealed together for a change. She managed to climb over him and get out of bed without waking him. She dressed quickly, teeth chattering in the frost-windowed morning, then reached down for Eliza in her cradleboard. Eliza had inherited her father's long, curled eyelashes, and mercifully hers were still sealed together as well. Before they could flutter open, Marie hefted her up and headed down the hall, leaving Eliza's father snoring peacefully. Eliza was definitely getting to be a load, stretching the seams of her mossbag. It was time to start weaning her and freeing her from her mossbag and cradleboard, to make room for her new little brother or sister.

In the kitchen, Father Picard was just getting up from his breakfast and struggling into his long blanket coat to go across to the little poplar log chapel next door. Josephte was making bannock. Maria Theresa and John were making faces at each other over their porridge. Eliza began to make it known to the world at large that Queen Elizabeth was waking up hungry. Marie unlaced her from her cradleboard for the day and gave her her breast.

Josephte interrupted her bannock making long enough to fill a bowl with porridge and carry it to the table. Marie sat spooning breakfast into her mouth while Eliza sucked it out of her breast. Josephte announced from the hearth, propping the skillet in front of the fire, "This is the last of the flour."

Marie hmmed around her mouthful of hot porridge to show that she'd heard. There were three bulging sacks of wheat sitting in the shed out back, besides the ones that had to be saved for seed. But it had been an unusually mild-mannered autumn. So when Wappeston had carted his harvest over to the colony windmill, several dozen carts had already been waiting in line to take advantage of one of the few blustery days. The miller had only gotten halfway through Wappeston's cartload before the wind had died.

There was a creaking on the stairs and Wappeston came into the kitchen, fisting sleep out of his eyes. Josephte slapped down a bowl of porridge at the head of the table and said: "The bannock I'm making is the last you're going to get. We're out of flour."

"Well, good morning to you, too. I was under the impression that Mary had sent over a few sacks of cattails in the fall. Don't people make flour out of cattail heads?"

Marie giggled. "Not unless you like the taste of pillow stuffing. It's cattail *roots,* and we used them all up already."

"Aren't there still three extra sacks of wheat still sitting in the shed?"

Josephte nodded. "Mm-hm, and maybe you'd like to grind them with your teeth."

He flung the back door open, letting in a blast of March lion peppered with snow crystals, and boomed cheerfully over its whistling: "Well, one thing we never have a shortage of in the winter is wind— nor in this kitchen, for that matter." He slammed the door and came back to his porridge, saying: "There appears to've been enough traffic back and forth between here and Red River to keep the trail packed down enough for a horse and jumper. I can easily be back in time for supper with three sacks of fresh-ground flour."

Marie said: "You don't have to do it today. We got plenty of other things to eat."

"I'm not exactly a dab hand at agriculture, Waposis, but I have managed to grasp the concept of making hay while the sun shines—or flour when the wind blows. Is there any sugar left from what we made last spring? . . . Ah, thank you."

By midafternoon the kitchen warmth had thawed the goose that she'd been saving in the freezing shed for the day when he was well and truly home. She stuffed it and spitted it and busied herself through the afternoon with basting and turning and side dishes. The goose had been rendered down to something more like a smoked duck by the time she heard harness bells jingling out of the night. She called the salivating children and Father Picard to come to the table while she and Josephte unspitted the goose and uncovered the wilted platters of wild parsnips, wild onions, wild berry leather, and potatoes, peas, and carrots from her garden.

He came through the door with a sack of flour sloped over each shoulder and an enthusiastic flush that the cold couldn't quite account for. He said: "Sorry to keep you waiting, but I discovered something. . . . Well, doesn't that look delicious! Roast duck!"

"Goose."

"Pardon me? Oh! Even better! Anyone seen my carving knife? . . . Ah—thank you. What I discovered was, it seems there's a company in Scotland that sells millworks, the whole mechanism, grindstones and all. Drumstick, John? No, Maria Theresa, I'm afraid you'll have to wait a few years till your hands get big enough. Where was I? Yes—it seems it's possible to order the whole works, lock, stock, and grindstones, through the Company. White meat or dark, Father Picard? What am I thinking of—there's only dark on a goose. Of course it might be difficult to convince the admiral of the boat brigade to haul a pair of grindstones all the way upstream from York Factory, except in this case the admiral is likely to be the same man who'd have to do the convincing. On the other hand, the Company's started a quarry up at Stony Mountain. Is that enough for you, Marie? You're eating for two again, remember—or three, including Eliza. . . . Well, I suppose that's enough to start with. Of course one would have to build one's own structure to house the ready-made works, and a water wheel to turn them— Did I mention I'm thinking of a water mill? That's the entire point. The winds may come and go, but the water runs steady from April through November. Sturgeon Creek seems the likeliest bet—halfway between here and the Forks, so we can grind the colonists' grain as well. Yes, and I found a book in the clerks' library: *The Complete Millwright.*

"Oh, forgive me, Father, I forgot about the grace. What say I finish carving up the bird, now that I've got it half-done, and then perhaps you'd do the honors. . . . Oh, did I mention Hargrave's being reposted to York Factory? He was quite adamant, Marie, that we invite him out here for a parting glass soon so he can bid you hail and farewell before he sets off north with the brigade and Admiral Grant. Proceed, Father."

As soon as dinner had been devoured, he excused himself and flung himself down on the hearth rug in the parlor to devour his book. Over the next few weeks, she watched him read through it again and again, when he wasn't making arrangements to have a full-size barn built come summer or charging off with his gun to where someone mentioned they'd seen deer sign. He was usually home for breakfast and supper and bedtime, and he never voiced one word that might suggest he wasn't happy to be home for a change, but Marie couldn't shake the feeling that she had somehow come to exist in a place just below his range of vision, except when both of them happened to be horizontal.

The ice on the river showed signs of rotting, and the woods beyond the kitchen window became a purple-and-amber Easter haze as the sap rose into the twigs of birch and willow. Pierriche stuck his head through the doorway one afternoon and said: "Got a spare cup of tea for a froze-moccasined man?"

Marie apologized, "I'm out of sugar to go in it. I almost made it through the winter, but I'm going to have to learn to measure a little better what we use from one sugaring-off to the next. All I got to sweeten your tea is brandy."

"Ah, well, in that case . . . Quiet in the house today. . . ."

"Eliza and Maria Theresa are taking their naps upstairs. Josephte and Father Picard went out visiting. John's checking his rabbit snares. Wappeston's off somewheres."

"I ain't butting in just when you finally got a momant to yourself? . . ."

"No—I was just praying for an excuse to pull my nose out of the mending basket before my eyes crossed for good. Sit down."

While she puttered with cups and liquids and prattled chirpy nonsense, he stomped the slush off his moccasins, pulled off his cap and gloves, flung his lanky body onto the nearest chair, and tugged open his coat. She added a dollop of brandy into his tea. He clammed his hand at her and winked, and she added a bit more than a dollop more. He took a sip and smacked his lips and said: "Well, it ain't maple sugar, but . . . Ain't you having none?"

She parted her lips to make some jaunty quip and burst out with: "What am I doing wrong, Pierriche?" To make matters worse, her eyes had flooded and her nose was suddenly stuffed up.

He lowered his eyes to study the rim of his cup for a moment while she sopped up the damage. When she lowered her handkerchief he raised his eyes and said with a confused, tentative smile: "Where'd you get the idea you're doing anything wrong?"

"From him! When he's not off fur trading or building a fort, he's captaining the boat brigade or going somewhere else where me and the children can't go with him. Then when he does come home for a while, he's out the door as soon as he's had his breakfast, saying he has to do some business at Fort Garry or talk over plans with a carpenter or see about buying a horse. And after supper he'll just pat me on the head and tell me what a good cook I am and go sit in front of the fire to read his book or clean his rifle or write down figures and plans in his account book. He must've wanted to be with me when he married me—so what am I doing wrong that he doesn't want to anymore?"

Pierriche rocked back in his chair, focused his hound-dog eyes on the ceiling, and pinched his sparse-mustached upper lip between his thumb and forefinger. He dropped the front legs of his chair back onto the floor and spread his hands on the table as though about to say something, then folded them together and didn't. He did the bullfrog trick with his upper lip, opened his hands again, and said: "Did you ever notice how a campfire changes as the sun goes down?"

She blinked at him.

"You see," he went on awkwardly, "when there's still sunlight, you look at the campfire and you see a pile of wood with a bit of flames licking out of it. But when it's dark, you don't see the wood, all you see are the flames and those bright-colored coals that were just lumps of gray ash when the sun was up.

"Well, back in the days when me and Wappeston was roaming footloose about the prairie, he was always the one to build the fire and tend it—and he still is, whenever we go off fishing or deer hunting for a day or two. It was always fine by me if that's what he wanted to do—I don't mind leaning back and puffing on my pipe and listening to the tree frogs and watching the pretty flames blossom and dance and keep me warm. But after a while of watching him looking after those fires, I realized he doesn't see the flames, even at night. What he's seeing is the wood burning, and how this big log end has to be shifted in over the coals if it's going to burn right through, and that smoldering branch has to be propped up higher if it's going to catch and stop blocking the draft to the other sticks around it.

"It's a sad thing for him, but a good thing for anybody who'd rather just sit back and enjoy the fire. And the fact is, he wouldn't be happy without something to fuss with. Sometimes you want to grab him by the throat and tell him the world won't stop turning if he put his feet up for a minute. I know you'll find it tough to believe, but he's got a lot better about it over the years. Back in the days when the New Nation was just starting, you just about had to hit him over the head with a hammer to get him to see anything except that point just over the horizon he was galloping for. I think that's a part of what happened between him and Bethsy McKay—her arms just got tired from swinging that hammer. You never been east, have you?"

"East?"

"I don't mean east to Lake of the Woods or Fort William, I mean east to what they call civilization." She shook her head, then realized he knew that already. "Most people here haven't, either, so they don't understand what he's fussing with this time. My father sent me out to Canada when I was a boy, to get a couple years of school. It gets you drunk at first—all the people galloping every which way, and the cobbled streets and stone buildings and fancy carriages. But then you start to see the habitants bowing and taking their hats off when the seigneur goes by, and the tavern girls packed off to jail by the judge they entertained the night before, and if you take a spring day to go fishing like any sensible person would, you find you might just as well be hanging your hook down an outhouse hole, and when you get back the priest whips you for missing the lesson. Wappeston didn't build the campfire we got here in the *pays d'en haut,* he's just trying to keep it fed and make sure it don't get trampled out before its time."

"I'm sorry, Pierriche—I guess I'm selfish, but whatever he might be doing to make you and other people happy don't help me and my children."

"It was you that wanted to ride the white devil horse, Marie. I don't recall me or anybody else putting a gun to your head. All you got to do is hang on tight and he'll gentle down once he's run himself out. You think you ain't got the strength, but I know different."

"And if I jump off he'll trample me?"

"Don't be ridiculous. When was the last time you saw him hurt anybody for spite? Except himself. If you cut and run, the only thing that'll come of it is you'll break both your hearts."

He suddenly snatched the top plate off the stack on the table and thrust it at her. She looked down at the empty plate and then up at him. He shrugged. "There's always supposed to be a collection after the sermon."

Chapter 24

When Grant got the news that he had a son, he was out in his barley field trying to convince his body and his new scythe to work together the way the proprietor of the new experimental farm at the Forks had told him they should.

Grant just couldn't seem to get the hang of allowing each backswing to carry him on through the next swath. Instead of a continuous, easy pendulum motion, he kept jerking the scythe to a halt in midsweep to plant his feet. He wasn't accustomed to this kind of physical frustration. But the frustration did serve to keep his mind off the fact that Marie was up in their bed having her insides torn apart as a result of the good time he'd had in there nine months ago.

Mary Falcon came running out of the path through the woods, shouting: "It's a boy!"

He turned toward her and said stupidly: "It's too fast. Eliza took all night." Something hard whacked him on the ankle. He looked down. He'd gone and let his hands go slack on the haft of the scythe. Fortunately it was the flat of the blade that had hit him.

"Eliza was different. First time's always the worst. And this time we had bethroot. Here—give me that before you cut your foot off."

He let her take the scythe out of his hands, then found himself running for the house. He registered a vague impression of Father Picard congratulating him as he charged up the stairs, then he was flinging open the bedroom door.

Josephte was stooped beside the bed, rolling together a bundle of rags. Marie was lying on her back with the blankets pulled up to her chin and her hair combed out over the pillow like black sun rays. He had a sudden twinge of déjà-vu and then remembered that Josephte and Mary had combed out Bethsy McKay's hair exactly the same way after James. But in Bethsy's case the sun rays had been gold, and her eyes had glittered, not glowed.

Josephte sidled out of the way as he moved forward to stand beside the bed. He looked down at his wrung-out, beautiful wife and said clumsily: "How are you feeling?"

She favored him with an attempt at a smile and whispered: "Better'n last time." Then she folded back the covers to show him a skinned frog squirming between her breasts with his thumb in his mouth—too dumb to realize that the real thing was there on either side. Grant knelt down and reached out to touch him. But the thumb suddenly popped out, uncorking a squall like a castrated calf. Marie said, "He ain't used to the cold," and covered him up again. "What should we call him?"

"I don't know. Anything but Cuthbert. Or Angus."

"What about Charles?"

"Why Charles?"

"I don't know, I just like it."

"Then Charles he is."

Josephte said: "Leave her to rest. They've both had a hard day."

"Yes, Doctor." He bent forward and kissed Marie's cheek. It was damp and warm and left a slight aftertaste of salt on his lips. Josephte and Mary Falcon hadn't quite managed to sponge off all the sweat.

He stumbled dazedly down the stairs and into the kitchen, where he shared a tot of rum with Father Picard and Mary and her husband, who had miraculously appeared at the back door just in time to help celebrate. After a toast to the child and another to the mother, Grant slapped his cup down bottom up on the kitchen table and said: "Well, I'd best be getting back to my mowing."

Mary Falcon shook her head and said impishly, as was her wont, "Not today you're not."

"There aren't many days left before the autumn buffalo hunt."

"You ain't going to run many buffalo if you got no legs to hold you on your buffalo runner—and that's just what's going to happen if you go playing with sharp objects in the state you're in."

"State?"

Falcon said: "That there cup wasn't empty." Josephte was already coming forward with a dishrag to mop it up.

Even with losing a day, he still managed to get all the mowing done before it came time to embark on the hunt. When the last sheaf was stacked in his new-built barn, he went up to the bedroom to inform Marie that their wheat and barley and oats would be ready and waiting for flailing when they got back from the buffalo hunt. He finished his report with: "And the threshing is going to be easy, because of the doors."

She obliged him by saying: "The doors? . . ." In the fecund sanctity of the birth room, he appreciated any encouragement that got thrown his way.

"Yes, when I was working out the plans for the barn, I incorporated a trick the Kildonan farmers came up with—or perhaps they brought it with them from the Highlands. The reason we went to all the trouble of putting big double doors in the north wall as well as the south wall is for threshing. Some blustery winter day, we'll just open up both sets of doors, scoop the flailed grain into the air, and let the wind do the threshing for us."

"Oh." She didn't appear to be astounded. "Wappeston, I was hoping things wouldn't turn out this way, but they have. I don't think either me or Charles is ready for a month or two of living in a cart and chopping pemmican. Josephte and John could do the butchering for you, and Josephte's a better cook than I am. Between Mary and Josephte there'd always be someone to look out for Maria Theresa if you want to take her along with you. I'm sorry, but . . ."

It threw him off and then some. He recovered his footing enough to say: "Well, if you don't feel up to it, then of course you mustn't come. On the condition that you'll be here when I get back."

"If you promise you won't go standing up alone in front of the whole Sioux Nation."

"If you promise you'll take a loaded gun with you when you go dancing."

"Dancing?"

"At the next full moon."

She just blinked her lustrous, opaque black eyes at him and went back to nursing their son.

In the three hunts that had passed since Grant last went out as Captain, the anarchic clans that gathered from all quarters of the prairie had grown even more accustomed to living under the eight commandments for the duration. Not that there wasn't the occasional argument or contretemps or knife fight, but by and large the duties of the Captain of the hunt weren't nearly as all-consuming as they once had been. Grant wouldn't have minded in the least, except that when he flung himself down on his buffalo robes at night, he wasn't too tired to notice he was sleeping alone. Josephte and John and Father Picard and Maria Theresa shared the tent with him, but that wasn't quite the same thing, although it was some consolation to be able to trot along at the head of a mile-long caravan with his daughter bouncing and chattering on the pommel of his saddle. He told her that the hunt was going to get so used to following her that he'd have to tie her to the flagpole in place of the blue-and-white standard.

There was a celebration when the hunt arrived back at the ford of the Pembina. There was a lot to celebrate. They'd crossed the wide Missouri and come back with packed-full carts, and the only losses had been two hunters who hadn't been paying enough attention, three buffalo runners who'd swerved left when they should have swerved right, one woman who'd died in childbirth, and a hunter and his son who'd stayed outside the cart circle after dark to take the meat off one last buffalo instead of leaving it to the wolves. They'd got butchered in turn by a wolf pack of Sioux gentlemen. Grant and Falcon and Urbain Delorme had chased the trail of unshod ponies for a day and lost them in the badlands.

The kick-up on the banks of the Pembina was also a parting celebration. The few families who were still wintering in the Pembina Hills would peel off in the morning. The place where Josephte had elected to pitch the tent turned out to be smack dab in the middle of the jigging and fiddling and hollering. She went to put the children and herself to bed, then came back and shouted to make herself heard over the bedlam: "It's too loud for anyone to sleep here! Mary's tent's way over at the other end and she said there's enough room for me and John and Maria Theresa and Father Picard to bed down with them."

Grant nodded and went back to watching the silhouettes of dancers against the bonfire and of the wild geese against the face of the moon. After a while and a few more cups of rum, he decided he was tired enough to sleep. The wild hunt was sufficiently engrossed in its festivities that he could slip away unnoticed.

He peeled off his clothes and groaned down onto his woolly mattress. Josephte was quite right, it was far too loud for anyone less than half-dead to sleep in here. Fortunately he was more than half-dead.

He was almost gone when he was jerked awake by the dry hissing and kissing sound of the tent flap sliding open and shut. He snapped open his eyes without moving his head, so whoever or whatever had slipped inside the tent couldn't tell that the lump on the bed was alive.

The side of the tent facing the bonfire was incandescent with a flickering orange glow. A woman appeared in silhouette against it. She was too short for Josephte and not wide enough for Mary. She moved toward the bed, going the long way around so as not to pass between the warrior and the firepit. Grant said: "What do you want?"

She gasped and jumped back a couple of feet, then started forward again, saying: "Mister Grant, it's me, Lucille."

The name meant nothing to him, but he reminded himself that more people know Jack Fool than Jack Fool knows. She drew in close enough to become more than a silhouette, but that didn't help. She was an auburn-haired young woman—a very young woman—in a beaded white doeskin dress. He remembered watching her dancing around the bonfire, prancing like a colt whose legs had just grown lithe, and remarking to himself on what a charming combination her coloring was, the waves of auburn hair against sun-baked skin and gray eyes. But he didn't recall ever having passed the time of day with her.

He said: "What do you want, Lucille?"

Her reply was to make an X with her arms reaching down to the hem of her skirt and sweep her dress off over her head in one smooth, magic motion. He swallowed a couple of times, cleared his throat, and said: "Um . . . Lucille, I'm, uh . . . old enough to be your father. . . ." *Oh, God, look at those teacup breasts with the areolae nubbled up like raspberries. . . .* "You're a lovely young woman, an extremely lovely young woman. . . ." *And that taut little belly with just enough fat on it to smooth out the muscles. . . .* "But I am a married man. . . ."

"So what? She's a hundred miles away. I don't want to steal you from her. So who would it hurt?"

Damned good question. "Uh . . . Lucille . . ." *And that dewy, downy triangle of auburn curls just aching for fingers to twine around. . . .* "When I was younger I would've asked the same rhetorical question, and perhaps I was right. But now, you see . . ." *Sweet Jesus, she's licking her lips. . . .* "I see—*now* I see, you see, that lies infect things. I'm too old to plead ignorance, and you're too young to be callous." *Now you've got her crying. The least you could do is console her a little, wrap your big, comforting arms around that tawny waist and . . .* "Ahem. It's very flattering of you to offer, but . . ."

She squatted down, wrapping her arms around her shins to cover her body and dropping her forehead to her knees so her hair would curtain her shame. He stretched one arm out from under the blanket to cup his hand against the side of her head. *Suffering Judas—spun silk cushioning a warming pan for a winter's night.* "Lucille, it's very hard—very difficult for me to resist the temptation. I wish I didn't have to, but I know I do. I'm sure there's no shortage of charming young men who can appreciate you. Thank you for making me feel for a moment that I'm more charming than any of them."

She scooped her dress up, snuffling, and draped it in front of her as she stood up and backed away. Once safely in the shadows, she pulled the dress back on again, giving Grant one last sweet silhouetted glimpse. She scuttled for the doorway and stooped to push open the flap. He hissed: "No, wait!" She turned back. "If anyone sees you going out, it'll be just as bad as if we had . . ."

"Then we might as well."

He laughed. "Not only beautiful, but . . . Here—" His eyes had lit on a glossy white cloud reflecting the filtered orange light. Maria Theresa's rabbit blanket. "Take this to Pierre Falcon's tent—there'll still be someone awake—and tell them I called you as you were passing by the tent and asked you to bring it over because I was afraid Maria Theresa might not be able to sleep without it. Don't lie more than you have to. And that, my dear, is the moral of the story. Good night, Lucille."

It was one thing to say good night and quite another to go to sleep. Maybe he should've kept Maria Theresa's rabbit blanket. When daylight struck, he bleared around the camp trying to give the impression that he was organizing the fording of the river. Whenever he passed by Mary Falcon she would toss him a glance that was even more impish than usual and clap a hand over her mouth as though stifling giggles. As he was saddling his horse, she punched him on the shoulder and said: "She'll get over it."

Marie seemed relatively pleased to see him; if it weren't for the ample cushion of her breasts, the impact of her chest hitting his solar plexus likely would have finished him for good. While he'd been gone,

Charles had changed from a skinned frog to a baby, and Eliza had learned to say "piss-face."

When the first snow came down, he loaded up a small train of carrioles and jumpers with trade goods, provisions, and hired hands and set off to reestablish Fort Mister Grant as open for business after the summer off season. Two American traders had already taken possession of Fort Mister Grant, assuming that it had been abandoned for good. Grant disabused them.

As soon as the cuckoos had been sent packing back south of the border and the store was once again in working order, Grant headed home, leaving Daniel and Donald McGillis in charge. They were young, but they were family.

He got home just before a week-long blizzard. The howling of the wind around the corners of the house, and the clatter of snow-shrapnel on the shingles, made it seem even warmer and cozier inside and exaggerated the luxury of just tossing another log on the fire. By the time the storm blew itself out, there was only a smattering of precut sticks scattered over the floor of the woodshed. Grant went to work with axe and saw on the tangle of deadfalls piled behind the shed. The thermometer outside the kitchen window read twenty below, but within a few minutes of starting each shift he was unknotting his sash to let his coat hang open. He'd gotten the shed half-filled and was sawing another oak branch into hearth-size lengths when he heard the trees rattling violently overhead.

He snagged a *shagganappi* rope out of the stable shed, strung it between the woodshed and the kitchen door, forked up a double armload of split firewood, and just made it to the house before the blizzard got its second wind. He stood looking out the front windows with the parlor hearth toasting the back of his shirt, watching the clumps of trees across the river turn into islands on a hurricane-tossed white ocean. Marie's voice came up behind his shoulder: "It don't look good."

"No need to fret, Waposis. We're safe and warm."

"Not everybody is."

"Donald and Daniel will be just as snug inside the fort as we are here."

"I wasn't thinking of them. I was thinking of the hunters."

He hadn't thought of that. Some of the families that wintered at Red River and didn't believe in gardening, and even some citizens of Grantown, made periodic forays to the buffalos' wintering grounds in the Pembina Hills. If they'd stayed snowed in in their tents and shanties for the last week, and then charged out across the plains and valleys the moment the storm seemed to be over . . .

The wind and snow ripped its claws against the house for three days. Grant was just getting adjusted to not having seashells clapped over both ears when the sound of harness bells jangled painfully close and Urbain Delorme banged through the door. "I got a letter for you from the chief factor at Fort Garry—or maybe I should call him the king for this year while George Simpson's off on the west side of the Rockies."

The letter read: "Mister Grant, The last words Mister Simpson had for me before his departure was that you were the man to be relied upon in case of any emergency. The situation upriver appears to be desperate. Many people exhausted their supplies during the first blizzard, so when it ended they rushed out onto the plains to hunt. The second storm caught them out in the open. We have many reports of people dead and dying from hunger and frost. We have collected a stock of provisions and blankets and medical supplies, but the devil of it is to get it all transported quickly to Pembina and then out to the people who are so desperate. I hope it will be possible for you to head the relief expedition."

Marie said: "I'll pack some food while you're getting your traps together."

With two feet of snow fallen in the last ten days alone, horses and jumpers were out of the question. A carriole couldn't carry as much, but a few hundred pounds of pemmican could go a long way. Less than an hour after Grant cracked open the letter, Falcon and Urbain and a half dozen others who were old enough to know what they were in for had their dog teams hitched up and their snowshoes strapped on.

They made Fort Garry at dusk and laid over till morning. Grant spent most of the night sorting through the mound of stores the chief factor had set aside, deciding what to take and what to leave behind. Taking it all would have meant dragging loaded toboggans behind the carrioles and taking longer to get to Pembina.

It was still dark when they left Fort Garry and dark again by the time they pulled into Fort Pembina. They flung themselves on the floor of the trader's store for a few hours' sleep and then fanned out through the hills and across the prairies. The cold was brutal, but at least the wind was as gentle as could be reasonably expected on a flat plate of snow stretching pretty much unbroken to the North Pole. The blizzard had done the job it had set out to do and moved on. Those it hadn't killed outright had been drained of all their resources. In sheltered coulees, Grant found eight-foot snowdrifts with smoking chimneys poking out of them; the families inside didn't have the strength left to dig themselves out and were burning their doors and shutters to keep warm. Out on the plains, he found standing ice statues of métis and Saulteaux hunters, frozen in place by the storm that would leave them preserved until the world turned green again. Some of them were missing arms or fingers. Grant hoped it had been wolves that had broken off the pieces to thaw in their mouths.

Grant kept on quartering his search area through the night and into the next day. His eyes started seeing things that weren't there, but he knew that if he dug himself a hole in the snow to take a nap in, he'd probably sleep around the clock, and a number of people were liable to go to sleep for good while he was snoozing beside their relief supplies.

It was about midday when he realized he'd made a terrible mistake. At the mouth of a valley running into the Pembina Hills he came across a snowed-in tipi housing a skeletal woman and two half-dead children. He ran back to the carriole to get a heart stimulant from his medicine chest and some food. The only food left was a corner of a bag of flour. He saw clearly in his mind's eye the bulging sacks of pemmican and potatoes and flour he'd left stacked in the storeroom at Fort Garry. All down the valley behind the starving family's tipi, there were other fingers of smoke and unnaturally shaped snow mounds. There was nothing he could do to help them.

He thought of killing his dogs, but they wouldn't fill many bellies, and then he'd be just as stranded and starving as the people he'd supposedly come to help—he was in no condition to make it back to Fort Pembina on foot. As though reading his thoughts, the team set up an unholy clamor, barking and snarling and jumping against their traces.

He snatched his rifle out of the carriole and strained his eyes to see what it was they were smelling or hearing. The dogs were directing their attentions north, toward the track of his own carriole. He whacked the dogs quiet and strained his ears northward.

An echo of their barking came out of the wind, then a tinkle of harness bells. Over the white crest came a loping snowshoer with a bristling black bearskin cap and matching mustachios, then a carriole with a big, fat, noseless man riding in it, then a loaded-down, one-dog toboggan with an Indian chasing it, then another carriole and another. The loper was Jean Baptiste Lajimodierre. The noseless fat man in the carriole—like a smoked oyster in a pastry shell—was Chief Peguis. The awkward pair of snowshoers bringing up the tail end of the line were the Point Douglas Sutherlands.

Grant sat down on the nose of his carriole and gawked. Jean Baptiste Lajimodierre crunched to a halt in front of him and said: "I was wondering when we'd catch up to you. We been following your trail all day, giving more food to the people that wouldn't've been alive to eat it if you hadn't got there first."

Peguis was shouting orders in Ojibway, pointing his warriors in the direction of the smoke wisps down the valley. Mister Sutherland was building a fire under a tripoded pot that his wife was dumping blocks of frozen soup into. Lajimodierre pointed his thumb at Mrs. Sutherland and winked at Grant. "She said she'd leave her son with my wife and come along. I told her she'd just slow us up. She said she could snowshoe at least as fast as her husband, and I once seen him hobble his way along from the Forks to the Mississippi in one February, so . . ."

Grant fished out a tin cup from his traveling gear and carried it over to the sizzling soup pot. "When it's ready, Mrs. Sutherland, there are some people in that tent who are in need of—"

"From the look of you, you are in more need of it yourself. When this is ready you will sit down and drink your cup of soup and let us take care of the others."

"But—"

"But me no buts, Mister Grant. I have no intention of being the one who has to tell your poor wife what your last words were. Mister Sutherland, Mister Grant needs something to sit down on."

In a trice, Grant was squatted on a buffalo robe beside the fire. He mumbled: "Thank you. I should've realized—I hadn't thought—that some of your people might have been caught out here as well."

"Our people?"

"Kildonan people."

Mrs. Sutherland said: "Mister Grant, I would have thought that you of all people would have realized that 'our people' means anyone who lives here. If we stop to worry whether the hand that is waving out of a snowdrift is white or brown or tartan, or whether the hand that takes hold of it is the same color, in a short while there are not going to be any hands left. Now drink your soup."

PART THREE

THE WARDEN OF
THE PLAINS

*How does Cuthbert Grant get on with his settlement at
White Horse Plains? I fear he has a turbulent set & not
very steady or easily satisfied to deal with. I sincerely wish
him every success. . . .*

FROM *THE HARGRAVE CORRESPONDENCE*,
PRIVATE LETTER TO JAMES HARGRAVE
FROM JOHN SIVERIGHT

CHAPTER 27

The blizzards that had killed so many people weren't done yet. The mountains of snow they had spread across the country bided their time till spring. As the sun melted the snow down low enough for the furry purple crocuses to poke their heads through, the rivers rose steadily up their banks and the feeder creeks turned into torrents. The Assiniboine seeped out onto Ghost Horse Plains, building an underfence of ice chunks against the deer fences bordering the fields behind Grantown. But the writhing, narrow channel that the Assiniboine became for that part of its course meant that most of its flooding was over islands or switchbacks and back into itself. The people of Grantown suffered sopping moccasins for a few days, but that was all.

At the Forks, though, the ice floes swept down by the Assiniboine and the Red met and locked together into an ice dam. As the currents behind it grew stronger with the onrush of the spring, ice boulders rammed into it with increasing velocity but couldn't break it open. The Point Douglas Sutherlands glanced nervously at it over their shoulders on their way back and forth from the house to the barn or the woodpile or the necessary. Every day the diamond-studded wall above the steel gray surface of the river sneaking under its base grew higher. Every foot the dam grew higher meant another foot of water trapped behind it.

Kate was in the barn milking Bessie good night when she heard her husband shouting outside. She cocked her ear in that direction for long enough to determine that he was shouting in English, not Gaelic—which meant he was not shouting to her. He was no doubt just passing the time of day with Jean Baptiste Lajimodierre on the other side of the river, in a language foreign to both of them but the only one they had in common.

She turned her attention back to rolling her fingers down Bessie's teats, pumping hot milk into the bucket. From time to time she glanced past Bessie's twitching tail to make sure John wasn't inadvertently crossing the goading line in his playing with MacCrimmon. MacCrimmon II, actually—named after her first black cat, who'd been hurled screaming into the flames of her father's house by the "improvers" of the Highland Clearances. A couple of summers ago several litters of ship's cats' kittens had been added to the manifest of the boat brigade from York Factory, to deal with a plague of mice at Red River. No one else had wanted the black one. MacCrimmon had rewarded her by slaughtering whole clans of rodents—some days he could barely waddle from one mouse hole to the next.

"Aaoww!"

"What is it, Johnny?"

"Nothing, Mama—just playing with MaQuimmon."

"MacCrimmon, dear."

"Yes, Mama—MaQuimmon."

"Well, you be careful playing with MacCrimmon. He has claws."

"Yes, Mama, I know. Hewe, MaQuimmon. . . ."

She went back to working her way around Bessie's squirted-out udder teat by teat, to make sure there were no drops left inside to foul tomorrow's milk. Since John had first started to speak in sentences, she'd been trying every way she could think of to get him to grasp the difference between r's and w's. She hoped he'd grow out of it, but if he didn't, she was hardly going to quibble about one tiny flaw.

The barn door jarred open and Sandy came stumping in with that lopsided gait that meant he'd come in a hurry. He said: "Lajimodierre says we should load up everything we can and head north *now*—to the high ground at Stony Mountain. He's packing up his family to make a run for the high ground on their side of the river."

"Why?"

"The *river*! Why else have we been gawking and nattering over that ice jam for the last week if we were not afraid of a flood?"

"It has never flooded here before."

"*Never* since we came here. Lajimodierre said he has seen times when the fur traders raced canoes around the trees. If you will put a halter on Bessie and bring her outside, I will hitch the pony to the cart." He turned and started for the door, then stopped abruptly, turned back, and stood there with his arms crossed.

She said: "I thought you said we were in a hurry. What are you waiting for?"

"For you to have the last word."

"Oh, go along with you."

He did, then jerked to a halt again as soon as he'd gotten out the door and ejaculated: "Suffering sheepshit . . ."

She scuttled toward him, hissing: "I have *asked* you not to use that manner of language in front of— Fucking Jesus!" A tongue of muddy water was poking its way across her garden patch, lapping in from the direction of the plains behind Fort Douglas. She looked to the Forks. The black-and-white barricade of ice and driftwood trees hadn't budged. The rivers it was holding back had given up trying to go through it and had simply overtopped the banks and gone around it.

Kate ran back into the barn and scooped up John, who was holding MacCrimmon, and then ran for the house. Her last three steps splashed ankle deep in icy water. She set John and MacCrimmon on the table. The floor of the house had been turned into a kind of shallow basin by years of footsteps packing it down a few inches lower than the level of the ground outside. It filled up quickly and kept on rising. Kate splashed about frantically, snatching up what they would need to take with them and piling it on the table around John and MacCrimmon: the sheet of sailcloth they used for a tent, blankets, the sodden buffalo robe that lay in front of the hearth, Sandy's musket, the half-emptied sacks of flour and oatmeal, the remains of the cheese she'd made last week, the tinderbox, the family Bible . . .

John sat with his mouth closed and his eyes wide, clutching MacCrimmon as the stack of household goods rose around them. MacCrimmon's eyes were even wider; the fur on his back had gone spiky and his narrow little chest was going in and out like a bellows. By the time Kate had piled up all the food in the house, the water was licking between her knees and the chairs were starting to float. Her legs were going numb, but she saw in a far corner that another piece of furniture besides the chairs was bobbing up and down—her spinning wheel. Her grandfather MacPherson had made it for her gran, and it had lived through three generations of house burnings and thousands of miles.

She rescued the spinning wheel and took it apart, wrapping the pieces in a blanket and adding the bundle to the stack on the table. The water was lapping at the rim of the table. She looked to John to make sure he'd curled his legs under him to keep his feet dry, then realized what else it meant that the water was almost as high as the table. The cartbed was no higher than the tabletop. If the water kept on rising, they didn't have a hope in hell of making it to Stony Mountain.

John burst into laughter and pointed at the door. His father came through the doorway paddling their crude log dugout of a boat. Sandy docked at the table and started taking on cargo, beginning with John and MacCrimmon. Kate stayed standing in the water, performing as a human wharf crane until the boat was crammed full and the table was half-empty. Then she settled her bottom onto the table, swiveled around, and gingerly maneuvered her nerve-dead legs into the open space in the bow. Once safely on board, she reached back to snag the blanket-wrapped bundle of her spinning wheel. Her husband barked: "Leave it!"

"It is my spinning wheel!"

"I know—but there is no room and no time to argue. If you think we are in danger now, wait till that ice jam breaks."

She clutched the bundle tighter and looked behind her at the midships of the little boat riding low in the water with its load of blankets, food, tent, gun, child, and cat. She put her spinning wheel back on the table and took up her paddle.

Bessie and the pony were standing up to their bellies in water, complaining loudly and trying to yank their halters free of the hitching ring Sandy had fixed to the huge old burl oak in front of the house. Sandy yanked open the slipknots and tied new ones around the ring at the stern of the boat while she waited with her paddle poised. He said, "All right," and she drove her paddle down hard. The lumbering boat lurched into motion with surprising alacrity. But when she was halfway through her second stroke, leaning forward to put her back into it, there was a yowl and a scream from behind her, then a splash. She looked back. John was reaching out over the water, threatening to swamp the boat. He had a slash of blood across one cheek and he was bawling: "MacCrimmon!" MacCrimmon was in the water, howling and spitting and swimming furiously back toward the barn.

She levered her paddle sideways to turn the boat around. Sandy shouted, "No!" and propelled them straight ahead. She wasn't accustomed to taking orders and was turning around to tell him so when she saw his face. It was what she thought of as his Corunna face—grim and fierce and inhuman. She'd only once heard him speak of the retreat to Corunna, where the remnant of his regiment who'd made it back through the mountains of Spain were those who'd marched eyes front past their messmates dying in the snow. She turned forward again and paddled hard.

John's squealing of "MacCrimmon!" behind her settled down to a snuffling sound and then a squeaky "I'm sorry. I tried to hold him. I did."

She said, "I know, dear," but didn't interrupt her paddling by looking back at him. It was only later that she realized he'd said "MacCrimmon."

As they came out of the channel that used to be the path through the woods, the sun was setting behind a red sea dotted with the silhouettes of canoes, pirogues, makeshift rafts, Company York boats, and swimming livestock. She was just barely beginning to discern the black line of the escarpment known as Stony Mountain when the air between the earth and sky behind her cracked with a crashing and rending noise like the teeth of a frost giant chewing a mountain. She forced her weary arms and shoulders to paddle harder. There was a sound of rushing wind. She stopped paddling and leaned forward to grab hold of both gunwales, shouting back at John to do the same. The nose of the boat dove down as the wave hit the stern. Water sloshed in over her hands. A horse-size boulder of ice shot by close enough for her to feel the cold air coming off it. The blunt prow disappeared under the water, then shot back up. She could feel the boat tilting to her left, so she leaned hard to her right, then back to her left as the boat threatened to swamp itself in the opposite direction.

As the wave rolled on away from them, she swallowed her heart, pried her fingernails out of the sides of the boat, and settled back to take stock. They had shipped a lot of water but were still afloat, surrounded by bobbing flotsam that included pieces of adze-squared logs and patches of roof thatch. It appeared that Bessie and the pony hadn't been hit by anything large enough to hurt them.

They baled out the boat as best they could with their hands and went back to paddling straight ahead for Stony Mountain. The only time they swerved aside was when a sheared-off tree floated by with a half-drowned rabbit clinging to it. Kate whacked the poor quivering creature with her paddle and Sandy scooped it out of the water as they went by.

Night came down while they were still on the water, but the new shoreline ahead was clearly delineated by the lights of campfires. The Point Douglas Sutherlands pitched their awning among their equally bedraggled neighbors, ate a meal of half-cooked rabbit, and bedded down on a soggy buffalo robe. But they were still alive.

After three days they could see that the water was slowly starting to go down, which would have been a cause for congratulations if it weren't that they were almost out of food. Sandy took his gun and rode north in hopes that the influx of wild creatures fleeing the flood would concentrate the game population to the point where even he might bag something.

Shortly after he'd left, a sail appeared on the new-made lake, tacking awkwardly across from the far shore. As it drew closer she could see that it was a patched-up relic of a York boat carrying half a dozen Des Meurons and a lumpy stack of cargo. They lowered their sail, beached their boat, and fanned out through the camp. One of them approached Kate. He looked to be at least ten years younger than she, which meant he couldn't have been more than sixteen when his regiment shipped across to North America to fight for the English King. He was wearing a fraying uniform tunic and holding up a haunch of a calf that hadn't even been skinned, just rough-gutted and quartered. He said: "To you, missus, good day. I have of beef to sell."

"I have no money."

"But it must be that you have something in trade to give? . . ."

"No. We could only take away the things we cannot live without."

"Please, missus . . ." He lowered his voice and looked back over his shoulder. "I do not feel well to see people be hungry. But if I do not go back with even some little thing given in trade, the others will—"

He was cut off by a bellowing of enraged male voices. Kate recognized the one outbellowing all the others—the parade ground roar of old Mister MacBeth, ex–regimental sergeant major of the Seventy-third Highlanders. Whatever it was that had got his goat, it had annoyed him to the point that he was trying to communicate in Gaelic to a chorus of Swiss-accented English.

Kate hurried over in the direction of the shouting, with the sheepish young beef trader trailing along behind. A horseshoe of Des Meurons was trying vainly to combine their voices into a match for the squat, white-whiskered, red-faced gnome in front of them. They all paused for breath just long enough for Kate to get in: "Whatever is the matter, Mister MacBeth?"

"Look!" He jabbed one stubby forefinger at the pinto-furred calf leg weighing down the hands of the fattest of the Des Meurons, whose bulge-seamed uniform coat still retained two tattered stripes on one arm. "Do you think I do not know my own animals? They are trying to sell me my own drowned cattle!"

The corpulent corporal said: "It is belonging to us! You want to eat what is ours—you pay us!"

The ensuing babel was drowned out in turn by the shrieks and moans of Red River carts approaching from the west. Everyone turned to look in that direction. Out of the bush, mashing down willow shoots under their wheels, came a train of half a dozen carts loaded down with sacks of pemmican and flour and potatoes. Driving the lead cart was

Cuthbert Grant. He reined his pony to a halt, cleared his throat, and announced with a surprising awkwardness: "We at Grantown were . . . fortunate enough to not take the brunt of the flood, as you did. So . . . since we lost nothing, we have plenty to spare. So . . ." He gestured at the cartloads of food behind him.

The fat Des Meuron shouted: "Oh, no, you won't! We come here to make what little bit of money we could for once! We will not lose it because of some rich half-savage playing Father Christmas!"

Kate had no intentions of hauling off and punching his fat head. But, by the tingling sensation in the knuckles of her right hand, by the pleasant released-spring feeling in her shoulder and arm, by the echo of a smacking sound, and particularly by the sight of the fat man sprawled in the mud, that was exactly what she'd gone and done.

The fat man's enraged scramble back to his feet was frozen halfway up by a diamond-hard baritone cutting down from the cart behind Kate: "Were I you, Corporal, I'd leave matters stand as they are. I haven't seen a right cross like that since Mister MacAndrew's demonstrations of the manly art at Inverness."

As the corporal and the rest of the Des Meurons grumbled back toward their boat, the young one who'd first approached Kate thrust his haunch of veal at her on the way by, mumbling: "We are not all like that, missus."

"If you do not wish to be thought of as the same, you should not wear the same uniform."

Mister Grant climbed off his cart. "Well, Mrs. Sutherland—I'm glad to see that you anticipated the flood in time to get yourself and your family safely to high ground."

"It was hardly 'in time'—we just barely rode it out in our boat."

" 'Boat'? How do you propose to get back once the waters recede?"

"I suppose we shall walk and drag the boat."

"You shall do nothing of the kind. I have more than enough carts and horses and will loan you this one, to return at your convenience. I can easily catch a ride back to Grantown in one of the other carts, once they've been unloaded. No—not another word about it."

It took another week for the Red and the Assiniboine to become rivers once again. The Point Douglas Sutherlands loaded their meager household goods and their boat onto Mister Grant's cart, hitched Bessie and their plow pony behind, and crawled across the sucking mud flats to Point Douglas. Long before they got there they could see that the riverbank had been shorn almost bald—those trees that hadn't been broken off at midtrunk had been uprooted and carried off entirely. Fort Douglas was a ragged remnant of shattered palisades and broken buildings. From what they could see of the Forks from Point Douglas, Fort Garry had fared even worse.

But there was one tree left standing—the old monster of a burl oak on Point Douglas. The barn, the sheds, and the necessary had been swept away, but the old oak tree had saved the house. The interior was a jumble of mud. Kate peeled the sodden bundle of her spinning wheel out of the mud, put it back together, and stood it up, then dragged out the feather mattresses to dry in the open air before they started to mildew. They laid the buffalo robe on the mucky floor and bedded down with all the windows and the door wide open.

In the middle of the night, she was brought awake by a pattering and intermittent wet plopping sounds. The moonlight through the door and windows showed a rank of gray furry lumps lined along the head of the bed on the floor. A patch torn out of the night trotted through the doorway—it was MacCrimmon, with another drowned mouse in his mouth.

CHAPTER 28

Marie kept surprising herself, and they weren't necessarily pleasant surprises. It started on the summer buffalo hunt, the first hunt she'd gone out on in two years. It was difficult enough to maintain a traveling household, keep her family well fed, and make pemmican out of all the buffalo her husband shot, without constantly watching out for where Eliza was toddling off to in a camp filled with cooking fires, guns, axes, and skinning knives. So she would ask Maria Theresa to keep an eye on her little sister. Unfortunately, whenever Maria Theresa's father would pass by on his way to take care of whatever the Captain of the hunt had to take care of at the moment, Maria Theresa would forget about everything except tagging along behind him and swinging her arms in imitation of his walk. Marie would glance up from the stew she was building and see Maria Theresa following Wappeston north and Eliza heading south to pet the pretty horses milling about on the prairie.

It never crossed Marie's mind to take a switch to Maria Theresa. One thing the New Nation had inherited from the uncivilized half of their ancestory was a general aversion to hitting small people they loved.

Late one night, when she was sure Wappeston was awake and the children weren't, Marie said: "Could you talk to Maria Theresa for me? I keep asking her to keep an eye on Eliza and she says she will and then she doesn't."

"Well, if you've only asked her offhandedly, she's bound to get the impression that it isn't all that important."

"I've told her it's important—over and over."

"She should listen to you."

"She does, most of the time. But there's no way around the fact that all her baby years, she got used to having no one to listen to but you."

In the morning he set his bannock-sopped plate on the grass and said: "Come here, Maria Theresa."

"Yes, Papa."

"Look at you—I turn my back for a moment and you've grown into a girl, not a baby anymore." She wriggled and blushed and looked down at the ground. "But the disadvantage of growing is that the bigger you get, the more other people grow to depend on you to help them. I'm afraid I need a good deal of help. As Captain of the hunt I barely have a moment from one day to the next to give to my family. I feel bad about it sometimes. It would help me a great deal if I knew that your mother and your aunt Josephte weren't constantly having to look over their shoulders to watch out for Eliza. They're very busy setting up our tent or cooking our dinner or patching our moccasins. If they could trust you to look after your sister, on those occasions when your mother asks you to, they wouldn't have to worry and I wouldn't feel quite so bad about all the work they have to do. Will you do that for me?"

"I will, Papa."

From then on, Maria Theresa stuck to her duties religiously—to the point where Marie sometimes had to pry Maria Theresa's hand from around her little sister's and shoo her off to run with the pack her own age for a change.

Marie surprised herself by feeling a bit annoyed about it all. She'd asked him to talk to his daughter, it had had the desired effect, so what was there to be annoyed about? She was well aware that it wasn't so much what he'd said to Maria Theresa that had done the trick; it was the fact that he'd said it. It did make her wonder how many times she herself had nodded her head eagerly at something he said. But that wasn't the reason for her annoyance. She didn't know what the reason was, and the most annoying part was that there was something tantalizingly familiar about it.

She realized what it was when they stopped to camp at Pancake Bay.

Pancake Bay wasn't a bay at all, just a slough that had been clear water when the hunt camped there on its way south and was now more like duckweed soup.

Once the cooking fire was going, she settled down beside it in the same way her maternal ancestors had since the dawn of time—kneeling on one hip with her pouches of herbs and roots and berries spread out around her. For at least a few minutes she could hum along happily in an enclosed sphere of smells twinned with sounds—the savory sizzle of the buffalo hump and onions browning in the pot, the aromatic crunch of the sweetgrass underneath her as she swiveled from her hip up onto her knees, the spiced-earth, smoky crackle of the buffalo chips laden with sage and wild mint.

Once the stew was simmering nicely, it was time to make tea. Josephte and John were still setting up the tent and Charles was sleeping safely in his cradleboard, so Marie went to fetch water herself. The level of the slough was barely higher than the kettle, and it took a lot of fussing and splashing to get the kettle full of water rather than duckweed. In the process, the bottom of the kettle got so imbedded in the sucking ooze that she had to yank the handle hard with both hands, spilling half the water as it smacked free.

She came back to the campsite scraping pond muck off the kettle and found her husband smoking his pipe with his back propped against the spokes of a cartwheel. She propped the kettle over the fire and said: "Why the hell would anyone call a mud hole on the prairie 'Pancake Bay'?"

He took his pipe out of his mouth and said: "I believe it was Falcon, actually, during one of his stints as Captain of the hunt. The original Pancake Bay is a place on Lake Superior where the old North West Company brigades would always camp—one day out from Sault Sainte Marie. On the way back from Fort William, everything left in the larder became fair game at Pancake Bay. And since this little mud hole on the prairie happens to be one day out from Fort Garry or Grantown—"

She said, "Oh," to stop him talking, and busied herself with the stew. Ever since his little talk with Maria Theresa, Marie had found that his voice started grating against her ears if she had to listen to it for too long.

After supper the sound of fiddles drifted over from the quarter of the circle where the Dumonts were camped. Wappeston offered her his arm and said: "I suppose we'd best put in an appearance." In the campsites they passed by, hunters were sitting patiently while their wives trimmed their beards, others were shaking out their gaudiest shirts and beribboned dresses in preparation for tomorrow. Marie felt shabby and slovenly but then reminded herself that there was no reason for her to prepare for the triumphal entry to Fort Garry—Wappeston would entrust his carts to Pierriche again and the Grants would wave good-bye to the hunt at the Passage of the Assiniboine.

The Dumonts had managed to leave a keg of brandy unopened all the way out to the plains and back again. It stood beside the fiddlers now with its head smashed in. Wappeston dipped a cup in and offered it to her. She shook her head and stood back as the old hunters congratulated each other on what a fine hunt they'd had and the young people her own age started the jigging.

Once again, as at that New Year's regale at Fort Garry, she could see in her husband the reluctance and awkwardness behind the jovial mask that everyone else seemed to take at face value. Only now it didn't seem sad to her, it seemed sickeningly false. And then it hit her that she was stabbing the same icicles of resentment at his back that she'd seen coming out of the eyes of George Simpson.

She pushed her way through the knot of people gathered around her husband, grabbed the neck of his shirt with both hands, and pulled him down low enough for her to get her mouth on his. When she let him go he said: "What did I do to deserve that?" There was a lot of laughter and lewd jokes, but she didn't mind. He said, "If you'll excuse us," put his arm around her shoulder, and walked her away from the kick-up.

They came to a halt at the deserted west wall of the cart circle. The sunset had turned the prairie into red-and-green shot silk, shimmering as the breeze ruffled the threads. The grasses were fat-stemmed and heavy-headed from gorging on the river loam the flood had spread out for them. Wappeston said: "I expect I'll have time to take off a good crop of hay before heading off again."

" 'Heading off'? Where?"

"To Fort Mister Grant and environs."

"Since when does anyone trade furs in the summer?"

"Since George Simpson came up with the notion of imitating the Russian army's scorched earth policy. It seems that for every pirate trader we send packing, another pops up to take his place. But if we encourage the natives in the border zones by buying anything they kill—molting buffalo hides, spawning fish, even the pelts of beaver cubs, which has been decidedly *dis*couraged in the past—in a few years we'll have a desert moat between Rupert's Land and the foreign traders."

"And then what happens to the people that live in your border zones, after they've turned their homes into a desert for you?"

"They can move their homes north or south. The country on either side of the line isn't exactly overpopulated."

"Tell that to the Sioux and the Blackfoot."

"The areas that've been stripped clean will rejuvenate themselves in a few years. By that time, the American and Canadian sharpers who hope to steal a quick profit out of the Company's pocket will realize the game ain't worth the candle."

"So who *cares* if a few little traders chip off a few hundred pounds from the Company's hundreds of thousands?"

He sighed extravagantly. "It seems to me, Waposis, that I've explained this once or twice before. A few hundred pounds this year becomes a few thousand next year, and so on. As long as the Company remains the sole authority here, you and I and everyone we hold dear can live pretty much as we please. But the instant the Company ceases to return a healthy profit, the London Committee will auction off its possessions, including us, to the highest bidder. And the only bidders I can think of are foreign governments looking to colonize any virgin territory they can get their hands on. I would've thought you understood that by now."

"What I understood by now—under*stand* by now—is what Mrs. Grant means."

"Pardon me?"

" 'Mrs. Grant' means that I get to hoe the garden and clean the house and raise the children while Mister Grant runs around on a chain being George Simpson's watchdog." She snaked her shoulders out from under his arm and headed back toward the tent. She hoped he wouldn't call or come after her, then was angry and hurt when he didn't.

They still hadn't made it up when it came time for him to leave Grantown for Fort Mister Grant. The night before he left, they made something vaguely resembling love, but when the heat had passed nothing had changed. Once he was gone, she settled back into the endlessly occupying, enclosed world of house and garden and children and neighbors.

She was sitting in the kitchen one morning feeding Charles when Josephte came in from outside with Maria Theresa trailing along in her wake. Josephte headed for the pantry, tossing over her shoulder: "You just sit and wait a moment, dear, and I'll get you a nice piece of bannock and a bowl of maple syrup."

Marie heard herself saying, in a lazy, heavy-lidded, nursing voice: "No, her teeth are bad enough already."

Josephte turned toward her with her pinched features adapting that expression of "I'm old enough to be your mother, dear," and said: "The poor child hardly ate a bite of breakfast."

"If she wasn't hungry enough for breakfast, she won't starve to death before lunch."

"But, Mama, I'm hungry *now!*"

"I know, dear. But if you go out and enjoy the sunshine a little longer, there'll be a real meal on the table before you know it. Babies like Charles have to be fed whenever they're hungry, but you're not a baby anymore."

"But everybody else eats whenever they're hungry. Just ask Jean Claude or Angelique or—"

"You're not living in anybody else's house, you're living in *this* house."

Maria Theresa stomped out. Josephte stood with her arms crossed and her sphincter of a mouth pinched in even tighter than usual. Marie negotiated Charles's mouth off her nipple and propped him against her shoulder to pry a burp out of him. Josephte went back outside without saying a word.

By the time lunch was ready Maria Theresa still hadn't forgiven her. She bolted her soup and was charging back out the door when Marie brought her up short with: "Maria Theresa—help your aunt Josephte with the washing up while I take Eliza and Charles upstairs for their naps."

"But Jean Claude found a turtle and—"

"It'll still be there when the dishes are washed."

"Yes, Mama."

Eliza was cranky and didn't want to sleep. Marie had just gotten her settled down when Maria Theresa hollered up the stairs: "Maman! Someone wants to see you!"

Josephte had left the visitor standing in the back doorway watching her and Maria Theresa sort out the kitchen. Although the woman in the doorway was silhouetted by the blaze of sunlight behind her, there was no mistaking that tall, broad-shouldered figure with the glint of red gold poking out from under the starched white cap. "Good afternoon, Mrs. Sutherland."

"And a good day to you, Mrs. Grant."

"Would you like a cup of tea?"

"Thank you—Mrs. Wills already offered, but, you see . . ." She gestured behind her. "I brought back the cart and pony that your husband loaned us in the spring, but I was not sure where you wanted them put."

Marie followed Mrs. Sutherland outside. The Sutherlands' little dark-haired son was perched on the cart rail, studiously holding the reins. A crude dugout boat and a pair of hand-carved paddles were propped within the cage of rails behind him. There was no sign of Mr. Sutherland.

Mrs. Sutherland said: "John—you remember Mrs. Grant? . . ."

He nodded. "How do you do, Mrs. Grant," he said with a gravity a bishop would envy.

"You sure got taller since the last time I saw you."

"Thank you, Mrs. Grant."

Mrs. Sutherland lifted out the paddles, saying: "It has taken us a terrible long time to bring your cart back. But there was so much rebuilding and planting to do after the flood, and it seemed whenever I could find a day to come here it was a day Mister Sutherland had to use our horse for plowing or hauling beams, so I would have no way to go back. Then it finally came to me that John and I could simply bring along the boat and let the current carry us home."

Marie reached up to help her lift out the boat, but it was more a matter of form, as the big, broad hands wafted the hollowed oak log out and down as though it were made of pressed feathers. As the hull thumped onto the grass, Maria Theresa came tearing out the back door. Marie called: "Maria Theresa!"

"We done all the dishes, Maman."

"Thank you, dear. I just thought maybe John Sutherland would like to go see the turtle, too."

John Sutherland chirped, "Yes, please!" then looked to his mother. "That is, if . . ."

Marie said: "You should have plenty of time to sit and have a cup of tea, Mrs. Sutherland—the current's still running fast for this time of year."

"You may go see the turtle, John—but do not stray so far that you cannot hear me when I call." He scrambled off the cart and took off after Maria Theresa.

Marie took hold of the cart pony's bridle and led him around to the side of the barn where the rest of their carts stood ranked—less those that Wappeston had taken to Fort Mister Grant. Mrs. Sutherland helped her with the harness, and the pony scampered off to join the herd running free on White Horse Plains. Now that all the mares had foaled at least once at Grantown, they wouldn't stray far, and the fences around the grainfields and gardens kept them from demolishing the crops.

Josephte was just setting a fresh-brewed pot of black tea on the kitchen table. Marie unshelved a pot of chokecherry jelly and a wheel of bannock and said: "It don't seem fair somehow that we got off so easy from the flood while so many other people lost so much."

Mrs. Sutherland said brightly: " 'It's an ill wind . . .' The flood turned out to be the final straw for the Des Meurons, or the worst of them. They have all packed off to the Ohio, where the American government offered free land. A few families of Kildonan people went with them. Not the old colonists, of course—oh, dear, listen to me, the 'old' ones. . . . But us 'old' ones are hardly likely to be scared off by a bit of mucky water after the locusts and the burnings and the half-breeds . . . Oh, dear, what a great oaf I am.

"You must understand, what with the Cree and Assiniboine and Sioux, we none of us slept quiet in our beds until your husband and his brave métis came to settle near us. . . . This jelly is wonderful. Do you sugar it, or is it just the sweetness of the berries?"

They talked a while longer about preserves and gardens and children and the weather—which in Rupert's Land was not an idle topic of conversation. Marie noticed that Mrs. Sutherland's eyes kept sidling toward the doorway into the parlor. She said: "So long as you're here, Mrs. Sutherland, would you like to get a look around at the rest of the house?"

The big, rawboned face flushed pink. "I am sure you have many other things to do than—"

"No. This is the time of day that belongs to me, when the little ones are sleeping. Come, I'll show you around."

Mrs. Sutherland followed her through the doorway into the parlor and stopped once she'd stepped across the threshold. Marie said, "We're still trying to fill it up bit by piece," then watched Mrs. Sutherland's gaze gawk its way around the room, from the stone fireplace big enough to heat the whole house through a winter's night, to the glass-paned windows with their woolen curtains that she and Josephte had whipped up quickly in their first January at Grantown, to the wolf- and bear- and deerskins on the floor or draped over lathe-turned chairs or tacked to the wall in between feathered coup sticks and oak candle brackets and the silver crucifix, to Wappeston's writing desk flanked by shelves of books and ledgers.

Mrs. Sutherland circled her widened eyes back to Marie and said: "It is so"—stretching her arms out—"big!"

"We keep talking about making it into smaller rooms, but till we get a real church built . . . If a feast day happens to fall on a day when it's raining or too cold to stand outside, that little chapel ain't big enough to hold everybody. I'll show you the upstairs."

Mrs. Sutherland followed her up the stairs and along the corridor with the closed doors of cupboards and bedrooms ranked on either side. Marie stopped at the opened doorway at the end to look in on Eliza and Charles where she'd laid them to sleep on her bed—she'd gotten out of the habit of thinking of it as "our bed."

Mrs. Sutherland's hand flew to her mouth at the sight of Eliza curled around her baby brother in his mossbag, and she whispered around her fingers, "The little dears—they look just like little brown angels sleeping on a cloud," then winked and added, "Too bad they have to wake up sometimes, hm?"

Marie giggled and shrugged and started back down the corridor. Mrs. Sutherland said softly: "They are so fortunate to be able to grow up with brothers and sisters—although I do recall wishing once or twice that I could have been an only child. But I do worry about John sometimes. He is so serious. And Mister Sutherland and I were no spring chickens when he came along. . . ."

"I think he's a lovely little boy."

"Thank you."

Halfway down the corridor, Marie stopped and pointed at the ceiling. "Do you think maybe you could pull that down for me? I have to stand on tiptoe, and even then . . ."

Mrs. Sutherland looked up at the dangling loop of *shagganappi*, glanced quizzically at Marie, then wafted up one crane-neck arm and snagged it easily. She gave it a tug and down came the counterweighted trap with its double ladder that slid out as the trap hit the end of its bracket. Marie gestured Mrs. Sutherland to go ahead and followed her up into the slant-walled, amber cell lit by one dust-speckled shaft of light through the parchment window Wappeston had sawn in the wall. She picked her way across the beams to the ladder to the roof peak, climbed up high enough to throw back the hatch that still had a tendency to leak despite all the experiments at making a seal from bull's hide, and beckoned Mrs. Sutherland to follow her out into the sunlight.

Up here, the wind was strong enough to take the edge off the heat of the sun. Marie took a firm grip of the iron railing. Mrs. Sutherland skipped around in a circle and said: "Oh, my! I have not stood on anything that felt like a hill in years and years. Look at the shadows of the clouds grazing across the plain! Oh, and look at her down there," pointing delightedly at a mourning dove brooding in her nest—or maybe it was his nest; the males of some species took their turn as well.

"I don't come up here very often. My husband does when he's home. They call it a widow's walk, from sea captains' wives watching for the ships to come home." She realized that Mrs. Sutherland probably knew that as well as she did, and also realized that, given the description, it might be assumed that Wappeston had had it built more for her than him. She let her gaze drift northward across the tops of the trees, to where the ripening plots of wheat and oats and barley made blocks of uniform metallic colors among the shifting waves of wild grasses. Her father and younger brothers—minus Daniel and Donald at Fort Mister Grant—were at work breaking another acre before the autumn hunt. Beyond them, a gaggle of boys was running foot races on Coteau des Festins.

Her eyes slid eastward, looking down over her father's roof at the patches of farmyards and other roofs and corners of houses that showed between the mottled thatch of leaves. There was some kind of bustle going on at the Falcons' place—perhaps Pierriche was finally getting around to adding on the side room that Mary kept teasing him about. Father Picard and François Morin were drifting around a bend, trolling hopefully for the caviar-fat monster sturgeon that got away last week. Chunks of sound wafted up into the treetop murmur of wind and leaves and creaking boughs—the wallop of an axe, gamboling hoofbeats, rough-sawn phrases of a half-learned fiddle tune, the crying of a baby that wasn't Charles . . .

Mrs. Sutherland murmured: "He has made his dream come true."

"Dream? Who? What dream?"

"Mister Grant. Your husband."

"What dream?"

"He told me once—oh, Lord, it must be ten years now, or more . . . It was by way of a threat, to make me understand that he and his warriors would stop at nothing to rid the country of us. I suppose I would have taken it to heart, if we had had anywhere else to go, because there was no question but that he meant it. What he said was that the oldest dream of the human heart is to return to Eden having eaten of the tree of knowledge—and that his New Nation had a good chance to make that real if left alone here. Well, now we all are doing just that."

"Anything I ever heard of the Garden of Eden didn't say nothing about blizzards and spring floods."

Mrs. Sutherland laughed. "You must admit the flood has succeeded in driving out the snakes—or some of them, at least. Oh, there are still those who call curses on your husband's head for Seven Oaks, and always will. Let anyone say what they like—he is a grand man."

Marie almost said, "You should try living with him."

"He is also . . ." Mrs. Sutherland trailed off.

"He is also what?"

"No, forgive me, I blather on."

"Mrs. Sutherland—after what happened on that first New Year's, I ain't likely to take offense at anything you have to say about my husband—or anything else, for that matter. He is also what?"

"The saddest man I ever knew. There, you see what kind of silly fancies come on women in their middle age. I had best be collecting John and starting for home."

"Wouldn't you care to stay for another cup of tea?"

"I would dearly like to, Mrs. Grant, but I have a half-weaned calf at home."

"A bull calf?"

"No—I made sure to line Bessie up north to south when Mister Macbeth brought his bull around. Not that we would not have got good money for an ox, but nowhere near the price of a heifer."

"So somebody's already bought her?"

"Not yet—as I said, she is not yet weaned. But when the time comes, I am sure there will be no shortage of—"

"I'll buy her—*we'll* buy her. If she isn't spoken for, and if it wouldn't make your neighbors feel—"

"If it makes them feel like fools for not speaking up sooner, so much the better. But you will want to have a look at her first, and see what your husband thinks, before offering a price. She should be weaned within the week."

"My husband should be back by then. We'll come to Point Douglas a week from today."

"We will not take any other offers until then."

They made their way back down the series of stairways and trap-doors, pausing en route so Marie could make sure Eliza and Charles were still sleeping and that Eliza hadn't inadvertently rolled over on top of the baby brother who had bumped her out of her position at the peak of the firmament. Outside, Mrs. Sutherland stopped beside the beached boat and cupped her hands around her mouth to bellow: "Jooohhnnee!"

A moment later her son appeared out of the willows fringing the stagnant backwater of the Assiniboine that plagued the McGillis properties with mosquitoes. His homemade shoes and trousers were thoroughly imbued with mud. He hunched his shoulders up around his ears and showed his mother the back of his neck. She handed him both paddles and he shouldered them as penance, staggering under the weight.

Mrs. Sutherland wrapped the end of the painter around her hand to drag the boat to the shore. Marie said: "Let me give you a hand. . . ."

"No need—it slides easy enough. Thank you for the cup of tea, and for showing me your lovely house."

"Thank you for bringing back the cart and the pony."

"Thank you for the loan of them, and— Oh, this is getting ridiculous. We shall look for you and Mister Grant at Point Douglas in a week."

But the week passed with no sign of Wappeston. On the morning of the appointed day, Marie climbed up to the widow's walk and scanned the misty vista to the southwest. Anyone approaching Grantown could be seen for miles across White Horse Plains, but no one was. Way off where the tree islands disappeared into the distance, there were a few antlike horsemen, but they appeared to be moving in the opposite direction.

Enough time had passed since he'd left for her to stop being angry at him. The unpleasantness of their last few days together meant nothing to her except that they'd parted on bad terms for no good reason. It had been pleasant for a while to be left alone with her children and her house and her garden, but she wanted him to come home now.

She could ache for him a few days longer, though, and find plenty of things around the house to keep her mind off it most of the time. The problem at the moment was Mrs. Sutherland's heifer. It was one thing to say they would buy it without asking him and another thing to go ahead and do it. She didn't even have the money. Maybe he couldn't abide cows. He'd seemed quite content in the past to leave her to make all kinds of decisions about managing the house while he was gone, but he'd never come home to find an unknown, troublesome animal roaming about the place. But if she waited one day longer, someone else would buy the calf, and all the happy notions that had been tripping over themselves for the last week—milk for the children, cheese, butter—would have to wait at least another year longer.

Her mind's eye showed her Mrs. Sutherland standing on the widow's walk beside her and not even blinking at promising the calf to her without consulting Mister Sutherland. But that was Mrs. Sutherland. When Marie had mentioned the name to her father, he'd said: "Sutherland? . . . Oh—Kate MacPherson! She's some big medicine around Kildonan. Sitting around a fireplace trading stories with some of the original colonists and Kate MacPherson crops up . . . Hell, you'd think it was a batch of old hunters talking about Lajimodierre."

But then again, that "big medicine" woman hadn't talked to her as Mr. Grant's child bride, or a little sister-in-law, or anything except as an equal. It had been a pleasant change. If that's how Marie wanted to be treated, maybe it was time she started acting that way.

She whirled around abruptly to start a resolute march down the stairs, but as she turned, her eyes caught another reason why she shouldn't go buy the calf. A line of black clouds was marching north across the purple ghosts of hills on the horizon. Perhaps they wouldn't march any farther, or perhaps the sky would explode with lightning and hailstones when she was halfway to the Forks. And it wouldn't just be her who got caught out in the open—she would have to take Charles along. As much as she might want to go, better she should keep herself and her child safe. The Sutherlands and everyone else would understand. . . .

She took herself by the scruff of the neck and slammed the trapdoors behind her. "John!"

"Yes, Auntie?"

"Please go catch one of the cart ponies—the gray one, if you can—and hitch him to a cart. Maria Theresa, Eliza—I have to go to Red River. I'll be back before supper. Be good and listen to your aunt Josephte while I'm gone."

She packed a pannier with jerked venison and bannock and another with clean moss for Charles. Charles whimpered and gurgled as she slung his cradleboard over her shoulder, but he went back to sleep. She hung the panniers and her son inside the railing of the cart John was hitching the gray pony to, added on one of the pipe-clayed buffalo-hide cart awnings from the stack in the shed, and set off, wondering if she'd lost her mind.

Halfway to the Forks, the ranks of storm clouds advanced far enough north that she could see them without the elevation of the widow's walk. But they stopped there, as though waiting patiently for further orders. As she passed by Fort Garry, blocks of pink flickered between the black gap-toothed remnants of the stockade—new-sawn log sheds thrown up among the old warehouses and countinghouse that had been too firmly anchored for the flood to budge.

The banks of the Red had been shaved down to a low stubble of broken trunks and tangled deadfalls, with green willow shoots poking up between. One of the few trees left standing was a big old burl oak that grew bigger as the cart drew closer to Point Douglas.

Mister Sutherland was planting a scarecrow among a ragged smattering of corn plants. John Sutherland was running around them, howling and banging a tin plate with a spoon. A fat black cat lay sprawled on a stump in the sun, watching the performance with mild interest. As the skreetch of the cartwheels drowned out John's caterwauling, the male population of Point Douglas stopped what they were doing and came out of the cornfield. "A good day to you, Mrs. Grant."

"And to you, Mister Sutherland. John."

"How do you do, Mrs. Grant."

Mister Sutherland shrugged back toward his motley patch of corn. "The flood made for late planting. I expect we might bring off enough to seed a real crop next year—if we can keep the blackbirds off. MacCrimmon appears to have lost his taste for blackbird. I cannot blame him—I expect we shall feel the same about the taste of pigeon a week after the flocks descend."

Mrs. Sutherland came out the door with her skirt bunched in front of her and called out something in Gaelic that included the universal "Chick, chick, chick, chick . . ." Two rust-splotched hens and a resplendent rooster came flapping and running around the corner of the house. Mrs. Sutherland shook down a shower of scraps and crumbs and came toward the cart dusting her hands together. "A good day to you, Mrs. Grant!"

"Hello, Mrs. Sutherland. I didn't know you had chickens."

"We did not, until last week. The experimental farm imported a few, but the experimental experts are so shoddy about collecting eggs that they soon had a flock that could take on the passenger pigeons. What with our crops and the garden going in so late, we thought it best we should lay our hands on anything that might make food through the winter. Well, I expect you will want to take a look at Bessie's girl. We have not named her, since we thought whoever comes to own her will want to do that for themselves. Did Mister Grant not come with you?"

"No."

After a quick look at Charles to make sure he was still sleeping, Marie climbed off the cart and followed the Sutherlands around to a shed of green poplar poles emanating a plaintive bleating and lowing. The lowing came from behind the shed, where a tethered spotted cow chewed her cud between mournful responses to the bleating from inside.

The shed was divided into two stalls. In one of them, a fawn-mottled creature with horn buds and a surprisingly big voice tugged against her halter and looked back over her shoulder, trying to melt her jailers with her big brown eyes.

Marie whispered, "Sssh," and shuffled her moccasins across the carpet of straw, holding her cupped hand out in front of her. A moist nose snuffled into her palm, and a pebbly tongue slurped at the salt taste. Marie turned back to the Sutherlands and said: "How much?"

Mister Sutherland cleared his throat and said crisply: "Two pounds."

Two pounds of sterling gold seemed like a healthy amount of money, but if that was the going price . . . "All right."

Mister Sutherland blinked his yellow bramble eyelashes several times, then barked, "Done!" spat in his palm, and extended his hand.

Before Marie could follow suit, Mrs. Sutherland slapped his hand aside, saying: "It is nothing of the kind! Mrs. Grant—you were supposed to say, 'One pound,' and then he would say, 'Thirty-five shillings,' and you would come back with 'Twenty-five,' and so on until you had worked your way together to thirty shillings—which is the price the Company has established for a female calf. And even that price is somewhat higher than when the deal is between two people. Say, 'Twenty-nine shillings,' Mrs. Grant, and spit in your hand and shake on it so he cannot take it back."

Marie did as she was told. As their hands slapped together, Mister Sutherland shrugged at her. "You cannot blame a man for trying."

They dragged the calf out past her bellering mother and loaded her, kicking, onto the cart. Marie shifted Charles's cradleboard to hang outside the cage of cart rails. Mrs. Sutherland said: "Would you like to stop for a cup of tea before you start back? Or a bite to eat? We have three fresh eggs."

"Thank you, but there's some storm clouds coming in. I want to get home before they get here. But, those eggs . . . If they weren't eaten, would they grow?"

"Grow?"

"Into chickens."

Mister Sutherland said: "I should hope so, the way that rooster has been—"

"Alexander! Little pitchers have big ears."

Marie said: "Could I buy those eggs from you? Not for eggs, but baby chickens."

Mrs. Sutherland clucked. "The price of eggs is not even worth adding up. Let me wrap them up for you, and if you can keep them warm and get them home whole, it will be worth it to us just to know if they hatch."

"If not," Mister Sutherland cackled, "we can eat the rooster."

Mrs. Sutherland went into the house and came out with three eggs wrapped in a hank of old blanket cloth. The question now was how to keep them warm and safe. Marie had an inspiration, stripped off her shawl, knotted it into a kind of sling with the eggs inside, slipped the sling over her head, turned her back on the Sutherlands, and hung the eggs down inside her dress to nestle between her breasts. She could feel herself blushing as she turned around again. Mrs. Sutherland giggled, "Well, that will certainly keep them warm," then pointed to the south. "Here come your storm clouds."

Marie turned to look. The black army was marching in fast now, stretching from horizon to horizon across the southern quarter of the sky. But there was no sound of thunder and no haze of rain as yet.

Mister Sutherland shook his head and said: "Perhaps you had best bide here until it passes over. You are welcome to stay the night if it comes to that."

"No—thank you, but I have to get home. I brought an awning in case it rains." She climbed onto the cart and left Point Douglas with the close-tethered calf clattering its hooves on the cartbed and squalling, "Maaa!" as its mother's plaintive bawling diminished into the distance behind them.

Where the trail rounded Fort Garry she turned in through the gates. She reined in in front of the countinghouse and climbed down carefully so as not to rattle the eggs together. Charles wasn't sleeping, but neither was he fussing. His eyes were as wide as saucers and he kept craning his neck around, as though he might be able to see through the cradleboard to the strange, loudmouthed creature making such a to-do behind him.

Marie decided they were both safe as they were and climbed the steps to the countinghouse. As she crossed the threshold, she realized there was one more hurdle she hadn't been banking on. James Hargrave wasn't at Fort Garry anymore, and she didn't know if any of the other clerks would recognize her. The only one in the room at the moment, painstakingly inking in a ledger at one of the stilt-legged desks, was a man she'd never seen before. He looked up from his ledger and said impatiently: "May I help you?"

"Um-hm. I'd like to take some money from Mister Grant's account."

"Wouldn't we all?"

"I am Mrs. Grant." She half expected him to reply "Prove it," or "That still doesn't give you the right to mess with his account."

"Yes, ma'am—it'll just take me a moment to pull the ledger. . . ."

"I want to move twenty-nine shillings from his—our—account to the Point Douglas Sutherlands'."

"Yes, ma'am."

When she came back out again, the clear portion of the sky had been reduced to a ragged blue ribbon caught in the teeth of the northern palisade. But the storm clouds still hung fire. She whipped the pony into a trot, jouncing and bouncing along the trail back to Grantown. Pretty soon there was no blue left at all and the birds were singing their evening songs in the middle of the day.

She had just forded Catfish Creek when the sky let loose with its artillery. The rain hit in a sheet that soaked her through in an instant. Between the thunder roars, she could hear Charles and the calf both shrieking. She hooked her arms around the front rail to keep the pony's jerking against the reins from yanking her out of the cart and hauled hard on the left rein to turn him off the trail and into the woods beside the river.

Just before they got there, a bombshell exploded in a tree ahead, blinding her and peppering her face with flinders and sending the pony into madder fits. By bracing one foot against the cart rails and putting every muscle in her body into straining back against the reins, she managed to stop his rearing. But the question was where to go now. The woods didn't seem the safer haven that they had a moment ago. But out on the prairie, their cart would be the tallest object for miles around. She reminded herself of the adage about lightning striking twice in the same spot, shifted the reins into her left hand, and whipped the pony into the woods.

When the trees closed in behind them, she jumped down, close-haltered the pony to a poplar, and fought her way back through the lashing branches. Even in the shelter of the woods, the rain pelted down so hard that she could only open her eyes for quick glimpses. She felt through the cart rails for the folded awning, snagged it, tied two corners to the back posts of the cart rails, and began to unfurl it. Charles's cradleboard still hung outside. She shifted it inside and carried on draping the awning over the cart and the pony. It wasn't quite long enough to cover the pony's head, so she tied it tight around his neck.

But when she went to climb back into the cart, she discovered that she'd battened down the buffalo-hide roof so snugly that there was no room for her to squeeze in over the top rail. Over the howl of the storm, she could hear the pony's back hooves battering the front of the cart and the calf's hooves drumming erratically on the cartbed, flailing in all directions, and over it all the wail of Charles's screaming.

Her hands took hold of two of the cart rails and pulled. They came apart, leaving a hole just big enough for her to crawl inside. She pushed the calf aside, getting a hoof in the cheek for her trouble, ripped open the thongs on the cradleboard, popped out Charles in his mossbag, and cupped him in under the yoke of her nursing dress. She put her free hand over the calf's nose, and, miraculously, both Bessie's child and hers settled down. Even the pony stopped his kicking, although the thunder claps still boomed like the crack of doom and the rain still clog-danced on the drumskin awning.

Marie discovered she was shivering. But the combined body warmth enclosed in the hide-roofed cave gradually stopped her teeth from clattering together. The eggs between her breasts just might survive after all. She started to cry, thinking of all those poor little eggs thinking they were safely mothered by a little fool playing at being a grown-up.

CHAPTER 24

At Fort Mister Grant, Mister Grant lay in the dark with the hounds of hell sniffing around his bed. It wasn't the first time they'd come calling.

He and Donald and Daniel McGillis and a brace of other young hired hands had just gotten back from a week-long swing through the upper Pembina country and had sat up after supper rewarding themselves with high wine and tobacco. But every fragmentary picture that now magic-lanterned itself onto the backs of Grant's eyelids showed Mister Grant flattering his vanity by making himself the center of attention to a roomful of down-mustached boys.

Some of the pictures showed quite clearly an appreciative and encouraging audience. He pointed out said fact to the hounds of hell. They replied that the boys hadn't had much choice, had they, now? After all, Mister Grant was the *okimaw*—the big man who gives the orders. Perhaps said appreciative flatterers wouldn't be so inclined to kowtow to said *okimaw* if they could see him toadying up to George

Simpson. The hounds put in a QED by forcing him to listen to his own voice actually saying "Sir" in his last interview with Simpson— just like some contract-bound little apprentice clerk.

Grant thrashed over into another position and instructed his mind to wander down another pathway, one that would lead him into sleep. He'd learned that the only way to throw the hounds off once they got his scent was to slip into a memory or fantasy too sweet for them to smell him in it. He put himself back roaming the pine-perfumed hills above Grantown-on-Spey where he was boarded between terms at Inverness. It was always a great delight to get away from the school and the town and be able to ramble wherever his legs would carry him, even if it was only for a few hours. As he skirted around the grounds of Castle Grant, he warmed himself with the fact that he wasn't just a misplaced orphan after all, he was a member of Clan Grant.

The hounds snickered in his ear at his blissful ignorance. Even if Clan Grant had still been what it had been in the days before Culloden and the Clearances, the folks at Castle Grant would have laughed themselves off their chairs at the notion of this black-eyed little mongrel presenting himself as part of the family.

Grant threw off the blankets and sat up, shaking his head like a terrier shaking a rat. This was getting him nowhere. He tugged on his trousers and moccasins, caped a blanket over his shoulders, snagged the brandy flask from his traveling bag, and went out into the clean night air.

It was a misty night, which was a rare treat on the prairies, softening the habitually sharp, dry air. A diffused flicker of orange light showed where the night sentry was dozing by the gate. The sentry jerked awake hearing the grass scuff of approaching moccasins, then scrambled to his feet when he saw who it was, dropping his musket in the process and scrabbling in the dirt to pick it up. Grant said: "Quiet night."

"So far, Mister Grant."

"I'm just going out for a stroll. . . ." The sentry dropped his gun again, giving the *okimaw* a hand unbarring the gate. "Bar it behind me. I'll call when I come back. Who knows—I may even nod off beside the river."

As the gate closed behind him, the hounds whispered in his ear the conversation that would be whispered around the mess table in the morning: "He went sleepwalking out the gate wearing a blanket and carrying a flask of brandy. . . ." Setting a fine example.

Fortunately, negotiating the dark path through the bush down to the riverbank was enough to occupy him beyond self-consciousness.

He came within an ace of plummeting headfirst into the Souris. As his moccasin splashed down into a void instead of thudding onto solid ground, he flung himself backward to reverse his momentum. The breath grunted out of him as his shoulders hit the path. He levered himself upright and fumbled over to a tree broad enough to lean his back against.

The sky was mostly matte black, with a few handfuls of spangles flung into the patches of lacquer brushed in between. There was just enough moonlight filtering through the clouds to illuminate the plumes of mist coalescing over the river. The peeper frogs and crickets fiddled a descant to the low murmur of the river and the sibilant rustle of the trembling aspens. A barred owl performed its series of rising huffs working their way up to a long hoot, paused to catch its breath, and then started all over again.

Grant squirreled the blanket around so that the two top corners overlapped one shoulder like a shepherd's plaid, unscrewed the cap on the flask, took a deep swig, shivered it down his throat, and then sighed as the warmth settled into his belly. The fading numbness from the evening's high wine kicked back up with the arrival of reinforcements.

The night put him in mind of another night twelve or thirteen years ago, the first misty night he'd ever spent beside a river in the *pays d'en haut*—or at least the first since the early childhood years before the MacGillivrays shipped him east. It was a pleasant memory.

He'd been camped on the Qu'Appelle with Bostonais Pangman when the mist came in. They'd spent the evening feeding the fire to keep off the ague, trading stories and jokes across the flames or leaning back in companionable silence to watch the firelight. It was the first night that Grant had gotten the impression that this granite-featured, laconic denizen of the wilderness had actually accepted a certain poncified, foreign-educated clerk as an equal and a friend.

"Some friend," the hounds chortled and panted. "He ran off with your wife and baby while you were locked up in a jail two thousand miles away." Grant pointed out to the hounds that there were a thousand other possible explanations for the fact that Bethsy and James and Bostonais had disappeared at roughly the same time. They replied: "You're right, she probably didn't leave you for anyone. Living with you was such a joy that she decided she and James would be better off running blind to nowhere. Probably the reason no one's heard anything of her and James since is because the Blackfoot or the Sioux or Gros Ventres chopped them up for entertainment or kept them for slaves."

"I realized I wasn't the best husband and father in the world. I was coming back to change that."

"A little late, wouldn't you say? And don't try to fob us off with that 'I was a young fool then.' You're doing precisely the same thing to Marie as you did to Bethsy—taking her for granted."

An acid laugh lacerated its way up his throat. He muttered, "For Granted," and washed it down with another burning mouthful from the flask. As though it weren't bad enough that every scrap of recollection came up against the same mannequin of shit masquerading as a human being, he wasn't even safe in the present.

He lurched to his feet to walk it off, only there was nowhere to walk. He wouldn't get far through the black jungle on either side of the path, and he couldn't very well go walking on the river—despite the impression he might try to give to the hired hands.

He snarled and whirled around, almost throwing himself off his feet, and blundered back up the slope to the open prairie. When the ground beneath his feet flattened out into the plantation between the riverside woods and Fort Mister Grant, he stopped for a moment to flip a coin in his mind and tilt his head back to suck in another ounce of brandy. He wheeled right and marched off through the crackling shortgrass of the Souris plain, clutching his blanket around his neck with one hand and his flask with the other, barking shards of words, bobbing and weaving against the faces that rose up in front of him sneering or weeping or bleeding, kicking back each step against the hounds baying and snapping at his heels. Out there somewhere there had to be something he could hold up between them and him, something he could do right for once in his life.

When he woke up there were bushes made of sterling silver, artfully constructed grass tufts of gleaming pink gold. . . . It was the sunrise hitting the dew. The bushes were the metallic-leaved silverberry, or snowberry, Grant could never tell them apart.

He stood up to see where he was. He had a vague memory of turning around and starting back to the fort at some point in the night. The forest belt flanking the river was only about a hundred yards from where he'd lain down. A ways to the south, the lookout tower of Fort Mister Grant poked over the crowns of the trees. He still had a good morning's walk ahead of him. But first he went to the river and drank a good deal of it, washed down with the last swallow of brandy. The Souris plain was sandier and drier than White Horse Plains and seemed particularly so today.

By the time he got back to the fort the sun was high enough that he'd switched to carrying the blanket instead of wearing it. He fumbled his way groggily through the business of the day. Fortunately there wasn't much that had to be done. And perhaps that was the problem. Now that the two swings along the border country—one to the east and one west—had been accomplished, there wasn't much to do but hang around the fort so that any Indian who stumbled across a stray muskrat wouldn't be disappointed.

He collapsed onto his bed after supper and announced over breakfast that he was going back to Grantown to prepare for the autumn buffalo hunt. The others were free to follow him in two weeks' time, provided they left two behind to man the store. They could draw straws or cut cards when the time came, or perhaps there were two of them who'd prefer to draw wages for two months longer instead of going on the hunt.

Once the fort dropped away behind the hooves of his horse, he began to relax. Going at an easy lope, he should be able to make it home in three days.

Late on the afternoon of the third day, he crossed the Assiniboine a few miles upstream of Grantown, by the time-honored expedient of stripping naked, tying his clothes onto the saddle pad, and wrapping one hand into the towrope of his horse's tail while the other held his rifle and powder flask out of the water.

As he trotted around to the back of the house, Maria Theresa came charging out of the woods hollering, "Papa!" and launched herself at his leg. He caught her in midair and settled her onto the pommel of his saddle pad. Marie came out the back door with Eliza clutching her skirt. He slid down, leaving Maria Theresa in possession of his horse, and stooped to enfold himself in his wife.

Marie said, after catching her breath: "Are you home for a while now, or just the day?"

"Till the fall hunt."

"That's good."

As he was elevating Eliza to the fullest extension of his arms, an alien voice came in under her squeals—a kind of bleating "maaa!" He looked over his shoulder. It appeared to be coming from a place that hadn't been there when he'd left, a fenced-in area beside the barn. Marie said, "I guess you better come meet Potacikin," which was Cree for "bugle."

"Who?"

"We got new additions to the family since you was gone." There was a strain of nervousness in her voice, coupled with something resembling defiance. He set Eliza back onto her feet and followed her mother to the new fence. Inside it was a long-legged, dappled calf. "I got my father to put the fence up so she'd have somewhere to go outside. The dogs wanted to chase her, and some of the horses didn't like her, so . . ."

"Wherever did you . . . ?" She told him the story of Mrs. Sutherland's serendipitous visit. "Well, I'm damned glad you took advantage of the opportunity. I'll go to Fort Garry tomorrow or the next day and see that the credit is transferred from my account to the Sutherlands'."

"I already did."

"Oh. Well, then . . ."

"You don't mind?"

"Mind? Why should I mind?" But he was beginning to feel a niggling sense of kinship with the nipples on a steer.

Maria Theresa jumped off his horse, shouting: "Come see the others, Papa!"

"Others?" He allowed Maria Theresa to tug him into the house. A basketlike pen of woven willow wands had been built beside a corner of the kitchen hearth. Inside it were two peeping, yellow-downed chicks, pecking at the straw around their feet and clapping their vestigial winglets.

Marie said placidly from the doorway: "I'm not sure if they're going to be hens or roosters."

"I expect they'll reveal themselves in due course." He was more than a little disoriented. While Marie didn't look markedly different from the wife he'd kissed good-bye, and she still laughed just as easily as ever—showing the pink roots of her teeth—there was something self-contained about her that wasn't there before.

Josephte appeared from the parlor with a hoop of needlework dangling from one hand. "Well, well—Cuthbert! And here I thought we'd have another month at least to teach Charles to say 'Papa.'"

By suppertime Father Picard and John had returned from their separate ramblings. The household was just sitting down to a dinner of roast prairie chicken and wild plum dumplings when Falcon stuck his head in the door and said: "Heard you was back. Mary told me if I said anything more than 'Hello' to you today I'd be making up songs for sopranos from now on. So: Hello, and I'll see you tomorrow. Oh, shit, that was more'n 'Hello,' wasn't it? Don't tell her. Damn, that was even more. I'm just making it worse. Good-bye."

Maria Theresa and Eliza were both pouty about being evicted from their mother's bedroom. Charles was just barely still young enough to be left hanging in his cradleboard at the foot of his parents' bed. When all the candles were blown out, Grant sighed his way into the soft, warm feather bed and his even softer, warmer wife, whose body was as tantalizingly familiar and exotic as an old song left unsung for far too long.

He was out in the barn hammering together a stall for Potacikin when a note arrived from George Simpson at Fort Garry.

My dear Grant,

The brigade from York Factory's arrived, including your personal outfit. Had to add on two more boats to accommodate it. I shall be in residence till October, so do stop by to have a word when you come to collect it.

Grant couldn't for the life of him figure out how it could take two extra York boats to carry a few pharmaceutical orders and sundries, then realized it was the millworks he'd ordered. The next morning he started off along the trail to the Forks with a train of half a dozen carts trailing behind. The brigade's timing couldn't have been more perfect; after a week of plowing and puttering he was starting to get restless. Once the millworks were stacked in his barn he could while away the time before the autumn hunt with figuring out which cog was supposed to fit into which gear.

At Fort Garry he left the drovers to deal with the loading and headed over to the countinghouse. Its corners still showed a bit of battering around the edges from the flood. Odd that no one had bothered to patch them.

Simpson extended his hand across his desk. "Good to see you, Grant. Take a pew. How goes it at Fort Mister Grant, Mister Grant?"

"Tolerable well. I think we've cleaned out the country, or nearabouts."

"Excellent. I expected no less. However, I'm afraid that won't solve our problem entirely. What I wanted to have a word with you about is a proposal I'm hoping to submit to the London Committee. Although I do believe we've pretty much put paid to any American or Canadian pirates foraging into Rupert's Land, that still leaves the possibility that some of—" He coughed delicately. "Some of . . . your people might feel the inclination to go into business for themselves—

buying furs in the north and then smuggling them down to the American peddlers on the Mississippi or Missouri.

"What I hope to suggest to the London Committee is that the Company create a position for you that would be a . . . unique sort of arrangement."

"What sort of arrangement?" Grant almost added "sir," but he bit his tongue.

"Unique in that it wouldn't precisely be a position of employment with the Company per se, but the Company would pay the salary—say . . . in the neighborhood of two hundred pounds per annum."

Two hundred pounds was almost double the unusually exorbitant salary the Company had paid him as a clerk. "That's a very interesting figure. What would the position entail?"

"Nothing terribly onerous—for a man with the right talents and background. The entire responsibilities of the position would be to keep an eye out for any local citizens who might be tempted to take advantage of the Company's liberality and the vastness of our southern border. I believe that the mere fact of Cuthbert Grant making it known that he intended to enforce the Company's monopoly would nip a lot of temptation in the bud."

" 'Enforcer' has a certain sinister ring to it."

"It do, don't it? A certain sinister ring is a prerequisite for the position. But in your case, that would be rather gilding the lily. I mean that as a compliment. When I was pondering on what title to define the position under in my submission to the committee, I found that the purpose put me in mind of the feudal sinecures for those men entrusted with patrolling the border counties in Britain: 'warden of the west marches,' 'warden of the fens,' and so on. I thought I'd propose to the committee that we create a position entitled 'warden of the plains.' "

"And what would be the tenure? A year or two?"

"Quite frankly, Grant, it would be a great relief to me if I knew I could count on a warden of the plains as long as I am governor in chief of Rupert's Land—which I plan to remain until I am called up to the House of Lords or carried out of here feet first, whichever comes first."

"I'll talk it over with my wife."

CHAPTER 30

It was the first year since moving into the big white house that Marie had had her husband home all winter. Of course, being "home" for him didn't preclude the occasional moose-hunting or ice-fishing expedition with Pierriche, or a jaunt to the rudimentary quarry at Stony Mountain with a gaggle of buffalo hunters willing to try their hand at carving millstones. But most nights found him warming the bed alongside her. Eliza and Maria Theresa got used to sleeping in their own room. The other people of Grantown got used to having him around, officiating at the snowshoe races, poking in and out of the carpenters' shed, taking a sack of flour over to a family where the man of the house hadn't had much hunting luck and slipping in a hint that maybe they might want to consider shoving a few potatoes into the ground come spring.

Marie got used to entertaining the possibility that his inborn afflic-tion of farsightedness might correct itself. He even seemed to be enjoy-ing the children—bundling Maria Theresa and Eliza into the jumper for a tear along the river, patiently coaxing Charles through his first toddling steps. It was just as well he was there to take them off her hands from time to time, since she was most decidedly pregnant again.

On New Year's Day he loaded her onto the jumper—literally, as she'd reached the waddling stage where clambering over cart rails was out of the question—and they set off for the governor's Hogmanay regale, waving good-bye to the children clustered around Josephte shivering in the doorway. He had put together a kind of traveling couch out of layers of buffalo robes and blankets banked up against the back rails of the jumper. She settled back down onto it, wrapping a few of the layers around herself, and watched the black-and-white banks of the Assiniboine skim by, tasting snowflakes on her tongue.

As the roofs of Fort Garry hove into view, an alien strand of sound weaved itself into the natural skein of hooves and runners and harness bells—the martial wail of the great Highland pipes. Wappeston winked back over his shoulder from his brace-legged stance at the reins. "The Little Emperor's unleashed his marching band."

The "Little Emperor" had become the accustomed tag for George Simpson all throughout Rupert's Land—although never when he was in hearing distance—courtesy of a certain warden of the plains. Last year the manifest list for the Little Emperor's personal outfit had included "Item—one bagpiper, slightly used." At the far-flung outposts of the Company's empire, the distant skirl of "Scotland the Brave" or "Cock o' the North" had come to mean a wild scramble to make everything as shipshape as possible before the imminent appearance of an express canoe on a surprise inspection tour.

As Wappeston ushered Marie through the doorway of the dance hall that had been a warehouse the day before, the piper paused to wet his whistle, and a brace of fiddlers picked up the slack. The hall was thick and bright with the gamy smells of roast beaver tail and moose nose, wood and tobacco smoke, and flame-lit flares of beaded dresses and embroidered waistcoats. Benches had been lined along the walls for those frail souls who couldn't jig more than four or five hours without a break.

Wappeston said: "What say you find yourself a place to sit and I'll fetch a couple of platterfuls of delicacies to restoke our boilers. Are you still feeling that craving for pickled buffalo tongue?"

"Um-hm." She didn't want to open her mouth for fear of dribbling.

There was an open space on a bench beside a woman nursing a newborn baby. The mother seemed tantalizingly familiar—a métis woman a few years younger than Marie, but taller, with an apricot complexion and delicate features. "Margaret Taylor? . . ."

The nursing-misted black eyes drifted up to her, and the heart-shaped lips smiled. "Marie."

The year before Marie became Mrs. Grant, Margaret Taylor had appeared at Red River with her mother and brothers and sisters. She and Marie had run with the same gaggle of girls until Marie's girlhood came to its abrupt end. Given the roaming habits of most métis, it wasn't odd that Marie hadn't heard a word of her since then.

"We're only going to be here till the spring," Margaret was saying. "Little George should be grown enough to travel by then, so we're going along on the inspection tour out west." She disengaged her breast and buttoned it away. Her baby gazed at Marie with blue eyes paler than a husky dog's.

Wappeston appeared with a plate of sliced buffalo tongue and gravied vegetables, a cup of punch, and the governor of the Hudson's Bay Company's North American Territories. George Simpson stuck out his hand to gently smooth the down on Margaret Taylor's baby's head and said: "Well, what do you think of our little *maudrillikens*?"

Wappeston said: "Well, there's certainly no question where he got the eyes."

Marie said: "They may change color yet."

"No!" Margaret Taylor put in. "No—I'm sure they won't."

Wappeston handed the mounded plate to Marie, and he and the governor circulated back into the crowd, stopping almost immediately in front of a black-haired young man in a new broadcloth suit. They were still close enough to the bench for Marie to hear George Simpson introduce the young man as "my new secretary, and my new brother-in-law, Thomas Taylor."

Marie choked down her half-chewed mouthful of brined tongue and parsnips and said to Margaret: "I didn't know you got married."

Margeret blushed. "Only *à la façon du pays.*"

"Well, like my father says, that's been good enough for him and my mother for twenty-odd years, or 'damned odd years' he calls 'em sometimes."

It was shaping up to be a new year of more surprises. Marie had only come to Fort Garry out of a sense of duty, or her husband's duty—the warden of the plains pretty much had to put in an appearance at the governor's Hogmanay. But now she found herself feeling a delightful sense of release in chattering away with Margaret Taylor—or Margaret Simpson. Although she hadn't realized it consciously until now, being Mrs. Grant meant there were certain guarded areas. Other wives could tell funny stories about their husbands' half-formed plans or private doubts. Mister Grant, though, was supposed to be the unshakable hub. But Mrs. George Simpson was hardly likely to panic at the thought that Cuthbert Grant might have human foibles.

She and Margaret kissed each other good-bye with many promises to see each other often over the winter. As she waddled off through the reveling mob with her elbow hooked around Wappeston's oak trunk of an arm, Marie kept shaking her head at the surprises of this New Year's Day and the impossible changes that had sneaked up on her through the old year. Not only was Cuthbert Grant turning into a husband, but George Simpson appeared to have started to become a human being. But when she turned to wave good-bye to Margaret, it seemed that another emotion besides a fond farewell flickered across those brushed-gold features. It only lasted for an instant before the rictus of a smile snapped in, but Marie was almost willing to swear she'd seen a flicker of naked terror.

Despite their best intentions, larger forces than Marie Grant and Margaret Simpson conspired to keep them apart. By the time the new Grant budding inside her had grown enough to release himself from her, the rivers had taken it in mind to break early and an inspection tour was paddling to New Caledonia with the pipes' bray setting time.

Giving birth to Angus Grant was a good deal easier for Marie than it had been with Eliza or Charles. His father's resolution against the name got melted down by his mother's certainty that it would please her father and by her insistent reminders that her father had gone so far as to name one of her little brothers Cuthbert.

Her husband gave birth some months later, between the summer and autumn buffalo hunts. The event took place on Sturgeon Creek, and two caravans of packed carts came to see it—one from Red River and one from White Horse Plains. They met at a large construct of stone, wood, and earth standing on the last shelf of high ground before Sturgeon Creek threw itself into the Assiniboine. The linchpin of the new structure was a waterwheel that wasn't turning. On one side of the wheel was a blocky wooden building with a stone foundation; on the other was a dam built out of earth- and stone-filled wooden cribs. Standing on the dam, with his beadwork-sleeved arms crossed, was Marie's husband.

When everyone had climbed off their horses and carts and taken up positions on the banks of the creek and the new pond behind the dam, Bishop Provencher and Father Picard blessed the mill, sprinkling holy water over the water. Then Wappeston bent down, took hold of the rim of the sliding gate holding the water back from the millrace, and tugged upward. It didn't budge. He shifted his feet to straddle the gate frame. Marie could see the rainbow geometric pattern she'd quill-worked on the back yoke of his coat swelling and twisting out of shape. The gate and Wappeston both flew straight up in the air and plunged backward into the pond spewing itself eagerly through the new opening. The current swept him into the millrace, but he managed to catch the corner of the dam with one hand as he went by and keep hold of the gate with the other before they were sucked in under the wheel. He tossed the gate out onto the shore and climbed up onto the dam. There was much laughter when they saw that he was safe, and then cheers as the wheel began to turn.

He bowed in acknowledgment and then flourished one dripping arm toward the door of the mill. Marie and the rest of the crowd followed him inside. The interior was dominated by a humpbacked, circular wooden housing, about as broad across as her and Wappeston laid end to end. The press of people jamming in to have a look squashed her knees up against its rim.

Wappeston shouldered a sack full of grain, handed her an empty sack, and pointed down toward her right knee. There was a troughlike, wooden spout coming out of the housing there. Manipulating Angus's cradleboard with one hand, the empty sack with the other, and the crowd with both elbows, she managed to negotiate the mouth of the bag open and poised under the lip of the spout. Wappeston pulled down a lever. There was a coarse, gritty roar as the shaft from the waterwheel engaged with the grindstones. Wappeston leaned forward to dip his grain sack over the funnel at the top of the wooden hump. A stream of golden wheat clattered in. A crunching sound joined the molar-grinding drone of the stones. Speckled puffs of flour belched out of the spout to fatten and overflow the sack in Marie's hand.

After a moment's hush, the crowd roared and applauded. Wappeston stood shrugging nonchalantly with his empty grain sack draped across one shoulder and a red blaze across both cheeks.

The crowd thinned out, separating itself into those of little faith and those who'd come in carts piled high with sacks of grain. Wappeston left John Wills in charge and toured Marie and the children around various ingenious details, such as the mechanism to lift the waterwheel out of harm's way come freeze-up.

On the way home he winked at her. "Well, I guess I'm a seigneur in truth now."

"Pardon me?"

"One of the ancient obligations of a seigneur—or a squire or a laird, for that matter—was to provide a mill for his tenants. Noblesse oblige. Nothing to do with the fact, of course, that the mill will have paid for itself in a year and keep us through our old age."

But in January the built-up pressure of the ice on the new pond burst the dam. He left the mill idle until high summer, when the water was low, and built a sturdier dam. It stood up against the next winter's ice, but the spring floods washed it away.

He didn't go out on the summer hunt that year. Both Pierriche and her father told Marie they'd seen him sitting among the buttercups and violets on the banks of Sturgeon Creek, "just like a beaver studying on a busted pond." This time he moved the entire mill upstream and redirected the creek so he could build a dam of stone and mortar. The mill was back in operation before the autumn hunt, and it looked like nothing short of a barrel of gunpowder could budge it. But the following winter piled snow higher than even her father could remember. The runoff swept away dam, waterwheel, mill, and all. Only a few corners of the foundation were left to show where Grant's folly had stood.

The wooden gears and drive shaft washed up along the Passage of the Assiniboine. Wappeston carted them back to Grantown.

Marie came downstairs from settling the children into their unaccustomed sleeping arrangements. Maria Theresa was getting too old to have Charles sharing a room with her and Eliza. Angus had outgrown the cradleboard. So now there was a girls' room and a boys' room. At the rate she was going, Father Picard and Josephte and John were going to get squeezed out soon.

When she'd gone up to put the children to bed, Wappeston had been sitting at his desk attacking ledgers and accounts. Now he was slumped by the hearth with a piece of paper in one hand, a half-empty pint bottle in the other, and a dead pipe in his mouth. He shifted the pipe stem into one corner of his mouth and muttered in her general direction, with an arch voice and hooded eyes, "That damned creek always had it in for me. 'Dammed' creek—ha! It was Sturgeon Creek forced us to Seven Oaks, pushing us farther east with its spring overflow when the plan was to pass by Fort Douglas too far west for them to see us. And now the son of a bitch has done it to me again."

He sucked on his pipe, producing not a hair of smoke, and focused on the column of figures scrawled on the piece of paper—as much as his eyes appeared capable of focusing. He sighed. "Well, there it is. No way around it. I've factored in the fact that we can still use the washed-up machinery. Thank God I didn't order cast iron. We'll build a windmill here. The only difference I've managed to create with my brilliant notion of a water mill is a small matter of"—he bleared at the piece of paper again—"eight hundred pounds."

"Is your pipe empty?"

"Hm?" He plucked it out of his mouth and stuck a finger in the bowl. "No—just seems to've expired for the nonce."

"Here—" She snatched the piece of paper out of his hand, twisted it into a wand, thrust the fanned end into the hearth fire, and brought the flame up to his pipe.

He cracked into a fit of barking that might have been laughter or choking, and just managed to get it under control in time to light his pipe before she burned her fingers. She flicked the nub of the twist of paper into the fire. He said, "I must admit, Waposis—" then was cut off by another fit.

She pointed her eyes down at her midriff and hips and then looked back up again to meet his eyes. "Maybe this here rabbit ain't so little anymore."

Chapter 31

Toussaint Lussier was the strongman of Grantown. He delighted in squat-lifting ponies on his shoulders, to the squeals and applause of mobs of children. All in all, he was the last man Grant wanted to have a contretemps with. But it looked as though he were going to have to.

The massed cart caravan was camped at the ford of the Pembina on their way back from the summer hunt—the same spot where little Lucille had bequeathed Grant the occasional twinge of regret. Marie and the children had stayed back at Grantown. Marie hadn't been excessively pregnant when he'd left, but it had been evident that she would be before the hunt was over.

Perhaps it was his temporary state of bachelorhood that had allowed Grant's attention to wander and linger on peripheral details he might not have noticed otherwise—details such as the fact that the string of carts Toussaint Lussier had started out from Grantown with had included three that were already fully loaded with baggage, although one should have been enough to carry the provisions and camp gear for his family.

Grant was just handing his scraped breakfast plate back to Josephte, and was standing up to proceed with the business of turning the camp circle into a line to ford the Pembina, when he saw Toussaint Lussier lumbering toward him. "Mister Grant . . . the hunt's done now . . . and we're close enough to home that no Sioux or Assiniboine's going to come after us . . . so it wouldn't really be breaking the rules if I was to split off now, would it?"

"Split off?"

"Split off from the hunt, instead of going along to the Passage of the Assiniboine with all the others from the Forks and Grantown. You see, my wife's got some relatives she ain't seen for a long time at Pembina—well, a little bit south of there—so we figured, since we're passing by so close anyway . . . My brother-in-law'll take my cartloads of pemmican to Fort Garry."

The buffalo steak and bannock in Grant's stomach congealed. If he'd known it was going to come now, he would've only had tea for breakfast, with perhaps an ounce or two of brandy. He started walking idly in the general direction of the Lussier carts, with Toussaint plodding along like a Clydesdale that had been taught to heel. "I think you're quite right, Toussaint, that you wouldn't be breaking the laws of the hunt. How do you plan to travel?"

"Huh?"

"Are you and your wife just going to take a couple of saddle horses or . . ."

"We got these three carts, you see, all loaded up with our traveling gear. The other ones . . ." He repeated as if by rote, "My brother-in-law's going to take my cartloads of pemmican to Fort Garry."

"Three carts seems like a lot of bother for a short trip. There's still time before we get under way for you to separate the load into what you need and what you don't and pack it all on one cart. I'll be glad to take charge of your other two carts back to Grantown."

"Well, no, uh . . . thank you, but . . . we're going to need all the things on all three."

Grant forced out as engaging a chuckle as he could manage under the circumstances. "Since when did a seasoned voyageur like you need three cartfuls of camp gear for a quick jaunt over to Pembina? Believe me, you wouldn't be putting me out in the least. Another cart or two added on to my string won't make a hair of difference."

By that time they had reached the carts in question. Toussaint's little bright-eyed wife was battening down their tent awning over the load on their lead cart. "Good morning, Madame Lussier."

"What do you want?"

"I'm going to give Toussaint a hand looking through the loads on your carts to—"

"No."

" 'No'?"

Toussaint said awkwardly: "He just . . . Mister Grant just thought maybe he could take a couple of our carts back to Grantown for us. I told him we're going to need everything on all three—"

"We will!"

"Come, come—I hate to think of you lumbering yourselves with a lot of unnecessary baggage, when it would take only a moment to shift the loads." He started toward the Lussiers' lead cart. "I'm sure if you'll only take a second look, you'll see that—"

"No!" Madame Lussier jumped in front of him. "What business is it of yours what we got in our carts?"

"In one sense, Madame Lussier, that is *precisely* my business. That's why I collect a salary as warden of the plains. A salary, I might add, that buys a lot of amenities for a lot of people in Grantown."

"Simpson's off in England. He won't know what you do or don't do."

"You're quite right, Madame Lussier—but I'll know. I have a prejudice against collecting wages for a job I haven't done; it seems suspiciously like thievery. And my job is to enforce the law."

"Whose law? The Company's law?"

"The Company treats us fairly."

Toussaint burst out with, "If they're so goddamned fair, how come the Americans'll pay us more for—" He cut himself off as his wife showed him her teeth and the whites of her eyes.

The blood that had been thudding softly in Grant's eardrums kicked up to a Sun Dance booming. He raised his eyes off Toussaint's wife and swiveled his head to face Toussaint. There were a good many other faces in soft focus behind the big, broad, black-bearded head. Grant swallowed to moisten his throat and said blandly: "Pay more for what, Toussaint?"

Toussaint's mouth opened and closed several times. He appeared to be in agony, shooting his eyes back and forth from his wife to Grant to the cart. Toussaint's mind was barely up to following one train of thought at a time, much less three contradictory ones. Grant turned toward the cart again and stepped around Madame Lussier, raising his right hand toward one corner of the buffalo hide tucked around the load. She shifted in front of him and threw her arms out. "No!"

A slab of beef wrapped itself around Grant's right shoulder. He turned his head to look at it, his eyes naturally crossing to focus on the knuckles that bore more resemblance to a row of kneecaps. Toussaint's voice rumbled painfully: "Please, Mister Grant, you don't want to—"

Grant shrugged off the hand and took another step toward the cart, reaching his right arm over the backpedaling Madame Lussier. Out of the corner of his left eye, he saw Toussaint launch himself forward with his arms sweeping into a bear hug. Grant's feet and legs stayed facing forward, but his torso turned and gave Toussaint a straight left in the mustache and nostrils, snapping his head back.

Toussaint shook his head and raised a hand to check that there was really blood coming out of his nose. Grant swiveled to face him. The intervening instant's pause was long enough for Grant to hear an analytical corner of his mind speaking in the voice of Mr. MacAndrew of Inverness College: "*This is a fine pickle. Well, you're in it now, no point in recriminations. There is something to be said for the uncivilized philosophy that if one must fight, one might as well go at it with knees and rocks and eye gouging and get it over with as soon as possible. But once yon lumbering lug gets his hands on you, you're done like King Alfred's cakes, lad. So I suggest you forget everything you learned in the* pays d'en haut *and give him a taste of the gentle science. I know it's a slim chance at best, but— Whoops, here he comes. . . ."*

Grant dropped back into the stance dunned into him through three years of gymnasium classes: left side facing the opponent, left elbow quarter-cocked to hold the left fist forward, right fist cradled halfway between chin and chest. As Toussaint came on, Grant gave him another straight left to the flat of his nose and stepped back quickly before Toussaint could catch hold of his arm. Toussaint kept on coming, and Grant shot out another straight left, fully expecting that even Toussaint could figure it out the third time in a row. Sure enough, Toussaint threw his left arm up in a big arc to block the blow, and Grant threw a right cross through the opening—he could've thrown a horse through it—to crack against Toussaint's jaw, following it up with a quick jab to the exposed neck.

There was no point in trying to work the body. He could punch away all day at that inches-thick padding of fat and muscle and accomplish nothing but wearing out his arms. So he drove Toussaint back with a succession of blows to the head, coming at him from all angles to keep him bewildered. It was too easy. Grant got too cocky and came in too close. The next thing he knew, one moose antler of a hand was wrapped around his arm and the other was eclipsing the sun and getting larger.

Grant flung himself sideways at the ground, turning on one heel and desperately kicking out his other foot to hook the back of Toussaint's knee. It just managed to connect. Toussaint went down as well. The concussion of hitting the ground jarred Toussaint's grip loose enough for Grant to yank his arm free.

Grant was back up before Toussaint was. Toussaint was in a perfect position to take a rugby kick to the head, but Grant didn't deliver it. The last thing he wanted was to push Toussaint across the line between annoyance and rage.

Toussaint found his feet and his bearings again, and Grant went back to work. They were both getting winded. Toussaint's face looked like a pounded steak, and Grant's hands felt so battered that he was afraid if he unfisted them for an instant, he'd never get them curled tight again. Toussaint managed to wallop him a couple of times, almost knocking him off his feet but not dazing him enough to let Toussaint get a hold on him.

Grant stumbled back from delivering his latest barrage. Toussaint stood bobbing his head like a baited bear, squinting against the blood seeping down from one eyebrow. Grant found enough breath to say: "Give it up, Toussaint, for God's sake."

Toussaint growled and came on again. Grant stepped out of his way. As Toussaint blundered by, Grant swung around and up, imitating the hammer tossers at Inverness Fair, and threw his whole body behind the heel of his right fist, driving down into the back of Toussaint's broad waist. Toussaint howled and bent backward like a strung bow, hands clutching at his kidneys, then went down on his knees. This time Grant didn't wait for him to get up but stepped in, looping a luxuriously long-handled right against Toussaint's left cheek. Toussaint's head swung around, spraying blood and spittle. The bearded chin crossed impossibly over the shoulder, and the bull-chested body followed it around and down into the dirt.

Toussaint Lussier was suddenly replaced by his wife, burying her claws in Grant's hair at both ears, yanking and spitting and screaming: "Leave him alone!" Grant grabbed hold of her forearms just in time to keep her from pulling his scalp off. But once he'd got hold of her there wasn't much he could do except stumble around in a tunnel-vision world walled with his hair and hers and his hands and her arms, with her snarling face at the other end. He was reluctant to punch a woman, even this one, and the fact was that if he did let go of one of her arms to do so, she would rip out half his scalp before his fist could connect. She was kicking at him furiously, but he was keeping her off balance enough that her feet didn't quite connect with their goal. At another time he could've just squeezed her wrists till her hands went numb, but with the state his hands were in at the moment it was liable to take a long time. All in all, it was a very unpleasant and embarrassing situation.

Four new hands appeared inside the walls of the tunnel—two longish, thin ones and two that were pudgy and stubby. The left one of the thin pair twined its long fingers in Madame Lussier's hair and pulled; the right one butted up against Grant's grip on Madame Lussier's right forearm. One of the stubby pair seconded Grant's hold on Madame Lussier's left forearm while the other clamped itself on Madame Lussier's left breast and twisted.

Madame Lussier screamed and let go. Grant cricked his back straight, pushing the hair out of his eyes, and had an instant to register Josephte and Mary Falcon twisting Toussaint's wife's arms behind her back. Then he was whirling around to see if Toussaint was coming up behind him.

Toussaint wasn't about to come up behind or in front of anybody.

He was still lying curled up where he'd fallen, although his fingers were making crab claws in the dust and his chest was emanating vestigial groans.

Grant slumped forward, propping his elbows on his knees, and waited for the air to stop tearing at his lungs and the blurred world to ease back into focus. He straightened his spine and walked over to the Lussiers' lead cart, gingerly exploring his hands along the way. Despite the pain and oozing blood and swollen knuckles, all of the bones appeared to be intact. He hooked his hands over the back rails of the cart—not difficult, since they had atrophied into hooks anyway—and ripped open the trellis. He started lifting things out. Underneath the cooking pots and buffalo robes was a fine collection of furs—glossy, frosted-black fisher, golden-brown marten, silky white ermine, and silvery lynx. There were no beaver pelts, but Grant expected he'd find plenty in the other two carts.

He scooped out an armload and headed back toward Toussaint. Toussaint was stretched out on his back now, with his immense head filling his wife's lap. Someone had brought a bucket of water and she was dabbing at the blood on his face with a rag.

Grant found Josephte's eyes in the crowd, mimed a tilting motion over his mouth with his free hand, and carried on to the Lussiers. Toussaint's eyes were open, to the extent the puffy bruises around them would allow. His wife's were nasty slits.

Grant threw the furs down in front of them and said: "Do you have the remotest notion of what would happen if the Company knew about this? At the very least, you would be refused credit at any of the Company's stores from this day forth. But if the Company chose to pursue it to the fullest extent of the law—the committee has approved a resolution to ban proven smugglers from building homes on Company land, and that means every foot of ground from here to the North Pole and from the Atlantic Ocean to the Pacific. You would lose your home in Grantown and would effectively be banished from the home territory of all your friends and relatives, unless you wanted to spend the rest of your lives wandering from campsite to campsite. You want to chance *that* for a few extra shillings in your pocket?"

Toussaint moved his mangled mouth, but nothing came out except a grunt. His wife hissed: "We got a right to trade furs if we want to."

"The Company doesn't give a fried goddamn if you and some passing Saulteaux trade a bit of tobacco for a muskrat pelt—provided you don't turn around and sell that pelt to the competition. Maybe the Company's prices aren't as good as the American traders'—but who is it that advances you powder and shot when you've got nothing to trade and nothing to hunt with? When you're starving in February, who gives you back the provisions that you sold them in November? If you went to the American traders for help, they'd chase you back out into the snow and bolt their gates. The Company lives here."

Josephte appeared with his brandy flask. He took a grateful swig and then handed it down to Toussaint, saying: "Throw it straight down at the back of your throat so it won't hit any cut spots." Toussaint did as he'd advised, gasped, and passed the flask to his wife. She pointedly handed it straight back to Grant.

Grant called out: "Pierriche? You take charge of crossing the ford. I'm going to take a couple of buffalo robes and lay my bruised bones down under a tree for an hour or two, or a week, or a month."

When the carts rolled into Grantown, Grant's hands still hadn't healed. He committed the sin of using a buffalo runner for a saddle horse so he could guide it with his knees. Maria Theresa and Eliza appeared as he trotted into the yard, but there was no sign of Marie or their little brothers, and the girls seemed strangely subdued.

The interior of the house was dark. Someone had drawn the parlor curtains and lighted a candle in the middle of the day. In the feeble orange glow within the gloom, Grant could just make out a nursing woman sitting cross-legged on the hearth rug. A toddling child was hiding behind her. The woman didn't look up at him, but the child at her breast did, black eyes catching the candlelight. Grant could make out just enough of the woman's shadowed features to see that they were too Botticellian to be Marie's, and then—as his eyes adjusted from the sunlight—he saw that she was Margeret Taylor. Or Margeret Simpson, rather.

Marie's voice came from above: "Wappeston?" He looked up and saw her coming down the stairs. She wasn't exactly hurrying to greet him, though, and her "Wappeston?" had been hushed.

Margeret Simpson was up and bundling her babies together and shuffling for the stairs, mumbling something he couldn't make out. Marie squeezed her very ripe body against the wall of the stairwell to let her pass and then came on at a pace not quite befitting a woman who hasn't seen her husband for two months. Grant said, "What . . . ?" and then got hung up trying to decide which of several Whats to proceed with. He finally settled on, "I thought she was ensconced at Bas de la Rivière, waiting to present him with their second child when he got back from furlough?"

"She was."

"Then what's she . . . I mean, she's welcome, of course—but I would've thought he'd be back by now."

"He is. If you hadn't been out on the plains, you would've heard the news by now."

"What news?"

"About George Simpson's wife."

"That's precisely who I'm asking you about."

"His white wife."

"His what?"

"It turns out when Simpson and his friend MacTavish went to England, they were planning all along on finding themselves nice white wives to bring back with them. They just didn't bother mentioning it to the ones they left here. Seems they both got lucky. Simpson married a cousin of his named Frances Simpson. The first that Margeret heard of it was when an express canoe came charging in to Bas de la Rivière telling her to clear out fast. They were just ahead of the brigade bringing Mister and Mrs. Simpson. They did give her two days 'cause the brigade wasn't moving too fast. Seems it's hard to carry a piano over a portage."

Grant muttered: "Oh, hell."

"Nice friend you got there."

"Friend? I never said George Simpson was a friend of mine."

"Maybe it's about time you told him he ain't."

"To what end? What the hell do you expect me to do—call him out? I think it's a disgustingly shoddy way they've treated Margeret and— damn, I've lost the name of MacTavish's—"

"*Nancy*. Nancy McKenzie."

"Yes. Old Roderick's granddaughter. But there's nothing that Roderick McKenzie or I or anyone else can do about the fact that Georgie Simpson wasn't content to be born a bastard, he has to go out of his way to prove it."

Marie dropped her eyes and then let out a sudden gasp and snatched hold of his hands. He gasped in response. She softened her grip but didn't let go, tugging him over to the candle and raising his hands into the light. She wailed: "What happened to your hands?"

"I was earning the money George Simpson pays me to keep us in the style to which we've grown accustomed."

CHAPTER 32

Marie became obsessed with Frances Simpson. It was difficult not to be. The governor's wife was the hottest new topic of conversation in a country whose snowed-in winters and campfire-lit summer nights elevated gossip into the realm of a basic need.

The opinions Marie heard were decidedly divided. Most of the Company men were in raptures over her delicate, pale beauty, her refined manners, and her pretty habit of dressing up in the Welsh national costume. The traders at the Rainy River post, which had got by perfectly well under that name for a hundred years, rechristened it Fort Frances. The Company's junior officers were all enthused about following the governor's advice to import a lovely, tender exotic of their own to give them a civilized home in the wilderness. Of course the Company men didn't have much choice but to express delight at anything that delighted the Little Emperor.

Marie was aware of the fact that, despite the vastness of the *pays d'en haut,* its thin population made it a relatively small world compared with the cities in the east. But she'd never imagined that so many ripples could come from simply dropping a Frances Simpson into their little pond. For one thing, in the quarter century since she'd first begun to pick out words from the various languages spoken around her cradleboard, she'd never heard the word *squaw* in an English or French conversation. Now it began to pop up all the time.

And then there was the matter of the new fort. George Simpson put a hundred men to work building a huge, stone-walled fort about twenty miles downstream from the Forks, to replace Fort Garry as Company headquarters. "Bloody foolishness," was Wappeston's opinion. "He justifies it to the London Committee by saying that Fort Garry's still dilapidated from the flood and that putting the headquarters at the foot of St. Andrew's Rapids will save the brigades a lot of work. The London Committee doesn't know any better, but the truth of it is it'd be a hell of a lot less trouble and expense to refurbish Fort Garry than build a whole new fort. And the brigades have been lining or shooting the rapids without thinking twice about it since the first fort went up at the Forks. He can't just wave his bloody scepter and change all the reasons why the Forks have been the crossroads of the country since the invention of the canoe."

"Then why . . ." She was going to say "don't you tell him so?" but amended it to, ". . . would he go to all that trouble and expense?"

Wappeston snorted a laugh, knocked back the dregs in his cup, and intoned: "In Xanadu did Simpson George a stately pleasure dome decree—with big stone walls to keep the rabble out, and sufficiently isolated from the habitations of Highlanders and half-breeds who might contaminate his precious transplanted flower."

Marie's third daughter came in the fall. Wappeston said: "God forbid I should tempt fate, but she's obviously born lucky—looks more like her mother than her father. What shall we call her? I've been thinking of—"

"Margeret Nancy."

The first opportunity Marie would've had to actually clap eyes on Frances Simpson was the governor's New Year's regale, except that Wappeston announced he'd had such a good time hosting their own Hogmanay at Grantown last year, he wanted to do it again.

She said: "But shouldn't you at least put in an appearance? As warden of the plains and all . . ."

"The description of the position of warden of the plains says nothing about enforced socializing. If the London Committee considers that an essential part of my duties, they can hire someone else."

Marie expected she'd get at least a secondhand view from Wappeston's occasional jaunts to Fort Garry on business, but somehow his path and Frances Simpson's never seemed to cross, and she got the distinct impression that he wasn't about to go out of his way to meet her.

She did manage to get a description of the birth of Frances Simpson's first child, from a very reliable source. The Simpsons had been in a quandary as her "confinement"—a euphemism Marie had never heard before—drew near. There were many women at Red River who'd midwifed other women's birthings, but they were all either coarse Highland women or even coarser daughters of the country. By a stroke of luck, though, there happened to be a young woman at loose ends at Red River who was generally acknowledged to have an aptitude for midwifery far beyond her years, and who also—despite her brown skin and black eyes— had a surprising air of refinement and education: Nancy McKenzie.

Nancy McKenzie set her teacup down on Marie's kitchen table and said, shaking her head, "I told her over and over again to squat on the bed and let it drop, instead of lying flat and pushing it out, but she wouldn't. It tore her up something fierce. I expect I'm going to be

nursing her for a while. I wish I could nurse her boy for her—those
tiny little pale tits couldn't hardly keep a kitten alive. Maybe it'll be
nice for her to have someone else around for a while, even just a nurse.
I expect she gets awful lonely sometimes. The only company she can
have is the missionaries' wives, and that piano. Well, and now she's
got the baby, too."

"What's it sound like?"

"The baby?"

"The piano! I wouldn't call a baby 'it'!"

"Well, maybe a Simpson baby . . . I shouldn't say that. He's a lovely
little boy, just so frail. . . . But the piano—I don't quite know how to
. . . It sounds sort of like a plucked fiddle, only louder and with more
notes together. I sure would like to hear a good fiddle player get his
hands on it. The way she plays is all tinkly, with no kick to it. Maybe
that's what they call music in England, but if that's the case, I don't
know how English people can dance."

The winter mail packet brought twice as many personal letters to
Wappeston as usual. Over the years, his lack of interest in the fur trade
gossip of promotions and misplaced indents had winnowed down his
correspondents to James Hargrave. Above Hargrave's habitual closing
of "My best regards to my old friend Mrs. Grant" was a by-the-way
quotation of Frances Simpson's description of Nancy McKenzie: "A
complete savage, with a coarse blue sort of woolen gown without shape
& a blanket around her neck."

Wappeston scaled the letter away to bounce off the hearth wall,
barking: "Silly little bitch! I don't object to anyone's private, nasty
narcissisms, but how much brains does it take to realize that Rupert's
Land is not an Edinburgh tea party? If the chief trader at Fort Edmon-
ton sneezes in the spring, the autumn boat brigade from York Factory
will arrive tugging out their handkerchiefs." He ripped open the
next letter and his anger dissipated into a chortling "Well, I'm
damned. . . ."

"What is it?" She knew he would tell her whether she expressed
interest or not, but everyone could do with a few extra crumbs of
encouragement now and then.

"It's Colin Robertson. An old . . . acquaintance from the fur trade
war. He's taking his furlough this spring, going to Lower Canada, and
is stopping by Red River to visit his sons boarded at the parsonage
school. He hopes that he and his wife might stop by at Grantown for
a day or two on their way out."

Marie had never met Colin Robertson, although the name was

vaguely familiar. But there was a spare bedroom upstairs and the pantry was full. "Why does that make you laugh?"

"Well, Robertson and I *did* spend the first five years of our mutual acquaintance shoving pistols up each other's noses. He was on the other side, you see. Several of our Grantown neighbors still harbor a deep resentment against Colin Robertson for absenting himself from Red River just before Seven Oaks; they'd been so looking forward to dicing him up in slow stages and pickling the pieces for souvenirs."

After that introduction, Marie wasn't quite sure what to expect of Colin Robertson. He turned out to be a boom-laughed, florid-faced man with receding red ringlets and a chest girth and height even larger than her husband's. His wife had the shy eyes and skittish manner of a deer and seemed more Cree than métis.

Colin Robertson stomped and scraped the mud off his boots on the iron boot scraper by the doorway before proceeding inside, booming: "Damned mucky time of year to be traveling! That horse was white when I set out, and my lady wife's was buckskin. Better mud than mosquitoes, though!"

Marie was only half-aware of Mister Robertson's florid flourishings. She was more aware of Mrs. Robertson balancing awkwardly on one stiff new high-heeled shoe while scraping the mud off the other in anxious imitation of her husband.

Supper was the usual riot of the extended Grant household around the extended table that was getting damned near to outgrowing the kitchen. It seemed to Marie that Mrs. Robertson loosened up a little once the children let loose. But she also noticed—in the sparse moments when she was allowed to notice anything beyond Maria Theresa kicking John under the table and Charles contemplating another try at putting his soup bowl on his head—that Mrs. Robertson seemed to be watching Wappeston like a cat at a mouse hole.

Marie came down from putting the babies to bed to find the rest of the family and their guests gathered around the parlor hearth. Wappeston and Colin Robertson had fired up their pipes. Mrs. Robertson wasn't smoking, but she'd placed herself between the pipes and the draft into the fireplace and appeared to be drinking in each whiff of smoke that wafted past her nose. Marie had never acquired a taste for tobacco, but most métis women were as adept at keeping a pipe alight in all weathers as their men. Perhaps Mrs. Robertson was doing penance for something.

Marie settled down on the hearth rug beside Wappeston's chair and cocked an elbow across his knee. Colin Robertson said: "The first time

I met your husband, Mrs. Grant, I was expecting some strutting little popinjay in a comic opera uniform. Well, what would *you* expect if all you'd been told was that there was this young nincompoop who'd got himself all puffed up about the North West Company declaring him captain general of the New Nation, when the only purpose behind the exercise was so the North West Company could use the half-breeds for its own ends—"

"As opposed," Wappeston put in, "to the Hudson's Bay Company using us for its own ends."

"Which I was damned near to accomplishing, when your husband rode in from the Qu'Appelle. Along with Bostonais Pangman. . . . Whatever happened to Bostonais Pangman?"

Although she was quite sure it wasn't apparent to anyone else, Marie heard an unnatural blandness in Wappeston's voice: "There are varying stories. No one knows for certain."

"He was a nasty piece of business."

"To anyone who tried to be nasty to him."

"At any event—instead of the little popinjay I was expecting, here were these two very large, stone-faced young men. I made a bit of conversation with Bostonais—which was hard work at the best of times. Your husband didn't say a word until I got someone to fetch us a hospitable round of rum—"

"John Pritchard," Wappeston tossed in.

"Little Pritchard—he's done well for himself. At any event—out comes the tot of rum, and finally your husband speaks. He poured his dram out on the ground and said—" He interrupted himself with sputters of laughter. "He said, 'Next time try blankets and beads.' Blankets and beads!" And the red-wreathed, florid face exploded in chair-arm-pounding guffaws.

"Well, you must admit," Wappeston said, "it was bound to be a trifle annoying for me to discover you using our own people to reestablish the colony we'd knocked on the head for good."

"I would've *done* it, too, if it weren't for that bloody idiot of a governor. Well, I suppose I oughtn't to speak ill of the dead." He exploded in guffaws again and boomed out: "You should've seen the furor when we got the news you'd skipped bail in Montreal instead of sticking around to hang like a gentleman!"

They went on trading stories. Marie found herself melting in the warmth of the fire and her husband's big, buckskinned thigh; floating along in those deep, complex voices—complex because there were so many conflicting currents swirling under the surface of each story.

Tonight's hearth fire burned in a place where regret and triumph and old fears converged to cancel out each other's names, so that all there was left to do was laugh so hard it hurt.

Josephte suddenly interjected: "The necessary's out behind the barn. I'll show you." Marie looked around. Eliza and Charles were asleep on the rug, but Maria Theresa was still wide-eyed. Mrs. Robertson was standing up gratefully, looking as though she were trying to swallow her back teeth.

When Josephte and Mrs. Robertson were gone, Colin Robertson leaned forward and said: "I want to ask you both a favor. You may have guessed that my notion to take a dogleg through Grantown wasn't just for auld lang syne. . . ."

Wappeston murmured: "What—you, Robertson? An ulterior motive?" And both men laughed again.

"The fact is, Grant, I'm looking to retire soon. Part of the reason I took my furlough when it came up is so we can scout out properties, and give my wife a chance to get her feet wet in civilized society. There ain't a finer woman in the world—with one possible exception, Mrs. Grant. . . . But people do grow up rather rustic in the *pays d'en haut*. Like it or not, there's a good deal of truth behind the old warning against transplanting a country family back east. Well, I hardly need tell *you*, Grant. After all, it was your father that—"

"Yes," Wappeston said crisply. "Oh, dear, Robertson—your cup looks to've run dry. . . ."

"Hm? Well, not quite—"

"Here, let me."

"Oh. Thank you. At any event—I was wondering if my wife might stay here with you for a day or two while I go back to the Forks and take care of the next step. I know you don't exactly keep Mayfair manners here, but there's not many people in the *pays d'en haut* housed like this. A couple of days here'd give her a chance to get used to staircases and china dishes and so on."

Wappeston said: "What 'next step'?"

"Well, I thought as long as we were stopping off at Red River it'd be a perfect opportunity for her to have tea with Mrs. Simpson once or twice—"

"And what," Wappeston cut him off, "does Mrs. Simpson think of this?"

"I haven't broached it to her yet. That's what I mean to do at the Forks while m'lady's staying over here—if you're agreeable to that. Well, actually I'll broach it to Simpson, since I haven't been introduced to Mrs. Simpson yet."

Marie was still leaning on Wappeston, so she heard the soft "Huh!" grunted deep. She looked up to see him studying the ripples in his cup with hooded eyes and sealed lips.

Josephte and Mrs. Robertson bustled back in out of the crisp spring night. Marie said: "Mrs. Robertson—we was just asking your husband if we could keep you here for a couple of days while he's going back and forth to the Forks on business. You and me ain't hardly had a chance to say more'n 'how do you do,' what with our husbands telling old war stories."

"Colin?"

"If you can put up with Grant's rantings for another day . . ."

When the candles were blown out and the bed warmed, Marie said: "What did he mean about your father?"

"Hm?"

"When Colin Robertson said: 'It was your father that . . .' "

"Oh." It came out in that brittle tone of voice that meant she'd stepped onto thin ice. "My father became a bit of a byword in the North West Company. In those days, before there was a Red River Settlement, someone like *your* father would've been faced with a grim choice when his time came to retire—and in those days you either retired young or died young. So when the time came, the choice was to abandon one's country family—though not in the shoddy way Simpson and MacTavish went about it—or to transport them in an alien environment. My father chose an unprecedented third choice—the same one old Roderick McKenzie is following now. Long after my father was due to take his reward in the boardroom in Montreal, he chose to stay here rather than abandon my mother. I'm going to sleep now."

The tautness of his body beside hers told her that wherever he had gone it wasn't to sleep. Marie couldn't puzzle out what had set him off. If anything, the story about his father seemed rather comforting and sweet. Wappeston had lived through so many deaths around him that he couldn't possibly still be disturbed by two that had happened so long ago—his mother when he was six and his father two years later. . . .

Then it hit her that Cuthbert Grant, Sr., had died of a fever on his way east to attend the annual North West Company rendezvous at Fort William—the first one he'd attended for many years, according to Cuthbert Grant, Jr. Fort William had been the halfway point where the canoe brigades from Montreal and the *pays d'en haut* met and then headed back where they came from. Maybe Wappeston's father hadn't had any intentions of coming back.

She felt a strong inclination to wrap her hands around the neck on the pillow beside her—or as much of it as her hands could encompass—and shriek: "For Christ's sake, let it go—all this happened before I was born!" But instead she lay there silently staring into the same dark he was staring into, skin to skin and miles apart.

After breakfast Colin Robertson went out to saddle his horse and came back laughing. Marie asked him what was funny.

"Your husband's in the barn, building a new stall for the new calf."

"I know."

"Well, I've never seen anyone so cheerfully incompetent in my life." He turned to his wife. "I won't be back before late tonight at the earliest. If it turns out I have to stay over, don't worry."

Marie went on about the business of her day, utterly flummoxed by the notion that anyone might think they could learn anything from her about how people conducted themselves in the outside world. Mrs. Robertson was fascinated by the process of making tea in a teapot instead of just tossing a handful of leaves in a kettle and awestruck that Marie, Josephte, and Maria Theresa could all read and write and even little Eliza could puzzle her way through a page of print if the words weren't too big.

While giving Nancy her midmorning meal, Marie said: "I think the white women—I mean, the ones in the east—go away into a private room to do this, and shut the door."

"Why?"

"I don't know. They think it's dirty or something. And they wean their babies a lot younger, too—maybe around a year or so."

"How can they eat before they got any teeth?"

"I guess the mothers make up a mush, or soup or something."

"Seems like a lot of trouble to go to when it's right there. Maybe they figure it's worth it so they can get pregnant again sooner. Though I don't see how they can be pregnant all the time wearing those things they got to wear."

"What things?"

"Coarse-lets. Colin says I should ask Mrs. Simpson when I meet her and maybe she'll show me one. He says they make them from the bones of a whale, and you have to lace it up tight all around your body to make your waist look small."

"How could you breathe?"

Mrs. Robertson just shook her head tremulously, eyes big with apprehension. "I'm sure he's making it sound worse than it is. It's probably just like a tight sash or something."

The back door crashed open and Maria Theresa and Eliza and several cousins came charging in, snatched up two of the kitchen chairs, and thundered back toward the doorway. "Hey! Where do you think you're—"

"We'll bring 'em back, Maman!" and the door slammed.

Marie shrugged at Mrs. Robertson. "I guess the women back east wouldn't stand for their children running wild like that. Me, I find it's all I can do just to keep them from throwing food at each other or playing on the ice in the spring."

"I got brought up the same way your kids are, and I bet you did, too. And we neither of us have shat on anyone's kitchen table lately, so far as I know. It made me feel funny, day before yesterday, seeing my boys in the parson's school with their hands clasped just so on their desks and saying 'Yes, sir' to the teacher. I guess it's good for them, but it did make me feel funny."

"Well, now that Nancy's got her fill, I guess I better be making dinner for the ones with teeth."

When she stepped out the back door to assemble the family to eat, Maria Theresa and Eliza were coming out of the bush carrying the chairs over their heads. "You scrape the mud off those legs before you take them inside."

"Ours, or the chairs?"

"Both. And tell your father there's food on the table."

"Yes, Maman. We got more company again."

She followed Maria Theresa's point to Colin Robertson turning his horse in from the cart trail. She waved and called cheerily: "Lucky I always cook too much. I thought you weren't going to be back till—" And then he was close enough for her to see his face. It was as red and raw-looking as if someone had flayed off the skin. The wine-colored laurel wreath of his hair looked almost purple by comparison.

He reined in his horse in front of her and said stiffly: "Would you be good enough to tell my wife to get her things together?"

"Does she have to see Mrs. Simpson today?"

"Mister Simpson informed me that the notion of his wife entertaining a native woman for tea was utterly preposterous and he couldn't imagine what could have possessed me to suggest such a thing.

"Would you please tell my wife to collect her things so we can get back to Red River and continue on our journey as soon as possible."

The Robertsons were gone before the soup had cooled noticeably.

Marie didn't feel much like eating, and it didn't appear that Wappeston did, either. As she and Josephte were cleaning up the dishes, he said: "Well, in a way, he's hoist on his own damned petard."

"Who is?"

"Robertson. In the old days, before he met his lovely half-breed girl, he used to humorously refer to other traders' native wives as 'Japan ladies.'"

"Why Japan?"

He just pointed his thumb over his shoulder at the shelf where the japanned tin tea canister stood—baked-on black lacquer.

She went with him on the summer buffalo hunt. The family had grown to the point where Wappeston had to get two new carts made. At least Maria Theresa was old enough now to drive one of them. When the hunt wound its way home, Marie got the belated news about Frances Simpson—her frail little son had died.

A few days before it was time to set off on the autumn hunt, Wappeston said: "I'll have to take a jaunt to Red River tomorrow. High time I brought our account up to date."

"I'll come with you. I haven't seen the stone fort yet." Although the new fort was officially Lower Fort Garry, even the Company men referred to it simply as the stone fort.

He shook his head. "If it was the old fort, it'd be an easy jaunt back and forth in a cart, but all the accounts are at the stone fort now, so—"

"I can still ride a horse. And Nancy's cradleboard slings over my shoulder just fine."

She hadn't thought of the fact that, at a trot, the cradleboard also bounced just fine. After the first hour she asked Wappeston to stop for a minute, unlaced Nancy and her mossbag from the cradleboard, and made a sling with her shawl, leaving the cradleboard on the prairie to retrieve on the way home. It would've been a lot longer journey if they'd followed the trail—paralleling the Assiniboine to the Forks and then a right angle north—but they just set a straight course across the prairie from Grantown to the halfway point between the Forks and the delta of the Red. Wappeston remarked: "Someday soon—though not in our lifetimes, if I have anything to say about it—people won't be able to do this."

"Do what?"

"Cut across country to wherever they want to go. All of this will be private property—either towns or fenced fields. If the public right-of-way winds forty miles to a point ten miles from Grantown, Nancy's children and grandchildren will just have to get used to swallowing the extra thirty. Either that or find themselves up on charges for trespassing. 'O brave new world . . .' "

"From what you said about the east, the people there'd be a lot happier living here, even if they have to go an extra thirty miles to follow the road."

"I would have to strain very hard to care less about the people in the east. What the hell—*après nous le déluge*."

Even traveling in a straight line, it took half the morning before the pink-grained white stone walls of the new fort appeared among the green fringe of trees flanking the Red. Marie had expected that they'd have to ride around to the wall facing the river to get in, but there was a gate on the inland wall as well. On either side of the gate, the walls sprawled out for several hundred yards to the fat, round bastions at the corners. The walls were dotted with rectangular loopholes for rifles and the bastions with square ones for cannons.

Inside the gate was a pink-and-white-graveled road that branched off at right angles. Wappeston took the left fork. Marie twitched her horse's halter to follow along, but she kept her eyes trained to the right, on a massive house made of whitewashed wood and pink stone.

He reined in in front of a big stone building with iron hitching rings fixed into its face, slid off his horse, and raised his arms to help her off hers. He said: "This shouldn't take long. Do you want to come in with me or . . . ?"

"No—Nancy's hungry." She found a shaded spot under an elm tree, settled down with her back against the trunk, nestled Nancy under the yoke of her dress, and looked around for an explanation for why the stone fort should give her this odd, tingly, twitchy feeling. The place was a series of boxes within boxes. Inside the stone square of the walls was another square, of warehouses, barracks buildings, bake houses, countinghouse, and stonewalled sheds, all fronting the hollow square of the roadway. Inside the graveled square was a square of manicured lawn, fronted by a white fence and bordered with rosebushes. The lawn surrounded the white-verandahed monument that housed George Simpson's pale flower.

In the time it took Nancy to drink her fill and fall asleep, nothing moved behind the white fence except the roses nodding in the breeze. It seemed to Marie that she'd just focused her eyes on the house when Wappeston's voice started calling: "Marie? . . ." He was standing by the horses, peering from side to side. She cradled Nancy in the crook of one arm, letting the yoke of her dress drop back over her breast, and stood up where he could see her. "Ah, there you are. Simpson's got a good crop of new clerks—didn't take as long as I'd thought."

She had just untied her pony's halter when George Simpson came trotting through the riverfront gate, accompanied by a woman in a candy-striped dress and a wide-winged straw bonnet, riding a glossy black horse. "Riding," though, wasn't quite the word—at least not in any way that made sense to Marie. Instead of straddling the horse's back where she could get a good grip with her knees, Mrs. Simpson was perched sideways on some precarious contraption that her voluminous skirts hid.

The straw bonnet swung in the direction of the countinghouse just long enough for Marie to get a glimpse of a porcelain face framed with dark ringlets, then it swiveled back toward the tall top hat on the little man bouncing along beside. Simpson leaned sideways to catch whatever it was she was saying, nodding his head gravely and flicking his eyes at the front of the countinghouse where Marie and Wappeston were standing.

Two grooms came running as the governor and his lady reined in in front of the white fence. Simpson helped his wife to dismount and then turned and started toward the countinghouse as his wife proceeded through the gate and up the flower-bordered walkway to her house.

"Good to see you, Grant; it's been too long. Mrs. Grant, you're looking well."

"Thank you."

"And what's this little fellow's name?"

"Margeret Nancy." As soon as she'd said it she felt cheap. She'd been hoping to have an opportunity to tell him someday, but that had been before they'd lost their son.

"Would you walk with me a moment, Grant? I just wanted to mention something to you that . . ." The voices faded out of Marie's earshot as Wappeston's moccasins and Simpson's boots crunched across the gravel roadway. Wappeston walked him back to the white gate and stopped there. They talked a moment longer, and then Wappeston turned and started back. It might have been just her imagination, but it seemed to Marie that she saw sunlit ice blue flares stabbing into her husband's back again, in the instant before George Simpson turned on his heel and proceeded through his gate.

As Wappeston swung up onto his saddle, she said: "What was that all about?"

"Hm? Oh, it seems that Mrs. Simpson would be quite delighted to have me drop around for tea someday, given my refined education and all. . . ."

"What did you say?"

"I told him that my wife and I would be more than delighted to receive an invitation."

He turned his horse and then reined it in again when he saw she wasn't falling in alongside. She said: "Maybe . . . maybe you could go back and tell him you wouldn't mind after all if it's just you. She must get awful lonely."

He laughed so hard he almost fell off his horse. He recovered enough breath to gasp out: "Oh, God . . . is there any living thing in this world, Waposis, that you can't find a soft spot for?"

The following spring, the brigade heading north to meet the ship at York Factory had to add on another York boat to carry Frances Simpson and all her possessions, except the piano. Wappeston said: "Apparently Simpson's promised to build her a big house in Lachine, just outside of Montreal, so they can at least live on the same continent. I'll lay you any odds you care to name, Waposis, that within two years George Simpson will be telling the new recruits—with the same earnestness he's been advising them to import a lovely, tender exotic of their own—that the only woman for a fur trader is a daughter of the country."

She didn't take the bet.

CHAPTER 33

The year that Frances Simpson left the *pays d'en haut* for good, Grant whiled away the winter with an interesting experiment. It started in the fall, when one of the Company clerks with a botanical bent happened to mention that a certain broad-leafed vine was wild hops. Marie knew it by a Cree name and also knew several places around Grantown where it grew in profusion. As luck would have it, Marie's father happened to possess a basic knowledge of the principles of beer making, culled from a junior clerk he'd wintered with once along the Qu'Appelle who'd started his working life as a brewer's apprentice.

Grant filled a sack with spikes of hop flowers and hung it up beside the kitchen chimney to dry. He then promptly forgot about it until the first heavy snow, when Marie asked him if he was ever going to take down that sack so she could use the wall peg for hanging up wet moccasins like it was intended.

With his scientific zeal reawakened, Grant went out into the barn and made a selection from the row of empty barrels left over from past years' personal outfits and indents. It wasn't easy manipulating the barrel into the kitchen and down into the root cellar. But he managed to get it down and set up in a corner next to the potato bin without crushing any of his children. Then he went next door to roust out his learned father-in-law. The two of them commandeered the kitchen hearth and Marie's largest pot to render a mixture of barley and water into a thick sludge. They dumped the sludge into the barrel, crumbled in a few handfuls of hops, and filled it up the rest of the way with buckets of river water. Then Grant went back into the kitchen to ask Marie for a cupful of yeast.

"What for?"

"We need yeast to ferment the beer."

She shook her head dubiously. "I don't know if you're supposed to use bread yeast for beer."

"Yeast is yeast, isn't it?"

"I ain't so sure. I don't know any more about making beer than you do. But yeast is tricky stuff. One batch don't necessarily act the same as another."

"Well, there's one way to find out. Where do you keep it?"

"In the *rogan* over there—the one with the cross on the front." He moved toward the shelf of stopper-topped, birchbark buckets of various shapes and sizes. "But don't use a whole cupful—just enough to cover the bottom."

He compromised with half a cup. He poured it on top of the tepid concoction, gave it a stir, and then hammered a lid on. Then he and Angus McGillis went off to find things to keep them occupied while they were waiting.

Three nights later someone fired off a gun inside the house. Grant fell out of bed, tugged on his trousers, and ran downstairs. He couldn't see or hear anyone moving, but that could be due to the feeble light from the coals on the hearth and the commotion of thumping and startled wailing from upstairs. He peered into the shadows, cursing himself for growing so complacent as to leave his rifle hanging up unloaded and his pistols locked in a trunk.

Marie's voice drifted dryly down the stairs: "Perhaps you should check the cellar."

He lit a candle from the hearth coals, carried it into the kitchen, and raised the cellar trap. A thick smell of sour bread and herbs wafted up, accompanied by a bubbling, dripping sound. He thrust the candle in front of him and climbed cautiously down the stairs.

Where the flat head of the barrel should have been, there was now a writhing dome of white bubbles with brown flecks boiling within it. In the growing brown lake at the foot of the barrel, the cracked midslat of the lid floated serenely. The candlelight showed a white, splintered scar on the rafter it had bounced off.

A sputtering and rustling sound came from above and behind him. He turned around to find Marie perched on the top step with one hand over her mouth and the other holding out a bucket filled with rags. She peeled her hand off her mouth as though intending to speak and then promptly clapped it back on again, shoulders shaking and eyes bugging out. She rattled the bucket at him until he took it from her, then she reached into her lap and held out his shirt and moccasins, finally finding enough of her voice to say: "So you don't catch cold while you're squelching around in the mud mopping this up."

"I can leave it till morning. Most of it will soak into the floor."

"If it soaks into my potatoes, you're going to have to do a lot of hunting and fishing come February. I'll keep the bed warm for you."

He set the candle on the step she'd vacated and went to work sopping up the lake with rags and wringing them out into the bucket. By the time the bucket was full there was only a puddle left, and the overflow from the barrel had settled down to an occasional dribble. He built a rag dam between the puddle and the potato bin, left his muddy moccasins on the top step, and went up to bed. In the morning he was carrying another couple of bucketfuls out to the horses, who seemed to have a taste for it, when Falcon ambled by. Falcon stopped to sniff the air and remarked: "You been making Irish oatmeal."

"Making what?"

"Last week I was riding by the farm of one of them old English Hudson's Bay men in what they're starting to call Little Britain, down around the stone fort. I smelled that exact same smell and I asked him what it was. He said he was making Irish oatmeal and then walked away laughing. I think maybe he's a little touched in the head."

"Well, well. . . . " Grant knew perfectly well that several of the Kildonan people had begun practicing the ancient Highland art the instant their barley fields started producing more than was necessary to feed their families. But he hadn't known that anyone at Red River was brewing beer. "How would you like to take a little ride with me tomorrow, and show me which old Englishman that was?"

It was a tricky proposition. Although the Company and the colony officially forbade the manufacturing of spirituous liquors, they were both content to look the other way, as long as no one sold it to the Indians. But anyone who was doing a little home brewing at Red River was still bound to be somewhat less than forthcoming if the warden of the plains came nosing around.

The old Englishman remained wooden-faced and purse-mouthed until Grant launched into a description of the recent experiment. When he got to the part about the exploding barrel head, the wooden face cracked into cackles of laughter. "*Yeast?* You put *yeast* in the beer?"

"Yeast is the necessary fermenting agent."

"*Brewer's* yeast! Brewer's yeast don't rise!"

"Oh. Well . . . how would one go about getting one's hands on such an article in Rupert's Land? Writing 'brewer's yeast' on the order for one's personal outfit would seem rather like rubbing the Company's nose in—"

"Don't be misled by the name. Brewer's yeast has many uses. For instance"—the old man's voice went grave—"you might not think it to look at me, but I have anemic blood. It's a well-known fact that a spoonful of brewer's yeast in an old man's morning mush will greatly increase the nutritional properties."

"Ah. So then you'd naturally tend to keep a more-than-adequate supply on hand."

"I might. I might. You might like to come have a look inside my barn. It's a curious fact about barns—the warmth from the animals keeps the temperature above freezing in even the worst of winters. It means that people don't have to trouble themselves with wrestling barrels in and out of root cellars, and blowing holes in the parlor floor and . . ."

Now there were three hardy scientists experimenting away in the Grantown laboratory—Grant and Angus McGillis and Pierre Falcon. They crumbled a corner of a cake of brewer's yeast into the barrel in the barn, hammered down the lid, crossed themselves, and waited three weeks. It didn't explode in the interim, but when they broached it what they found was rather thin and bitter. They tried more yeast and less hops in the next batch. It was an improvement, but not much. Next time they left the barrel sealed for six weeks. When the great day came, the snow was almost gone and every other man in Grantown was scattered out to the sloughs and lakes with bulging pouches of birdshot. Grant and his father- and brother-in-law assembled in the barn with a hatchet and three tin cups.

Grant gave Angus the privilege of stoving in the latest barrel head. Inside was a black-brown, effervescent well. They skimmed off the splinters, dipped in their cups, and took tentative sips. Grant tongued his lips and said: "Not bad."

Falcon shook his head, "You're just getting used to it," then swallowed half a cup. They emptied their cups and dipped and drank again and laughed and congratulated each other. After another cup it seemed like a good idea to sit down in the straw to drink the next one. The point when Grant realized they'd succeeded better than they'd hoped was when he stood up to refill his cup the fifth or tenth time and found the mouth of the barrel opening and closing like a spastic sphincter.

Marie's voice and a male voice were bellowing, "Wappeston!" and "Mister Grant!" He managed to focus his eyes on the barn door as the two of them came pelting in—Marie and one of the Red River métis. Out of the jumble of their voices hitting his thick ears, he finally heard: "The Sioux are at the Forks!"

Grant had been shocked sober before. This time it only made the difference between falling down and stumbling. He shouted at Falcon and Angus: "One of you ride north and one south! Get all the men you can find. I'm going to get the Saulteaux." Then he headed for the door, shooing Marie ahead of him. "Get my rifle and pistols while I saddle up."

It took a few minutes to catch one of the grazing ponies and even longer to get a saddle and bridle on it, and then there was the question of mounting. Grant managed to get aboard on his third try. Marie was standing at the back step holding several objects in both hands. He stopped beside her, flopped the pistol holsters across his horse's neck, slung his powder flask and bullet bags over his shoulder, snagged his rifle, and galloped west toward the Saulteaux mission that had grown up as an offshoot of Grantown.

The ride for the Forks with the Saulteaux was a patchwork blur of cobalt-blue runoff ponds, sap-rising yellow-and-red willows, and gleaming white streaks of stubborn snowdrifts. As his horse splashed up the east bank of Catfish Creek, Fort Garry came into view. He wouldn't have been able to see it from there if the trees had been in leaf. There didn't appear to be any smoke rising from it, beyond the usual thin columns out of chimneys. He strained his ears ahead for gunfire without hearing any, but that could have been because of the cacophony of hoofbeats and war songs surging along behind him.

As the fort drew closer, he could make out a large number of men and horses milling about on the Assiniboine side of the plantation. They were separated into two distinct groups. One group was dressed in black broadcloth or dun-colored homespuns, the other in beaded buckskin and dyed feathers. But every man of them was brandishing a weapon. In the front rank of the gaudier contingent, Grant picked out the green-daubed horse and red horned hat of La Terre Qui Brûle.

Grant's horse was foam-flecked and gasping, but he whipped it mercilessly through the last few hundred yards and then reined in hard at the edge of the melee. Unfortunately the world continued jouncing up and down as though he were still passing through it at a gallop. Several hundred voices were shouting, in Sioux, Saulteaux, French, English, Gaelic, and maybe Italian, for all he knew.

He focused his eyes on La Terre Qui Brûle and cocked his rifle. The hollering voices were suddenly underscored with a percussive medley of answering gun clicks and the hammering of war clubs on bull's-hide shields.

Grant was about to wave Urbain Delorme forward to tell La Terre Qui Brûle that the Sioux were outgunned and had best clear off back where they came from, when he noticed an odd thing. The guns of the colony and Company men were pointed not at the Sioux, but at him and the Saulteaux. The colony governor and the chief trader of Upper Fort Garry came toward him with their rubbery maws working in unison. He managed to separate the timbre of their voices from the general din so he could pick out a phrase here and there—first "drunken fool" and then enough scraps of sentences to piece together the gist.

The Sioux had come to the Forks to ask the Hudson's Bay Company to establish a trading post in Sioux territory. The chief trader had regretfully informed them that the Company wasn't allowed to operate south of the American border. So the Sioux had been about to start back home with nothing to show for their long journey except a few kind presents from their good friends the "Hussens Bay Men."

A wiry man with grizzled blond hair limped up beside Grant's horse. Grant looked down into the stricken face of Alexander Sutherland, who hissed in Gaelic: "For God's sake, man—clear off before you start another massacre."

Grant turned his horse around to face the line of Saulteaux shouting taunts and insults at the Sioux. He chopped his hand through the air to silence them and said, "They came in peace. Urbain—tell La Terre Qui Brûle we'll guarantee him safe passage," then nudged his horse forward. The Saulteaux parted reluctantly to let him pass. He didn't look back, but he gauged from the hoof sounds that enough of the Saulteaux had fallen in behind him to give the rest no choice but to do the same.

The ride home was at a much slower pace. They encountered several groups of Grantown men along the way, galloping for the Forks. Grant told them it had been a false alarm, and they fell in grumpily at the end of the line.

By the time they reached the Passage of the Assiniboine, the sun was going down and Grant was brutally sober. He heard a rustling and thudding sound off to his left and turned to look. The Saulteaux were peeling off, taking the side trail south to the ford. Grant trotted his horse around to head them off. Pointing west, he said: "Your homes are that way."

"If we cross here and ride all night, we can get ahead of the Sioux and surprise them."

"We promised them safe passage."

"*You* did."

"That's right—I gave them *my* word. Would you steal my word from me? Your homes are that way." There were some surly mutterings, but the Saulteaux turned their horses west. Grant suspected it had less to do with his moral authority than with the authority of several dozen métis buffalo hunters who'd come galloping to a fight and hadn't gotten one yet.

As his horse plodded into the yard, Marie came flying out the back door, yelling: "What happened?"

"What happened? What happened was that your drunken fool of a husband almost precipitated a wholesale slaughter. He managed to avoid that by a hair, but still managed to disgrace himself."

By the end of the summer buffalo hunt, Grant had gotten to the point where he could look people in the eye again, if it wasn't for too long. He didn't go out on the autumn hunt. There was an epidemic of whooping cough among the children of Grantown. It brought on, or was coupled with, some form of influenza, as far as Grant could diagnose it from his medical books. For weeks he made a daily pilgrimage from one end of Grantown to the other and out to the Saulteaux village, handing out purgatives and emetics and advice he hoped was right. Apparently it was just as bad at Red River, but they had the Company doctor there and Grant had all he could do at Ghost Horse Plains. Marie did as much as she could to help, but she was eight months pregnant and had their own children to care for.

Eliza and Charles and Nancy came down with it. They all recovered, or seemed to, but then Nancy started coughing again. Finally she was the only sick child left in Grantown; the others were either running wild across White Horse Plains once more or lying under the row of little crosses behind the chapel of St. François Xavier.

The end of the epidemic gave Grant a chance to look around, particularly at Marie. She and Nancy had both faded to blue-white ghosts. He said: "I'll take care of Nancy now. You have another child to think of, and that means taking care of yourself."

He put Nancy in a room of her own and, as often as not, spent the night there with her, although it became increasingly difficult to separate the nights from the days. She would appear to rally, then develop other complications. One of them was a diarrhea that left her dehydrated. Marie suggested bethroot soaked in milk, which seemed to help a little. It wasn't possible to keep Marie away entirely, but he would let her have only an hour or so and then shoo her back out. Gradually she began to look like a pregnant woman again instead of a distended-bellied corpse.

Nancy wasted away to a translucent doll with immense black eyes, but she wouldn't quit. The worst times were when he had to stand her in a basin of cold water and sponge her to bring down her fever. She would scream and cry and flail her tiny hands at his as he told her over and over that he didn't want to torture her, knowing full well he could never make her understand.

One evening, or perhaps it was morning, he was cupping her naked body against his chest with one hand while his other hand emptied out another mossbag soaked with shit soup, when Josephte stuck her head in the door and hissed: "It's time! We need the bethroot."

He fumbled around for the bethroot pouch. When he picked it up, it flapped slackly, with a rattle of dry fragments in the bottom. "Take it." Then he repacked Nancy's mossbag—he was getting adept at doing it one-handed—and squatted down on the buffalo robe on the floor to go to work rocking and crooning his baby bunting back to sleep.

Sometime later he began to hear grunting and gasping sounds from down the hall. It took him a while to figure out why he'd suddenly begun to hear them clearly, even though they had the texture of sounds that had been going on for some time. It was because the wheezing, bird-chest sound his ears had been attuned to for so long had stopped.

He lifted Nancy's mouth to his ear, then put the tip of his forefinger against the side of her neck just under her jaw, then laid her down on the buffalo robe and creaked slowly to his feet. His journey down the stairs was more in the realm of skidding than stepping, with his hand skimming along the banister rail to keep his balance. There was a still-sealed bottle of brandy in the kitchen. Falcon was sitting at the kitchen table. Grant went by him without saying a word, but when he emerged from the pantry Falcon was on his feet with two tin cups hooked over one finger and two blankets slung over his shoulder. Falcon said: "There's a nice spot by the river where we can dip our cups to wash it down."

The next morning Grant woke up to an orange sky that the orange starbursts behind his eyes were trying to merge with. In front of him, a bed of orange coals was flickering out within the ashes of a campfire. Falcon was sitting on the other side of the fire with a blanket around his shoulders and his back against a tree. Falcon leaned sideways to dip a cup in the river and then handed it across the dying coals. Grant took a sip, then fumbled for the brandy bottle. Falcon puffed out his upper lip like a bagpipe bellows, let the air out with a soft pop, and said: "You got a son."

Grant grunted. He seemed to remember someone telling him that earlier. Falcon said: "That was some good song you made up last night."

"Song?"

"I don't remember it too good. It was a funny-sounding English. Something about not blaming your partial fancy and 'Nothing could resist my Nancy, But to see her was to love her. . . .' "

"Robert Burns."

"If you're up to walking, you better go see Marie."

Grant took hold of the poplar trunk behind him and climbed up it to his feet. The house was a long way away, but he managed the march to the door and up the stairs. Josephte sniffed at him as he lurched through the bedroom door, then got out of the way as he thudded down on his knees beside the bed. He opened his mouth to say something to Marie, but nothing came out. She levered out one stubby hand from under the covers, exposing a glimpse of the translucent-skinned head sucking on her breast, and pressed her warm palm against his temple. He said: "Nancy . . . she—"

"Ssh. I know."

"I'm sorry."

"You did everything you could, and so did I. We ain't God, Wappeston—no matter how many people expect you to be."

"I've thought about what to name him."

"I thought we'd settled on—"

"Louis for a boy or Louise for a girl"—he nodded—"and Louis's what we'll call him. But now that they've started registering births at St. Francis Xavier he'll need a full baptismal name. I thought perhaps 'Cuthbert-Marie Louis George.'"

" 'George'?"

"They lost theirs."

Her eyes slitted for an instant. Then she said: "One of these days you're going to regret being so good to that son of a bitch."

"As good as you are to this one?"

Part Four

GONE TO SEED

Grant has not yet returned from the War. I daresay you will hear the result before I can.

NICOL FINLAYSON TO JAMES HARGRAVE

There was a magistrate there, a Mister Grant; he was one of the best there. . . .

LIEUTENANT COLONEL WILLIAM CALDWELL,
IN TESTIMONY TO THE COLONIAL SECRETARY,
SELECT COMMITTEE OF
THE IMPERIAL HOUSE OF COMMONS

CHAPTER 34

In the winter of 1837, a ragged party composed of three dog sleds and eleven men staggered out of a blizzard through the gates of Fort Garry. It was all that was left of the expedition of Montezuma II, General James Dickson, the liberator of the Indian Nations, that had set sail from Buffalo six months earlier with flags flying and cannons booming.

General Dickson spent his first two days and nights at Red River flat on his back, sipping buffalo broth and burning with frostbite. On the third day he sprang up jauntily, shaved his saber-scarred cheeks, and did an inventory of the two paltry trunks of his personal equipage that had survived the journey. There were a dozen uniforms in various resplendent hues and styles, a sack of extra gold and silver braid and epaulets, his inlaid general's sword, a coat of chain mail, and a collection of false beards and mustaches. A lesser man might have sat down and wept at the thought of all the crates of rifles and ammunition jettisoned or bartered along the trail, but General Dickson decked himself out in his white hussar's uniform and requested an immediate interview with the officer commanding. All in all, prospects were far from grim. The Hudson's Bay Company would certainly recognize a letter of credit when they saw one, and the liberator had several. Most important of all, Mister Grant, the Chief of the Red River half-breeds, was just around the corner.

The general was ushered in to see the chief factor of Upper Fort Garry, who said: "Do sit down, General. Glad to see you up and about. I'm afraid Mister Simpson is wintering at Lachine this year, so . . ."

"No need to apologize. I asked to see the commanding officer, and if that's you, you're just the man I want to see. I have several bank drafts here I'd like to draw on."

The chief factor looked them over, raising his eyebrows appreciatively at the numbers, and then shrugged. "I'm sorry—I would like nothing better than to add portions of these to our accounts, but I'm afraid I've been instructed not to honor your bank drafts."

"Not to *what*? Can't you read? Barclay's Bank, Lloyd's of London, the Bank of Montreal—"

"I'm sorry, General, but I have my orders. I don't determine Company policy. As much as it pains me to say so, you are of course perfectly free to take your business elsewhere."

"Such as *where*?"

The chief factor didn't rub it in by saying something along the lines of "Go straight south to the Mississippi and bear left four or five hundred miles." Instead he coughed delicately and said: "I've also been instructed to extend every hospitality to you and your six followers—"

"Eleven."

"Well, as it turned out, five of them happened to be experienced voyageurs, the ones you'd hired on in Montreal. We informed them that the Company is always looking for experienced tripmen, and they . . ."

"Deserted."

"Come, come, General—they aren't soldiers, only workmen hired on for wages. Given that they haven't seen any wages for several months now . . . But as I was saying, I've been instructed to extend you every hospitality during your stay here, and I expect you've had your fill of winter traveling for one year. You'll find the winters at Red River aren't nearly so grim as might appear. The winter is our social season, and several of our local social set are champing at the bit to have you as their guest of honor."

"What you mean to say is if it's inevitable I might as well lie back and enjoy it."

"Pardon me?"

"Oriental philosophy."

"Oh. I'm C of E myself, but you'll find we've learned to be broadminded in Rupert's Land."

"Where would I find Mister Grant?"

"We don't see him often at Red River. His home is in Grantown, some miles west of here. It seems to me I heard he's out on the plains just at present. There's been a bit of an outbreak of typhus and Mister Grant is by way of being a bit of a doctor. I do hope you'll honor us at the factor's table this evening. The cook's managed to get his hands on a couple of beaver tails."

What with the Upper and Lower Forts Garry, the mansions of retired fur traders, the Anglican and Catholic bishops, and the most prosperous elements of the Kildonan and St. Boniface farmers, General Dickson soon worked his way through every article of apparel in his trunks, excluding the coat of chain mail and false facial hair. The procession of dinners, teas, and dances reached the point where he had to start mixing and matching pieces of different uniforms so as not to repeat himself. At every event he scoured the assemblage for anyone who looked as though he might be Mister Grant, and he asked his hostess if Mister Grant was in attendance. Invariably the chief factor's "We don't see him often at Red River" was borne out.

Very early one morning, the door of General Dickson's room crashed open and a large figure filling the doorway said flatly: "You been looking for Mister Grant."

It was difficult to discern details in the half-light of a winter dawn, not to mention the blurring effect of half-awake eyes, but the general managed to make out a thick mane of blue-black hair blending into a black fur cap, flares of beadwork encrusting the knee-high moccasins, and white clumps of snow falling off the white blanket coat onto the floor. He said: "It's a pleasure to meet you at last, Mister Grant."

The fur-hatted head swiveled slowly from side to side and a thick-tongued tenor voice said: "I ain't him. Me, I'm Jean Baptiste Falcon. I got a message from my uncle saying come get you. I give you breakfast on the road."

The carriole went past a large white house on the right side of the road and turned in at an even larger one, with a widow's walk crowning its roof peak. There was a bell-towered church next door with a rectory behind it.

The dogs pulled up at the front step of the house. General Dickson climbed out of the carriole as Jean Baptiste stripped off his snowshoes, panting a bit from the twenty-mile run. Jean Baptiste beckoned him to follow and opened the door without knocking.

Beyond the doorway was a vast sprawl of a room filled with firelight and fur rugs and people with black eyes and high cheekbones. The vast majority of the people were children, ranging from pudgy toddlers to gangly adolescents. The adults consisted of three women and two men. One of the men was a loose-jointed scarecrow with grizzled, wispy whiskers and eye pouches like a bloodhound. The other was a big man with a coarse-cut black mane and a bloated, battered face that might have been quite handsome once—giving an overall impression rather like a heavyweight boxer gone off his training. The strange thing was that the battered boxer's eyes and those of the shortest woman's were exactly alike, although otherwise there wasn't the slightest resemblance. Both pairs of eyes were hooded and opaque, with a Mongolian fold in the corners. They weren't exactly threatening or challenging, just utterly direct and utterly unreadable—like looking into a black mirror. Undoubtedly the man was a onetime stalwart strong-arm that Mister Grant kept around for old times' sake. The hound-dog-eyed fellow must be another retainer of one kind or another, perhaps court jester, given his glum, purse-mouthed expression.

There were many shouted jovialities at Jean Baptiste, in the French-Cree patois that was so tantalizingly frustrating to someone whose Parisian French was as good as General Dickson's. When the jovialities died down, he employed it to say: "Would someone be kind enough to inform Mister Grant that General Dickson is—"

"You just did." The crisp-consonanted baritone had emanated from the down-at-the-heels boxer, in English. "How do you do, Montezuma? Would you care for a cup of homemade gin—my lady wife is a dab hand at locating and gathering juniper berries."

General Dickson's checkered past had given him a wealth of experience in imbibing spirituous liquors, running the gamut from knocking back vodka toasts with Russian counts to swilling tequila with Mexican bandits. But he'd never seen anyone put it away like Mister Grant without showing any noticeable effects—although by the end of the evening the general was hardly in any condition to notice slurring or stumbling on anyone else's part.

He woke up in a feather bed to the sound of several dozen children's voices chanting through the floorboards. It would be fair to say he had a bit of a head on. There was a pitcher of water and a basin on a stand by the bed. He poured half of it down his throat and used the other half to tidy himself up as much as possible without a mirror. He buckled himself into his mauve-and-silver uniform, tugged on his boots, and stepped into the corridor.

There was a slim girl of about sixteen or so taking some linens from a blanket press. He assumed she must be the Maria Theresa who'd stayed out late at a dance last night—or a "kick-up," as the local parlance would have it—which had appeared to cause her mother some concern. A pair of black eyes flashed over her shoulder, and she chirped: "Good morning, General."

"Good morning."

"My father's downstairs at his desk." She brushed past him, carrying an armload of bedclothes, giving the general second thoughts as to whether "slim" was entirely accurate. Out of all the pieces of evidence the general had noted as proof of the Métis Nation's innate good sense and taste, none was more decisive than the fact that they did not believe in ladies' undergarments.

As he came down the stairs he discovered the source of the chanting voices. The floor of the big main room was covered with rows of black-haired boys sitting cross-legged. A priest was going up and down the rows examining their slates. The priest glanced up at the stairwell and, without interrupting the lesson, pointed the general toward a corner of the room that had been partitioned off to make a separate room.

The general rapped softly on the door and pulled it open when *"Entrez"* came through it in Mister Grant's whiskey baritone. Inside was more of a cubbyhole than a room, with oiled oak walls sporting a few shelves of books, a brass-bound English rifle and matching fowling piece, a pair of holstered horse pistols, a feather-bedecked coup stick, and various other implements and trophies of a life in the Indian territories. Mister Grant was sitting on an upholstered armchair that had been created by the simple expedient of draping a buffalo robe over a captain's chair. He was holding a goose quill poised over a ledger that was being crowded off his clerk-size desk by a teapot, a square-shouldered green bottle, and a Royal Doulton teacup.

"Ah—good morning, General. Come in, come in," gesturing with the quill pen to close the door behind him. "I'm afraid we're a bit sardined around here on winter mornings. Our parlor happens to be the only enclosed space in Grantown big enough to squeeze all the boys in, consequently . . . One of these days we're going to get around to building an addition to the rectory, but what with this and that . . . What did I do with that damned penknife? The Company clerks keep telling me to switch over to steel pens, but, quite frankly, the amount of writing I do these days isn't worth the effort to adjust myself to newfangled— Would you care for a cup of brandied tea?"

The general swallowed his gorge and muttered: "No, thank you."

"Ah. Well—my wife's been keeping breakfast warm for you. I thought perhaps you might care to take a stroll around the town with me, once I've finished this up. Did you bring along a change of clothes? . . ."

"No. I assumed—"

"A natural assumption. I should've told Jean Baptiste to tell you you'd be staying over. But you can't go tromping through the snow in cavalry boots, though—unless you've got more toes than you can use. Tell Mrs. Grant I've offered you the loan of a pair of winter moccasins, and a woolen shirt and trousers. Won't be exactly Mayfair tailoring, I'm afraid, but around here clothes make the man warm and dry and that's about it. I should be done with this by the time you're done with breakfast."

Mrs. Grant chirped, "Good morning," in that odd, husky, melodious voice. She pointed to a chair and drew out a warming pan of biscuits, smoked goldeye, beef sausages, skillet-crisped potatoes, and a dab of caviar that wasn't quite up to Beluga but damned close and quickly fried up four eggs to go with it. Around his plate she arranged several jars of wild plum or berry jam, a dish of fresh butter, a quarter round of country cheese, and a gargantuan cup of black tea—thankfully without alcoholic flavoring.

Over the years, General Dickson had grown adept at stuffing his face while entertaining his hostess with amusing stories, some of them bordering on true. But Mrs. Grant surprised him. She wasn't exactly impressed and she wasn't unimpressed. She carried on bustling about the kitchen, shooing the children in and out, coordinating her efforts with those of the hatchet-faced Mrs. Wills, squatting by the hearth to give her more-than-ample breast to the baby hanging on the wall . . . Whenever Dickson was sure she wasn't listening at all, and had decided to make this story the last, the tripwire of the punch line or one of his polished bon mots would spring out a sparkling burst of alto giggles. He had steeled himself against being overawed by Mister Grant, given the reputation. But Mister Grant's reputation was a drop in the bucket of the fact that this beguiling little rock of a woman was his wife.

Mrs. Grant rummaged out a pair of quillworked, high-topped moccasins and a shirt and trousers of thick red blanket cloth. Dickson changed upstairs and came back down holding up the trousers with one hand and drowning in the shirt. Mrs. Grant threw up her hand to cover another cascade of pink-gummed giggles, then pattered out of the kitchen and came back with a woolen sash woven in a multicolored arrowhead pattern. As General Dickson knotted himself together, Mister Grant loomed into the doorway, shrugging on an immense black buffalo coat and chortling jauntily: "Well . . . 'Tybalt, you ratcatcher, will you walk? . . .' Oh—just a moment—" reaching up to extricate a silver flask from one of the kitchen shelves. He shook it against his ear, nodded, dropped it into one of the pockets of his buffalo coat, and beckoned General Dickson to follow him outside. On the way outside, Dickson glanced back over his shoulder and caught a glimpse of Mrs. Grant looking at the floor.

The sky was gray cotton wool, which Dickson had learned to interpret as a sign of a relatively gentle day for prairie winters. Mister Grant ushered him through the church next door, with its lathe-turned candlesticks and remarkably ornate carvings, and then along the trail running westward through the village. "That's Urbain Delorme's place on your right—second-best buffalo hunter alive. That lean-to on your left's for ice fishing—leave a net in overnight and you'll have enough to feed your family and sled dogs for a week. Care for a nip to keep the cold off? . . . No? Well, I suppose I'd best, then, so long as I've got the cap off."

As they trundled along on the sled-packed snow, Mister Grant's running patter was interrupted incessantly by good-mornings and snatches of pragmatic gossip from shirtsleeved woodchoppers, tobogganing children, women bearing yoked buckets up the riverbank . . . Mister Grant would toss off a jovial reply or a wave and carry on without breaking stride. The general could discern nothing remotely resembling forelock tugging from the people of Grantown to their Chief. But he also noticed that no one, outside of the people who'd been inside the big white house when he'd arrived yesterday, ever addressed Mister Grant by any name other than "Mister Grant."

General Dickson's guided tour carried on a little farther, through the well-equiped work shed of a pair of carpenters and cartwrights and the interior of the windmill, which unfortunately didn't have enough wind today to turn the sails. Mister Grant glanced at the sun and said: "I'm afraid we'd best be getting back. Court's in session this afternoon."

"Court?"

"Yes. The Company had to create district courts. A few years back, the London Committee finally got around to buying out the earl of Selkirk's proprietorship of the Kildonan colony. It's simplified matters immensely, since the days of two separate governors and administrations, but it did make the Company entirely responsible for the affairs of everyone in Rupert's Land. Consequently, I am the magistrate of the western district."

Mrs. Grant was just setting out another vast meal for her family and several guests, among whom was an Indian who preferred to sit on the floor rather than at the table. When everything on the table had been demolished, Mister Grant stood up and said: "Well, I suppose we'd best get down to business."

Dickson fell in with the rest of the guests trooping along behind Mister Grant into the big open parlor. Mister Grant ducked into his cubbyhole of an office, emerging with a folded piece of paper. The rest of the luncheon guests were settling themselves on the parlor chairs or on the floor. The general followed suit. Mister Grant squatted with his back against the hearth wall, lit his pipe, passed his tobacco around, snapped open the piece of paper, and said: "The first case on the docket is MacDougall versus Kitchikew. . . ."

Most of the evidence was given in métis French and an Indian dialect, but General Dickson managed to pick out the gist. Kitchikew had killed and eaten one of MacDougall's bullocks. When both parties had had their say, Mister Grant pulled his pipe out of his mouth and said: "Well now . . . the Company's current purchase price for beef on the hoof is nineteen shillings. I have it on good information that Monsieur MacDougall was planning to sell said bullock to a Monsieur Delorme, and the price of a cow when the transaction is between one man and another—as opposed to dealing with the Company—is more in the neighborhood of fifteen shillings. Monsieur Kitchikew encountered the bullock in question rambling about the bush many miles north of Grantown—which for all intents and purposes made it in his eyes just another wild creature like any moose or deer. Monsieur MacDougall's negligence in providing sufficient fodder to his animals—to the point where they feel constrained to wander so many miles foraging for themselves—puts at least half the blame on him, which reduces the damages to seven and a half shillings. I also understand that Monsieur MacDougall was able to recover the hide, worth approximately two shillings and a half. That leaves five shillings. Now if Monsieur Kitchikew *had* five shillings, he wouldn't have murdered his neighbor's bullock to feed his family. Come spring, though, I'm sure Monsieur Kitchikew's larder will be as brim full with geese and ducks as anyone else's. The Company's currently paying a shilling the brace for goosemeat. So this court sentences Monsieur Kitchikew to deliver ten geese, or the equivalent in ducks, to Monsieur MacDougall by the time the kinnikinnick bells bloom. Next case."

There were two further cases. One involved a pony that had tripped in a gopher hole during the intervening time between a handshake deal to sell it and the new owner's delivery of the purchase price. The other case had to do with a question of the boundary between two farms. General Dickson couldn't quite follow all the ins and outs, but it appeared as far as he could make out that the residents of Grantown didn't own their homes, they were tenants of Mister Grant.

After disposing of the third case, Mister Grant said: "If no one has any surprises to spring, the quarterly session of the Court of White Horse Plains is now adjourned."

It took a moment or two to register on General Dickson. The petitioners and witnesses had all filed out by the time he ejaculated: "*Quarterly?*"

"Hm? Yes, quarterly. And an unusually heavy docket. The last two quarters I had no cases at all."

"How many people are in your district?"

"Well . . . nomadic peoples do have a tendency to come and go. . . . And the northern and western boundaries of the western district are rather nebulous. . . . But at a rough guess, on any given day, I'd say about two thousand more or less."

"Two *thousand?*"

"Excluding the Blackfoot and the Assiniboine, who are nominally in the western district, but . . . Ah—you think three disputes in three months is low. I'd like to say that it's because the citizens of Rupert's Land are innately moral, but the fact is"—with a wink and a crooked grin—"the truly contentious disputes tend to get resolved on the spot, leaving the case sans plaintiff or defendant, one or the other. I'd say you and I are about due for a pot of beer or two. Handing down the law do tend to parch the throat, as Moses used to say."

After supper, Dickson entertained the household in the parlor with adventure stories and Spanish songs. But he had resolved to get down to business before the night was through. The children were packed off upstairs in stages, until finally there was no one left but the general and his host and hostess and Mrs. Wills. He was about to start working his way around to the purpose that had brought him across half a continent when Mrs. Grant chortled to herself and said to her husband without looking up from her baskets of dyed porcupine quills and the swatch of moose hide she was inserting them onto: "I heard you capsizing old MacDougall for letting his cattle roam—"

The general burst into laughter and sputtered: "I *think,* Mrs. Grant, you meant 'chastising.' "

"Marie, perhaps you would be so good as to brew us up another pot of tea to take our rum with." The flat, cold tone of Mister Grant's voice cut off the general's laughter. Mrs. Grant set her work aside, stood up, and headed for the kitchen, with her eyes downcast and her chipmunk cheeks blazing red. Mister Grant's eyes followed her out of the room and then swiveled to General Dickson. They weren't the same eyes Dickson had grown accustomed to over the last day and a half. The hooded shapes were the same, but their opaque, dark centers had been replaced by flamelit black ice.

In his time, General Dickson had been shot at, stabbed, and chased by an irate Corsican husband with a meat axe, but he'd never felt the temperature of a room go from toasty to arctic so immediately. When Mister Grant spoke, it was in a voice barely above a whisper, but General Dickson had not the slightest difficulty hearing every syllable. "General Dickson, my wife has not had the advantage of the kind of formal education to which you and I were privileged. If and when I choose to correct her occasional tendency to overreach herself, I shall do so. Do you understand me?" The general nodded. "Oh, dear, your cup's gone and evaporated. Here, take a drop of the pure while Mrs. Grant is brewing tea."

After Mrs. Grant had come back with the teapot and Mrs. Wills gone off to bed, Dickson decided to take the bull by the horns and said: "You got my letter in the spring? . . ." Mister Grant swallowed his latest sip and nodded. "My purpose remains the same, to march south to Santa Fe with you and your soldiers of the buffalo hunt and sufficient equipage to arm the Indian Nations there to throw off the yoke of their Spanish oppressors. I admit it might sound like an overbold enterprise, but with you and your half-breed cavalry to bolster your oppressed brothers—"

"You needn't convince me that bold enterprises only seem mad until they've succeeded."

"Your reputation led me to expect I need not. However . . . perhaps you've heard that the Company won't honor my letters of credit."

"I had heard something along those lines, yes."

"I have them upstairs in the pocket of—"

"No need to show me. I'm sure they're perfectly valid."

"Well, then you know—and you could explain to your soldiers— that there's plenty of places between here and Santa Fe where those letters of credit could be turned into armaments and provisions and wages."

"Ah. I was wondering when we were going to come down to it. Before you ask me 'yes or no,' there are a few questions I would like to ask you. Imprimis—you don't think that our little tour of Grantown, and the coincidence that you happened to be brought out here on court day, was just a matter of sight-seeing, do you?" The general hadn't thought about it one way or the other, but he kept his mouth closed. "Why should I or anyone else here be even remotely interested in an invitation to build a brave new world five thousand miles away?" Dickson opened his mouth to come up with some reasons, but Mister Grant held up his hand to stop him. "No need to trouble yourself with sophistry, General, because my next question is decidedly *not* rhetorical. Namely: Where did you get your money?"

"There's a lot of gold in Mexico—or there *was*." The general winked. "And a lot of soldiers of fortune running their own private armies."

Mister Grant grunted, "It's possible. I've seen even more fantastical tales proved true. But there is another possibility that occurred to me."

"What possibility is that?"

"News of the outside world does eventually find its way into our little backwater. The Republic of Texas has liberated itself from Mexico, with the help of a good deal of money and arms from the United States of America. In time the Republic of Texas seems bound to become another state of the Union. To the west of Texas is another vast parcel of Mexican land—Santa Fe and California—that the United States would dearly love to get its hands on. And if we of the Hudson's Bay Company's territories were to enlist ourselves in that cause, wouldn't it legitimize the American Republic looking north to annex us next? I have no grudge against the United States of America, but I have no wish to live under her rule, or Canada's or England's or any other country's, for that matter.

"Now all of that may or may not be what you had in the back of your mind when you wrote that letter. Or you may be just as much an unwitting tool of Washington, D.C., as they hope to make of us. Or perhaps your story of Mexican gold is gospel truth. Regardless, my answer is no. You're a charming guest and a good fellow whom I hope to see more of during your stay in Rupert's Land, so let's not hear another word about it. I'm going to bed. Marie? . . ."

"Go on up, Wappeston. I'll follow you as soon as I got this border done."

As the Chief of the Red River half-breeds disappeared into the dark at the top of the stairs, his wife set down her handiwork and said softly: "Maybe you noticed my husband's got a kind of dangerous streak in him sometimes."

"Something along those lines had crossed my mind."

"You see, sometimes, though, he's the most dangerous to himself. Usually when he's making decisions for a whole lot of people, and he knows at bottom he's right, but someone else throws a doubt in that makes him wonder and chew himself up. Like he said, it's a good change to have someone like you here in our home as a guest, and I hope we see you here a lot. But he's gave you his answer and I hope you leave it at that. If you don't—if you keep harping at him about it and get him gnawing at himself—I'm just about the right height to chew your balls off bit by piece, and that's what I'll do.

"Well, it's about time I was climbing up to bed. Wappeston told me you said you'd never had duck dumplings, so that's what we're having for breakfast. Hope you like 'em."

In the spring, after the festival of sugaring off the maple groves at Rivière aux Îlots de Bois, Dickson the liberator embarked from Grantown with the carts and drovers that Mister Grant had appointed to convoy him south to St. Paul. On the morning of his departure, the people of White Horse Plains assembled in the churchyard to bid bon voyage to the general, who stood on the church steps beside Mister Grant.

General Dickson thanked them profusely for their hospitality, then clapped his hands on his shoulders and ripped off his gold epaulets—which he'd spent a portion of the evening cutting almost loose—and clapped them on the shoulders of Mister Grant. Then he flourished his saber out of its scabbard—an official British general's sword, as certified by the College of Arms and the Tower of London—and presented it to Mister Grant, announcing: "*You* are the general. I am but a fraud." The crowd went wild.

CHAPTER 35

Marie was pouring melted tallow into candle molds. It was a tricky business. The pot was heavy and the handle was hot, the wicks didn't want to stay straight, and the steaming, bubbling stream coming out of the spouted pot lip was less inclined to go into the mold than to splatter on the kitchen floor. At least she didn't have to worry about splashing Louis or Angus, because Maria Theresa was keeping an eye on them from her post at the rendering kettle on the hearth. Tending the kettle didn't require much concentration, but Maria Theresa wasn't singing or chattering cheerily as she usually would when performing some task she didn't have to think about. For the last few days she'd been dragging about, bleary-eyed and silent. Maybe she was finally beginning to get the message that even a girl her age couldn't dance till dawn every night without feeling some effects. Marie had given up trying to get the point across through lectures and had simply initiated a policy of rousting her out of bed every morning at the same time as the rest of the family.

A pair of tiny hands were suddenly clutching at Marie's skirt about knee high and a high-pitched voice was wailing: "Mama! I want a cup of—" The voice turned into a muffled squawk as little Angus got himself entangled in the yards of wool around her legs. She could feel her equilibrium starting to go and the pot starting to dip sideways. She could right herself or the pot, but not both. As she started to fall, everything slowed down, to the point where she had time to make sure that Louis was still snuggled peacefully on the hearth rug beside Maria Theresa and then to swing the pot up and back past her shoulder, slinging the boiling tallow out behind her.

She hit the floor with a bruising thump on her right knee and hip. Angus was squealing from somewhere inside the folds of her skirt. The pot was burning her fingers. Maria Theresa was running forward from the hearth rug, where Louis was still snoring away.

Marie let go of the pot, extricated Angus, looked him over to make sure he wasn't hurt, and then rocked him against her breast and told him so. His screams subsided. Maria Theresa, who'd supposedly been minding him, was bending over them with her hands awkwardly clutching at the air, saying: "I'm sorry. . . ."

"*Sorry?* Your little brother just about got boiled in oil! And look at that mess!"

Maria Theresa dropped her head so that her hair covered her face and murmured: "I know. I'll clean it up. I'm sorry. . . ."

"I don't know what the hell's got into you these days!"

"Pascal Breland."

"What?"

And then Maria Theresa was blubbering: "I'm going to have a *baby!* . . . He told me it wouldn't happen if we didn't do it at a full moon."

Marie's first thought was to look around to make sure none of the other children were in hearing distance. Her second was to pick up the pot and whack Maria Theresa across the head with it. But she left the pot where it lay, patted Angus's bottom toward the parlor, climbed to her feet—shaking off Maria Theresa's hands—and thudded down on the nearest chair. By then her fury had settled down to white rage. She said: "Cows go into heat and can't help it, but you're supposed to be a human being."

"Please, Mama—don't you remember what it was like to be young?"

"I'm only thirty years old, for Christ's sake! It wasn't that long ago since I was your age that I can't remember your father and me managed to wait till our wedding night."

"My mother and my father didn't."

Marie looked down at her lap, where her right hand had taken to twisting the ring around the third finger of her left. She fumed and steamed in silence for a moment and then latched on to the name that Maria Theresa had blurted. Pascal Breland was a good ten years older than Maria Theresa. She snapped her head back up to point that out to her, then changed her mind and looked back down at her lap. She muttered to her hands: "Well, at least he isn't married."

"What? I didn't hear you, Maman. . . ."

"I said, 'What did Pascal say when you told him?' "

"I haven't. No one knows but me, and you. . . ."

"You haven't made confession yet?"

"No, I—"

"Go and do that now. Wait! Put a shawl on unless you want to catch your death."

"Maybe it'd be better for everybody if I did."

"Don't talk silly. Go along with you." After Maria Theresa had gone, Marie sat counting her knuckles a while longer, then exhaled a long sigh, grunted up off the chair, and got down on her knees to swab the larger pieces of congealed fat off the floor. She dropped the rags into a basket to save for torches. After swiveling the hook with the kettle on it off the fire, she carried Louis into the parlor and called up the staircase: "Josephte?"

"I'm just making the beds."

"Would you mind looking after the babies for a while?"

"It'd be a change."

Wappeston and John Wills were out in the fields, extending the fence to encompass this fall's new-plowed acre. When she came stumping across the frozen stubble toward them, Wappeston called, "What's wrong?" and came to meet her. John picked up the message that he should keep on working out of earshot.

Wappeston's eyes went dark and murderous as she told the tale. When she was done, he glared off across the dun-colored sweep of White Horse Plains and then laughed brittlely. "Isn't it odd, Waposis—when I was Pascal's age I was carrying on in exactly the same way, and now my immediate inclination is to get out the knife we use to make bull calves into oxen."

"A little late."

"John!"

"Yes, Uncle?"

"Would you be so good as to trot over to the Brelands' place and tell Pascal I want to see him yesterday?" On the way back to the house he shrugged and sighed "Well, Pascal's a pleasant enough young man. With a quick mind, if he ever gets around to applying it to something useful. It's about time he settled down with a home and family of his own."

"Shouldn't that be up to him and Maria Theresa to decide?"

"I'd say they already have."

She was nearly finished helping Josephte mop up the floor, and Wappeston was smacking his lips over the dregs of a cup of brandied tea, when John came back with Pascal Breland. "*Bonjour*, Mister Grant, Madame Grant. . . ." Marie looked up from the floor but didn't reply. No question but that he was a devilishly handsome young man, with high, narrow cheekbones and a diamond-cut jaw and honest-looking eyes. At the moment, though, the overall effect was marred by a chalky tinge in his complexion.

Wappeston stood up and said: "Good of you to come so quick, Pascal. Marie—we'll be in my office. Do give us a knock on the door when . . ."

She nodded. After they were gone she tried sitting down with a cup of tea and waiting, but her hands kept fidgeting. So she put the babies upstairs for an early nap, swung the rendering kettle over the fire, and went back to making candles.

It was another dozen finished candles later before Maria Theresa came back from confession. Marie said: "Sit down a moment. Your father's talking to Pascal."

"He's *what?*"

"Sit!"

Maria Theresa sat. Marie went into the parlor and knocked on the door. Wappeston came out, saying over his shoulder, "Wait here," and hooked his arm into hers to walk her back into the kitchen. Maria Theresa stood up as they came in. Wappeston extended his free hand to cup Maria Theresa's down-bent chin and raise her eyes to meet his. "Pascal has something to say to you."

The wedding took place in the little church of St. François Xavier next door to the house where the newlyweds were going to live for the winter. It was too late in the year to put up a cabin on the lot they'd chosen on the western edge of Grantown, and the groom's home had been with his older brother's family, whose house was already crammed to the rafters with Brelands. So Pascal and Maria Theresa Breland settled into the bedroom that had housed Dickson the liberator.

It took Marie a while to get used to having a son-in-law in the house, especially one who was barely five years younger than she was. But that wasn't near so difficult to get used to as the fact that she was about to become a grandmother. She consoled herself with the thought that she was actually only going to be a stepgrandmother, and that Eliza wouldn't marry as young as Maria Theresa. For the sake of her future husband she'd better not, because she still had a great deal to learn about running a household. Marie hadn't realized how many tasks there were—from milking a cow to smoke-curing moccasin leather—that Eliza knew nothing about except "Maria Theresa will do it."

When spring came, and the new cabin at the edge of town was caulked and thatched, the Pascal Brelands loaded all their possessions onto a cart behind the big white house. Pascal climbed aboard and took the reins while Maria Theresa came back to take little Patrice from his grandmother's arms. But her reaching hands stopped midway to her baby, and one veered up to touch Marie's cheek. "Don't cry, Maman. We'll only be two miles away."

"Then why are *you* crying?"

"I'll miss you."

"Pascal won't. Just ask your father what it's been like living next door to his mother-in-law all these years."

Wappeston said: "Not bad, actually—at least on those days when you can't remember what goes into *tortierre* dough."

Maria Theresa turned to say good-bye to her father but ended up just letting out a strangled squawk and hurling herself against his chest. He smoothed her hair and kissed the top of her head, murmuring: "You're all grown up now."

"No, I'm not!"

"Sssh . . . don't tell Pascal. And the truth of it is"—he lowered his voice to a conspiratorial whisper—"none of us are."

When the cart had rolled past the church and out of sight, his arm came up across Marie's shoulders and he turned to walk her back inside, remarking jauntily: "One down, four to go."

"Five."

CHAPTER 36

Two days after Sophie Caroline was baptized, Grant saddled up the current favorite of his string of saddle horses and rode to Upper Fort Garry for the summer meeting of the Council of the Assiniboia. The horse was the product of a visit from the English stud horse—appropriately named FireAway—that the Company had imported to improve the chunky little breed of prairie horses. The Council of the Assiniboia was the product of George Simpson's desire to occupy himself with business rather than petty domestic squabbles. So he had created the District of Assiniboia to encompass all the permanent settlements in the Northern Department—namely the scattered clumps of farms along the Red and the Assiniboine—and had appointed eight councillors: the Anglican and Catholic bishops and representatives from Kildonan, St. Boniface, the retired fur traders in the vicinity of the stone fort, and White Horse Plains.

Grant was geographically the representative of White Horse Plains and biologically the sole representative of the ninety percent of Assiniboia's population who had at least a touch of the tar brush, if not a thorough coating. He was also one of the two sheriffs of Red River, as well as councillor, magistrate, warden of the plains, and any other title George Simpson cared to dream up—next week perhaps grand panjandrum of the mystic sword.

The sun poured down like melted gold, in terms of both color and heat. Grant stood in his stirrups and peered around to make sure there was no other traffic on the trail before stripping off his shirt. He was not concerned with offending the dignity of his various offices, but rather with offending the eyes of passersby with the sight of a naked forty-five-year-old torso.

The purple thistles flanking the trail were all blown out now, gray and puffed up and ragged around the edges. Gone to seed. They might not be as lovely to look at, but they were accomplishing their purpose.

Grant's current purpose was one he didn't relish. There would be a new seat at the council table today, occupied by a man Grant had never met before. He would have met the man a few weeks earlier when the other councillors had, upon his arrival from Lachine with George Simpson, if it hadn't been for the minor matter of captaining the buffalo hunt. But Grant already knew a good deal about him, and all of it suggested an impending mess that he didn't want to have to clean up.

The man's name was Adam Thom. He'd come to Red River to embody yet another of the Little Emperor's seemingly endless capacity for inventing titles. The recorder of Rupert's Land would essentially be chief justice and codifier of laws for the Court of Assiniboia. Grant thought the invention of a recorder an excellent idea. Filling the office with Adam Thom was another matter.

Grant had first come across Adam Thom's name in the reports of the recent rebellions in Upper and Lower Canada. During the French habitants' agitation for equal rights under English colonial rule, Mister Thom had thoughtfully poured oil on the troubled waters by firing off reams of pamphlets and letters and articles in the Quebec journals, all of which basically said that there would never be peace in Lower Canada until the frogs were forced to speak white and become British citizens in fact as well as in name.

Adam Thom's history didn't bode well in a chief justice placed over a population that was more likely to speak French or Cree or Gaelic than English.

The subject of the Canadian rebellions shifted Grant's mind gratefully from Adam Thom to several extravagant ironies that were probably appreciated by no one on the face of the earth but him—except perhaps the Point Douglas Sutherlands and a few other front-line survivors of the fur trade war. He paused on the bank of Catfish Creek to appreciate them once more and to put his shirt back on, unscrew his flask, and watch a pair of otters initiate their brood into the serious business of mud sliding.

The ironies grew out of the first time Grant had burned the Selkirk colony, the year before Seven Oaks. Duncan Cameron, the North West Company's counter to Colin Robertson, had convinced most of the colonists—including Mrs. Sutherland's brother—to head east to Upper Canada. Twenty years later the boneheaded die-hards at Kildonan were living in peace and plenty, and the clever deserters to Upper Canada had grown desperate enough to rise up in one of the saddest excuses for a rebellion that ever went off half-cocked. One of the stalwarts who'd helped crush it was Duncan Cameron.

Grant toasted his old friend Cameron's impeccable loyalty. Whatever the quarrel or the odds, old Duncan could always be found on the same side—the winning side.

The first toast tasted so good, Grant decided to have another before proceeding to his appointed meeting with the new grand poobah of the little courts in the wilderness. As the whiskey warmth filtered through the walls of his stomach, it began to seem more likely that there was no reason to get his sporran in a knot. Probably Adam Thom's Quebec polemics had only been in response to a particularly tumultuous environment, which Red River certainly wasn't—at least not yet. And even if Adam Thom did turn out to be as much of a disturbing element as Frances Simpson, she had come and gone and the *pays d'en haut* was still there.

He recapped his flask and clucked his horse across Catfish Creek. A few miles farther on, the bastions of Fort Garry loomed over the trees. The Little Emperor had finally given in to geography and caused a massive new fort to be erected at the Forks, leaving the stone fort to languish as a secondary depot. As Grant trotted through the gates he glanced toward the new courthouse with its attached shed of a jail—first sign of impending civilization. The courthouse steps were bereft of councillors having a last nip and a gossip, which meant the meeting was already in session.

The council met in the magistrates' chambers behind the courtroom. As Grant opened the door, his fellow councillors looked back over their shoulders and George Simpson looked up from his sheaf of papers at the head of the table. In a rare bit of coincidence, Simpson's current inspection tour had placed him at Red River at the same time as a council meeting, so the governor of the District of Assiniboia, aka the chief factor of Fort Garry, had given up the chair to the governor in chief.

Simpson said: "Ah, Grant—watch running slow?"

"Not at all. But my horse doesn't seem to be eating up the miles at quite the same pace as she did last year."

The sheriff of Red River said: "She might say you don't seem to be quite as light in the saddle. . . ."

"Pots and kettles, Sheriff."

Simpson said: "I don't believe you've met Mister Thom."

At Simpson's right hand sat an improbable cross between a bull and a badger—a largish man with forward-thrust shoulders and grizzled side-whiskers joined to a fluffy tuft of beard under the jaw, leaving the chin and the rest of the bull-thick features exposed. "How do you do, Mister Thom."

"Mister Grant."

They shook hands across the table, and Grant took his seat. Simpson carried on with the current item on the agenda, which was the matter of declaring a date for the annual race to stake out haying privileges on the prairie behind the strip farms of Red River. After they'd all contributed their opinions as to whether it looked to be an early autumn or a dry August, they reached a consensus and moved on to the perennial question of whether pigs should be allowed to roam free as cattle were. The next item on the agenda was a motion to increase the salary of the volunteer constabulary, who never seemed to do anything. Grant pointed out that a constabulary that never had to be called upon to enforce the law must be doing an excellent job of upholding it, and the motion was passed.

Simpson shuffled his papers together and said: "And now I'll hand the floor over to Mister Thom, who's spent the past weeks familiarizing himself with the lay of the land so he could establish a judicial system that suits. Mister Thom? . . ."

Adam Thom didn't have to be asked twice to take the floor. He cleared his throat with a resonance that made gavels redundant and proceeded to lay down the law from an elaborate system of notes, covering everything from the precise dates for the quarterly sittings of the Court of Rupert's Land to the exact maximum amount of damages that the petty magistrates would be allowed to assess without forwarding the case to the superior court.

They were all nodding off under the inundation of quid est demonstratums and quid pro quos when Thom slipped in: "Any defendant, plaintiff, or witness requiring the services of a translator must inform the court in writing, not less than two calendar months prior to the quarterly session."

The sheriff of Red River interjected: "Oh, I wouldn't worry too much about finding translators. There's enough of us here in this room who speak Cree and Bungee—even a little Sioux, some of us. And if it comes to some of the stranger dialects from way north or west, you just have to holler out the courthouse door and there'll be some old voyageur passing by who can translate it into French."

"And then who," Mister Thom asked rhetorically, "will translate the translators?"

"Pardon me?"

"The Court of Rupert's Land shall conduct its business in English."

There was a pause, then Bishop Provencher said: "Forgive me, but I was under the impression—given your years in Lower Canada and university—that you would be conversant with the French language."

"All cases that come before the Court of Rupert's Land," the recorder intoned, "shall be tried in English. Now, as to the process of jury selection . . ."

The sudden tingling through Grant's fingers made it very difficult to maintain his sprawled-back posture and blandly receptive expression. But the dozing cat mustn't twitch its whiskers when it's wakened by a whiff of rat and the skittering of little paws.

A little further on, some of the other councillors who also happened to be magistrates began to cavil at Mister Thom's declaration that all petty magistrates—whether permanent or temporary—would be required to join the recorder on the bench for every sitting of the Court of Rupert's Land. Grant caught Thom's eye and said: *"Hic quae habus munum ergo exsequi munus."*

The pedantic badger mask broke into a delighted grin—not only in agreement that "he who would possess the office must perform its duties," but in discovering another liberally educated man among all these backwoodsmen and priests. Thom barked back jovially, *"Et munum, Grante,"* underscoring the alternate meaning of the word for office as a gift or gratuity.

Grant gave him back the most ingenuously companionable nod and winking smile that he could muster under the circumstances and waited. When Thom had finally exhausted his notes, and everyone else, the meeting adjourned into a scrum of "Good to see you again!" and "How's the wife?" Grant negotiated his way toward where Adam Thom was filing his notes into a much worn leather valise embossed with cabalistic symbols. Grant's mouth and eyes were straining under the burden of false warmth.

Adam Thom looked up and grinned again when he saw Grant coming. Grant extended his right hand and pumped Thom's enthusiastically, gushing: *"Je vous remercie du bon travail!"*

"De rien, je—" The modest growl of a voice, the gratified blush blossoming up from the grizzled side-whiskers—all froze at the same instant, as Adam Thom finally felt the trap snap across his nose. The suddenly cold hand clasping Grant's tried to snatch itself away, but Grant caught it and held it and nodded acknowledgment at the fury in the badger's eyes. Then he let go of Thom's hand, turned, and headed for the door.

He was intercepted in the doorway by Bishop Provencher. "Do you have a moment to take a stroll with me, my son, before you mount up for the long ride home?"

"Certainly, Eminence."

They were held up on the courthouse steps for a moment by the obligatory exchange of farewells and flask tastings with Grant's fellow councillors. As the bishop's moccasins and Grant's crackled over the tramped-dead grass of the fort's central square, the bishop made conversation about the weather, the healthy blossoming of the next crop of Grants, the arrangements to transfer the bell from the old church of St. Boniface to the chapel of St. François Xavier . . .

Grant was expecting the bishop to switch over to the business of Adam Thom as soon as they were out of earshot of the other councillors, so that Grant could tell him honestly that he had no idea what to do about the recorder of Rupert's Land except to wait and see what developed. But the bishop kept ambling and prattling all the way across the square to the fort gates and out onto the riverbank.

The bishop finally came to a halt beside a clump of wild roses, looked back over both shoulders, and then directed his gaze across the river at the shining twin bell spires of St. Boniface Cathedral. "What I wanted to speak to you of, my son, is a matter of some delicacy, but one that has been weighing heavily on the hearts of many of our people. I know you well enough to know that you are the only man in the country who does not suspect the deep concern that so many of the people of Red River and White Horse Plains have been feeling for you."

"For *me*?"

"It is a delicate subject, as I said. I would not presume to broach it to you, if it weren't that I could see so many people longing to ask me to do so. I know that there are many reasons in your past that could drive a man to drink. So many ghosts. No doubt they wouldn't haunt someone without a conscience, but you are a man of conscience. But the haze of alcohol is no solution. Those same ghosts will be waiting in the morning. The only way to free yourself is to unburden your soul to God and—"

"Uh, Your Eminence . . ."

"Yes, my son?"

"I do appreciate your concern. And I do appreciate that you are aware of many of the reasons I might be driven to drink beyond what some people might consider moderation. But I believe there is another reason you haven't taken into consideration."

"What is that, my son?"

"I like it."

CHAPTER 37

Marie was nursing Sophie Caroline and watching the last of the frost embroidery melt off the kitchen window when Wappeston came in stomping mud off his boots. The only time he wore boots anymore was in the spring. He poured himself a cup of gin and water, took a tentative swallow, and nodded. "Not bad. So how's our little white-mud factory this morning—still taking it in and churning it out?"

"She does like to drink."

"Comes by it honestly."

Marie let it lie. It was difficult to berate him about his drinking when the only noticeable effects were that he got a bit more bright-eyed and good-humored, or occasionally a little snappish when he hadn't eaten. And on some mornings his hands would shake before he'd had a few sips of brandy or a cup of beer, then settle down to fine tremors. And perhaps the puffiness in his face wasn't due entirely to encroaching middle age.

Sometimes she almost longed for the days when she could get him to rein back for a week or two by not letting him forget how drunk he'd gotten at a wedding dance or trading stories with Pierriche and her father. But the last occurrence had been years ago.

He settled into his chair at the head of the table and said: "What would you say if I proposed we don't go out on the summer hunt?"

She was moved to say "Hooray!" but she wasn't entirely sure that the response came from a healthy place. She'd noticed herself becoming increasingly reluctant to leave the enclosed world of her house and farmyard and the home territory surrounding Grantown. Maybe she was growing old before her time. She said: "What would we do instead?"

"Camp up at the lake for a few weeks." In Grantown parlance, "the lake" meant the little lake just north of White Horse Plains, one of the dozens of Rice Lakes scattered across the country. "You may have noticed that the portion of Grantown that stays behind when the hunt goes out has been growing year by year. Lord, when even Angus decides it's time he hung up his buffalo gun . . . And various circumstances have created a number of widows and orphans with no one to hunt for them. For the ones that stay behind, the Hard Time Moon doesn't end with the spring. So, I thought we might pack up all of the stay-at-homes, or most of them, and spend a month or so up at the lake netting fish and decimating the wild fowl population.

"Besides, there's a number of the younger hunters who should be given a chance to try their hand as Captain of the hunt. And besides all that, I want to be here for the summer sitting of the Court of Rupert's Land. If someone doesn't counterweight that bastard Thom, we're going to have a civil war on our hands.

"At the last quarterly session, Aicawpow Dumont—who's just about the easygoing-est young giant you'd ever hope to meet—was shooting sparks out of his eyes when Thom interrupted him to demand a translation for *mon père*. So, what do you think?"

"Of Adam Thom?"

"Sometimes, Little Rabbit, I suspect you of harboring a sardonic wit. What do you think of my proposal to go up to the lake instead of out on the hunt?"

"I think, given a choice between eating hoof dust, hacking up dead buffaloes, and listening to four thousand cartwheels shrieking all day long, or lying around in the sun on the lakeshore . . . I will follow along where my husband thinks best."

His laughter was interrupted by the back door opening and Charles crouching on the threshold to strip off his mud-and-snow-caked bull's-hide moccasins. Poor Charles had gone and hit all his awkward stages at the same time.

His father said: "I thought you were mending that fence?"

"I did."

"That was remarkably swift work. I'll just go out and have a look at it, shall I?"

After Wappeston had gone and Marie had manipulated Sophie Caroline into her freshened mossbag, Charles was still standing staring daggers at the door. Marie stood up and said: "Would you like a cup of tea?" She was growing accustomed to looking up at him. Even though it seemed unlikely he'd ever come close to his father's height, that still left him a lot of range to outgrow his mother.

"Yes, thank you, Maman." But he didn't move from where he stood, even when she'd set his cup out on the table.

"Come and sit, Charles, before it gets cold."

"Yes, Maman." Once he'd maneuvered his gawky body onto a chair and taken a sip, he said: "I'm going to need a new gun. The little bird gun I got for my last birthday won't do for buffalo."

"You're not old enough yet for running buffalo."

"Lots of boys my age ran buffalo last year—Pierre MacDougall and Patrice Falcon and Jean Delorme and—"

"If their parents want to take the chance of throwing them into the herd before they're ready, that's up to them. There's no point in us arguing about it, anyways. We're not going on the hunt this time."

"What?"

"Your father decided—"

"*He* decided? Don't we get any say in it?"

"He talked it over with me and I agreed with him. When the hunt leaves we'll go up to the lake with the old folks and widows to fish and shoot geese. You'll like that."

"*Like* spending the summer with the old folks and widows? The rest of you can do that if you like. I'm going on the hunt."

"You're too young to—"

"Look after myself, I know. But I can hook myself up with Uncle Pierre's family, or Uncle Daniel's. . . ."

She sighed. "It shouldn't be up to me to decide about things like buffalo hunts. You should talk to your father."

"Well, that settles it right there, doesn't it? You know he'll say no. All he ever says to me is 'No' or 'You're doing that wrong.' "

"I know it seems like that to you. All fathers want for their oldest sons to be perfect."

"I'm not his oldest son." That caught her by the throat. But then he added: "Pascal is."

She couldn't dispute that the strange bond between Maria Theresa and her father appeared to have expanded itself to include her husband. There had been many a winter's night when Wappeston and Pascal Breland had sat up talking by the fire in the parlor, of fur trading and plows and horses, muttering abstracted good-nights over their shoulders as the rest of the family trooped off to bed.

She said: "It's only because he can talk to Pascal like one man to another. In a few years, when you're not a boy no more—"

"Maman, someday you got to wake up and stop living in this dream where you and him and us make up a family. Half the time I swear he's got to stop and think twice to remember my name."

"That isn't true."

"Sure it isn't. Just like it isn't true he's never had time to be here more'n one day out of twenty—he's too busy being Mister Grant the magistrate or Mister Grant the sheriff or the chief of the half-breeds or the fur trader or the warden of the plains or—"

"He does all those things so we can have a good life."

"He does all those things to make himself a big man!"

Her right hand snapped out across his cheek. It was more of a tap than a slap—she'd caught herself just in time to pull it a little. But from the look on his face she might just as well have horsewhipped him. The look lasted only an instant, then he clamped his shock-gaped mouth and eyes into slits and hunched his shoulders and chin into his bony chest.

"Oh, God, Charles—I'm sorry! I—"

The back door opened and Wappeston stuck his head in for long enough to say: "The top rail needed refitting, but other than that it seems like a serviceable enough job. I'm just going to take a jaunt over to Pascal and Maria Theresa's to see how his negotiations for a private trader's license are coming along. Should be back in time for dinner." The door closed again and Marie turned back to Charles, but he was already out of his chair and disappearing through the doorway to the parlor.

Charles didn't forgive her until halfway through their sojourn at the lake, and even then there was no overt forgiveness, just a gradual thawing of his cold sulks. Not even a fifteen-year-old boy could keep ill-tempered for long in that golden time of lolling on the lakeshore in the sun or poking crackling goose into one's mouth with greasy fingers while the old ones told stories around the fire. Her happiness was complete the night Wappeston crawled into the tent abstractedly and kept shaking his head and muttering to himself as though he'd forgotten something, even after they were settled into bed. He suddenly sat up, spilling the blankets off, and laughed. "*That's* what it is."

"What what is?"

"I haven't had a drink all day."

But on the night before they had to pack up camp if they hoped to be settled back in Grantown in time for him to attend the court session at Fort Garry, he sat up long after the Great Bear had shown its tail, feeding the campfire with one hand and his brandy cup with the other. She lay in bed watching his distorted silhouette flicker across the tent wall. She dozed off for a moment and was wakened by a rasping, coughing, barking sound somewhere out in the night. She crawled to the door flap and looked out.

The fire had sunk low but still cast enough light to show he wasn't there. She tugged on her moccasins and followed the sound along the shore of the moonlit lake. He was sprawled across the end of a rocky point, dry-heaving into the water. He heard her coming, glanced back over his shoulder, and waved her off. But she kept on picking her way across the mossy rocks. As she came up to him, he gasped in a few lungfuls of air and scooped up a handful of lake to sluice his face. She squatted down and maneuvered his head onto her lap. His chest made a few saw-toothed hiccuping sounds and then quieted down. She said: "Why do you have to do it?"

"I suppose . . . I suppose I have to admit I've become addicted."

"Addicted?"

"That's where . . . where you have to have your regular dosage . . . where you can't leave something alone, even if you don't enjoy it, even if it makes you sick."

"But all the time we been here you didn't hardly drink at all."

"*Drink?*" He sat up, laughing and belching, and slapped his chest to regain control. "Oh, dear, that wasn't what I . . . Well, what the hell, I suppose even were I to come to my senses, there'd still be other reasons why I have to keep at it. But not for too much longer, Waposis. There's a lot of bright young men coming along. The question is . . . I think it's time for bed."

A week after he came back from sitting on the bench with Adam Thom, the hunt came home. They'd had some trouble with the Sioux and responded in kind. Marie listened in silence as Pierriche told the story by the parlor fire, ending with: "So you better come out on the fall hunt, Wappeston."

"No need. Tit for tat. It's over."

"Well, then at least let me take the cannon—"

"No! As I said—it's over."

It wasn't. When the fall hunt came home with more stories of scalpings and retaliations, Wappeston sighed. "I'm sorry, Waposis—it looks like I won't be spending next spring up at the lake after all."

That turned out to be true, but he didn't go out on the hunt, either. The spring brought a message from the newly elevated George Simpson. Sir George was traveling from Lachine in company with two young British lords eager to do some trophy shooting on the fabled plains of the Saskatchewan. Sir George had assured them that they would be guided and cared for by the warden of the plains himself.

Only a few years ago, the notion of taking a jolly shooting party into the hunting grounds of the Assiniboine Nation would have been ridiculously suicidal. But the smallpox had left few remnants of the wild Assiniboines except horror stories of warriors scraping their pustulating faces against the gates of trading forts to give the white men back their disease, and of ghost camps where the only life within the circled tents was the dogs eating the corpses. Wappeston had lined up everyone in Grantown to have their arms scratched by a needle dipped in fluid from a sick cow. When she'd begged him to go out on the plains and do the same for Unpredictable Loon and her people, he'd exploded: "I can't save everybody! I don't even know whether I can save anyone here, or whether I even picked the right damned cow!" But it seemed that he had. Grantown didn't lose one citizen to the smallpox.

After he'd handed her Sir George's letter to read, she said: "What's 'trophy shooting'?"

"It's a charming custom among civilized peoples. It means killing the biggest and healthiest elk you can find—or bear or buffalo or whatever—for the sake of displaying a bigger pair of antlers on your library wall than your neighbor down the road. But I'm afraid I don't have much choice."

"It's more important you show these lords some trophy shooting than go out to captain the hunt against the Sioux?"

"It is important that the Little Emperor be assured that he can rely upon me to make his bragging true. The hunt caravan is far too large for the Sioux to take on. The only danger is to anyone fool enough to stray too far."

"Then there's no reason we can't let Charles go on the hunt."

"Charles? He's too young to—"

"He's getting almost too *old* to take his first buffalo run. Pierriche can look after him."

"Pierriche will be coming with me to help guide the lords and keep them entertained."

"Donald can look after him, then, or Daniel, or François . . ."

"Well, if you think it's a good idea . . ."

"And he'll need a new gun."

With only a skeleton population left at Grantown, Marie was allowed to entwine herself in the things that mattered—the garden performing its alchemy of turning sun and earth and rain into fresh food for her family, the hummingbirds blazing and buzzing through the morning dew, the cows lowing their way back to their milking stalls at dusk. The placid surface was cracked from time to time by rumors making their way up the moccasin telegraph from the south. The skirmishes between the Dakotah Nation and the allied Saulteaux, Cree, and métis were escalating into a full-scale war.

· · ·

The wild roses were painting the prairie pink when Wappeston came back from the west escorting the lords with their cartloads of animal heads and skins. As soon as the lords had been waved on their way, he disappeared into the house. She found him standing on the widow's walk, looking down on the gold-thatched cabins showing between the leaves and the smattering of stick figures moving between them. He said, "I wonder how many of them have the vaguest inkling just how fragile this all is?" then looked out over the prairie again. "It all seems so permanent, doesn't it? As though nothing can change except the seasons. But when we first stood here, Waposis, and looked that way"—pointing west—"we were looking at the gates of a tribal territory that stretched from here to the Shining Mountains. And now it's a vacuum that the Cree and Saulteaux are pouring into from the north and east, the Sioux from the south, and the Blackfoot and Gros Ventres from the far west. That's why there's a war on now." He drew in a long breath through his nostrils and blew it out again. "And then there's also the fact that one of the main reasons the Company gave us the land here was to stand as a bulwark against the fearsome Assiniboines. . . ."

He turned around and slapped his hands against the ends of her shoulders with a jaunty grin she could see through like cheesecloth, saying: "All of which means, my love, that I'll be saddling up to ride south tomorrow morning—along with Pierriche and anyone else I can scrape together who isn't already off on the hunt. With luck we'll find the hunt caravan before the Sioux find us. And then, if the Sioux want a war, we'll take it to them."

"You said there was no need to worry about the hunt."

"There wasn't, then. This isn't nip and run anymore."

"Don't go."

"Don't worry."

She tried not to. The rumors that had been shuttling up from the south multiplied themselves tenfold once Mister Grant had been shuffled into the deck. The whole buffalo hunt had been knocked on the head. Mister Grant had massacred entire villages of Sioux. La Terre Qui Brûle had ambushed a métis war party and danced with Mister Grant's scalp. Marie had to remind herself over and over again of what she'd learned years ago about the moccasin telegraph—there was always something at the base of it, but it was like the game of sitting in a circle and passing a whispered phrase around to where it had started.

White Horse Plains was gaudy with purple blazing stars and goldenrod when the tortured symphony of a thousand dry-wood axles announced the return of the buffalo hunt. Wappeston rode in front, with Charles behind him balancing the staff of the blue-and-white flag on the base of his stirrup. Wappeston's face looked like a rusted iron mask scored with a chisel. He climbed off his horse, hugged her stiffly, and pronounced: "The war is over."

"What happened?"

" 'Happened'?"

"How did it end?"

"In the usual way. There was a lamenting of widows."

CHAPTER 38

Shortly after Hogmanay, Grant received a delightful Christmas present. It came in two parts, one part being the list of cases for the upcoming sitting of the Court of Rupert's Land, the other a letter from the sheriff of Red River gleefully drawing Grant's attention to the third case on the docket. The other half dozen cases were the usual array of strayed horses, breach of promise, or selling beer to Chief Peguis. But the third case was quite unusual, in that the name of the defendant was one Adam Thom.

It seemed that Mr. and Mrs. Thom had brought a Scottish housekeeper cum nanny with them to Red River. It seemed the housekeeper had become friendly with one of the Company's Scots carpenters and that Mister Thom had unceremoniously ejected her from his home when it became evident that "friendly" was an understatement. But instead of slinking away to hide her shame, the housekeeper, bless her, was suing Mister Thom for her back wages—which amounted to a considerable sum, since Mister Thom had volunteered himself as her banker from the beginning, only doling out the occasional bit of pin money. She was also suing for the amount of her passage back to Scotland, as had been agreed upon in her initial contract.

On the morning of the quarterly session, Grant slipped out of bed while the window was still black, bundled himself up, and went out back to hitch the dogs to the carriole. When he came back in to fill his flask and fetch his rifle, Marie was waddling about the kitchen barefoot, with her hair down and only a worn-thin shawl over her nightdress. He bent down to kiss her temple and pat her swollen belly, saying: "You should be snug in bed."

"And then who would put together something for you to eat? I don't suppose *you* have."

"I thought I'd stop in at the fort mess for breakfast."

"Unless court's already started by the time you get there, and then you'd spend the whole morning sitting on the bench with nothing in your stomach but gin."

"Brandy, actually. Gin simply won't do for a long ride through the snow."

"Here." She handed him a bulging rawhide pannier. "There's some bannock and cold beef and cheese and onions. You can munch along in the carriole without having to stop. Wrap it up next to you or it'll freeze solid."

"Thank you. If it turns into a long sitting, I'll stay over at the fort, so don't fret if I'm not home tonight. Is there anything you'd like me to pick up at the store as long as I'm there?"

"I made a list. It's in there with your breakfast." She reached up to tug on his left ear. "If you don't want it obvious how much you're planning to enjoy this, you're going to have to stop smirking."

"Smirk? I? I am a duly appointed officer of the law, madame. We magistrates do not *enjoy* dispensing justice—it is our duty."

It was a mercifully cloudy night, the cloud canopy providing a buffer between what little warmth there was in the planet and the infinite black vacuum above. Driving a dog carriole while riding in it was a tricky business. Once ensconced in the fur-lined cockpit, the driver/passenger was pretty much at the mercy of the dogs. The whip could egg them on or turn them, but not rein them in. Fortunately Grant's lead dog was a quarter-wolf bitch martinet who'd been trained by Jean Baptiste Lajimodierre, who was not only the wiliest hunter in the *pays d'en haut* but also had an uncanny way with dogs. She prided herself on her ability to understand verbal commands better than most two-legged creatures and to enforce them on the rest of the pack. Unfortunately she was growing as grizzled and cantankerous as Lajimodierre himself. Grant made a mental note to board her entire next litter with Lajimodierre to see if he could make a successor out of one of them.

The sun was coming up as he approached the gates of the upper fort, which at this time of year made it almost nine o'clock. The tail end of the usual court-day crowd was just making its way in to the auditorium, knocking out their pipes and stomping snow off their moccasins, so Marie had guessed right about providing him with breakfast for the trail.

On his way up the aisle he took a last pull from his flask, engendering a glare from Mister Thom and appreciative chortles from the gallery. The other three petty magistrates were already in their places, flanking the recorder. Grant dropped his coat across his chair for upholstery and settled in as Adam Thom announced: "The Court of Rupert's Land is now in session."

The first two cases went by quickly. Hugh Matheson was ordered to pay two shillings for the damage his wandering hog had done to John Pritchard's turnip bin, and Honoré Lepine was sentenced to two days and nights in jail for shooting Wataskawin's dog. Then the recorder of Rupert's Land stepped off the bench and the governor of Assiniboia took his place as president of the court. Like most Company officers these days, the governor/chief factor was in a state not unlike an older sister left in charge while the folks are away—half-tyrannical and half-apprehensive. Sir George Simpson had taken a two-year leave of absence to take a trip around the world, leaving Lady Frances in her castle at Lachine. The summer and winter mail packets would bring letters from Murmansk or Edinburgh, ordering that this chief trader be denied promotion or that that district trim its indents.

Adam Thom's ex-housekeeper stood up to state her case. And when she stood she definitely stood—six feet tall and at least eight months big with child. The sight of her looming in the witness box immediately explained at least part of her attachment to her carpenter. Although the age difference was even greater than the one between Grant and Marie McGillis, the carpenter was one of the few men in the country—or any other country, for that matter—who could make her seem even remotely delicate and diminutive. Grant had to exercise his imagination and memory to stand the carpenter beside her for comparison, because wherever said carpenter was at the moment, it was nowhere in the vicinity of the Court of Rupert's Land.

When the housekeeper had stated her case, in plain Aberdonian English, Mister Thom stood up to take his innings. After quoting a phalanx of precedents and Latin homilies, he finally got down to: "The plaintiff is proffering a misapprehension when she testifies that she was never paid her wages. At the end of every calendar month, from the time she was first engaged in service up until the day she *chose* to leave, the agreed-upon salary was duly remitted into her hands in coin of the realm."

The governor said: "No doubt, Mister Thom, you have signed receipts to—"

"Receipts? Receipts, sir? Since when does a man protect himself with receipts against a trusted domestic servant—the nanny to his children, a woman clutched to the bosom of his household—as he would against a usuring shylock? We shook hands, sir! No doubt the Court has heard the story of the wise old man of Aberdeen, who lived not far from where my housekeeper was born. One day a young man asked him for a loan of a sum of money. The wise old man agreed to provide it. But when the young man drew out a contract to be signed, the old man slammed shut his money box and said: 'If you cannot trust yourself on your sworn word, I shall not trust you on a piece of paper!' "

Grant didn't like the way this was shaping up. If the whole case came down to a question of her word against Thom's, the petty magistrates were going to find it difficult to find against the recorder of Rupert's Land. There was a momentary lull as the president of the court tried to figure out if he was supposed to ask any more questions. Grant cleared his throat and said: "If the Court will allow, and if Mister Thom won't mind me backtracking for a moment to allow me to catch up . . ."

Thom's bullock head and shoulders hunkered even closer together, and he squinted suspiciously at the bench. It suddenly occurred to Grant why Thom's eyes had that badgerish look to them—he was extremely shortsighted. But that wasn't going to make it any easier to catch him out a second time. He'd been wary of every word Grant said since their first meeting.

Grant reached over to retrieve the contract from the stack of papers in front of the president of the court, saying: "I'm afraid that part of the time when I should have been paying strict attention to the two preceding cases, I was studying the contract that the plaintiff and defendant in this case signed in Scotland. I'm assuming, Mister Thom, you were the author of this document? . . ."

"I was."

"It merits some study. It appears to be a remarkably meticulous piece of work, with all the i's dotted and t's crossed."

"I have been privileged with a classical education, sir, as well as studying the law. We were taught to caulk a contract or a thesis or a translation from Tacitus as tightly as a shipwright would a hull, sir."

"Well, I must say that this document is a testimony to the masters at King's College, Aberdeen."

"Thank you, sir. I would be flattered to consider myself a credit to the finest staff of educators in the British Isles—no slight intended against the masters of Inverness College."

"None taken."

The governor sighed. "If the gentlemen could save their old school songs for the next recess, perhaps we could get on with—"

"If the Court pleases," Grant cut him off. It looked like the president of the court decidedly did not please, but Grant bulled on regardless. "There is just one aspect of this contract that I'm afraid is"—shrugging apologetically—"a bit beyond my grasp. It has, after all, been thirty years since I waved good-bye to the quad at Inverness. I'm sure it would take Mister Thom only a moment to explain it, and it would be educational for us all."

The badger-bullock positively preened himself for a moment before cooing: "If the Court pleases; if Mister Grant's question is one that can be answered in a moment, I would be more than happy to elucidate."

The president of the court put his hand over his eyes, which Grant chose to interpret as acquiescence. "What I find difficult to grasp, Mister Thom is . . . how is it, that out of all this meticulous education in the dotting of i's and the caulking of contracts, you were somehow neglected to be taught to keep written accounts and receipts with the people you pay wages to?"

There was laughter from the gallery. The governor gaveled for order. Adam Thom's fur-framed features took on a glow like the grate of the little iron stove in the corner. His mouth opened and closed several times, but nothing intelligible came out.

The president of the court moved on to the question of whether the defendant had ejected the plaintiff from his household or whether she'd left of her own accord. Thom's contention was that the housekeeper had elected to take the last six months as paid sick leave. Once again, it was coming down to a question of his word against hers.

Grant couldn't fathom why Thom was digging in so fiercely over that one question, unless he was just being cantankerous for the sake of cantankerousness. If he did manage to browbeat the court into accepting that she'd invalided herself out at full wages—as stipulated in the clause regarding "Incapacitating Illness or Injury"—then he'd still have to pay her the six months' wages. And Adam Thom hardly seemed the type to care whether the hoi polloi thought him cruel for throwing a pregnant servant out into the snow or generous for continuing to support her long after she'd ceased to be useful.

Then something twigged in the back of Grant's mind. He looked at the contract again. Sure enough, the clause regarding her return fare to Scotland specified that it would be due to her only after four years of service in the household of the Thoms. The contract had been signed four years ago last month. If Thom could put across the notion that she'd declared herself incapable of performing her duties, that left her five months short.

As Adam Thom carried on with his pedantic harangue, Grant began to peer quizzically at the pregnant Clydesdale of a housekeeper, doing his best imitation of a setter encountering a stuffed owl, cocking his head, *hm*ing under his breath, scratching his chin, and even leaning forward across the magistrates' communal podium. The housekeeper began to blush and look down at her hands. Grant could feel the court-day crowd, and the participants in other cases who'd stayed on to watch the show, gradually shifting their attention from Adam Thom to him and the housekeeper. Finally Thom ground to a frustrated halt and the president of the court said exasperatedly: "Mister Grant! . . ."

"Hm?"

"Do you have something you'd like to say?"

"Well, I do find it a bit confusing."

"*What* do you find confusing *now?*"

"Mind you, I'm only an amateur doctor . . . but I keep looking and looking and I keep seeing the same damned thing."

"And what is it that you keep seeing, Mister Grant?"

"Well, she looks to me to be positively *bursting* with health."

The laughter from the gallery this time was an explosion. Even some of the magistrates couldn't cover their snickers. The housekeeper's face and hands burned even redder, and she looked as though she wanted to dig a hole through the floor. Grant tried to catch her eyes with his, to try to tell her he was sorry he hadn't been able to think of another way to do it, but suffering that one moment of ridicule had probably won her all her back wages plus her passage money home. She wouldn't look up.

The president of the court and his empaneled magistrates retired to the back room to deliberate and moisten their throats. When they came back out, the court filled up again quickly. The governor gaveled for order and announced: "It is the judgment of this Court—of *all* this Court, you understand . . . that is to say, of a *majority* of the magistrates sitting today . . . and majority rules— The Court finds in favor of the plaintiff on all counts. Mister Thom is instructed to pay her the entirety of her four years' salary, plus the amount of her passage back to Scotland. Until such time as full payment has been made, Mister Thom's house and all his household goods shall be bound over to the plaintiff as security."

The mob in the pews cheered and applauded. Adam Thom looked as though he were about to start chewing the furniture. The housekeeper stood up and stepped toward the bench. Once the noise had died down enough for her to make herself heard, she said: "Please, sirs

. . . there is no need for that. I only want what's owed me."

Grant said: "Dammit, girl—don't you understand? We've found in your favor. If he doesn't pay up smartly, you *own* the house you used to be a slavey in."

"No, sir"—she shook her head ponderously—"I only want what's mine." Grant threw up his hands.

When the quarterly session was adjourned, the sheriff of Red River ambled over to where Grant was heaving his coat back on and murmured: "Tell me, Grant—were you born with a genius for making enemies, or was it something you had to work at?"

"Who—Adam Thom? I'd say our revered recorder doesn't harbor warm feelings for any of us."

The sheriff shook his head. "None of the rest of us have made him look a fool. I've seen you do it twice now."

Grant laughed. "I don't see what he can do about it—except perhaps dust off one of his learned lectures and *bore* me to death."

"I wouldn't be so cavalier. He and Sir George are thick as thieves—"

"Then when the time comes for me to get crucified, they'll have to hang on either side."

Within three days all the magistrates of the Court of Rupert's Land received a thirteen-page dissertation from Adam Thom, enumerating all the legal reasons they should acquiesce to his demand that the case be tried again in front of a jury. The unanimous response was "No." In the interim, the housekeeper gave birth to an enormously healthy baby girl. Three weeks later she married her carpenter and they settled down to build a farm with the dowry Adam Thom had provided.

But by the time of the happy ending, Grant had other things on his mind.

Although there was no question that the Sioux had lost the war, they still hadn't formally sued for peace. It wasn't customary for a war between the Plains tribes to end without a lot of poetic embroidery on the theme of "If you won't come hunting us, we won't come hunting you."

As the willow twigs sprouted litters of furry catkins, the people of Grantown were busily splicing the last bits of mending into their cart harnesses and bridles and the buffalo runners were frisking in the pastures, but there was still no word from the Dakotah Nation.

CHAPTER 39

Marie was hoeing earth into potato hills. Actually it was more like mud, but if she waited for the ground to sop up all the spring melt-off, the garden would only be half planted when it came time to head up to the lake. By rights she shouldn't be hilling them at all until they'd sprouted to a decent height, but they were going to have to get along untended for their first few weeks of life.

She was finding it increasingly difficult to stoop around the basket of flesh belling out between her pelvis and her rib cage. This one was definitely not going to be the runt of the litter. Fortunately Eliza was there to poke the quartered potatoes into the hills and cover them up, and Angus was doing the necessary stooping at the rows Marie had hoed that morning—drilling holes in the ground with his fingers and dribbling in carrot or turnip seeds. She hoped he wasn't getting them mixed up. Well, she'd find out when they came back from the lake.

As Eliza attended to the latest hill, Marie leaned on her hoe and let her eyes drift to a cowbird perched on a fence post, its beady eyes tracking the flitting sparrows to scout out a nest to leave her egg in. Beyond the garden fence, the cows were chewing up the last of last summer's hay. It was time to start drying them off again if they weren't going to be too much of a handful for the handful of people who would keep Grantown from being a ghost town for the first part of the summer. Drying off the cows would also be good for the calves growing inside them. Even old Potacikin, the grandmother of them all, was shamelessly showing the effects of her latest rendezvous with Urbain Delorme's bull. But then, Marie giggled to herself, you're one to talk—edging forty and still waddling around like a heifer relieved of its first heat.

There was something moving through the green haze of budding trees between the graveyard and Ghost Horse Plains. It was large and white and it bobbed along with that easy, rolling gait of a horse running free in a meadow and with the eerie soundlessness of a horse close enough to see clearly but just too far off to hear its hooves. She should have been able to hear this one from there, though. She reminded herself that ghosts didn't walk by daylight, or gallop, for that matter. But the roots of the hairs on her arms started tingling nonetheless.

Eliza broke the spell by saying: "Mama—I'm ready for the next one." Marie heaved her body farther along the row and started hoeing up another hill, clucking at herself for being so foolish.

As she finished scooping the next section of muddy clods into a melting approximation of a mound, she heard Angus's voice chirping hopefully behind her: "See, Papa? I got it just about all done."

"Yes, I see, Angus. I hope you haven't used up all your seeds before the end of the row."

"No, Papa."

Marie turned her hoe into a leaning post again. Wappeston was standing at the border of the garden in his billowy white shirt, with the empty rawhide seed bag flapping slackly against his hip. The spring sun was already starting to alter his coloring, although it couldn't be held responsible for the gray flecks in his hair. It wasn't fair that men grew better looking as they grew older. Or at least this one did. Or at least to her. The wind-scoured lines around his eyes and down his cheeks, scored deeply into the puffiness of dissipation, just made him look more like the Chief people had been trusting their lives to for thirty years. He said: "I've been debating, Waposis, whether we ought to not go up to the lake this year after all."

"What would we do instead?"

"Go on the hunt. I don't like it that we still haven't had an envoy from the Sioux."

"I thought you said the war was over."

"It is—or I believe it is. But if I'm wrong, I should be there to deal with it."

"I thought you said there was plenty of young men who should be given a chance to captain the hunt?"

"There are. But if anything were to happen . . ."

"Well, if you figure that's what you have to do . . . I'll herd the old folks up to the lake and do the best I can to see they don't starve to death." He blinked at her. "In case you ain't noticed, I'm a bit fatter than I was last month—or last week, for that matter."

"You were equally pregnant with Eliza when we went out on the first hunt."

"I was also nineteen years old."

"I don't see the difference. Whether on the hunt or at the lake, you'll still be living in a tent when—"

"At the lake it'll be a tent that's been set up in one place for long enough to make it a place we live in. And most of the tents around it will have at least one old woman in it who's midwifed a hundred babies and won't have nothing else to take care of except me."

"Well, as I said, I've merely been debating it with myself; I've yet to make up my mind."

In the end he made up his mind that even if the Sioux hadn't learned their lesson from last year, they still weren't likely to try anything this year beyond the usual tentative stabs at horse stealing. When the hunt caravan embarked east toward the Passage of the Assiniboine, Wappeston boosted her up the attic steps so they could wave good-bye from the widow's walk.

The lake hadn't lost its medicine. Once again, the more they got settled in at the camp among the spring-fragrant spruce and balsam poplar, the less he drank. Although he did stay more than a bit anxious to corral every family band of Cree or Saulteaux that happened to wander by Grant's Lake and pump them for any news they might have heard from the south.

In between potting ducks by the canoeful, he burned off some of his excess nerves by setting to work with an axe and spade to build a green log shanty in the pines. "After all, Waposis, if we plan to be coming back here every spring . . . And you said yourself you were getting a bit long in the tooth for giving birth in a tent."

"Maybe I'm getting a bit long in the tooth for giving birth."

"Well . . . nonetheless, you'll have a roof over your head this time."

She didn't. She beat him to it. Or, rather, Elisabeth did. Marie had decided ahead of time that they would name a girl Elisabeth. It wouldn't be like having two of them in the family; Eliza hadn't been called by her full name since her christening. And if he wanted to call this Elisabeth Beth or Betsy or even Bethsy, Marie no longer minded.

She'd guessed right that this was going to be a big one, but it still didn't take very long. Not that it felt like a short time while it was happening. But when her mother and the flock of assistant midwives eased her down onto her back and settled the squealing hulk between her breasts, the oval of sky through the smoke hole had only deepened from violet to purple. She found enough breath to whisper: "Guess I'm getting to be an old hand at this."

Her mother grunted: "Maybe a bit too old a hand."

They built up the fire and let her husband in. The faces of Eliza, Angus, Louis, and Sophie Caroline filled the door hole behind him. He knelt beside the bed of buffalo robes and Hudson's Bay blankets and took hold of her hand. From the flexing and twitching going on under his cheekbones, he was still grinding deeper valleys in his back teeth. He pried his front teeth apart and said hoarsely: "No matter how many times, I'm still never sure you're safe until it's over. *Are* you?" She nodded. He lowered his eyes to the new Miss Grant. "And I never fail to be astounded by . . ."

When it came time to head back to Grantown, both Elisabeth and the new cabin on the lakeshore were ready to face the elements, if the wind didn't blow too hard. The buffalo hunt came home minus only a few horses lost to Sioux night stalkers and one Saulteaux hunter who'd interrupted them. Charles brought home a cartload of pemmican and an unpunctured skin, as did another young man named Henry Pagée.

A few weeks later Marie said, after she'd blown out the candle, "Maybe you could find a way to let Henry Pagée know you wouldn't mind if he was to talk to you. I don't know if he'll ever get up the nerve otherwise."

"Henry Pagée? What would he want to—"

"Eliza."

"Eliza?"

She knew that rolling her eyes in the dark wasn't likely to have much effect, but she did it anyway.

Except in cases of dire emergency, weddings at Red River and White Horse Plains always took place in the winter, when everybody needed every celebration they could get their hands on. Marie was pleasantly surprised when Eliza came up with no pressing reasons why they shouldn't simply post the banns now and wait a few months longer. Maybe she'd actually been listening all those times when she'd looked to be dozing off in church, or maybe she just hadn't inherited her mother's fertility. In which case Marie might yet have a few years' grace before she had to succumb to full grandmotherhood instead of just the step variety.

The day after the banns were posted, one of the Red River métis came pounding into the yard on a lathered horse, yelling for Mister Grant. Wappeston came out of the barn with a pitchfork in his hand. Marie set down her half-filled basket of pea pods and went to see what was going on.

"Mister Grant—there's a bunch of Sioux heading for the Forks!"

"How many?"

"Maybe ten tents."

"Women and children?"

"Some."

"It sounds to me like they've just come to trade, or to try to wheedle some more presents out of the Company."

"But if there was an accident, Mister Grant! All it'd take is one spark and the whole place'd—"

"I might *be* that accident, if I go charging in there like I did the last time. I'll see to it that everybody here stays ready, in case any real trouble starts. Send a galloper and we'll come immediately. You should have a cup of beer before you start back—give your horse a chance to breathe himself out."

The next morning Pierriche ambled in at the tail end of breakfast and accepted the offer of a cup of tea. Once he was sat down with Sophie Caroline on his knee, he said offhandedly: "So what do you think about the shooting?"

Wappeston said: "What shooting?"

"Ain't you heard? Jean Baptiste told me last night. I would've come over and told you then, except I figured . . . When the Sioux came into Fort Garry there was some Saulteaux there. One of them was the brother of the one the Sioux got on the last hunt. He took a shot at one of the Sioux and missed and killed one of his own cousins."

Wappeston was on his feet, shouting: "I *told* them to send a message if there was any trouble!"

"Calm down. That was the end of it. The sheriff and Adam Thom did the smart thing. The sheriff had the Saulteaux under arrest before his gun stopped smoking, to show the Sioux they didn't have to defend themselves. And Thom's trying him this morning before the Sioux leave, so they can see they don't have to make their own justice."

"Trying him on what charge?"

"Murder."

"He can't *do* that! The Court of Rupert's Land isn't empowered to try capital cases—they have to be forwarded to the courts in Upper Canada."

"Maybe he figures that only applies to white men. . . ." But by that time Wappeston was through the doorway to the parlor. He was back in an instant, with his rifle in his hand, ducking his head through the shoulder straps of his shot pouch and powder flask.

Marie said: "What do you think you're going to do—shoot Adam Thom?"

"Don't tempt me."

As the echoes of the slam of the back door faded, Pierriche shrugged apologetically and mumbled: "I thought he knew." A moment later came the sound of a horse galloping out of the yard and fading eastward.

She was giving Elisabeth her afternoon feeding when she heard his horse plodding back past the side of the house. His face was pale when he came through the door. He didn't move to sit down, just stood there in the rectangle of summer sun. In a voice that sounded as though he had to keep swallowing, he said: "I got there just as they were cutting him down."

"Cutting him down?"

"They hung him. I'm told an experienced hangman can make it instantaneous. Unfortunately for one poor bastard, there are no experienced hangmen at Red River."

"If they had to kill him, why couldn't they just put a bullet through his heart?"

"That's what he wanted. He didn't mind dying, not after killing one of his own, but he didn't want to hang. But the recorder of Rupert's Land said any method other than hanging would not be a legal execution. I need some air."

She didn't point out the fact that he'd been galloping through the open air all day. She didn't even call him back to close the door he'd left gaping for the flies. She burped Elisabeth, laced her back in her cradleboard, closed the door, and started shelling her way through her basket of peas.

He still hadn't reappeared when the cows came trooping in off the prairie to be milked. Marie and Eliza and Charles went out to separate the calves from their mothers and herd the girls into their milking stalls. At the end of the row of stalls was one whose permanent occupant neither lowed nor gave milk. Wappeston was in there, sweeping clinging bits of straw and chicken droppings off the cannon.

Marie stopped in the mouth of the stall and said: "What are you doing?"

He sloped his broom and rasped: "I'm afraid this old thing is going to have to go on one more buffalo hunt after all."

"Which old thing?"

He laughed. "*Us* old things, if you feel up to it. Adam Thom's summary justice may have prevented a running fight through the farmyards of Red River, but he didn't consider—or didn't care—that there will be a number of Saulteaux accompanying the fall hunt into Sioux territory. Should make for a perfect opportunity for another stupid cycle of blood feuds escalating into another bloody war.

"I'm sorry, Little Rabbit, but I'm afraid I really can't think of anyone else at the moment who stands a better chance of being able to prevent that. You know I wouldn't even entertain the notion of you coming along if I weren't certain you'd be safe."

"It wouldn't be right for Elisabeth and Sophie Caroline to grow up without ever watching how their mother made pemmican."

CHAPTER 40

At the rendezvous on the meadow where the Pembina River joined the Red, the combined hunts from Red River, White Horse Plains, and Pembina totaled some 1,200 carts, 650 hunters with their wives and children, 2,000 horses, 500 oxen, and innumerable barking shoals of dogs.

With Mister Grant in attendance, it was a foregone conclusion who'd be Captain of the hunt. But Grant preferred to go through the formality of the election and of declaring the eight laws that, by now, every toddling child knew by heart. There would come a time when those toddling children had children of their own, who would have to learn by tradition.

Once the armada was under way across the rolling ocean of the plains, following the blue-and-white admiral's flag and the bright polished cannon, Grant was surprised to discover how much he'd been missing it. It was ridiculous for a man to allow himself to become entirely sedentary in a country made for nomads. Every day brought a new range of misty hills purpling another quarter of the horizon or a new series of variations in the endlessly shifting pallet of the prairie.

The hunt ascended from the tall-grass prairie to the drier shortgrass plains and encountered the herd and the Sioux on the same day. Grant and the other hunters—scattered over ten or twenty square miles— were wearily walking their buffalo runners back from the first run when one of the boys too young to hunt came galloping. "Mister Grant—the Sioux!"

"How many?"

"Not many—maybe a dozen. One of 'em's got a white flag."

Grant waved a few of the nearer hunters to fall in and kicked his exhausted buffalo runner into a trot in the direction the boy had pointed. The Sioux halted their ponies and held up the palms of their hands when they saw them coming. Grant twitched the halter and clamped in his knees to stop his horse in front of the one with the white flag and bade him howd'you do in sign talk. Fortunately one of the Sioux spoke a halting kind of French, courtesy of some suicidally zealous missionary. He informed Grant that they had come from several bands camped together a half day's ride to the west. The Sioux hunters had been meaning to run buffalo today, but now the wagon men had come and driven the herd out of reach. The Chiefs wished to come and smoke tobacco with their half-breed friends and discuss the situation.

Grant said: "We have a lot of butchering to do before the night comes down. Tell the Chiefs to come to our camp at sunset. Just the Chiefs, mind—we only have so much tobacco." They parted with the usual declarations of undying friendship and mutual respect.

Grant rode back to where the carts were waiting and set up a relay of scouts to patrol the perimeter of the outdoor abattoir, instructing all the hunters to make sure their guns stayed loaded and close to hand. As the sun stepped down onto the horizon, he shucked on his resplendent quillworked and embroidered antelope-skin coat—interrupting Marie's pemmican pounding to ask where she'd packed it—and settled down beside the fire with Falcon, Urbain Delorme, the headman of the Saulteaux hunters, Jean Baptiste Lajimodierre, big Toussaint Lussier, and the Dumont brothers. There were only two Dumont brothers now; crazy Gabriel had long since disappeared into the foothills country.

Grant didn't expect Toussaint or the Dumonts to contribute much to the oratory; they were just there to loom. They didn't have to wait long before taking up their duties. As the western hem of clouds turned magenta and cobalt, there was a shout from one of the sentries and a cart was wheeled aside to make an opening in the circle. Six painted horsemen pranced in through the gap, trailing streams of feathers and ribbons and foxtails. The lead one wore the red-dyed pronghorn-crowned bonnet of La Terre Qui Brûle. Grant caught him glancing sideways at the firelit brass gleam of the cannon, which just happened to have been placed behind the cart that had been wheeled aside to make a gate.

La Terre Qui Brûle climbed off his horse and unwrapped the long-stemmed pipe crooked in his arm. Grant proffered his tobacco pouch. After an hour or so of pipe ceremony and sonorous pronouncements on how the weather'd been down Dakotah way for the past year or three, La Terre Qui Brûle decided it would be within the realm of politeness to get down to business. "It is not right for our friends to

come into our country and kill our buffalo without giving us at least
a little something in return. The wagon men should—"

He was cut off by a crackle of gunshots and shouts from somewhere
in the night beyond the east wall. Grant wanted to leap to his feet but
stayed cross-legged on the ground, looking across the fire at La Terre
Qui Brûle, who looked uncomfortable. The gunfire ended, but the
shouts didn't, growing louder as they grew nearer. There was a tidal
wave in that direction, sweeping up everyone within the circle of carts
except the fourteen men circled around the council fire.

The shouting voices multiplied into two thousand voices roaring
and wailing. The wave washed back toward where Grant was sitting.
At its crest was a knot of hunters staggering under the deadweight of
three bodies.

Grant rose to his feet as the corpses were carried into the firelight.
He recognized all three of them, although one had to be identified by
the beadwork on his vest because his face had been skinned. All three
had been scalped. The third one wasn't all that much of a burden even
as deadweight, since she wasn't yet fourteen years old. The hunter
holding her said two things: "They got away"—nobody needed to be
told who "they" were—and "She's still alive."

Grant found Marie's eyes in the crowd. She nodded that she would
fetch his medicine box. Then he turned to La Terre Qui Brûle. He had
to hand it to him, the Chief had sand. With the whole camp howling
for his blood, La Terre Qui Brûle stood loose-shouldered and impassive. One of the other Chiefs opened his mouth to squawk out some
kind of excuse. La Terre Qui Brûle just raised his furled hand to his
chest and unhinged the fingers with a short, slicing motion. The other
Chief closed his mouth.

La Terre Qui Brûle raised his eyes to meet Grant's and said: "None
of us here had any part in this."

Grant believed him. Not that he had any doubt La Terre Qui Brûle
had it in him to smile and stab at the same time, but arranging a bit
of gratuitous butchery to coincide with a time when he was trapped
defenseless in the enemy camp didn't exactly fall under the heading
of sly. Someone in the mob who spoke Sioux bellowed: "It was *your*
warriors!"

A roar of agreement went up. Grant waited until he had some
chance to make himself heard and then blared over the receding
howls: "No! *We* don't butcher the innocent! La Terre Qui Brûle—will
you and your brothers seek out the ones who have done this and see
they are punished?"

"You have my word on that, Mister Grant. As surely as the sun will rise and the dew kiss the grass, La Terre Qui Brûle will see that justice is done."

Portions of the throng made it clear that they doubted that. Grant doubted it himself, but slicing up six Sioux Chiefs over a slow fire wasn't the best way to go about forestalling another war.

Toussaint Lussier boomed thickly: "If Mister Grant he says we let 'em go, that's good enough for me."

One of the Dumont brothers—their Cree names were He Talks and He Stands—said: "We can wait to see tomorrow."

It still took some doing to escort La Terre Qui Brûlé and the others through the mob to where their horses were picketed and see them safely on their way. Grant was leaning on the cannon, watching the painted rumps of their ponies melt into the dark and hatching options for the developments tomorrow might bring, when an unearthly shriek tore out behind him. The scalped girl had surfaced. He ran back to the council fire, and he and Marie went to work with bandages and poultices and morphine.

In the morning Grant strapped on General Dickson's sword, borrowing an awl from Marie to add a hole to the tongue of the waist belt, primed his pistols, and called for the Captain of the day. It turned out to be Falcon's turn in the rotation.

Grant changed his mind. His original plan was to take the Captain of the day and his ten soldiers and form a kind of flying squad, to patrol the outer reaches where various butchering parties were going out to salvage the remnants of the carcasses that nightfall had forced them to leave to the wolves. On the off chance that La Terre Qui Brûle's speech about justice had just been an excuse to get his hide out in one piece so his warriors could carry on playing wolf pack without putting him in jeopardy, it might be handy to have a dozen armed men trotting about in a body within earshot of the scouts posted around the perimeter. But Grant didn't fancy Pierriche being one of them. Not that Falcon wasn't a good man in a fight, but if he went down, there'd be no more songs.

"You and your soldiers," he told Falcon, "are to stick close to camp and keep an eye on the horse herd." Two of Falcon's ten soldiers—his nephews Charles Grant and John Wills—scowled disappointment. Grant tried in vain to remember what it felt like to be eager for a chance to prove himself in a situation where he had to kill men who were trying to kill him. One thing about the *pays d'en haut*, Charles and John would get all the chances they ever wanted without having to look for them.

In the end, it was probably better to hand-pick his flying squad instead of going with the Captain of the day. He took a stroll through the bustling city of tents, culling out hard-cases: the Dumont brothers, Urbain Delorme, François Morin . . . Marie's full-bearded little brother Daniel hadn't killed anybody yet that Grant knew of, but he rode like a demon and had somehow contrived to get his hands on a Kentucky rifle. Once Daniel was added in, his older brother, Donald, had to come along as well.

The ground shuddered as Toussaint Lussier trotted forward to volunteer. Grant shook his head. If it came down to a contest of which tribe could shoulder the most horses, Toussaint would be the first he called.

The sun quickly gained enough of an angle to burn off the lingering night chill as Grant trotted his troop in a five-mile oval. Within the oval, a trickle of carts was making its way out from the circle—now a pemmican factory working full tilt—toward the last kills of yesterday's run. Halfway through the second circuit, Grant spotted something inside the oval that disturbed him. A cart was parked beside a buffalo that three people were carving up. Two of the three appeared to be men.

It offended Grant's sense of propriety. Once one family established a precedent, it wouldn't take long before all the hunters found themselves grabbed by the collar as they slumped exhausted off their buffalo runners and told that if Jean Baptiste or Keewatin could help with the butchering . . .

Grant told Urbain to carry on trotting the hedgehog of mounted riflemen around the perimeter and turned his horse toward the precedent-breaking butchers. As he drew closer he saw that they were neither Saulteaux nor métis. A little closer in he recognized the Point Douglas Sutherlands, Mr. and Mrs., working with a strapping, dark-haired young man. All three were hacking away at the dead cow as though it were an obstreperous log and their knives rather dullish axes.

Mrs. Sutherland straightened up to her full, gawky height when she heard his horse approaching. A fair sprinkling of silver had been woven into her copper hair. Her face and dress were streaked with dried blood and sweat. She was still one damned handsome woman. She said in Gaelic: "A good day to you, Mister Grant."

"And to you, Mrs. Sutherland. Mister Sutherland."

"You remember our son, John. . . ."

"Good Lord—didn't you barely come up to my knee just yesterday? I must say I'm astounded at the energy of both Messrs. Sutherland. It was all I could do to crawl off my horse after yesterday's run, much less heft a skinning knife."

Mister Sutherland said: "We were not in on the running of the herd." It was only then that Grant remembered Mister Sutherland's gammy knee, which might do well enough for following a plow but not for clutching the ribs of a buffalo runner. "John is a better rider than I am," Mister Sutherland went on, "but *good* horsemanship is not the same as running buffalo. We came in company with Mister Lajimodierre, who has a habit of shooting buffalos faster than his wife and all his children can turn them into pemmican."

"Mister Grant," Mrs. Sutherland put in, "perhaps you could explain something Mister Sutherland and I were arguing about—"

"We were not *arguing*—"

"You see, Mister Lajimodierre has made a practice of throwing down a glove or something else that we can recognize as his beside every buffalo he shot. But most of the other hunters' kills have no mark to show which is whose. How can they tell?"

"Well . . . if I recall, you are both dab hands at reading and writing. . . ."

"She is better at it than I am, although I can manage well enough. John does better than both of us put together."

"Well, most of those six hundred–odd buffalo hunters would find it remarkable that six hundred scholars could each sign their names on a piece of paper—or a sheaf of papers, rather—and be able to go back and identify at a glance which was whose."

There was a gunshot from the south. It might have been someone scaring off a wolf or perhaps someone administering a coup de grâce to a buffalo who'd lain half-dead all night, but Grant wheeled his horse and kicked him into a gallop without bidding the Point Douglas Sutherlands good day.

Two moving objects—one much larger than the other—separated themselves from the drumming, bouncing horizon line ahead. The larger one was angling forward from Grant's left and shooting sparks out in front of it—his flying squad of reins-in-their-teeth gallopers. The smaller object grew larger as it charged straight on toward Grant—an unhorsed scout trying to run and reload at the same time. As Grant whipped past him to link up with Urbain and the others, he saw that it was Jean Baptiste Lajimodierre, who was as sharp-nosed a watchdog as a man could ask for but getting a bit grizzled for long sprints across broken country.

The hedgehog of horsemen fanned out into a line. Grant fell in on the right flank. There was nothing in front of them but yellow tufts of buffalo grass and a few blue clumps of sage. The man on Grant's left spun around on his saddle and fell away—the Sioux were down in the grass, aiming up at the horsemen silhouetted against the sky.

A panicked urge threw itself head on at Grant and his charging horse to shout a frantic order to rein in and drop down to the ground. He ducked sideways to let the urge whizz past his head and kept on going.

A painted body separated itself from the prairie. Grant fired both pistols. One misfired and the other plain missed. Grant yanked his horse to a squealing, rearing halt and slid backward off its rump, drawing General Dickson's saber on the way down. A snarling mask with a green feather in its hair and a spear in its hand erupted in front of him. He took the head off the spear with a parry *en carte* and drove his left fist into the painted face. The Sioux spun around, throwing the spear haft aside and tugging out a knife. The saber's returning arc from the neck of the spear took him in the neck.

As the Sioux went down, Grant yanked his sword free and spun around to see if anyone was coming up behind him. No one was. The remainder of the pack of Sioux were running for where they'd left their horses. Some of the more youthful members of the métis patrol were reloading to get another shot at their backs. Except for Aicawpow Dumont, who was using the butt of his rifle as a pile driver to silence something shrieking in the grass.

Grant's rifle was still hanging sheathed and loaded on his horse standing ten feet away. But at the moment he thought he'd leave it hang and just lean on his sword for a while. Urbain Delorme was slumped against the flank of his own horse, wheezing. He shook his head at Grant and said: "I think you're getting too old for this kind of nonsense."

Jean Baptiste Lajimodierre, who had somehow contrived to catch up but was paying for it on his hands and knees, nodded and panted: "Yeah, I think he is, too." He spat out a rusty-looking blob of sputum and growled: "Sons of bitches killed my horse."

Grant found enough breath to gasp out: "Accident . . . no doubt they were aiming at you."

"Goddamned Sioux never could learn to shoot straight."

On the way back, the jig rhythm of Grant's heart pumping blood into his brain slowed enough for him to start considering whether to turn the hunt around and head for home while they were still ahead of the game. He decided to hell with it—they'd come south to fill up their carts with pemmican. If the Sioux hadn't learned to let well enough alone, it was their lookout.

When the bulging carts shattered the skin of ice across the Passage of the Assiniboine, Grant had yet to see any further sign of the Sioux, and didn't until the morning of Eliza's wedding. He was trying to fasten a clean collar around his throat without strangling himself—the damned thing had fit perfectly when he'd bought it in Montreal twenty years ago—when Josephte bellowed up the stairs: "Cuthbert! There's someone here to see you!" He bounced the collar button off the wall and stomped downstairs.

Enough ice had melted off the man huddled by the kitchen fire for Grant to recognize one of the métis who'd chosen to stay on at Pembina when the rest of the tribe shifted their wintering grounds north. One blue-tinged hand clawed itself inside the flap of the blanket coat and produced a smoke-stained sheaf of folded papers. "I wrote this down from what the Chiefs said, Mister Grant."

Grant waved Josephte to give the man a bowl of soup and went into his study to crack the icy leaves apart. It was addressed to "Mister Grant, Chief of all the Half-Breeds" and read: "Friends, we hang down our heads, our wives mourn and our children cry. Friends, the pipe of peace has not been in our council lodge . . ." It went on to establish a benchmark in impudence, complaining that the wagon men had sent them away from their last parley with no gifts of tobacco or ammunition, and that the Dakotah Nation was owed at least eight cartfuls of pemmican in recompense for the eight murdered warriors. The document concluded with pious prayers for peace and justice, over the names and hieroglyphs of La Terre Qui Brûle and three other Chiefs.

Grant had just cut a sharp nib onto a fresh goose quill when the door of his study popped free of the frame like a champagne cork and Marie asked: "Why ain't you ready?"

"Hm? Oh, I just have to dash off a quick reply to—"

"Your daughter's getting married in five minutes!"

"Well, I'm sure she can wait the few extra minutes it'll take me to—"

"How old is that letter you got to dash off a reply to right now?"

"Hm? Let's see if it's . . . yes, dated just three weeks ago today."

"Then they can wait one goddamned day longer, can't they?"

It turned out to be three days, actually, before Grant recovered sufficiently to heft a pen again. He began his reply with: "Friends— The messenger which you sent us found us all as sad as yourselves, and from a similar cause: a cause which may give a momentary interruption to the pipe of peace; but should not, we hope, wholly extinguish it. . . .

"Friends—you say your people have been killed: we believe what you say, and sincerely regret it; but at the same time you forget to express your regret that our people were killed also. . . ." He went on in the same vein, either expressing himself or culling half-remembered phrases from Xenophon or Virgil, he wasn't certain. "They who would have friends must show themselves friendly. We have violated no faith, we have broken no peace. We will break none. We will not go to find you to do you harm. We will always respect the laws of humanity. But we will never forget the first law of nature: we will defend ourselves, should you be as numerous as the stars and powerful as the sun. . . ."

The wild geese were winging north across the face of the moon when the reply to his reply arrived—a letter enclosed with several wrapped bundles. "Friends . . . your message is now spread before us in council. Ne-tai-ope called for the pipe. Wa-nen-de-ne-ko-ton-money said no. All the men were then silent, but the women set up a noisy howl outside. Nothing was done till they got quiet. The council then broke up. It was the same the next day. The third day the council received your message as one of peace. . . ."

After the preamble came a series of statements by the relatives of the eight dead warriors. "Friends— You killed my son, he was brave. He who pointed the gun at him, I wish to be my son. My dead son had a feathered coup stick in his hand. I send it to my new son."

When Grant had skimmed on to the end, he leaned back in his chair, rubbed his eyes, and bellowed: "Marie!"

After a moment she spoke from the doorway behind him: "Yes?"

"That cabin we built by the lake last spring—"

"*You* built. I don't want no blame for it."

"Well, regardless . . . I'd say we're going to get a lot of use out of it."

"If it's still standing."

CHAPTER 41

When it came time to start putting things together for the annual relocation to the lake, Marie was left to manage it alone. Her husband had loaded a small tent and other camp gear onto a packhorse and disappeared into the southeast, toward a new trail that several enterprising young métis had cut through the bush that covered the border country east of the Red. The trail had ostensibly been cut for safety, so that small family groups traveling back and forth between the Forks and Pembina wouldn't have to pass through Sioux territory. By coincidence it also provided a handy back route for enterprising young men who might want to pay a call on the American trader who'd set up shop in Pembina, without the inconvenience of having their carts inspected by the warden of the plains.

He was only supposed to be gone a week. The week had stretched to ten days and Marie was beginning to get worried. After all, if he did find any smugglers, they'd be armed to the teeth like any other band of métis travelers, and he was only one man. She shook it off—no métis would dream of raising his hand to Mister Grant—and threw on her blanket to fetch the axe that Daniel had borrowed in December.

Despite the crisp, early spring air, the earth was almost dry and turning green. Her mother and Donald and his wife were working in the garden behind the big white house next door to Marie's. Donald and his family had moved in after her father had died—of pneumonia caught from falling through the ice chasing a wounded deer at the age of sixty-seven.

Marie stopped to pass the time of day and exchange comments on how fast the spring was advancing this year. Not fast enough, though, to be comfortable standing around outside gossiping for more than a few minutes. Soon she said: "Well, I'd better be getting along. I'm just going over to Daniel's to get our axe back."

Her mother said: "Your father'd say, 'Never could get that boy to grasp the notion of private property,' " doing a passable imitation of his snort when he was enjoying being curmudgeonly. "Yes, that's what he'd say all right."

"While you're at it," Donald put in, "tell him I want my skinning knife back. I think I just seen him heading out behind his barn."

Marie carried on across the somewhat fuzzy boundaries between the various McGillis properties and turned up the rutted path leading behind Daniel's barn, skirting the fenced pen squealing with piglets. Daniel was hunched over the tailgate of a cart, arranging the load in preparation for the summer hunt. On the ground beside him was a stack of camp gear, topped by Wappeston's felling axe. She called: "Hello, Daniel—"

He whirled around and straightened up, pressing his back against the cart. His startled expression relaxed into a strange wariness. "Oh, it's you. . . ." Then something white slithered out of the back of the cart and slid down to the ground. Daniel turned to snatch it up and put it back, but two more followed it out, as sinuously slippery as swatches of silk. They were ermine skins.

Marie shot a glance over her shoulder and hissed: "Have you gone crazy?"

"There's no law against me doing a bit of trapping."

"There's a law against selling them in Pembina!"

"Who said I was going to do that?"

"Why else would you be sneaking them onto a cart you'll be taking south to the rendezvous?"

"For Christ's sake, Marie, what harm does it do? Oh, I see. It might do harm to *you*, 'cause if your husband can't stop furs from leaving the country, maybe the Company'll stop paying him all that money every year. Well, maybe some of the rest of us want a little money from time to time, too!"

"I can see you're real hard done by; and your children sure look to me like they're starving."

"And that's supposed to be enough for the rest of us, ain't it? Just as long as we got enough to eat and a roof over our heads. Well, maybe sometimes *we'd* like to be able to buy a little present for our wives or our children, too—something we can't grow in our gardens or make with our hands, or something we can't afford from the Company stores 'cause the Company sells everything for three times what it's worth and buys our furs and pemmican for a third what they're worth. But I guess that don't matter to you."

"If the Company treats you that cruel, why don't you move down to the States or Canada—I hear they got a lot of fancy things in the stores there."

"So that's it? Toe the line or leave the country?"

"Oh, God, Danny—" She had to pause to stem a flash flood threatening to block the back of her nose. "Can't you be happy with the way things are?" He looked down at the ground, then crossed his arms and shook his head. "I won't have to say a word about this if you just promise me you'll take whatever you got hid in the cart to the Company store."

He just snorted. The bull-like sound and head toss was so much like their father, and the truculent pose was so much like the toddling little brother Marie used to lead by the hand, that the moisture she'd managed to stem behind the bridge of her nose flooded around to gush out both her eyes.

Daniel looked down at the ground again, nudged at a thistle root with the toe of his moccasin, and rasped: "What are you going to do?"

"I don't know!"

He raised his eyes to hers and said levelly: "It'd be better—better for *his* sake—that he don't find out. There's a lot of us have just about had it up to the bloody teeth with Mister Grant sniffing around like the Company's sheepdog."

"And you figure on being the one to tell him so?"

"I wouldn't want to. He's a sad old man who was good to me in his day. But if he tries to lord it over me, I'll—"

"Because you've had it up to the bloody teeth?" He crossed his arms and nodded. " 'Bloody teeth' don't touch on it, you bloody little idiot. You say something to him like you just said to me and he'll pull your head off and kick it across the river."

"I don't think so."

"Maybe you're right. Maybe he's gotten too softhearted. Maybe if he thinks he ain't wanted as Chief anymore, he'll just let it all go and tend his own garden. And then who's gonna speak on the council for all the people that don't happen to be white? Who's going to keep the Court of Rupert's Land from treating everyone that don't speak English like shit? Who's going to keep going back and forth between George Simpson and us to make sure the Company don't get fed up and pull out and leave us to the Americans or the Canadians or English to plow under?"

"There's a lot of younger men willing to do those things. James Sinclair, Louis Riel—"

"Did James Sinclair or Louis Riel stand up alone on the prairie between us and the Sioux? Was it one of them that put together a buffalo hunt that can go anywhere it damn pleases? Was it one of them that got you the land here to live on, or pulled the arrow out of your chest last year?"

"Like I said, Marie—I know he's been good to me in his day. But his day's gone."

She snatched up the axe and fled home.

Wappeston came home the day after the hunt pulled out, looking and smelling much like a man who'd spent the last two weeks living in a bush tent and on horseback. As she was firing up the kettle to fill the hip bath in the kitchen, she said: "So, did you catch anybody?"

"Some." He named a couple of the young Red River métis. "They'll spend the next few weeks living in that shed of a jail and chopping firewood instead of going out on the hunt. That should be enough to make them think twice. Where should I put this shirt?"

"Out the back door. If it ain't crawled away by next laundry day, I'll see what I can do."

"Did anyone get up to anything interesting while I was off making the country safe for the shareholders in London?"

"No, nothing out of the ordinary. We're all packed up to head up to the lake. Pierriche and Mary are coming along this time. Elisabeth got her first tooth—I got the scars to prove it. I think your water's ready."

After the first lie, it got easier. By the time they were packing up the cabin at Grant's Lake to head back to Grantown, she'd succeeded in building a wall in her mind between her husband and her brother. It took no effort at all anymore to keep them separate, so she could stumble across a memory of either without any danger of the other one popping up to make her uncomfortable. But when the hunt came back, with Daniel and his family all sporting new store-bought hats and shoes, a few cracks spread through the wall.

As the maturer denizens of Grantown were abandoning the moonlit dance yard of the homecoming to the younger generation, Wappeston sidled up to her and said: "What's Daniel done?"

"Daniel?"

"Your brother, remember? A rather crisp and wintry air's developed between you two. Did he do something to offend you?"

"No . . . just because I don't throw my arms around him every time I see him . . . with the amount of family we got living on all sides, I'd spend my whole life hugging and kissing."

"It doesn't sound like a bad way to pass the time—at least for a night. . . ." He took her arm and walked her toward the house.

. . .

In August a message came that Sir George Simpson had completed his circle around the world to the stone fort and would like to have a few words with the warden of the plains. Wappeston saddled up FireAway's daughter, whistling jauntily. Marie leaned her elbows on the fence and said: "What's got you so frisky all of a sudden?"

"Today's the day the cat learns what a certain Thom rat has been playing at while he was away."

He came home much less frisky. She ladled out a bowlful from the soup pot she'd left standing on the hearth and said: "Well?"

"Well what?"

"Well, what about the Little Emperor and the recorder of Rupert's Land?"

"Oh. Mister Simpson was decidedly not inclined to hear a word regarding Mister Thom."

"Then why'd he want to see you? Just to say hello?"

"What— Sir George indulge in conviviality for its own sake? He wanted to discuss the fact that the illicit trade in furs is getting out of hand. He has a point. Although the Company has nothing to worry about from the young men of Grantown." She bit her lips and breathed through her nose. "The more I've got settled in here, the more I've been neglecting the métis at Red River. There's an entire generation there that's grown up under the influence of malcontents who portray the Company as some sort of Oriental despot.

"But Sir George appears to have come up with a solution. While he was in London he managed to convince the imperial government that the American Republic's expansion into the Oregon Territory means that Rupert's Land will be next, unless we have a garrison of stout British soldiers on hand to scare the Yankees off. By the end of the summer Red River will be graced by the redcoats of the Sixth Royal Regiment of Foot. By pure happenstance, good British troops also serve to enforce good British laws—such as the trade monopoly of the Governor and Company of Adventurers Trading into Hudson's Bay."

"Well, that's good."

"What is?"

"That the soldiers'll stop the smuggling."

"Good?" He rolled the word around in his mouth and tasted it again. " 'Good . . .' That was supposed to be my job, Waposis. I'm not all that hungry. Where did you shelve that crock of gin?"

The troops were garrisoned at Lower Fort Garry, so Lady Frances Simpson's pink limestone bandbox came to some use after all. Although the soldiers never ventured out as far as Grantown, except for a few officers on hunting trips, and although Marie only ventured to the stone fort once to join the crowd of curious Saulteaux watching the red files march for hours without going anywhere, the Sixth Royals still had their effects on Marie's circle of domesticity. For one thing, as the soldiers' pay packets began to spread themselves around, the old habit of doing business by barter or exchanging credit at the Company store began to be replaced by cash—to the point where Marie grew to recognize a shilling or a penny at a glance, instead of having to peer at the engraving.

Another effect was that the fur smuggling came to an abrupt halt, leaving Wappeston nothing to do but putter around the farm and worry about how he was going to prove himself useful to the Company. After the first year, though, it sank in to a few of the bolder smugglers that five hundred foot soldiers drilling smartly at the stone fort weren't much of a threat to a cart or a carriole slipping through the backwoods or the hills along the border. So the warden of the plains was back in business.

As soon as the ice was off the rivers and the spring gumbo had dried enough to make cart travel possible, Wappeston saddled up his horse to take a swing southeast through the gap between the Pembina Hills and Turtle Mountain. Marie considered mentioning that maybe he was getting a little old for long rides and cold camps. But the boyish bounce that had come back to him at the prospect of making himself useful made her wave good-bye without saying a word, except: "Come back safe."

He'd been gone for a week when Mary Falcon announced breathlessly from the kitchen doorway: "Have you heard?"

"Heard what?"

"Then you haven't. It'll take a while to tell. . . ."

"Would you like a cup of tea?"

"I don't mind, me whatever. You better sit down."

"I have to get the—"

"They arrested Father Belcourt!"

"Father Belcourt? For what?"

"Smuggling furs. He was sending some carts to Pembina to pick up some stoves that'd been shipped there. The governor gave orders to have his carts searched. They didn't find any furs, but they arrested him anyways."

Marie had to sit down. Father Belcourt had baptized Sophie Caroline and Elisabeth and Julie Rose and had performed the sacrament of marriage for Eliza. Marie said: "If they didn't find any furs, they can't arrest him."

"They did anyways. The Red River métis say they're going to pull the jail apart."

Wappeston came home that afternoon, bouncing off his saddle, brandishing two fat, leather-bound books with the pages still uncut, crowing: "Here it is! George Simpson's—"

"Is it true about Father Belcourt?"

"Probably. I'd believe anything of the reverend father. Here, take a look: *A Journey Round the World in Two Volumes*, by Sir—"

"Is it true Father Belcourt's in jail?"

"Last time I looked. Can't you offer a man a drink after a week in the saddle? Angus, would you be so good as to take care of the horses?"

"Yes, Papa."

"Mind the packhorse, he's got into a habit of kicking."

"Is it true you arrested Father Belcourt even though you didn't find any furs?"

He groaned. "Well, at least let me get sat down, if you're going to . . ." Once he was settled into his chair at the head of the table with a cup of brandied tea, he said: "Now, who's been bending your ear about Father Belcourt?"

"Mary."

"Ah. I should've known." He took another deep quaff and smacked his lips. "In the first place, I didn't arrest Father Belcourt. That was our esteemed governor's doing. In the second, there's no shortage of other evidence. Father Belcourt's been preaching increasingly loudly with each passing year that the Company has no right to restrict trade, and that the natives of the *pays d'en haut* have every right to engage in—"

"That don't mean he's doing it himself!"

"You don't say. Any idea why Father Belcourt hired a train of freight carts to go to Pembina?"

"Mary said there was some stoves there he'd ordered."

"Remarkable. My sister actually got part of it right. Now, why do you figure the Company chose to slap a heavy tariff on Carron stoves?"

"I don't know. Because they'd rather sell them through their own stores?"

He shook his head. "Because a portable heating stove is a damned handy article if you plan to throw up a trading shack on the Qu'Appelle for the month of February and move on to the Souris come March."

"Well, that still don't mean—"

"*Ten* stoves? What do you think he was planning to do—found a chain of nunneries?"

"He still could be innocent."

"You know and I know different. It makes no difference, anyway. The Company isn't interested in convicting or punishing him, just in coming up with a plausible excuse to eject him from its territories."

"It isn't up to them where a missionary goes, it's up to the Church."

"Unless I miss my guess, Bishop Provencher will say a hundred Hail Marys when he sees the back of Father Belcourt. And so will I."

"Mary said the Red River métis are going to pull the jail down if the Company don't set him free."

"No doubt they also plan to pull the bayonets off five hundred British muskets while they're at it."

"But if—"

"All the ifs have been blanketed, Waposis, take my word for it. Now, if you don't mind, I'd like to repair to the study to study the gospel according to the Little Emperor."

After a few moments Marie began to hear muffled chortles from the parlor. They built up to wolfish howls of laughter. She went into the parlor and pulled open the door of his little office. He was doubled over on his chair, rocking back and forth precariously, with one of the leather-bound volumes cracked open in his hand. He wiped the tears off his cheeks, looking up at her. She said: "I wouldn't've thought George Simpson would write good jokes."

"George Simpson wrote nothing! Adam Thom wrote his book for him!"

"How can you tell?"

"Believe me, Waposis—after nine years of being forced to listen to Adam Thom's—Adam *Tome's*—pronouncements . . ."

She was willing to take his word for it, but he was proved wrong about the situation building at Red River. Although it did end with Father Belcourt being banished across the border to Pembina, it wasn't before lots of feathered rifles had been brandished around the courthouse and the good Father carried in triumph to St. Boniface. She began to worry about what was building up in front of her husband and told him so.

He laughed. "What's to fear? Didn't it end exactly like I said?"

"Yes, but . . . it wasn't as easy as you thought it'd be, was it? I'm getting afraid for you."

"For me? Don't you fret for me, Little Rabbit. I may not be quite so limber as I once was, but I flatter myself that I can still go toe to toe with any man in—"

"Toe to toe didn't help you on a New Year's night when you were twenty-five years younger."

His voice went hard. "Perhaps you failed to notice that I have not made the mistake of sitting with my back to a door since that night. Or to a tent entrance, for that matter—usurping the warrior's privilege from the traditions of our maternal ancestors."

"There's other ways someone can get hurt."

"And I know them all. It's good of you to be concerned, but there's no need. What's this—tears? I told you—there's nothing to be afraid of for my sake. After the entire Dakotah Nation and all the others who've done their damnedest to take this scalp . . . Ssh . . ." But she couldn't "ssh," nor find a way to make him understand what she was trying to warn him about.

Fortunately something came along the next day to take her mind off it. It came out at one of her favorite times of the day, those few moments when she had finished eating her supper but couldn't start clearing the table until everyone else had. She could lean back in her chair and gaze at Wappeston at the far end of the long avenue of plates and platters and gravy-sopping children: butterball Sophie Caroline, long, lean Betsy—whose short form for "Elisabeth" didn't bother Marie in the least—earnest Angus, Louis with his eyes twinkling at some new-hatched inspiration for mischief, Marie Rose with her eyes barely overtopping her plate rim, humming to herself as she ate, and Julie Rose gurgling in her cradleboard on the wall. Julie Rose and Marie Rose had proved all the experts wrong about Betsy being their mother's last. So it was just as well that their Aunt Josephte and cousin John were no longer part of the household or there wouldn't have been room to graduate to the table. John had a place of his own now, next to the Brelands', with an added-on back room for his mother.

Charles folded his hands on the table, coughed to clear his throat, and announced: "I guess now's as good a time as any. While I was away on the hunt I decided—well, we decided . . . Me and Euphrosme Gladu are getting married."

His brothers and sisters goggled at him, but their whoops and giggles died aborning in the face of their father's reaction. He didn't alter his expression or his posture on his chair, just slowly slid his eyes sideways toward Charles and then reached into his belt pouch for his pipe and tobacco. Angus and Louis leaped off their chairs and raced to be the one who got to light a straw from the hearth fire. Louis got there first, but Charles ostentatiously tugged out a pipe of his own and beckoned his littlest brother to bring him a light.

Once Wappeston's pipe was going, and the blown-out straw handed back to Louis, he said in Charles's general direction: "I'm sure both you and Euphrosme sincerely believe you'll still want to marry each other when the time comes. But a lot can change in four or five years."

"It won't be four or five years. Or even one. We're gonna go right to work putting up a house so we can be settled into it before the fall hunt."

"You're too young to get married."

"I'm a lot older'n Eliza was."

"It's different for a girl. A man should get himself a start in life before he thinks of taking on a wife and family."

"Like Pascal did?"

"Yes, like Pascal, for instance."

"Well, I ain't Pascal—did that ever cross your mind? I want to live my own life my own way!"

Marie could see the embers starting to flare up in Wappeston's eyes. She stood up abruptly and said: "Charles—you just caught us flat-footed. You got to give us a little time to think over what we think. Tomorrow you and me and your father can sit down and talk." Wappeston arched his eyebrows at her, but she started stacking plates together with as much clatter as her Crown Staffordshire seemed likely to survive. Betsy and Sophie Caroline, bless them, leaped up to give her a hand.

In the night, after she'd blown out the candle, she said: "Charles don't mean to get that yelling tone in his voice when he talks to you. It's just he's scared to death of you, so by the time he works himself up to saying something . . ."

"Why would he be scared of me? I'm his father!"

"Well, that's one reason. Euphrosme's a good, smart girl, and Charles wants badly to get out from under us and start his own life."

"I'm sure he *thinks* he does. I'm sure *Angus* thinks he'd like to have a house of his own where Mama can't tell him not to burp at the table."

"That ain't hardly the same thing. Charles has been taking care of himself just fine on the buffalo hunt for years now."

"*That's* hardly the same thing. For God's sake—at twenty-one years of age it's still a struggle for him to sign his name! And I swear he has to ask the Company clerks to read out the figures on his little account."

"Maybe he's just gone out of his way to make himself as different from you as he can, so he won't seem like just a smaller copy. Maybe he'll surprise you once he's off on his own."

"Well, we'll try to have a reasoned conversation with him tomorrow. And with the girl's parents."

"I think the Gladus ain't likely to kick up a fuss."

"Were I them I would."

"Wappeston—I know it's hard for you to get used to, but we can't stop him from doing what he wants to do anymore. The only difference we can make is in how far away he has to go to do it."

Among the rambling row of strip farms that made up Grantown there were a few houses and barns standing empty, due to the cruel arithmetic of the buffalo hunt or to the occasional family of dyed-in-the-wool nomads who decided they weren't made for farming after all. But instead of taking one of those places, Charles and Euphrosme elected to build on a virgin lot at the downstream edge of Ghost Horse Plains—the opposite end of town from the Brelands and as far away from the big white house with the widow's walk that one could go while still remaining part of Grantown.

Wappeston put up a pretty good show of good humor at the wedding, although he did make one too many jokes. Marie had insisted that they should hand over Potacikin's healthiest great-granddaughter as a wedding present, and Wappeston had thrown in two hundred pounds of credit at the Company store. Marie said: "You didn't have to do that."

"Well, hell, the way that boy earns money, they're going to need it."

In November Jean Baptiste Falcon brought a letter from the chief factor at Fort Garry. Wappeston said: "Well, well . . . it appears that after two years with no discernible invasions by the Army of the Republic, the imperial Parliament has decided that Rupert's Land will be just as safe under the protection of a small troop of Chelsea pensioners as under a full regiment of the line that could be better put to use against the Zulus or Afghans or Russians or any of the other barbarians nibbling at the borders of the Empire."

"What are Chelsea pensioners?"

"Chelsea Hospital, in London. It's the warehouse for British soldiers who've been invalided out for one reason or another: infirmities of age, recurring fevers. Should be quite a show when the Sixth Royals strike up the band for auld lang syne."

In the spring Marie and Wappeston loaded the children onto two carts and traveled to the stone fort to watch the pomp and circumstance of the old guards' fare-thee-well. In the fall they went again to see their new protectors disembarking from the York boat brigade.

The officers of the Chelsea pensioners were as spit-polished as the Sixth Royals. But the few of the seventy rank soldiers who weren't hobbling or shuffling looked to be growing mold out of their red uniforms and gray cheeks.

Wappeston chuckled low in his throat. Marie turned to see what the joke was. He murmured: "They remind you of anyone?"

She looked again. "The Des Meurons?"

"Exactly."

"Why's that funny?"

"Because, Waposis . . . if this is all the Company's got to keep the peace with, it's going to find itself increasingly in need of the services of the warden of the plains."

He was proved right almost immediately. The District of Assiniboia turned into a nursery with no nanny. By the spring, four métis had been nabbed trying to sneak across the line with loads of furs. Two of the four were from Red River and two from White Horse Plains. The Grantown métis were Guillaume Sayer and Daniel McGillis.

CHAPTER 42

The day before the trial of Sayer, McGillis et al, Grant saddled up FireAway's granddaughter Elisabeth and rode to the Forks. She had inherited more length of leg than her mother had and was a joy to ride, eager to test her newly filled-out muscles. Grant held the reins loose and let her gallop when the fancy took her.

It had been an early spring, and when spring came on the prairies it had a habit of bursting straight toward summer with breakneck speed. The meadows and sloughs and woods were riotous with courting birds. The air was sweet with the blooming tang of balsam poplars, what the Kildonan people called the Balm of Gilead tree. The pussy willow catkins were already bloated and brittle and blowing away, gone to seed.

Adam Thom had gone and scheduled the trial for Ascension Day, apparently on the clever assumption that all the fractious Red River métis would be occupied at mass instead of loitering around the courthouse. It didn't appear to have occurred to him that anyone who felt inclined to assemble a mob would have one ready-made the instant mass let out.

A mob around the courthouse seemed to be exactly what was in the offing for this Ascension Day, which was why Grant was traveling to the Forks a day early. His long-ago attempt at water mills had left him with no illusions about his capacity as a millwright but had given him enough hands-on experience to guess at how a real millwright would respond to the sight of a spar about to swing in among the cogs and gears of his machine: keep calm, take hold of the right levers, and put his hands on the appropriate tools. The spar that was about to get itself caught up in the works of Rupert's Land needn't do too much damage, depending upon two men Grant was going to have words with beforehand.

One of them was Louis "Irish" Riel, who in five short years' residence at Red River had elevated himself to spokesman for the Red River métis. Grant wouldn't have thought that a fractional trace of Cree blood and a background as a wool carder and seminarian would qualify a man to speak for half-breed buffalo hunters, but Riel had added to his credentials by marrying one of the daughters of Jean Baptiste Lajimodierre. Jean Baptiste and his wife were both white, but Irish had hit upon the happy notion that métis and French were the same thing. Various métis with names like Sinclair or MacDougall might have objected to that, if Adam Thom hadn't done such a marvelous job of drawing a line between the English and French sides of the river.

It was all so damned ridiculous. Most of the "English" faction spoke Gaelic before English, and most of the "French" were more comfortable speaking Cree or the hybrid patois that might just as well be Chinese to anyone from Paris or Montreal. Ridiculous or not, Grant told himself, there it is and you'll have to play it as it lies.

He hobbled Elisabeth to graze the plantation around Fort Garry and commandeered one of the Company's smaller canoes to cross the river. The tip of a windmill sail poking over the treetops on the east bank gave him a compass point and reminded him of Irish Riel's other nickname—"the Miller of the Seine," earned by his having inveigled the Company into financing a fulling mill that was no more successful than Grant's attempts on Sturgeon Creek. The Miller of the Seine hadn't appeared to detect even a whiff of sarcasm in the title, but then that was his major qualification as a voice crying out against the Company's tyranny in the wilderness—he was as earnest as the grass was green.

Grant beached the canoe downstream of St. Boniface Cathedral and climbed up through the riverside woods to the Riel segment of Jean Baptist Lajimodierre's vast portion of the east bank of the Red. There was a clay-plastered log house, a few sheds, and a garden. Between the house and the garden, a lean woman with blue-gray eyes was manhandling a canoe paddle through an immense pot squatted over a bed of coals. From the smell, she was rendering tallow and ashes to make soap. Perched on the woodpile behind her was a gray-eyed boy still pudgy with baby fat.

Grant said: "*Bonjour*, Madame Riel. Is your husband about?"

"Jean Louis!"

Irish came around the corner of the house with an axe in his hand, stopped in his tracks, and said warily: "Mister Grant. What brings you here?"

Before Grant could reply, Irish's father-in-law came ambling out behind him and held up the palm of his hand. "*Wakiye*, Wappeston."

"*Wakiye, Kichee Omachew*, Great Hunter."

"Oh, I ain't all that *kichee* and *omachew* no more. Joints're getting too stiff."

"That'll be the day." Grant turned back to Riel. "I just stopped by to have a word with you, Irish, about tomorrow—hoping that between the two of us we might be able to forestall any unpleasantness that might be in the offing."

"Unpleasantness?"

Could the man really be that obtuse? "You know as well as I do that Sayer and the others are guilty. But there is a segment of the population that believes the law is unjust. They should be made aware of the fact that the Company is hardly going to stand Sayer and company against a wall and shoot them."

"The Company has no right to put a yoke around our necks! We have the right to—"

" 'We'? To which 'we' are you referring, Irish?"

"We who live here! We have the right to trade freely with whoever we please!"

"Why not let the courts decide that?" Riel opened his mouth to protest. "I don't mean Adam Thom's court. You know as well as I that the Company's charter is an ongoing question in the British courts. If they decide the monopoly's invalid—"

"They won't! You know as well as I that the rich English judges will back up the rich English Company!"

"Well, so what if they do?" Grant attempted to moderate his voice to a cajoling tone. "Look around you—you have a comfortable home and a lovely family. And no one's going to interfere with your continuing prosperity so long as you sell any furs that come into your possession to the Company. Is that too much to ask in exchange for all you have here? And if the life you have here is so damned miserable, why the hell did you leave Quebec?"

Madame Riel let go her paddle with a gasp and whirled around to clap her hands over her son's ears. Irish said stiffly: "I will thank you not to speak evil within hearing of my son."

Grant knuckled the bridge of his nose, inhaled and exhaled twice, and said: "Forgive me. I didn't come here to create bad blood, only to point out that while the Company's rule may not be perfect, its shortcomings are hardly good cause to find ourselves with a riot on our hands tomorrow."

"That isn't up to me to decide, Mister Grant. If the Company refuses to listen to the will of the people, tomorrow's sun may set on a Fort Garry that's been pulled down stone by stone!"

"Or it may set on me riding home with your balls in my hand. Good day." Grant regretted it as soon as he'd said it, but he'd already turned on his heel and started back toward the canoe waiting on the shore.

"Wappeston!" Jean Baptiste Lajimodierre called out and caught up with him. "I'll walk you down to your boat, in case you might get lost in the bush." Once they were out of earshot he murmured under his breath, shaking his head: "Ain't no question he's a good boy, but he still seems like a damned odd boy to me."

" 'Boy'? He must be thirty years old if he's a day."

"He's barely out of his cradleboard!"

"In some ways, perhaps. . . ."

"Who the hell are you talking about?"

"Louis Riel."

"So am I—my grandson."

"Oh."

"Marie Anne'd skin me for it, but I still think there's something damned odd about a boy that can tell you how Saint Polycarp got martyred but ain't interested in how to tell the difference between a perch and a trout, much less how to go about catching 'em. I guess it's better that Julie finally got herself married instead of becoming a nun like she wanted, but sometimes I can't help thinking it'd be healthier for her to have been a bride of Christ instead of raising her own little baby Jesus."

By that time they'd reached the canoe. Lajimodierre scratched his beard and said: "Well . . . well . . . come tomorrow, why don't you do a favor to yourself and leave your rifle and your pistols at home?"

"I don't usually make a habit of going armed to court."

"Tomorrow's court ain't going to be usual. Most people on this side of the river don't have anything against you, but there's a few who'd take any excuse, and a lot of heads getting just a bit too hot for anybody's good. You don't want to go losing your temper tomorrow like you did just now. But what the hell do I know?"

"Quite a bit. Are you coming across the river tomorrow?"

Lajimodierre shook his head. "I've had enough excitement for one life. Maybe you have, too. I don't know what the hell to say to you. I never seen a War Chief like you in my life, or any kind of Chief, for that matter. But I don't want to see another war here."

"Nor do I."

"Well . . . good luck to you, then. I got this bad feeling you're gonna need it."

Grant let Elisabeth break into a canter on the trail winding north toward Kildonan. It was just as well that her natural inclination was to go wherever she was going at a gallop or a canter; further acquaintance was making it clear that her trot was an open invitation to kidney damage.

Just before Point Douglas, he turned her off the trail toward a very spruce and well-ordered farm, where he was due to have supper and spend the night.

Grant was expecting that supper with the sheriff of Red River and his delightful Okanagan "princess" of a wife would be a respite between the two men he'd come to see for reasons other than the pleasure of their conversation. Perhaps it would even calm him down enough to do a better job with Adam Thom than he had with Irish Riel.

While carving the roast, the sheriff of Red River announced that he'd formed a resolution, now that the children were grown, to write a book about the Red River Settlement—perhaps several. Grant said gravely, "Were I you, I'd think twice. I hear Adam 'Tome' doesn't come cheap," provoking a scowl from the sheriff and a whoop of laughter from his wife.

For all the sheriff's cranky posturing and fierce side-whiskers, he could never manage to disguise the fact that he was hopelessly in love with the place he'd come to live in and had been since the day he'd first laid eyes on it. He still delighted in telling the story, to anyone who hadn't heard it more than ten times, of encountering one of the local farm boys out on the prairie and inquiring as to where he could find the trail to Red River. The farm boy had replied: "You're on it."

"I see no trail!"

"There ain't none, but that's the way we goes."

After supper the sheriffs of Red River and White Horse Plains climbed onto their horses and rode north. As they passed the base of Point Douglas, Grant could see through the fringe of budding poplars that there was a big new square-beam house where the Sutherlands' thatched cabin had stood, and that the three Point Douglas Sutherlands were out working in their rose-lit garden in company with a sturdy-looking, young, blond, pregnant woman. He'd heard last winter that John Sutherland had finally allowed himself to be caught. He would've liked to take a detour up the path onto Point Douglas, but he kept Elisabeth's nose pointed ahead along the trail through Kildonan to Little Britain and Adam Thom.

With his wife no longer within earshot, the sheriff of Red River dropped his sanguine pose and said: "If there's trouble tomorrow, we'll get no help from the Chelsea pensioners. Since the major's the governor now, he's got to stand in as president of the court, so there'll be no one to order the soldiers out and line them up."

"What about the captain?"

"The captain and the major had a tiff, and the major's suspended him from duty."

"Is this whole place turning into a madhouse? Oh, well, I suppose it's just as well the soldiers stay out of it. The casualties might have been appalling. If one métis were to cock his buffalo gun in the face of our stalwart Chelsea pensioners, half of them would drop dead from heart failure." The sheriff of Red River laughed, but the sheriff of White Horse Plains didn't feel near as cavalier as he'd sounded.

As they turned off the trail, a choral chanting emanated from the Thom house—the unmistakable, stentorian bass-baritone of the man himself, accompanied by several higher, thinner voices. Grant looked a question at the sheriff of Red River, who shrugged. "He leads the family in prayer services twice a day. Very religious man, our recorder. But do you think he could trouble himself to help us persuade the Company to send us a kirk minister as they've been promising these forty years? . . ."

By the time they'd climbed off their horses, hitched their reins to the iron post ring, and stepped to the door, the catechizing had stopped. Grant plied the brass lion's head knocker and the door was opened by the harried-looking métis girl who was the latest in a long line of replacements for the Scots nanny. "Mister Grant!"

"*Bon soir*, Marie Hélène. Would you be so good as to inform Mister Thom we'd like to have a word with him?"

"Oh!" She shot a flustered glance back over her shoulder. "But, Mister Thom, you see, he's *reading*. . . ."

"I don't believe he'll object to the interruption, under the circumstances. Or if he does, he can make his objections known to *me*." She stepped aside reluctantly and Grant crossed the threshold.

A spit-polished little boy was solemnly perusing a schoolbook at the dining table, overseen by Adam Thom's anemic, deferential wife, who was busying her hands with needlepoint. In a leather wing chair by the hearth sat the man of the house, with a weighty tome in one hand, a Bavarian churchwarden in the other, and a tassled, squat version of a Turkish fez perched on his blocky head. Although his starched collar was still fastened firmly around his neck, he'd discarded his customary broadcloth day coat in favor of a quilted velvet smoking jacket. He didn't look up as they came through the door. Grant called: "Good evening, Mister Thom."

"Hm? What? Oh—didn't expect to see you two till morning."

"We thought there might be one or two things that ought to be discussed beforehand."

"Such as what? Oh, very well. Mary Helen, fetch some tea."

"Oui, monsieur— Oh! I mean, yes, Mister Thom, I will do so right smartly."

Thom closed his book, marking the place with a needlepointed bookmark, and said: "Forgive me for being a bit gruff. Once one gets hot on the trail of the obscurer Hebraic scriptures . . . Had to teach myself Hebrew, you know. All they taught at Aberdeen were Greek and Latin. And the proper use of English, of course. Did you know that the life span of our Lord—thirty-four years, or possibly thirty-five—explains all of human history? Every decisive event since the Creation can be charted at intervals of between thirty-four and thirty-five years. I mean to write a book about it someday."

"Seems to be a lot of that going around these days." Since their host showed no signs of offering a chair, Grant squatted down Indian fashion on the hearth rug. His knees didn't bend quite as spryly as they used to, but the gesture was worth the strain.

The tea arrived. Thom waved the girl away and played mother with the tea caddy, then hoisted his cup and gruffed: "Now, what is it that's so urgent it couldn't wait until tomorrow?"

The sheriff of Red River said: "It's not so much *urgent*, as that we might not be given the time tomorrow to stop and make plans."

"Plans? Plans for what, sir?"

"For how we intend to respond"—Grant elucidated what should have been obvious—"if several hundred sulky buffalo hunters appear on the courthouse steps. The Chelsea pensioners won't be of any help."

"I hardly expected they would. But what about this Red River constabulary to which we've been paying wages all these years?"

Grant shook his head. "I'm not sure how they'd take it if they were asked to line up against their brothers and cousins and uncles. And even if they did, there's not enough of them to make a difference."

"Nonsense. I've seen a dozen disciplined officers, or even a half dozen, face down unruly mobs numbering in the hundreds."

"Mister Thom . . ." Grant rubbed his forehead to keep his voice level. "Allow me to point out that any unruly mobs you may have seen in Lower Canada or Scotland were composed of disgruntled farmers or factory workers or grocery clerks. The men who are likely to come knocking on the courthouse door tomorrow morning will come carrying guns and knives and axes and know how to use them."

"This is preposterous. Are you telling me you *expect* your people to run riot tomorrow?"

Grant let that "your people" go by. "No, I don't. I expect them to make a lot of threatening noises, but I don't expect them to go any further, as long as they're not provoked."

"Provoked, sir? How could they be *provoked* by the impartial administration of justice?"

"That depends. How do you plan to proceed with the cases of Sayer and McGillis, etcetera?"

"How else? If the jury convicts them on the evidence, they shall be punished with the full rigor of the law."

"What exactly do you mean by 'full rigor'?"

"The law is perfectly clear: fines up to the full retail value of the contraband in question, the immediate revocation of the guilty party's leasehold—"

"You can't!"

"I can and I will, sir. The resolution of 1828 states unequivocally—"

"I know that. I was here when the resolution was approved. But it's never been used."

"And perhaps that is precisely why we've seen a steady increase in smuggling and other lawless acts with every passing year. What's the use of giving the law teeth if we don't use them?"

Grant yanked his eyes off Adam Thom's bull neck before his hands could sieze the urge to follow them. He looked into the hearth fire to see if it could divert him for long enough to avoid committing homicide. Every home and farm in Rupert's Land was technically on lease from the Company, except the Kildonan colonists' freeholds. The Company hadn't gone into the landlord business for profit. Grant had seen one deed on file leasing two hundred acres for nine hundred and ninety-nine years at an annual rent of one peppercorn. But each and every lease the Company drew up contained the condition that the lessee not engage in trading furs, except through the Company.

On paper, the Company had a perfect right to revoke the lease of anyone found guilty and to refuse them any future lease, effectively banishing them from the northern half of North America. The people who'd been living there for generations didn't care much for pieces of paper.

Grant managed to slow his breathing enough to take a sip of tea and came across a possible out. "All of that's academic in the cases of Sayer and McGillis. They both live in Grantown, so they hold their deeds through me. You can't go evicting another man's tenants."

"You can take that up with Sir George and the London Committee. In the meanwhile, I intend to do my duty and enforce the law, without bending it to the will of any surly batch of half-savages or Frenchmen."

Grant took another sip of tea and found himself shuddering and tasting bile. The words that came out of his mouth burned his throat on the way up, as though he'd seared it raw with dry-heaving acid. "Perhaps there *is* some merit to your theory of history's cycle, Mister Thom. But perhaps you don't have the life span of our Lord exactly right. You see, it will be thirty-*three* years ago tomorrow, less a month or so, that a certain upstanding governor of the Selkirk colony marched out to read the law to a motley group of half-savages and Frenchmen, at a place called Seven Oaks."

"Ah, but there is one overwhelming difference between that poor, deluded gentleman and I. And though I appreciate the show of concern and prudence on the part of my two sheriffs, you will see there's no need whatever to be alarmed about tomorrow if you but keep that difference in mind."

The sheriff of Red River said: "Which difference would that be?"

"I should think it was obvious. When I take my place on the bench tomorrow, I shall have at my right hand the warden of the plains, the laird of Grantown, the general of Seven Oaks, and the Chief of all the half-breeds."

CHAPTER 43

In the morning, Grant persuaded his brother sheriff to part with a stirrup cup of his precious Glenlivet, then climbed up on Elisabeth and turned her nose toward Fort Garry. The sheriff of Red River would follow along after milking his cows and strawing his strawberries and dealing with the other living parts of Colony Gardens that didn't alter their schedules to suit the Court of Rupert's Land.

The farmsteads that the trail wound through were bustling with sowers and plowers and noisy squads of child scarecrows. The other side of the river was bustling as well, but not with gardening. Horsemen were galloping from house to house. Milling family groups were making their way to mass. From the profusion of black pencil lines of gun barrels among the gaudy flocks of Assumption sashes and Sunday shawls, the bishop must have added target shooting to the litany.

On the shore fronting the cathedral, it appeared that every birch-bark canoe, dugout pirogue, or homemade rowboat in the parish of St. Boniface was moored and waiting for when mass let out.

In the vast open square that took up half the area enclosed by the palisades of Upper Fort Garry, a few of the less religious Red River buffalo hunters were already gathered, leaning on their buffalo guns and muttering around the mouths of their pipes. Grant nodded at them as he rode by. Some of them looked away; some gave stiff, perfunctory nods in reply. He handed Elisabeth into the tender care of the fort ostler, who whispered nervously: "Is there going to be trouble, Mister Grant?"

"Of one sort or another. Don't give her too much oats. She'd bloat up like a walrus if she had her way."

Adam Thom and the other three magistrates were already assembled in the chamber behind the courtroom. The major wouldn't make his entrance until the moment before court was declared in session. Grant sat down at the end of the table, and Adam Thom proclaimed: "Well, gentlemen, we have a full slate of administrative matters that have to be discussed before they can be submitted for the approval of the Council of Assiniboia. To begin with, the question of whether to amend the law regarding bull owners who allow their animals to roam free in spite of their neighbors' programs for controlled breeding. . . ."

Not far into the agenda, a gathering storm of shouting voices began to penetrate the stone walls of the courthouse. The recorder of Rupert's Land droned on obliviously, but a couple of his magistrates began to exhibit distinct signs of distraction—to the point where Mister Thom had to remind them which resolution they were about to vote on.

There was a knock at the door, and the sheriff of Red River stepped in. There was a grim set to his jaw, and his eyes were unnaturally bright. He said: "I walked here in company with a delegation from the other side of the river. They were kind enough to stop by Colony Gardens to inform me in advance that they will not permit their brothers to be tried under an unjust law."

" 'Not permit'?" Adam Thom bellowed. "I'd like to see their credentials from the imperial government or the London Committee that empower them to permit or not permit!"

"From what I saw on the way over," Grant remarked, "they were all carrying a good many credentials. I'm sure they'll be more than delighted to present them to you when the time comes."

"The next item on the agenda is . . ."

A few items farther on, the noise of voices began to emanate from inside the courtroom itself. Adam Thom tugged out his pocket watch and announced: "It's time." On cue, the chamber door swung open and the major made his entrance in full dress fig. He customarily came escorted by a ceremonial bodyguard composed of the few Chelsea pensioners who still remembered how to spit-shine a boot. This time he seemed to have wisely concluded that it would be a good day to make his way across the courtyard simply as a private citizen, albeit a uniformed one.

The magistrates trooped out to take their places on the bench. The courtroom was jammed, but the defendants in the first four cases on the docket were nowhere in evidence.

The major gaveled the table and announced: "The Court of Rupert's Land is now in session! First case: that of Regina against Guillaume Sayer, for illegally trading in furs."

The sheriff of White Horse Plains stood up and declaimed as resonantly as his dry throat would allow, "Call Guillaume Sayer," then sat back down again as magistrate of the western district.

From his post at the back of the courtroom, the sheriff of Red River stepped into the anteroom and shouted out the courthouse door: "Call Guillaume Sayer!" The cacophony outside died down for an instant, then erupted again at treble the volume. The sheriff of Red

River came down the aisle alone and chalky-faced and approached the bench. "He won't come. They say if we try to bring him in, they'll kill us."

Grant planted his hands on the table and levered himself to his feet. His upper lip was oozing sweat. He wiped his clammy mouth with his clammy hand and said to his brother sheriff: "This is where we earn our wages." He negotiated his way around the copious belly of Magistrate Hugh Polson at the end of the bench, strode up the aisle with the sheriff of Red River at his side, and stepped out into Hogmanay at the Asylum.

At a rough guess, there were about three hundred and fifty smoothbore trade guns in evidence. All were imaginatively decorated with brass nail heads or feathers or paint. Some of them were being brandished in the air, some of them were being leaned on, some were cradled in the crooks of bare brown arms. The brandishers, leaners, and cradlers were sprinkled in various-size clumps around the courtyard. Runners were shuttling from clump to clump, shouting messages and questions such as "Who are you going to shoot?" In one particularly large clump on the far side of the square, Guillaume Sayer and Marie's little brother Daniel stood bending their heads toward an earnest piece of advice from Irish Riel.

The shouting and gesticulating gradually faded as the shouters and gesticulators turned their heads toward the two sheriffs standing on the courthouse steps. Grant was surprised at how many of the faces he couldn't put a name to. So many boys had grown to manhood without his laying eyes on them from one year to the next, except occasionally as anonymous members of the massed hunt.

Grant glanced sideways, caught the eye of the sheriff of Red River, and pointed his chin at the knot of armed men around Sayer and Daniel. The sheriff of Red River gave a jerky little nod, and they stepped down into the courtyard.

It was a long walk. Another, larger knot of buffalo hunters was planted directly across the straight course from the courthouse steps to the group collected around Daniel, Riel, and Sayer. It would have been easy enough to swerve around them, but Grant kept walking straight on toward where he wanted to go. As he got close enough to appreciate the beadwork on the headband of the hatchet-faced young man whose place at the edge of the clump happened to be squarely in his path, Grant asked himself just exactly what it was he planned to do if they didn't step aside.

At the last instant before his nose collided with the beaded headband, the hatchet-faced young man sidled out of the way. The rest of the clump parted, but just barely wide enough to let the two sheriffs through, and closed up again behind them. By the time Grant reached his destination, he and the sheriff of Red River and Guillaume Sayer, Daniel McGillis, and Irish Riel were in the center of a circle packed ten men deep.

Grant came to a halt in front of Guillaume Sayer and said: "We're ready to try your case, Guillaume."

Riel trumpeted, "We won't let you take him!" and the crowd let out a roar. Out of the corner of his eye, Grant caught a glimpse of someone stepping out from the front rank of the ring to take up a position directly behind his back. It didn't take more than a glimpse to know who it was bound to be. Grant didn't particularly dislike James Sinclair, but it was generally acknowledged that he expected to step into the moccasins of Mister Grant the instant the old man finally put his feet up.

Grant refrained from looking over his shoulder, but the muscles in the middle of his back remained acutely aware that James Sinclair was breathing on them. When the crowd had yelled itself out for the moment, he said to Guillaume Sayer: "We've heard what Monsieur Riel has to say, and what they have to say—what do *you* have to say about it?"

Guillaume didn't look so much defiant as confused. "Well, Mister Grant, I don't mind standing up to a fair trial. . . . Like my father told me, if I just tell the truth, I got nothing to be ashamed of. But they say I won't get a fair trial in there."

"I can assure you you will."

Riel bellowed, "Not from the Company's court and the Company's law!" which bought another round of roaring and ululations from the mob. It would have been pleasant if the man could learn to occasionally express himself in a sentence that didn't end with an exclamation point.

Grant was getting a queasy feeling about this mob, namely that that was exactly what it was. Riel wasn't in control of it, and neither was James Sinclair or anyone else. Whatever individual reasons had originally brought them all across the river, they were now simply several hundred angry, armed men who were feeling their oats and intoxicated with the power of the herd.

Grant said to Riel, "And just what will you do"—raising his own voice to an oratorical level—"what will *all* of you do, when you've succeeded in driving the Company out of the *pays d'en haut,* and the armies of the American Republic or Upper Canada or some other foreign country come rolling in to enforce *their* laws?"

James Sinclair shouted into his ear: "We don't want to drive the Company out! But they have no right to dictate to the New Nation!"

Grant offered admiringly over his shoulder: " 'The New Nation . . .' Wish I'd thought of that." He turned to Guillaume Sayer again. "Well, Guillaume? . . ." Guillaume dropped his eyes but shook his head. Grant looked to Daniel McGillis, who crossed his arms and shook his head emphatically.

And just what, Grant asked himself, will *you* do now? For a fleeting instant he saw himself hammering James Sinclair and Irish Riel on the top of their heads to drive their feet into the ground like fence posts, then grabbing Daniel and Guillaume by the scruff of the neck and marching them into the courthouse. He'd committed bolder idiocies before and got away with them. But then he'd never had second thoughts before.

He said to the sheriff of Red River, "I suppose we'd best apprise the Court of this," then pivoted on his heel to bypass James Sinclair and beat a strategic retreat. A narrow avenue opened in the circle to let the sheriffs out again. Grant had his doubts that they would step aside a third time.

The spectators and witnesses who were jammed into the courtroom all turned their heads when the sheriffs came back in. Grant carried straight on down the aisle without acknowledging the questions in their eyes. He approached the bench and leaned across the table toward the major. The recorder and the other magistrates huddled in. When he'd apprised them of the situation, the recorder snorted: "If they fail to present themselves in court, they forfeit their bail and their right to a defense."

"I don't think that would be wise—"

" 'Wise'? It's the law!"

The major murmured tautly: "What would you suggest, Mister Grant?"

"Well, there are several other cases on the docket besides the four in question. I suggest we proceed with those and let the parties involved get their business over with, so they can clear off home if they've got the sense God gave a yard hen. It will also give our friends outside some time to talk things over further and perhaps come up with some coherent notion of just what it is they want."

The major nodded. Grant squeezed his way back past the testimonial to Mrs. Polson's cooking. The court proceeded with the case of the widow with a wood lot versus her axe-happy neighbor.

As the cases progressed, though, the noise outside didn't abate as Grant had expected. If anything, it grew louder. Halfway through the case of the deceased ewe versus the team of sled dogs, the courthouse door crashed open and a scrawny wild-haired métis burst in flourishing a musket almost taller than he was and hollering: "Which one's Adam Thom?"

The sheriff of Red River grabbed the barrel of the gun. The sheriff of White Horse Plains didn't waste time squeezing past the nebulous waist of Hugh Polson; he just heaved himself up and over the table, scattering papers and inkpots, and charged up the aisle.

The sheriff of Red River was doing a good job of keeping the muzzle pointed at the ceiling, although it took some wrestling. But at this point it didn't matter whether the musket went off into the ceiling or into Adam Thom—just the sound of a gunshot and Fort Garry was going to explode. As the jouncing musket bounced closer into view, Grant could see that the flint was fully cocked and ready to fire the instant one of the wrestling hands blundered a finger through the trigger guard. Some of the powder was dribbling out of the priming pan, but not all of it. He skidded to a halt beside the wrestlers, hauling in a deep breath and stooping forward, and expelled all the air in his lungs at the gyrating priming pan. His eyelids snapped themselves shut as some of the particles in the black cloud bounced off them. He blinked them open again as he straightened up and found himself staring into a narrow pair of mirror-sheened black eyes. The man was either crazy or drunk or both.

Grant would have liked nothing better than to apply his right fist to the spot between the crazy eyes. But if one of the mob's own were to be hurled bleeding out the door, the whole courtyard would react in exactly the same manner as they would to the sound of a gunshot. So instead he shifted around behind the would-be assassin, making a sandwich of him between two sheriffs, took hold of both scrawny forearms just above the elbows, and squeezed hard while pulling inward and upward.

Either the lunatic wasn't as scrawny as he looked or Grant's arms weren't quite as strong as they once were, but it still ended up with Grant clutching a limp and helpless and musketless scarecrow to his chest, although the scarecrow's legs continued to kick and dance frantically to get its moccasins back on the floor where they belonged. Grant swung around, breathing through his teeth. At the far end of the little cloakroom of an entranceway, the doorway was filled with bearded faces, among which were James Sinclair's and Irish Riel's. Grant took a few steps toward them, lowered the dancing mocassins to the floor, hissed, "Get him *out* of here!" and propelled their occupant toward the beards.

As Riel's and Sinclair's hands caught and held the squalling scarecrow, Grant slammed the door and turned back into the courtroom. The spectators, jurors, and officers of the court had got all mixed in together. Some of the magistrates were down on the floor, picking up the papers and inkpots that the magistrate of the western district had scattered on his way along the shortest distance between two points.

The magistrate of the western district was currently quite giddy and breathless. By the time he'd made his way back to the bench, the other occupants of the courtroom were back in their places. He sucked in and held a breath in preparation for squeezing past Hugh Polson and then discovered he had more than enough room to get past, because Magistrate Hugh Polson's chair was now occupied by the sparse frame of Alexander Sutherland. Grant said: "What are you doing here?"

"I know—at my age I should know better. But there was so much hurly-burly drifting downstream, curiosity got the better of me."

"I meant what are you doing in Hugh Polson's chair?"

"Oh. He offered five American dollars to anyone who'd take his place for the day. Five dollars is five dollars. He's long gone out the back way. Just tip me a nod or a wink when to say yea or nay or guilty or not guilty."

Even with drawing out every other case as long as possible, the time eventually had to come when there was nothing left on the docket but the matter of Sayer and McGillis et al. The two sheriffs went to the doorway to try negotiating with the gentlemen outside. A compromise was finally struck. Guillaume Sayer would voluntarily surrender himself up for trial, but only if accompanied by a delegation that would be allowed to speak for him and challenge jurors. The delegation magnanimously agreed to leave their guns outside, propped against the courthouse steps.

Grant settled back into his chair beside Mister Sutherland and folded his arms. It was a decidedly odd feeling to be sitting on this side of the table with the New Nation raging on the other side. In his time, he'd looked down the barrels of Selkirk colony cannons, fur traders' pistols, and shotguns decorated in the fashions of every tribe between the Shining Mountains and Thunder Bay. But he'd never entertained the possibility of being torn apart by his own soldiers of the buffalo hunt.

James Sinclair and Adam Thom had both come armed with copies of the Royal Charter of the Governor and Company of Adventurers Trading into Hudson's Bay, along with various pronouncements from the imperial Parliament and editorials from the Times of London. They went at each other for a while on the question of whether the Company really had the authority to pass laws restricting trade. Grant was hard-pressed to decide which of the two was more ridiculous. It seemed astounding that either of them wouldn't know that their little Punch and Judy show was just delaying a decision that was going to alter the shape of their world. Either the Company was going to back down and admit there was only as much law in Rupert's Land as the inhabitants would stand for, or the mob outside was going to prove it.

After exchanging preliminary harangues, both Thom and Sinclair retired to their corners and came out at the sound of the bell for jury selection. Nine potential jurors were challenged and rejected, which didn't signify a damn one way or the other—because when Guillaume Sayer was called to the stand, he freely confessed that he'd been caught with a cartload of furs he'd been planning to sell to the American traders at Pembina. If that weren't enough to put paid to the sparring, Guillaume's twelve-year-old son bore witness that he'd seen his father give a pint of gin to some Saulteaux in exchange for a brace of silver fox pelts. Madame Sayer had instructed him to tell the plain truth because his father wouldn't want him to tell a lie. The residents of Rupert's Land still had a long way to go on the way to civilization.

The major handed it over to the jury. Grant continued to lean back and breathe deliberately, with his eyelids at half-mast. Mister Sutherland whispered out of the side of his mouth: "What happens now?"

"I wish to God I had an inkling. By the way, do extend my congratulations to your son upon his marriage. I'd meant to stop by and congratulate him personally when I passed by Point Douglas yesterday, but . . ."

"There'll be plenty of time to get around to it."

"There will?" It seemed an optimistic prognosis.

"It took John long enough to get around to it. Maybe he was just holding out. She's a fine girl, Janet—daughter of old ex-Sergeant Macbeth, RSM of the Seventy-third. Remember? . . ."

"Hm? Oh, possibly . . . short man, white beard?"

"Just so. She's a good, hardworking girl. And the way she's going it'll be no time before Kate gets what she's always wanted."

"What's that?"

"A house full of children."

"Ah. That's a grand thing, for anyone with the wit to appreciate it."

"I get the feeling, Mister Grant, that we're getting damned close to 'Fix bayonets.' Except it appears we have no bayonets to fix, have we?"

"I'm afraid not—which is probably for the best. It's not your fight, Mister Sutherland."

"You may not think so, Mister Grant, but if you have to stand up, be wary of jumping too fast in this direction or you'll bump my shoulder."

The jury returned from its deliberations. Grant leaned forward, coming back to life with a tingling vengeance. The blessed foreman of the blessed jury delivered the only verdict that had a hope of satisfying both the law and the mob—guilty with a recommendation for mercy. There was a ground-rumbling grumbling when the verdict was relayed outside, but they hung fire and waited to hear the sentence.

It was up to the recorder of Rupert's Land to determine the sentence the president of the court would hand down. Grant glanced across at the recorder. Mister Thom was rolling his fleshy lips back inside his mouth to try to moisten them and darting his squinty eyes here and there at those members of the jury or the spectators' gallery who happened to have powder horns and shot pouches slung over their shoulders. Well, finally, Grant said in his mind to Adam Thom. You stupid son of a bitch, you've finally caught on to what's happening here.

The recorder whispered in the major's ear. The president of the court cleared his throat and said to the defendant: "Do you have anything to say before we pass sentence?"

Guillaume Sayer shook his head. "Only that . . . well, there was one of the Company's factors I talked to last year, and he said he figured the Company wouldn't mind if I was to buy a few trade goods and trade 'em to the Indians."

The major said: "Ahem, well, since the defendant appears to have sincerely believed that he had a right to engage in private trade, the Court takes his statement on good faith and we warn him not to do so again in future. And since it seems likely that the cases of McGillis etcetera will resolve themselves in the same fashion, the Court declines to proceed in—"

Whatever else the major might have intended to say was drowned under a jubilant rush up the aisle from the jury box and gallery. Someone shouted from the courthouse steps: "Le commerce est libre! C'est vrai!" No one detoured by the bench to share their jubilation with Mister Grant.

Adam Thom barked: "How could anyone be so ignorant as to misconstrue the verdict in this case as a license to—"

"Well, gentlemen," Grant interjected as he levered himself out of his chair, "It appears to me this court is adjourned." As he made his way up the aisle between the empty rows, a raspy thought-voice hissed in his inner ear: "What, all my pretty chickens come home to roost in one fell swoop?"

The sheriff of Red River ambushed him with: "What did you say?"

"Hm? Oh—I didn't realize it came out aloud. . . . It's just a somewhat mangled quote from Shakespeare I was trying to place."

"Shakespeare? Good God, Grant. Amidst all of this, and you're pondering poetry? Well, no one can say you're not a cool one."

"No, I suppose no one would ever say that." Beyond the courthouse door, the sunlight had shifted to pink gold. The sounds of the celebration in St. Boniface carried clearly across the river. Grant wiped his eyes, squared his shoulders, and carried on across the courtyard toward Elisabeth and the long ride home.

Part Five

GONE TO GROUND

Grant has taken a sober fit lately, which, if he continues it, may keep him alive a good while yet.

EDEN COLVILLE,
GOVERNOR OF RUPERT'S LAND;
CONFIDENTIAL LETTER TO
SIR GEORGE SIMPSON

CHAPTER 44

The chief factor of Fort Garry was sitting with his head in his hands when the clerk announced that Mister Grant had come to see him. The chief factor didn't want to see anybody, he was busy wallowing in the gossip about the First Lady of Red River—as his beautiful young métis wife was affectionately known throughout Rupert's Land—and the captain of the Chelsea pensioners.

The clerk at the door cleared his throat and said again: "Mister Grant is—"

The chief factor scrubbed his hands off his face, straightened his spine against the back of his chair, and said: "Yes, I heard you. Send him in."

The clerk stepped aside to let Grant's shoulders through the doorway. It appeared to the chief factor that it was no longer just Grant's shoulders and the crown of his head that were liable to leave scuff marks on door frames—the man was getting a decidedly bloated look to him. But at the moment the chief factor wasn't all that concerned with life's effects on anyone else. "Good afternoon, Grant. Pull up a chair. Afraid I'm up to my neck just now, but always glad to spare you a moment or three. Just passing by? . . ."

"No, actually. I rode over from Grantown expressly to see you. I'd heard that you'd got back last week from the annual meeting of the Northern Department at Norway House—"

"Week before, actually. Oh! You're wondering about the upshoot from the Sayer mess. The Company's decided to try letting some of the steam off by issuing new licenses to a few private traders to act as middlemen. Your son-in-law Breland, for one, and Sinclair, and . . . I can't remember who else."

"I think that's a wise move. But, in point of fact, that wasn't what brought me here. You see, I suppose I'm as much a creature of habit as anyone, and over the last twenty years I've grown accustomed to receiving my confirmation within a day or two of the chief factor or chief trader's return from Norway House. . . ."

" 'Confirmation'?"

"Yes. It's only a formality—no doubt that's why it slipped your mind. But every year the Council of the Northern Department has to go through the motions of confirming my appointment and salary as warden of the plains, and I usually receive a formal notice within—"

"Oh, damn. No, it didn't slip my mind, but I assumed that you'd assume . . . I should've thought to send a note with someone traveling by White Horse Plains, save you the trip. Sir George and the rest of the council decided—given that conditions change in Rupert's Land the same as in the rest of the world—a little more slowly here, maybe, but they do change. . . . But anyway, the upshot is the Company's decided to abolish the position of warden of the plains."

Grant didn't say anything in reply, which allowed the chief factor to feel a twinge of another business reminder buried somewhere under his personal preoccupation. "Damn! And there was something else as well . . . I can distinctly remember your name coming up at Norway House in some other context. . . . Ah! Yes, there was some discussion about this notion you seem to've got from somewhere that the township at White Horse Plains was granted to you. 'Granted,' ha ha. Of course your own farm is yours, as everybody else's there is theirs. No doubt you just misheard something Sir George might have said twenty years ago. But it was never the Company's intention to create a . . . a kind of squire's county, or a seigneury, as I believe they call it in Quebec."

Grant still had nothing to say, so the chief factor went on, "You can take it up with the new governor when he gets here. You knew we're going to have a new governor of Rupert's Land? Only whenever Sir George happens to be absent, but that seems to be more often than not these days. Word is Lady Frances is pining for her family in England. Well, marriage does mean your life ain't your own, as I'm sure you know. Well, it's always a pleasure to pass the time of day with you, but . . ."

The chief factor cracked open the dust-skinned ledger on his desk. Grant stood up. The chief factor pushed his chair back to shake Grant's hand good-bye, but the ex–warden of the plains had already turned and started for the door. As the door closed, the chief factor sat down and put his head back in his hands, reviewing for the hundredth time the magic lantern show of his wife and Captain Foss accidentally dropping their forks on the floor at exactly the same instant during dinner last night.

· · ·

Grant managed to negotiate his way through the countingroom and out the front door without meeting any of the clerks' eyes. But once he stepped outside he discovered that the courtyard was even worse, filled to bursting with Company servants and Kildonan farmers and métis hunters bustling about in the bright summer sun, and all of them had eyes. He wondered how many of them knew already. The ones that didn't would hear soon enough.

He was trapped inside one of those dreams where he found himself naked on a busy street. At least, whether by pure luck or premonition, he'd gone and hitched Elisabeth to one of the rings set into the face of the countinghouse, rather than taking her to the stables at the other side of the courtyard or leaving her hobbled out on the plantation. He popped her reins out of the ring, climbed onto the saddle, swung her head around, and clucked her into a brisk trot, training his eyes straight ahead at the gate. The gatekeeper called something to him as he went by, but he didn't look back.

Grant yearned to let the reins go slack and let Elisabeth gallop him away, but he held her to a businesslike trot until Fort Garry sank behind him.

Once there were no sounds around him except the lapping of the river and the whisper of the leaves on his left hand, and the sighing of the wind-blown prairie on his right, and no eyes but the blackbirds' and the wheeling swallows', he slowed Elisabeth to a walk and slumped forward, leaning his hands on the rolling nape of her neck. He supposed he should have seen it coming. But he couldn't think of anything along the chain of events that he could have done differently, except perhaps to not be quite so confoundedly certain of his own importance.

He asked himself why what had just happened should disturb him in the least. He certainly didn't regret that he'd never have to stop and search another métis cart or carriole or saddlebag. He could regret losing the income, but he hadn't managed to burn through all his father's money yet, and he wasn't planning on building any more big houses or gristmills. No one in Grantown was going to be harmed by the fact that he wasn't the laird of the manor as he'd claimed to be; after the Sayer debacle the Company certainly wasn't about to try confiscating anyone's home.

Nevertheless, it was a relief when Elisabeth's saddle sloped forward, signifying the trail was dipping into the gully of Catfish Creek and the cool, dark curtain of the woods closing in to hide him.

"Good day, Mister Grant!"

His head snapped up so fast he almost fell off the saddle. A gaggle of adolescent boys and girls, skirts and trousers hiked and rolled for wading, were weaving a willow-wand weir across the mouth of the creek. Grant straightened his shoulders, forced a perfunctory nod in answer to their waves, splashed Elisabeth through the shallows, and kicked her into a trot up the opposite slope and back out into the unforgiving light.

From then on he kept the shell up, trotting rigidly along toward the moment when he could escape across the threshold of his house and close the door behind him. The worst part of the ride was when the Assiniboine Trail angled into the switchback-widened tree belt at the beginning of Ghost Horse Plains, where the cozily slipshod cabins and farmyards of Grantown began to appear among the leaves. The people of Grantown called out and waved to their supposed seigneur as he passed by. Grant contorted his features into something resembling a cheerful expression and nodded in the general direction of the cart-wheel menders, or garden-patch weeders, or rabbit snare riggers, or tobacco puffers without meeting their eyes. The important Mister Grant had important business to deal with a little farther down the road. At least he could be grateful that the summer hunt was still out on the plains, so there were only a quarter as many people between the edge of Grantown and his house as there might have been.

When he was finally in his own backyard, he let his breath out, climbed off the saddle, dropped Elisabeth's reins to the ground, swung open the back door, and immediately realized he'd been horribly mistaken. His home wasn't the safe haven he'd expected; in fact, it was the worst of all. His wife and children were looking up expectantly from the kitchen table or emerging from the parlor to see what news the paterfamilias had brought back from Fort Garry.

Marie started to say: "So what did—"

"Louis, would you be so good as to strip down Elisabeth and put her out with the rest of the horses?"

Louis beamed, "Sure, Papa," and made a grab for his big-boned little sister. Betsy applied her cudgel of an elbow to his ribs. There was much groaning and eye rolling at the ancient family joke, which allowed Grant to slide on into the parlor and through the doorway of his private office. He closed the door behind him, reached down his flask off the shelf, and filled the cup sitting on his desk.

There was a rap on the door. It opened before he could say "Who's there?" Marie came in and closed the door behind her. She said:

"What happened?" He told her, in as offhanded and matter-of-fact a manner as he could manage, which became progressively easier as the level in his cup grew progressively lower. When he was done she said: "Well, that's a relief."

"Pardon me?"

"I been praying for years there might come a time when you didn't have to spend your life being the Company's policeman, and carrying all of Grantown around on your shoulders, and fighting Adam Thom, and—"

"I *am* still a magistrate, so far, and a sheriff."

"Well, that ain't too bad, so long as that's all that you got to do. You brought home good news."

He should've known that that would be exactly what she'd say. She could lie like a prime minister when she knew the truth would hurt.

CHAPTER 45

Marie was just sitting in the sun for a change, on one of the kitchen chairs brought out for shelling peas. Julie Rose came running and crying out of the woods, making for the back door. Marie intercepted her with: "What's the matter, dear?"

"Sophie pulled out my hair!"

Sophie Caroline came running after her, shouting: "She tried to pull out mine! Just 'cause I told her she's got a nose like a pig!"

"Shush. She has a perfectly lovely little nose. And look, Julie—all your hair's still there on your head where it's supposed to be."

"I can't see it."

"Well, you can feel it, can't you?"

"It hurts!"

"That means it's still there. Now if you two can't do anything but fight, you better stay away from each other. And if you keep on hollering and squalling like that, you're going to wake your father." That did it. They went off quietly in opposite directions.

Even though the sun had been up for some time, Wappeston was still in bed. He'd been sleeping a lot lately, and when he was up and about he moved from room to room like a ghost who didn't feel much like haunting anybody. He'd always been punctilious about shaving. Marie suspected it was because he'd only inherited a few sparse clumps of whiskers from his father. But now he'd left his razor gathering dust, to the point where a patchy growth of grizzled wisps tendriled his jawline. Whenever people came to call he'd be polite enough, but he always retained a sort of shambling aura, as though he were working his way up to apologize for something. Even Pierriche couldn't manage to pry more than the occasional dry chuckle out of him. Except for a few nights when the two of them sat up late in the parlor, and Marie would hear from her bed bursts of cutting-edged metallic cackling that was worse than no laughter at all.

Julie Rose had asked her last week if Papa was sick. "No, dear, just tired." Marie was hoping he would pick up when the summer hunt came home from the plains and Grantown became filled and bustling once again, bubbling with tall tales of the latest adventures and boiling over with all the refurbishing and harvesting that would have to be crammed into the short weeks before it came time to set out on the autumn hunt.

She was just starting to put together a midday meal when the happy groaning and creaking of several hundred approaching carts penetrated the walls. She went out onto the front steps. Wappeston stayed inside the house, so she did her best to fill in for him, standing on tiptoe waving and shouting at her relatives and neighbors as the procession filed by. Although they all waved back and called out jovial-sounding replies, it seemed to her that there was something not quite right, something forced in the joviality. As far as she could see, every cart that had gone out empty had come back loaded to the gunwales, but there was still something subdued about what had every right to be a triumphal return.

She found out what was wrong later in the afternoon. She and Betsy were picking more peas, dropping the fat pods in willow baskets, when Maria Theresa came to call, carrying a laden cradleboard slung over one shoulder. She stopped by the garden to say hello and then surprised Marie by staying there, as though she actually wanted to have a few words with her stepmother before going in to renew acquaintance with her father.

Marie remarked: "Looks like it was a good hunt."

"It was a bad hunt."

"It looked to me like all the carts were filled and then some."

"It wasn't the hunting that was bad. Even Pascal filled up all his carts. It was the fighting."

"Sioux?"

Maria Theresa shook her head. "Ourselves. Pascal got into two fights. And I got into one. It's hard to keep your temper when Guillaume Sayer's sister is crowing about 'I guess we sure showed old King Grant he ain't king no more.'"

"Oh, God."

"It was mostly the Red River people, and not all of them—just enough to draw a line between them and us. It just about got to an all-out war after Toussaint Lussier tossed one of the Sinclairs over a cart and broke his arm. If Father LaFleche hadn't been there . . ." She shook her head again. "I don't know what's going to happen on the fall hunt."

"You mustn't tell him."

"He's going to find out anyway. But all right, if you want me to lie to him, I will."

"You don't necessarily have to lie—"

"Just not tell the truth."

"But if you have to, lie like hell."

After supper, when the sound of fiddles began to drift over from the other side of the churchyard, Wappeston stood up and said: "I guess we better put in an appearance." He went to the door and stood waiting, without showing any inclination of detouring upstairs to shave or of reaching down the resplendent coat she'd spent so long embroidering and beading. She threw on a shawl and went out with him.

The sky had clouded over and it was starting to drizzle. If the sprinkle turned into an exceptionally hard rain, the homecoming would move inside a string of houses whose furniture had already been piled outside. But at the moment the tribe was dancing and singing and feasting around bonfires behind Urbain Delorme's house and in the two adjoining yards.

The Grants made their rounds, Wappeston nodding painfully in response to the ebullient cries of "*Mister Grant!*" and "You shoulda seen the shot Jean Baptiste made when . . ." They got separated for a while. Marie was listening to Euphrosme tell her how she'd worn her brand-new knife down to a sliver with cutting up all the buffalo Charles had brought down when Wappeston shuffled up and murmured: "I suppose it's about time we started home."

As they crossed the churchyard, Marie cranked as much of a chirp as she could into: "Sounds like they had a real good hunt!"

"Does it?"

Over the years since the first cabin went up at Grant's lake, it had become the custom for the Captain of the hunt to visit the big white house with the widow's walk the morning after the homecoming—late enough in the morning for everyone to have recovered—in order to paint Mister Grant a coherent overall picture out of all the garbled stories he would have heard the night before. On the occasions when the hunt elected a Captain who wasn't from Grantown, the report would be delivered by whomever the White Horse Plains caravan had elected to captain them back and forth from the rendezvous at Pembina. Lately, more often than not it would be Jean Baptiste Falcon who appeared at the door. And it was Jean Baptiste again this time. Except this time his father came with him.

Marie carried a pot of tea and four cups into the parlor. Wappeston had already set out the pewter brandy decanter. Marie settled down on the hearth rug beside his chair. Jean Baptiste began to tell them how many carts had been in the caravan, how many bags of pemmican and dried meat they'd brought back, how many bladders of tallow, how many hides, how many days they'd had to travel from Pembina before finding the herd—

"But none of that," Wappeston interrupted softly, "has anything to do with what made this hunt different from all previous ones, does it?"

Jean Baptiste looked down at his hands and muttered: "No."

"It seems," Wappeston said to the wall, "that as long as I'm around to be the bone of contention, that isn't going to change."

Pierriche nodded. "So we got to *make* a change."

"Such as?"

Jean Baptiste blurted: "Take out our own hunt! Leave the people from Red River to go their way and we'll go ours."

There was a pause. Marie stepped into it with the story of what had happened with Sophie Caroline and Julie Rose yesterday morning. She could feel Wappeston looking at her as if she were losing her mind to interrupt such an important conversation with some furry little tale of family squabbles. It made her rush and trip over her words. But when she got to the end, Pierriche slapped his hands together and laughed. "That's just exactly what it is, Marie. If us and the Red River métis can't do nothing together but fight, we better just stay away from each other."

Wappeston shook his head. "A White Horse Plains hunt wouldn't amount to more than a hundred rifles at best. The Sioux would—"

"Not if they knew you were along," Jean Baptiste jumped in. "And Urbain Delorme and the other tough old hunters. Even my old gray father's said maybe he ain't too old to take a few more runs at the buffalo."

Wappeston shrugged his shoulders up around his ears and said wispily: "Well, I suppose the cannon would make a difference. . . ."

Marie burst out: "Goddammit, don't you hear? *You* make the difference. If you don't think people around here think so, why'd they waste all that effort punching other people in the head and throwing them over carts?" His head snapped around murderously in her direction, but the hard flares in his eyes lasted only an instant before diffusing once again into that misty, downcast look.

He was wrong about the hundred rifles. When the White Horse Plains hunt lined up in front of the big white house, there were less than fifty. More than a few carts had already left Grantown to join up with the Red River hunt. Wappeston had shaved his face and polished the cannon and put on his rainbow coat, and Pierriche and Urbain were doing their best to buoy him up, but it seemed obvious to Marie from her place in the lead cart that he wasn't being tremendously successful at putting a bold face on it.

When the hunt rolled up the first slope of the Pembina Hills on the trail toward the ford of the Pembina River, one of the scouts came galloping back to report that there was a camp in the valley ahead of them. Wappeston said: "Sioux? Cree?"

"Métis."

"The Red River hunt? . . ."

"No. Only about a dozen tents."

Wappeston shrugged, "Well, I suppose we'll find out," and swung his arm ahead. Marie snapped the whip to set the ox back in motion.

When the camp came into view, several horsemen came trotting forward to meet them. Wappeston held up his arm again, and Marie halted the cart. As the horsemen drew closer, Marie recognized the two remaining Dumont brothers, along with three of their hulking, adolescent sons and little, gnomelike Gabriel, who'd inherited his crazy uncle's gun-barrel eyes along with his name. As they reined in, Wappeston said: "Good afternoon. Aren't you a little ways out of your way from St. Boniface to the rendezvous?"

Skakatatow, He Talks, said: "We ain't headed for the rendezvous. We heard Mister Grant was going hunting, so we thought"—jerking his thumb back over his shoulder at the rest of the Dumont clan camped below—"maybe we could tag along with you."

Aicawpow, He Stands, nodded his tombstone of a head and added gravely: "If that's all right with you, Mister Grant."

"Well, if . . ." Marie doubted that anyone else knew her husband's voice well enough to make out words in that abortive croak. She heard him swallow to moisten his throat and saw the wrinkled, wilted wild roses smooth out and swell around the shoulders she'd embroidered them to fit. Mister Grant's reverberant, crisp-edged baritone boomed: "If that's what you choose, we'd be more than delighted to have you along."

If Marie had been ten years younger, when it might still have been an appealing prospect to the men of the Dumont clan, she would have been hard-pressed not to drag them bodily off their horses and thank them then and there in the grass.

A few days farther on, a couple of families of Pembina métis—including Joseph Wilkie, who'd served as Captain of the hunt most times Jean Baptiste Falcon hadn't—were waiting to go hunting with Mister Grant. As Wappeston snuggled into the tent one night, he said: "Well, there may not be many of them, but if offered a choice . . ." She didn't have to ask what he meant. The White Horse Plains hunt might not have bucketfuls of hunters, but they had the cream.

They came home with cart rails creaking as loudly as their cart-wheels. They'd seen no sign of the Sioux beyond an occasional distant wisp of camp smoke. When the rivers broke into ice shards in the spring, Grantown turned nomad again for the annual jaunt to the sugar bush at Rivière aux Îlots de Bois. Marie had climbed off the cart to join everyone else in the rush to set up camp before sunset when she felt a twinge and looked back.

Wappeston was still standing in the cart, with his chin in his hand, shaking his head from side to side. She followed his gaze to their accustomed stand of trees and the hide-covered mound of the iron kettle filled with birchbark rogans and wooden tapping spouts standing where they'd left it last year. She looked back at him. He murmured: "Remarkable. . . ."

"What's remarkable?"

"Well, that's a very expensive monster of a kettle sitting there. We left all those things stacked up in the open all year long and no one's touched them. No one's tried to sneak a march on us by tapping our trees. No one's—"

"That's just like it's been every year since Grantown started."

"I suppose it has. But, given all the bands of Cree or Saulteaux that wander by here over the course of a year, and other métis, and Kildonan people . . ." He chortled behind his hand and lowered his starry-night eyes toward her. "Well, isn't it just goddamned remarkable?"

She stretched her arms up to try to grab hold of his ears and pull his idiot mouth down to hers. "Something is, Wappeston."

CHAPTER 46

When the snow-capped ramparts and roofs of Fort Garry poked into view over the lead dog's head, Grant found himself feeling a little queasy. The last time he'd passed through those gates had been that nasty, brutish, and short interview with the chief factor. And the time before that had been the Sayer trial and the mob. But it was impossible to feel queasy for long with the carriole skimming him along over the wind-crusted waves and the air tingling with ice crystals.

When the list of cases for the winter sitting of the Court of Rupert's Land had arrived in Grantown, Grant had seriously considered sending a message to the effect that it was high time someone else tried his hand at the job. But then, as he'd said to Marie: "If only the court weren't in such a shambles. . . ."

"You mean if Adam Thom wasn't running it."

"Something along those lines. But I want to make damn sure that whoever takes my place is from Grantown as well, or at least métis, so I ought to stay on long enough to see that whoever it is isn't stepping into a snake's nest. Or maybe I'm just fooling myself for the sake of holding on to one last puffed-up title."

"You know I'd like it better if you stayed home, but I think you should go."

So he did. It was remarkable that he hadn't noticed over the years how much he'd come to rely on the undistorted mirror she held up to him. Perhaps if he had noticed, he could have saved himself and the rest of the world a lot of unnecessary posturing.

And there was another reason he probably would have ended up going even if she hadn't encouraged him. If the Company couldn't govern Rupert's Land, some foreign power would. The recorder of Rupert's Land was rapidly making its inhabitants ungovernable, except by the kind of choking structures that ruled every other corner of the world.

As the carriole swung through the gates, Grant popped the whip over the lead dog's head to let her know he was thinking of her. Lajimodierre hadn't done quite as good a job on her as on her late, lamented mother. Or perhaps the strain got played out in the second generation.

There were a half dozen other dog teams staked out beside the courthouse, far enough apart that the packs couldn't get at each other. Grant was just straightening up from hammering his own stake into the frozen ground when the sheriff of Red River came around the corner and stopped dead. "Good God, Grant, what's happened to you?"

" 'Happened'?"

"You look ten years younger. Have you taken the pledge?"

"That's for Protestants. Why do you think I converted? But as a matter of fact, I do seem to be going through days at a time when the bottles sit corked and forlorn. Just happenstance."

"Well, something seems to be agreeing with you. Although I doubt today will."

"Why ever not? I would have thought case number two alone would be worth the trip." The defendant in the second case on the docket was Adam Thom. He'd hired one of the Kildonan farmers who was by way of being a bit of a carpenter to build a porch onto his house and then refused to pay him. Thom did seem to have his problems with carpenters.

Grant had expected the sheriff of Red River to chortle and rub his mittens together with glee. Instead he shook his side-whiskers dourly and growled: "I'll have no part in this sham trial. The case should never even have come to court. There is no doubt the man did the work—the porch is there for all to see—and that he would never have done it without agreeing upon a price beforehand. But since a written account wasn't presented, Thom claims the agreement is void."

"Couldn't the carpenter find someone to write up an account for him? Hell, give me five minutes with him and some ink and paper—"

"The man can write perfectly well for himself. He thought it was a handshake agreement. When he found out it wasn't, which was after he'd finished the work, he went straight home and wrote up an account, but Thom refused to sign it. The whole thing's bloody ridiculous. The instant I saw the case on the docket I went straight to the major and told him, 'This is bloody ridiculous! A dispute over twenty-five pounds shouldn't even come to trial! Hand it over to one of the petty magistrates and they'll have it decided like Bob's-your-uncle!' But the major would have none of it, so I'll have none of this trial. Which means, I'm afraid, you'll have to stand in as sheriff."

"Oh, hell, here we go again."

"How's that?"

"Nothing. Sometimes I should listen to my first instincts. Oh, well, if that's how it lies, I suppose that's how we'll have to play it."

"Play through, Mister Grant."

The courtroom was as jammed with spectators as it had been for the Sayer trial, and the atmosphere was just as taut, but in a different manner. Kildonan people weren't in the habit of resolving disputes with guns and knives, but neither were they in the habit of forgetting a wrong done to one of their "ain" folk. They might have been driven out of the Highlands forty years ago, but they were still the same people who would never seat a Campbell beside a MacDonald because of what had happened at Glencoe in the winter of 1691.

When it came time for the Thom case, the major announced, "The defendant has elected a trial by jury," which was unheard of for such a petty dispute. "As the sheriff of Red River refuses to act in this case, the sheriff of White Horse Plains shall call the jury."

Grant stood up and pointed out twelve good men and true from among the spectators—six each from what Adam "Tome" had managed to delineate as the "English" and "French" halves of the Red River Settlement.

As the jurors were shuffling into the jury box and Grant was settling back into his chair, the defendant rose up and proclaimed: "As a British citizen, I am entitled to a jury of my peers."

Grant paused and hung poised with the seat of his trousers just kissing his chair seat while he asked: "Are you suggesting, Mister Thom, that these twelve men are somehow not your equals under the law?"

"Not at all. But half of them, with the exception of Mister Marion there, are incapable of understanding the evidence, though I put it in as simple English as possible."

The major nodded. "Point taken, Mister Thom."

Grant found himself back on his feet, banging the table and shouting: "If the Court of Rupert's Land continues to insult and degrade half the community it purports to serve, I refuse to remain a part of it!"

The major nodded. "As president of this Court, I can only say that if Mister Grant chooses to relinquish his seat on the bench, we will accept his resignation with regret."

Grant swallowed his pride, which was becoming increasingly less of a mouthful, muttered, "You'd love that, wouldn't you?" and sat back down.

The case finally got started. The plaintiff, a plain-faced young farmer with a spade-shaped blond beard, stood up to tell his story and sat back down when it was done. Then it was the defendant's turn.

Thom had half a dozen law books stacked up on the table in front of him, with several needlepointed or embossed leather bookmarks projecting out of each. He began with, "As the only man in Rupert's Land who has been educated in the law, I feel it is incumbent upon me to . . ." and then proceeded to read out a plethora of precedents and learned opinions regarding contract law. When he'd succeeded in thoroughly confusing everyone who hadn't nodded off, he thumped his last book shut with: "This case has naught to do with money. It is a matter of principle: of personal principles and a principle of law.

"The plaintiff offered to reduce his price by three pounds rather than proceed with a suit against me. I told him it mattered not one whit to me whether the price was twenty-two pounds or twenty-five or twenty eight; the laborer is worthy of his hire. But I will not pay one penny that is demanded from me on the assumption that I'm afraid to go to court!

"As to the principle of law, it is quite simple. As you've heard"— thudding a blunt-ended forefinger down on his law books—"without a written account, there is no contract."

Grant leaned forward to catch the major's eye. "If the Court pleases . . ."

"Proceed, Mister Grant."

Grant turned toward the plaintiff. "Have you drawn up an account?"

Adam Thom went apopleptic. "Who told you there was an account, sir? Who told you there was an account?" Then he seemed to catch himself and swung bodily back to the major, modulating his tone considerably. "Allow me to point out to the Court that even if the plaintiff has written up an account, it should have been presented in evidence when he stated his case. Now is not the proper time."

The president of the Court of Rupert's Land said: "The Court rules that now is not the proper time to present an account."

And with that, Adam Thom picked up his law books, sidled out from behind the defendant's table, and turned up the aisle toward the door. Grant blinked incredulously at the receding back of the oversize badger stumping up the aisle and then turned to the major. The president of the court was complacently glancing over the affidavit in front of him, as though it were an everyday occurrence for a defendant to dismiss himself from court before his case was concluded.

From the back of the courtroom, the sheriff of Red River bellowed: "You may as well all go back to your homes, for you'll get no law nor justice here!" Then he rattled out the door just ahead of Adam Thom.

Shouting voices erupted from the anteroom that served as a cloakroom in the winter. Grant slammed to his feet, kicking his chair back, and headed up the aisle. The major clutched at him as he went by. "See here, Grant . . ."

"I'm still the sheriff."

In the cloakroom, Thom had donned his coat and hat and muffler and was stooping down to retrieve his stack of law books from the floor. Several métis—some of them blond cousins of the plaintiff—were standing between him and the exterior door. Several other métis were pushing their way off the back benches to join them. The sheriff of Red River was standing off to one side with his arms crossed. It was becoming rather a crowded little vestibule.

Thom straightened up, looked at the knot of buffalo hunters barring his way, then turned to the sheriff of Red River. "Sheriff, would you kindly instruct these men to—"

"I will *not*."

One of the blond métis shouted across the four feet between him and the recorder: "You ain't done in there!"

"Do you presume, sir, to read the law to me?"

"You can wave all the law books you want, but you're going back in there." When Thom didn't move, they started toward him. Grant stepped in front of them and held up his hand. "I'm sorry, Mister Grant, but we're taking him back in there."

Grant shook his head. "Let him dig his own grave." They looked at each other dubiously and then stepped aside. Adam Thom made his exit without sparing a glance for the rabble, including the two sheriffs.

Grant came back into the courtroom just in time to hear the president of the court pronounce: "The legal evidence presented makes it clear that the plaintiff has no case under the Law of Contracts. The Court sees no choice but to unsuit the plaintiff and dismiss the jury."

One of the blond métis hissed at Grant: "I thought you said he was digging his own grave?"

Grant glanced around at the faces of the Kildonan people who'd come to see justice done and replied: "That's precisely what he's doing. In fact, I doubt he could do a better job if he applied himself to it." Those métis and transplanted French-Canadians who hadn't hated Thom from the start had learned to do so during the Sayer trial; the local Saulteaux and Cree had hated him ever since he'd condemned their brother to hang; and now the Kildonan people hated him as well. The only segments of the population he hadn't yet managed to turn against him were the Company officers, the Protestant missionaries, and the Chelsea pensioners.

When the rest of the docket had been dealt with and Grant was shrugging on his coat to head home, a mild voice murmured from behind him: "What are we going to do about that man?"

Grant turned around. It was John Bunn, the blue-eyed métis who had gone away and come home with a medical degree from the University of Edinburgh. Besides being the only real doctor in the *pays d'en haut,* as well as the most universally liked and respected man at Red River, not to mention a delightful drinking companion, he also happened to be one of the three permanent magistrates of the Court of Rupert's Land, along with the sheriffs of Red River and White Horse Plains.

Grant said: "Which man?"

"Surely you jest."

"Well, what I'm moved to do is inform the London Committee that I can no longer pretend to administer the law under a recorder who makes it up to suit his own purposes. But, as you no doubt saw me realize in mid-dudgeon, all my resignation would accomplish would be to create an opening that Thom could fill with some dupe that the rest of you would have to deal with."

"If you resign"—the mild blue eyes twinkled—"so will I."

The voice of the sheriff of Red River came out of the corner behind Doctor Bunn. "And so will I."

Grant shifted sideways to make a triangle and stuck his right hand out, knuckles up. The sheriff of Red River slapped his right palm on top of it and the Doctor completed the stack. "Done."

Shortly after Grant shipped off his letter of resignation, a petition was circulated throughout the District of Assiniboia demanding several reforms in the Court of Rupert's Land, most particularly the dismissal of the current recorder. Grant was about to sign it when he considered that the whole affair might be starting to look too much like a conspiracy or an in-house coup d'état. He settled for advising the petitioners to change the clause demanding "a Recorder who could speak the French language" to "who *would* speak the French language."

And then the outburst of spring made him forget all about law and politics in the rush to accomplish the sugaring-off and seeding before it came time to set off on the summer hunt. Although the hunts from White Horse Plains and Red River still stayed separate, they traveled on a parallel course and scouts went back and forth between them to exchange news of the herd and the Sioux. Amazingly, the Sioux still didn't try to take advantage of the little caravan from Grantown.

Perhaps it had something to do with the fact that the seven hundred rifles of the Red River hunt were never more than a day's ride away.

As often as not, when it came time to run the herd Grant would appoint Jean Baptiste or one of the Dumonts to take his place for the day and stay behind with Pierriche to trade old stories and play with the children. Sometimes he would just sit with his cheek on his fist covertly watching Marie showing the girls how to cook up a buffalo hump or sharpen a knife. He could watch her for hours, feeling his insides turn to pudding, but he couldn't for the life of him find any way to tell her so.

The hunts came home to a place that was imploding with the reaping of whirlwinds. The captain of the Chelsea pensioners had launched a suit claiming "defamatory conspiracy" against several members of Red River society for spreading malicious rumors regarding him and the chief factor's wife. The lawyer representing him happened to be the only lawyer in the country and also the only judge left to sit on the bench—the recorder of Rupert's Land.

Marie said: "He can't be all bad, then."

"He can't?"

"You said so many times he looks down on everybody who isn't white, but now he's standing up for Sarah Ballenden against his own people. Mary told me he's even opened up his house for Sarah while the trial goes on, so she can have a place to stay that's neutral territory from her husband or the captain."

Grant laughed. "When are you ever going to stop straining your eyes to see something good in everyone? On second thought, don't—just save it for me. Although it'd be nice to think that our recorder's biases are loosening up, I'm afraid this has nothing to do with anything except that old Adam just can't resist playing knight errant for the lovely Sarah."

"You don't really believe she and Captain Foss—"

"I don't really give a damn, so long as they don't do it in the road and frighten the horses. Except for poor John Ballenden's sake. The important thing for our sakes is that good old Adam Thom seems about to shoot off the few toes he's got left."

True to form, Adam Thom did just that, with a little help from Sarah Ballenden. Lawyer Thom bullied the jury into finding against the various Company officers and clergymen's wives for slander, allowing Judge Thom to assess several hundred pounds in damages, a good deal higher than the maximum amounts the Court of Rupert's Land was legally empowered to make judgments on, and to deliver a stinging lecture on the evils of unfounded gossip. Bright-eyed Sarah returned to hearth and home, where she promptly took advantage of her husband's first absence on an inspection tour to have Captain Foss over for a weekend. It wasn't the brightest or most thoughtful thing to do in a community where people knew where you were going before they met you on the road. The fall ship from York Factory carried a holdful of letters to the London Committee, whose governor just happened to be the uncle of one of the convicted slanderers. The return ship brought a deed revoking Adam Thom's appointment as recorder of Rupert's Land.

When he got the news, Grant grabbed Marie and danced her around the parlor. She batted at his shoulders, giggling. "What's got into you?"

"Nothing compared to what's about to get into you. Let's see, now . . . Once they appoint a new recorder I'll have to stand again as magistrate for, oh, perhaps a year at most—to prove I only resigned because of Thom. But after that I'm free—*we're* free. Free of it all."

"Have you lost your mind?"

"And found my heart."

Chapter 47

The trilling of a song sparrow told Marie it was time to start checking over all the cart harness if they wanted it shipshape for the summer hunt. Wappeston and Louis and Angus would do most of the actual mending once she'd pointed it out to them, but none of them would get around to thinking of it on their own until the night before the hunt was due to start. She cloaked herself in her heaviest wool shawl—actually a green-striped Hudson's Bay blanket—and went out through the melting snow to the harness shed.

The song sparrow was suddenly drowned out by fifty girls' voices singing "Au Clair de Lune" from the old presbytery behind the church. Marie fancied she could pick out Julie Rose, Marie Rose, and Sophie Caroline's from among them. The coming of the Sisters of Charity had made Marie's days less hectic, but sometimes she felt a little wistful that she would never again spend an afternoon shuttling between the half of the kitchen table where she was rolling out pastry dough and the half where her daughters were hunched over paper and pencils.

She was just about at the door of the harness shed when she became aware that the melt-off on the ground was starting to soak through her moccasins. It made her stop and peer across the churchyard at the timber stacked beside the presbytery, to make sure it was covered. Part of Wappeston's campaign to lure a couple of the sisters from the convent in St. Boniface had been a promise to build them a house. Every now and then over the course of the winter, the spirit had moved him to organize an expedition of axe men and oxen up to the oak bluff near Grant's Lake. Today he'd had more pressing business. Urbain Delorme had bought another of FireAway's many descendants and was bragging that anyone could tell just by looking that the colt was going to grow up to be longer-legged and faster than Elisabeth.

Marie satisfied herself that the cart awnings draped over the pile of lumber looked adequate to keep the snowcap from melting through to the wood, and she carried on toward the shed. Someone had left the door ajar, and a few veins of snow had drifted in. She propped the door wide open for light and maybe enough sun warmth to melt the snow into the floor. On her way across to open the shutter on the far wall, a spitting and mewling out of one of the dark corners told her not to be too hard on the culprit who hadn't closed the door tight. One of the barn cats had decided that the harness shed would be a perfect place to make a nest.

With the sun coming in from both ends, there was enough light to start sifting through the piles of buffalo-wool-stuffed yoke pieces and the hanging vinery of braided harness straps. She'd just gotten a good start when she heard her husband's voice calling her name.

"I'm in here!"

Approaching footsteps mulched through the snow, then the light through the doorway dimmed to a halo around a buffalo-coated silhouette. He said: "While Urbain was at Fort Garry picking up his colt, one of the clerks handed him a letter for us that got misplaced from the autumn brigade. It's from James Hargrave."

"He hasn't written in years."

"Well, I suppose I wasn't exactly holding up my end of the correspondence. He extends his regards to his old friend Mrs. Grant, 'now and always.' He enclosed a letter for Miss Elisabeth Grant from one of the young men that works for him. It seems that this Willie McKay got acquainted with Betsy when he was at Red River last summer, and now he's approached Hargrave 'in a manly, frank manner' to ask permission to marry and establish a household at York Factory."

"What does Betsy say?"

"She's busy having her knuckles rapped by Sister Marie Eulate

Lagrave. According to Hargrave, this Willie McKay's an honest and prudent young fellow, actually managing to accumulate some savings at an assistant interpreter's salary. Hargrave says he and Mrs. Hargrave would be delighted to have Betsy as a guest until the wedding. She can hitch a ride there with the spring brigade—"

"No!"

"No? What happened to 'What does Betsy think?' "

"Two months alone in the bush with forty voyageurs?" On top of which, the notion of sending her daughter eight hundred miles away to marry a man Marie had never met made her stomach turn over.

"There's any number of freighters I can vouch for personally, who'd watch out for—"

"All the watching out in the world can't cover two months and eight hundred miles of rivers and lakes and bush camps. And some of those boatmen would make a Blackfoot's hair curl."

"Well . . . perhaps Betsy won't prove quite so enthusiastic as young Mister McKay and the whole question will be academic. Funny, hearing from Hargrave after all these years. One can't help but feel sorry for him."

"Why?"

"Well, he's only one of many—just about all the other career men in the Company are in the same case—but in his case it seems particularly a pity. Here he is in the midst of this beautiful, untouched country—well, it *is* a tad swampy right around York Factory, but he wouldn't have to go far. . . . And by all accounts he has a lovely flock of little Hargraves and a grand wife, the only imported wife to make a go of it in the *pays d'en haut*—but then, Hargrave had the sense to marry a good Highland girl instead of a hothouse flower like Frances Simpson. . . .

"Now, given all that, how does Hargrave spend his life when he's not working? Battened inside his office pursuing his letter-writing campaign to secure a transfer to a more prestigious posting, agonizing over whether the wording of Sir George's latest reply means he's next in line for a promotion. And the fact is, the Little Emperor's the saddest case of all."

"*Simpson?*"

"Well, you have to feel a certain amount of sympathy for the poor little bastard."

"No, I don't."

"I know it seems ridiculous from the outside, but when you're in it, it becomes so easy to be seduced by sonorous titles and spangled accoutrements. They appear to put the seal on each stage of a life lived well, when in fact they're just painted bones thrown to a dog who's allowing himself to be used. When George Simpson is no longer up to setting speed records for inspection tours between Rainy River and the Athabaska, he'll retire to his mansion in Lachine where his alabaster wife sits displayed on the mantel beside his knighthood and his other trophies.

"I know it's probably a bit mush-hearted of me, Waposis"—he moved forward out of the doorway, turning into himself again instead of a haloed silhouette—"but I was always taught to be charitable toward those who've been less fortunate. And George Simpson just hasn't been as lucky as me.

"Oh, hell, it's all bound to sound abstract to you. You've always been who you are, not what you do. Speaking of which, what *are* you doing?"

"Sorting out the harness that'll need to be patched before the hunt. That's the good pile, that's the mending pile."

"Oh, damn, I should've told you—well, I was still mulling it over. . . . But the end of the mulling is that after the last two years the Ghost Horse Plains Hunt is on a safe enough footing to get along perfectly well without us. That is, if you don't mind going back to whiling away our springtimes at the lake."

"You could've told me before I started laying out all this."

"You're quite right"—sweeping the workbench clear with one arm—"especially when it could be put to so much better purpose."

"Are you crazy? Don't! What if one of the children was to—"

"They're all at school, bless the Sisters of Charity. . . ."

Even without mending the harness for a dozen carts, there was still a lot to be done before abandoning the place to its own devices. Wappeston actually helped her with the last weeding the garden was going to get for a month, crawling about on his hands and knees among the fingerling rows of radishes and beets. At one point he straightened up onto his knees, cricking the small of his back, and announced: "I believe I've finally figured it out."

"Figured what out?"

"I could never understand how you could tell the difference between the weeds and the garden plants at this stage, when they're all just green shoots. But now I think I know how you do it."

"How's that?"

"Well, if they pop right out with the merest little tug, they probably weren't weeds."

She sat down in the mud and laughed.

The cabin at the lake needed a bit of refurbishing after sitting empty for two years. The boys had used it for a fishing shack a few times, but sweeping the floor and plugging up mouse holes wasn't high on their list of priorities. After a few days' work the place was tidy and weather-proof again, and they all settled in for a month of fishing and fowling and feasting.

Marie came out of the cabin one morning to fetch a bucket of water from the lake. It was what her father used to call a soft day—with a constant light drizzle that was more like droplets of mist. Wappeston had told her that most days in Scotland were like this. It was a pleasant change in a country where the rain came with a vengeance when it came at all. Wappeston was out on the lake with Louis and Angus, angling instead of spreading nets. With the mist and the distance, they weren't much more than hazy silhouettes, but Marie didn't need much in the way of details to picture him clearly. He was leaned back against the stern of the canoe with his feet propped on the midstrut and his imported, split-cane fishing rod dangling in his hand, drifting with what little current there was.

Pierriche came ambling from the collection of cabins and tents spread along the shore. He stopped beside her and stood looking out over the lake, with his head cocked to one side and his reedy arms crossed. After a moment he shook his head, puffed up his upper lip and let the air out with a soft pop, and said: "You remember once a long time ago I told you about Wappeston and campfires? How he's always too busy making sure the wood's burning right to see the flames?"

"I remember."

"Well, I don't know how you done it, but if that ain't a man laying back and watching his campfire dance, I never seen one."

But it only lasted until they packed up their kegs of pickled goose and salt fish and went home to Grantown. The day after they got back, a wandering family of Woods Crees stopped by and were surprised that no one in Grantown had heard the news. La Terre Qui Brûle and a dozen other Sioux chiefs had combined their bands into one massed war party that had swept down on the Ghost Horse Plains hunt and massacred them all.

Marie was as horror-stricken as anyone, but she forced it down and said to Wappeston: "You know how stories can get twisted around on the moccasin telegraph. You told me yourself that the story that went around after Seven Oaks was that the whole colony'd been rubbed out."

"Yes." He nodded rigidly. "When the truth of it was we'd only killed a couple of dozen of them."

For Marie, the ensuing days and nights were a brutal fog of trying to go about the mechanical tasks of gardening or preparing meals while her mind and ears were constantly replaying the latest rumor or hearing the distant squeal of cartwheels that were never there. Wappeston barely slept at all. During the day he would go up to the widow's walk every hour or so to strain his eyes at the horizon. He'd loaned his little brass telescope to Jean Baptiste Falcon for the hunt, which wasn't much of a substitute for the little brass cannon still sitting in the barn. She tried to tell him that the cannon wouldn't've made any difference. "No one knows how to use it anyways."

"They would have if I'd showed them."

At night he would sit staring into the hearth fire with a jug of gin at his elbow. The crevices in his face grew jaggeder, and a gray tinge crept into his skin.

One morning he came down from the widow's walk and announced: "They're coming."

"Are you sure it's them?"

"I'm sure. There's not enough of them for the Red River hunt."

"How many?"

"Impossible to tell at that distance. They'll still be a while yet, but they're coming."

She went upstairs to kneel in front of the crucifix on the bedroom wall and say "thank you" that the worst of the rumors weren't true. She wanted to pray that none of her children were among the dead or wounded, but she would have been praying that some other woman's were. She began to hear a distant amalgam of plodding hooves, lowing oxen, and keening wooden wheel hubs grinding on wooden axles. This time it didn't fade away when she listened harder. She washed her face with cold water and went downstairs. The front door was open. Wappeston was standing on the front steps with the children who were still at home gathered around him. She went out and stood beside him.

At most homecomings, a storm of whooping horsemen would come galloping ahead of the carts. This time the outriders all hung back behind Jean Baptiste Falcon, who was walking his horse beside the flag fixed to the lead cart. Marie spotted Charles. He wasn't wearing any bandages that she could see, and there didn't appear to be any holes in his coat.

Usually the caravan would dissolve on its way into Grantown, with various segments peeling off into their own separate farmsteads. This time the hunt stayed intact and didn't halt until Jean Baptiste Falcon reined in his horse in front of Mister Grant and held up his hand. The old folks who'd stayed behind came running, calling out joyfully to Isidor or Madelaine or Ian Pierre. But the people of the hunt didn't shout back or jump off their carts and horses, just nodded grimly or held up their hands stiffly in reply.

Jean Baptiste said: "*Wakiye*, Mister Grant."

"*Wakiye*, Jean Baptiste. You were the Captain this year?"

"I was."

"We heard . . . rumors. Of a battle."

"It's true. It's one long story, but I'll just tell you the bones of it for now. It was when we were getting close to the Missouri. We sent some scouts up Le Grand Coteau and they found the Sioux waiting—maybe two thousand warriors. We were sixty-four hunters, along with maybe a dozen boys old enough to shoot a gun. We made a circle with the carts, locked the wheels together, put all our families and the horses and oxes inside, and dug rifle pits about a hundred yards out. They came at us for two days. I think we killed about eighty of them, but it's hard to say for sure. At the end of the second day La Terre Qui Brûle came out and said the Sioux wouldn't ever fight with us no more."

Marie could feel Wappeston's rib cage haul in the first deep breath he'd taken for weeks. But it was still only a ghost of his voice that came out with: "And how many . . . how many of our people . . . ?"

"One of the scouts went down making a run for the cart circle—Malaterre. And Aicawpow Dumont got an arrow through his leg, but it's healed up. Oh, and a long shoot downed an ox, but we ate him."

"And . . . ?"

Jean Baptiste's black hedge of a beard split into the grin he couldn't hold shut any longer. "There ain't no 'and,' Mister Grant. We whomped the whole goddamned Dakotah Nation and only lost one man."

At various points during the ensuing evening, Pierriche or one of the other founding soldiers of the New Nation would holler over the music at Marie that there hadn't been a kick-up like this since the night of

Seven Oaks, and maybe this one was even better because Wappeston didn't look to have that same bitter taste in his mouth. Late at night, though not so late that the sounds of fiddles and laughter weren't still barging through the bedroom window, Wappeston murmured: "The breadth and depth of human self-centeredness is awe-inspiring. I should be swept away with joy and gratitude by what happened at Le Grand Coteau. And I am. But, within that, I can't quite manage to rub out a certain . . . disappointment that I wasn't there."

"Sounds to me like you were."

CHAPTER 48

It seemed a waste for a man to own an iron-tipped plow and only use it for turning the same old furrows. Especially when those old furrows were surrounded by open grasslands. So Grant yoked up Bruno and Bertram and led them out beside the fence protecting the green barley sprigs sprinkled across the last acre he'd broken ten years ago. He was supposed to be attending to the preparations for Betsy's wedding, but all work and no play . . .

Over the course of the last ten years it had somehow slipped his mind just how fiercely prairie grass roots clung together. Even with Bertram and Bruno putting their massive backs into it, his arms and shoulders felt as if they were going to crack from keeping the plow blade in the ground and holding it to a straight course. He considered the possibility that his age might have something to do with it and then rejected it. Back in civilization a man of sixty was considered not much good for anything except warming a rocking chair. Out here if you'd managed to make it to that age, you could expect another couple of decades of relatively robust health.

His wobbly new furrow finally grew roughly parallel to the corner of the fence. Grant gratefully ordered the oxen to a halt and slumped over the plow handles to catch his breath for a moment, or maybe fifteen. He felt a tingling at the back of his neck and looked up. There was a horseman standing watching him. The horseman had the sun behind him, and Grant's eyes were full of sweat. He wiped his eyes with his shirttail and looked again.

Even with the sun behind it, there was no mistaking that suety, noseless slab of a face that always put Grant in mind of an immense smoked oyster. It occurred to him that here was the perfect example of his theory about longevity in the *pays d'en haut*. Old Chief Peguis had been "old" when Grant first met him forty years ago, but apart from a few more gray hairs he didn't appear to have aged a day. On second thought, maybe he wasn't much of an example after all. How could a smoked oyster age?

Grant raised his hand and said: "*Wakiye,* Chief."

Peguis nodded and grunted, "Wappeston," then leaned far down from his saddlepad, which was a remarkable feat for a torso like a bladder of tallow, and scooped up one of the newly turned clods of earth, with its severed grass roots pointing at the sun. "Wrong side up."

Grant had to catch his breath again, this time from laughing, before he could reply: "You might have a point there, Chief. What brings you out this far from your stomping grounds?"

"When Father Belcourt set up his mission up the Assiniboine, some of the people from my band went with him. Most of them've come back, but a few thought they wouldn't be welcome. I hear they ain't doing so good. I thought I'd go tell them not to starve stupid when we got all the fish in Lake Winnipeg and all the birds in the delta." He studied the clod of earth in his hand and added contemplatively: "And maybe I needed a day of rest. My newest wife expects a lot from an old man."

Grant snorted: "You've been calling yourself an old man since I was a young man."

"Ah, but then, you see"—the black eye holes above the black holes where the nose had been twinkled—"if *I* do, no one else has to." He looked back down at the clod of earth, turning it over and over in his hand without breaking the mat of roots holding it together. "I had a vision, Wappeston. That all this"—sweeping his arm out across the unbroken vastness of Ghost Horse Plains—"is going to be that—" pointing at the fenced black field with its sprouts of barley. "Not tomorrow, maybe not even the next day, but someday soon."

"Someday, but not soon. We still have a lot of good years left."

"Might be. Well, we gave 'em a good run for it—can't ask for much more'n that. Did you hear Kichee Omachew Lajimodierre went down?"

"I saw them put him in the ground."

"Yup, not many of us left. Funny thing, when you first came back out here with the North West Company, I thought they'd made you into one of them."

" 'Them'?"

"One of those with no heart for the earth but how to use her. I was wrong." He handed the clod of prairie back to Grant. "Even if you do scratch her skin up from time to time. She don't mind a little of that. Have you seen the white horse yet?"

"Not yet, Chief."

"I got this feeling you're going to. *Wakiye*, Wappeston."

"*Wakiye*, Peguis."

Marrying off Betsy was a good deal more complex than it had been with the others. For one thing, it had taken a devilish long time for young William McKay to get a long enough furlough to come to Grantown, and even longer for Betsy to make up her mind whether Willie McKay might be worth living on the shore of Hudson's Bay for the foreseeable future.

For another thing, the wedding seemed a perfect opportunity to take another step toward healing the rift between Red River and White Horse Plains. Although the hunts still traveled separately, relations had grown more cordial, particularly since the Red River hunters yearned to bathe in the reflected glory of Le Grand Coteau. It wouldn't hurt if one of Mister Grant's daughters were to be married in St. Boniface Cathedral, with all and sundry invited back to Grantown for the kick-up. Although if someone were to put a gun to Grant's head, he'd've had to admit that he'd grown far less interested in political ramifications than in the notion of several hundred people feasting and toasting and dancing themselves silly in his backyard.

The procession back to Grantown was a mile-long parade of beribboned carts and galloping outriders. The gallopers were careful to run their races only as far ahead as the lead cart bearing the bride and groom and then drop back. Grant ambled along on Elisabeth beside the second cart bearing Marie and the paltry handful of children left to rattle about the big white house.

There had already been several rude jokes about the fact that Mister Grant wouldn't be the one riding Elisabeth tonight, which had found Marie palpably not amused. Marie didn't have a priggish bone in her body, which made it all the more amusing to watch her button on her respectable matron's mouth whenever one of her daughters got married.

The space between the back of the house and the front of the barn had been lined with trestle tables crowded with platters of buffalo tongue, venison steaks, moose stew, grilled whitefish, smoked goldeye, pea soup, potatoes, wild parsnips, *tortierres*, turnips, gooseberry pies, maple tarts, and God knew what else. Barrels of beer and wine stood with their heads smashed in. Taps were a bit of eastern decadence that had yet to find their way into celebrations in the *pays d'en haut*.

Grant drank a lot, but only beer, and he'd refined his brewing skills a good deal since that first successful batch that had just about caused a bloodbath at Fort Garry. He sat at the head table in the red sunset light with his right hand plying his beer mug and his left clasped in Marie's hands in her lap, drinking in the music and the capering of the young folks of all ages. And then someone bellowed a toast to Bethsy McKay.

Grant whirled his head around and then remembered that his daughter Betsy had just married Will McKay. He took another quaff of his beer. It didn't help. If his son James was still alive, he'd turned thirty-seven on January 16, born in the year of Seven Oaks. Grant told himself not to be bloody ridiculous. Marie was ten times the woman Bethsy ever could've grown into, and she'd given him three good sons and five lovely daughters to replace James. Ridiculous or not, he still found himself feeling a bit morose and couldn't shake it. He squeezed Marie's hands and extricated his own, saying: "I'll just go have a look at the horse racing." She sparkled her eyes at him abstractedly and then returned them to the mob of bright-sashed White Horse Plains métis jigging with their cousins from Red River.

Grant wove his way through the mob toward the churchyard. Father LaFleche might not be too enamored of having his church steps transformed into a platform for gambling, but he was also smart enough to know that the wilder members of his congregation found it difficult enough to swallow that God frowned on polygamy, much less horse racing.

It took him a while to get to the church. It seemed that every dancer or lounger or beer quaffer had to call out "Mister Grant!" as he went by and shake his hand or kiss his cheek. It had mainly to do with appreciation of his extravagant hospitality and congratulations on his daughter's wedding, but Grant was also beginning to get a niggling feeling, strange as it seemed, that people seemed to be rather fond of him, even though he was no longer warden of the plains and laird of Grantown or even a magistrate or sheriff.

The focus of the horse race crowd at the moment was an argument between Urbain Delorme and the new magistrate and sheriff of White Horse Plains—Pierre Falcon and Pascal Breland. Pascal was avowing: "You could never take her."

Urbain expostulated: "We taken every-goddamn-body else, ain't we?"

Falcon saw Grant coming and called: "He says his pony can take Elisabeth."

"Does he, now?" Grant let his eyes drift over to Urbain's horse, which was nuzzling the shoulder of its jockey, one of Falcon's wiry adolescent grandsons, who was looking bored with no new worlds to conquer. The horse was a big black beast that Urbain had christened Démon Noir. There was no question he'd inherited several inches more of FireAway's legs than Elisabeth, but there wasn't much muscle on him yet. In fact, if he'd been Grant's horse, he wouldn't have started running races until next year.

Grant turned to Urbain and offered blandly: "One pound sterling says you're wrong."

"Why not make it two?"

"Why not make it ten?"

Urbain blanched. It was probably three times his winnings for the day. But he took the bit in his teeth and nodded his head. "Done. Who's going to ride her for you?"

" 'Ride her'? I ride my own horses, Urbain—don't you?"

There were chortles from some of Urbain's recent victims when they saw how he'd been caught. Although Urbain wasn't quite Grant's size, he would still tip the scales against two of the jockeys Démon Noir had been carrying. Elisabeth had been galloping under Grant's weight all her adult life. But Urbain couldn't back out now, and he couldn't very well run a sixteen-year-old boy against a sixty-year-old man, not if he didn't want to make himself and his horse an object of contempt and ridicule. He put a good face on it and took the whip from his jockey, who'd initially perked up at the prospect of a worthy opponent and now kicked the ground in disgust.

Grant dispatched Angus to saddle up Elisabeth and bring her back at a trot to warm her up. While he waited, he looked over the course the other racers had been running: to a lone oak tree about a quarter mile out on White Horse Plains and back to the church steps. He would've preferred a longer course, to give Elisabeth a chance to play on her stamina, but he could only jig the odds so much.

When Angus came bouncing back, straining his arms to hold Elisabeth to a trot, Grant checked the saddle girth and blew into her nostrils before climbing aboard. Urbain did the same with Démon Noir. No doubt about it, neither of them sprang into the saddle with the same élan they once had. Grant was tingling and finding it difficult to keep his face impassive. These days ten pounds sterling meant almost as much to him as it did to Urbain, but that was only a bit of priming for the pump of giddiness inside him. Urbain looked across at him and laughed. "You're one crazy old man, you know that?"

"Tell me that when I'm pocketing your ten pounds."

Falcon walked out in front of them with a handkerchief held up in his hand. Grant shifted the reins into his right hand so he could hold the whip in his left, clucking at Elisabeth and holding her in, focusing his eyes on the hank of calico in Falcon's hand and the crown of the lonesome oak behind it. Even with tricking Urbain into weighing down his horse, it was by no means a sure thing. Démon Noir could sprint like hell.

When Falcon released the handkerchief, Grant whooped and kicked his heels against Elisabeth's ribs. In an instant it was all behind him: the fluttering shard of colored cloth, Falcon, the shouting of the side bettors, the fiddle music from the wedding dance. There was only the kettle drumming of hooves beneath and behind him, the taste of the wind in his teeth, the blur of prairie and the growing tree bouncing up and down between Elisabeth's ears, and the surge of her body between his legs.

A black nose poked into the edge of his peripheral vision. He leaned forward into Elisabeth's flailing mane and flailed the whip against her rump. Not that Elisabeth needed coercion. Once she hit her stride, all her rider had to do, or could do, was hold on for dear life and pray against gopher holes. Grant could already feel the strain in his thighs from clutching her rib cage.

The green mane of the bouncing tree began to separate itself into serrated leaves. Urbain cursed Démon Noir into another burst of speed. Whoever got to the tree first would have the inside track for the turn. Grant bellowed something wordless at Elisabeth. She kicked ahead and he reined her hard around the black trunk, with Démon Noir skirting wide around her back hooves.

But as Grant glanced back to see that Urbain had lost a length on the turn, he felt his right moccasin squirt out of the stirrup. He let it dangle and squeezed tighter with his weakening knees. The empty stirrup kept bouncing up and smacking the blade of his shin, but that was a small price to pay.

And then the prairie exploded under Elisabeth's nose. It was a covey of grouse. One of them flew straight up into her face, booming and batting her eyes with its wings. She shied and reared back. With only one stirrup to plant his weight on, Grant felt himself slipping sideways off the saddle. He made a grab for Elisabeth's mane and then changed his mind before he pulled her down on top of him. Something, either one of her hooves or the ground, hit the back of his head like a mallet hitting a melon.

After about as much time as it took for him to become thoroughly comfortable where he was, jarring sounds and shapes began to spiral out of the darkness. Urbain was leaning over him, holding Elisabeth's reins in one hand and Démon Noir's halter in the other. There was an inordinate amount of shouting going on, and the earth was shaking with approaching hooves.

Grant sat up gingerly and tried to focus his eyes. Half the crowd from the churchyard were rearing their horses to a halt around him and jumping down; the other half were coming running. All of them were hollering: "Mister Grant! Mister Grant! Are you all right?"

Although it hurt like hell even to think of it, Grant put his hand to the back of his head. It came away with no trace of blood. That didn't mean he was even remotely all right, unless "all right" had suddenly come to include pinwheels of light and double and triple vision. But he was quite sure it would pass, and the last thing Betsy needed was for her one and only wedding day to be ruined by her father getting drunk and falling off a horse. He shouted in a voice that hurt his head: "I'm all right!"

They boosted him to his feet. He forced what he hoped looked like a dismissive grin through the vertigo and then turned to look concernedly at Elisabeth, as though he were capable of discerning whether any of her eight legs had been injured.

She didn't scream when he heaved himself back onto the saddle, so she must have been all right. But from the mutterings around him as the race crowd made its way back to the churchyard, and the palpable shortage of joshing and laughter, they weren't at all convinced that he was. This wouldn't do. As the church steps hove into view—several sets of church steps, actually—he had an inspiration and whipped Elisabeth with the trailing ends of the reins. She squealed with joy and leaped into a gallop. As the several sets of church steps shot closer, they narrowed down to two. Grant flipped a coin in his mind, opted for the left set, reined Elisabeth to a halt and jumped down onto them. They were still there when the soles of his moccasins hit them. He whirled around, slapping the knuckles of his right hand into the palm of his left, and cackled: "Ten pounds, Urbain! Pay up!"

That did it, at least as far as the general run of the wedding guests went.

Angus came to collect Elisabeth. "Are you all right, Papa?"

"Just a little knock on the head. Give her a good rubdown, would you? She's earned it."

"Yes, Papa."

Grant navigated by the stars through the swirling wedding mob. Marie was still sitting on the chair he'd left her on, although the look on both her faces suggested she'd spent several of the last few moments standing on it to peer at the race course. She said: "Are you all right?"

"Perfectly. I'll have a sore head in the morning, but that wouldn't be the first time." He groped his hands onto the back of the empty chair beside her, glanced down nonchalantly at the two chairs his four hands were holding, decided that what had worked for the stairs would work for the chairs and sat down on the left one. He guessed wrong.

The next thing he saw, after the table rim and Marie's stricken face rocketing into the ether, was the mild blue eyes and professionally placid features of Doctor John Bunn. There was a candle burning, and Grant was lying in bed. Doctor Bunn said: "We've been pretty damned silly, haven't we? Damaging brains we don't appear to use."

Marie darted out from behind Dr. Bunn and knelt down by the bed. Grant reached out and settled his hand on her shoulder, glad to see that there were only two of them to choose from. He swallowed to moisten his throat and said in a voice that still scratched: "There's no music. . . . Did I spoil the—"

"It's Sunday night," Bunn informed him. "The party's been over for three days. You had a mild concussion. Or at least I hope it's mild. I'll look in on you again tomorrow."

Marie had reached both of her hands up to shift his hand off her shoulder and was kissing the tender valleys between his knuckles. The candlelight appeared to make the gullys around her eyes deeper. She said: "You made me a solemn promise you weren't ever going to leave me."

PART SIX

THE WIDOW'S WALK

He was the husband of Dame Marie MacGillis [sic].

PARISH REGISTER OF
ST. FRANÇOIS-XAVIER

Chapter 49

On a blistering summer day, Kate and Sandy Sutherland were ambling along the Assiniboine Trail in a Red River cart with two of their grandchildren. The other four were still too young for long journeys in this kind of heat. Donald and John Hugh wore hand-woven straw hats just like their grandfather's. Their grandmother wore a frilled white mutch, starched within an inch of its life, that was made for a climate with a softer sun. She was also wearing her best dress, petticoats and all, and her Sunday shawl, and the boys and Sandy had been forced into starched shirts and clean trousers. Kate had gotten into the habit of planting almost as many potatoes for starch as for food over the last three years, ever since Red River finally got a real kirk minister and Kildonan Kirk went up downstream from the *sassenach* St. John's.

Donald rode perched between his grandparents on the plank seat, and his little brother rode on his grandmother's lap. Kate loved all her grandchildren, but red-haired Hugh was her Christmas boy, born on Christmas morning with a caul on his head. He still hadn't lost that perpetually intent expression of a kitten, where everything he encountered, from a cart horse to a ball of string, was a wonder previously unrevealed.

At the moment, though, he'd pretty much exhausted the wonders of the wooden Highland soldier his grandfather had carved for him, at least as far as marching it back and forth across the narrow confines of the cart seat, and was growing fidgety. "Gran? . . ."

"Yes, dear?"

"Is it much farther?"

"A little ways yet, dear. After we have made our visit we can stop and have our picnic on the way home. You can look for a nice place along the way that we can come back to."

"Howzabout . . . there!" pointing his stubby little arm at a green and verdant willow swamp.

"I think there might be a lot of mosquitoes there, dear. And remember, whatever place you pick, the nearer it is to where we are now, the farther we will have to go before we can stop on the way back."

" 'The nearer it is, the farther we have to go. . . .' " He repeated the enigma several times with awe.

Once he'd played that one out and started fidgeting again, she said: "If he is feeling well enough to visit with children, you will be able to tell your grandchildren you shook the hand of Mister Grant."

"Mustn't shake his hand," Donald cautioned. "He's as big as two grizzly bears and twice as ornery."

"Donald! Mister Grant is nothing of the kind. He is a very courtly gentleman who has been very kind to a great many people."

"Granda says he's as big as two grizzly bears and twice as ornery."

"Granda" appeared to have discovered something intensely interesting in a cloud formation. Kate said: "Your grandfather has been known to pull the long bow from time to time."

"You mean he lies?"

"Not exactly. Perhaps there have been times when Mister Grant seemed as . . ."

"Big as two grizzly bears and twice as ornery."

"But I do not think today will be one of those times."

The trail dipped into the shade of the woods along the edge of White Horse Plains. But almost immediately they encountered a barrier across the road, a trimmed poplar trunk fixed to two stumps about three feet high. A voice called out of the mottled shadows, "Hello, Sutherlands," and Pierre Falcon uncoiled his lanky body from the base of an oak tree.

Kate said: "Good morning, Mister Fall-coe."

Her husband said: "Why have you barred the road?"

"Wappeston—Mister Grant—he's laid up, and it's hard for him to get good rest with carts squealing back and forth under his window all day long. So we figured . . . there's another gate up at the other end of town."

Kate said: "But Mister Grant is who we came to see. I brought some soup. . . ."

"That was sure a kind thought. He'll perk up to see you, if he ain't sleeping. What we been doing with our carts is skirting around to the north—you'll see the ruts—and leaving 'em by the edge of the fields. What you can do is go around till you see the cage on the top of his house straight by your left hand and walk in from there, if it ain't too much for the little fellows' legs."

"You'd be surprised," Sandy grumbled, "what those little legs can get up to."

Kate said: "Thank you, Mister Fall-coe. How is he?"

"Oh . . ." The sketchy eyebrow lines turned into flying arches. "Some days he's good, some days he ain't so good."

Sandy turned the horse around to follow the lane of flattened grass around behind the fields of Grantown. When the widow's walk poked over the crowns of the trees, he reined in the horse and they climbed down. Kate reached back into the cart for a quart-size *rogan*. "Now Donald, and Hugh, we are going into the house of a poor, sick man who needs rest and peace. Will you both promise to keep your voices soft and walk as though we are in the kirk?"

"Yes, Gran."

"If you do not," their grandfather growled, "Mister Grant might eat you."

"Alexander Sutherland!"

"Well, if he does not, I might."

There was a pathway leading between the fields and through the trees. Mrs. Grant and two beautiful black-eyed girls were working in the garden. Mrs. Grant looked up when she heard them coming. There were dark circles under her eyes and her face looked roweled.

"A good day to you, Mrs. Grant."

"Mrs. Sutherland, Mister Sutherland. . . ."

"These are our grandsons, Donald and John Hugh."

"Hello, Donald and John Hugh."

"It is all right to speak when you are spoken to, boys. Say hello to Mrs. Grant."

"Hello, Mrs. Grant."

"And these are my daughters, Marie Rose and Julie Rose."

"How do you do. We heard that Mister Grant was laid up. I brought some beef and barley soup. There is a lot of blood in it, very good for the bedridden."

"Thank you, that's very kind of you. He'll be glad to see you."

"We do not wish to disturb him if—"

"I think he's having a good day today. Maria Theresa's sitting with him. Come on inside."

"What does the doctor say?"

"He says it's very hard to tell with head wounds. Just rest and time."

Kate pointed the boys toward the boot scraper fixed into the back step, but Mrs. Grant shook her head. "No need, I haven't had time to wash the floors since . . ."

Hugh's hand came up for Kate to take hold of on the way through the kitchen, clutching even tighter as they entered the vast, open parlor with its worn-dark chairs and looming stone fireplace. His little legs just managed to cope with the stairs, given a pull-up from his grandmother's hand at strategic points. He started to giggle at the sensation of becoming airborne at the top of each step, then choked it off.

Partway down the corridor, Kate began to hear a slow, deep, heavy breathing. The room at the end of the hall had a curtain drawn across its window. Once they'd adjusted to the gloom, Kate's eyes went straight to the bed. He was lying back against a mound of feather pillows, the top ones banked up to pad his head and hold it in one position. His eyes were closed. He was dressed in a loose-necked cotton nightshirt. He had lost some weight and gone back to his winter pallor, except without the brushed-in flush of wind and cold. A green glass bottle half-filled with some thick dark liquid stood on the trunk beside the bed.

Mrs. Grant said softly: "This is my daughter, Maria Theresa Breland."

Kate looked to the other corner of the room and a pregnant woman sitting on a chair, then whispered: "Of course. I knew you when you were no bigger than a biscuit."

Mrs. Breland said: "You must make fat biscuits."

"We are—"

"I know. The Point Douglas Sutherlands. Papa always talked about you."

Mrs. Grant started toward the bed. Kate hissed: "There is no need to wake him—"

"I don't think he's sleeping. And after you come all this way, he'd hate not to see you. Wappeston. . . . Wappeston? . . ."

"Hm?" The long-lashed lids fluttered open. The big black eyes fastened on Kate, lowered to John Hugh pressing himself back into the front of her skirt, and then misted over as though about to weep. He said in Gaelic: "I did not mean to hit your mother. . . ."

Kate said: "This is my *grand*son, John *Hugh*. He has only a little of the Gaelic."

"Oh. Oh, of course. For a moment there . . ." The snap-edged baritone she'd known had become slow and deliberate, as though his tongue had grown too big for his mouth. "I was back in your bed thirty years ago." The black eyes shifted to Sandy without the head moving, and a twinkle of life sparked within the unnatural sheen. "I suppose I might have phrased that differently. . . ."

"If I recall, you were incapable of cuckolding a mouse at the time."

"Alexander Sutherland!"

"This is another one of our grandchildren, Donald. Shake hands with Mister Grant, Donald."

Donald wrapped both arms and one leg around his grandfather's leg and whimpered: "No. . . ."

Hugh said, "I will," and marched to the bedside with his right hand thrust out.

The massive right arm wafted up off the bedclothes, and the hand that could have crushed Hugh's like a bundle of matchsticks settled around it gently. "How do you do, Master Sutherland. Well, good Lord, your son may have started late, but two grandchildren already. . . ."

"Four more at home," Sandy groused, "and another on the way."

"Good Lord. You must be having to add on to that big new house I saw on Point Douglas."

Kate said: "We no longer live on Point Douglas."

"How's that?"

"We still farm the fields there, and keep the garden, but we boat back and forth. Last year's flood carried the house away. When we came back from Stony Mountain we found it settled among a stand of elms on the other side of the river—"

"Damned snug piece of carpentry," Sandy interjected.

"So, the Lajimodierres—or rather, Mrs. Lajimodierre now—were willing to sell us the piece of land, and it seemed a waste to build a whole new house. . . ."

Mister Grant started to laugh, rocking his head back among the mounded pillows. His laughter broke off and his face contorted into a silent scream, with his hands clawing rigidly at the air. Mrs. Grant jumped to the cup sitting between the green glass bottle and a water pitcher, looked inside it, and held the rim to his mouth. Some liquid spilled out over his chin, but he managed to swallow some. After a moment his features went placid again. Mrs. Grant wiped his chin with a damp rag. His eyes were still open, but he didn't appear to be in them, just as he hadn't when they were riveted open with the scream no one heard.

Kate said: "We should let you get your rest."

"Vair gu . . ." he mumbled thickly, "very . . . good of you to come. Regards to your son."

Back in the cart Sandy said: "What are you weeping about?"

"Oh . . . oh, just to see that great hulk of a man so helpless, with a wandering mind. And the pain . . . And his poor wife . . . Mister

Lajimodierre was no surprise, he was such an old man. But I never thought that Mister Grant would—"

"I would not count that one out if his head had been cut clean off and stuck on a pike."

CHAPTER 50

Marie and Maria Theresa were partners and rivals in nursing. Every morning and every evening, Maria Theresa would leave her children with Pascal while she came over to feed her father powders and concoctions from his medicine chest, following his instructions. While Maria Theresa was upstairs making the medicine her father taught her, Marie would be in the kitchen brewing up herbal mixtures and building poultices the way her grandmother had taught her.

It was hard to believe that either of them was accomplishing anything beyond keeping their hands busy. Whatever was wrong with him was inside his head, and there wasn't even a scratch to bandage. All they could hope to do was try to stop the pain. Sometimes it only showed itself by a tightness around his eyes. Sometimes he would clutch the mattress with both hands and breathe through gritted teeth. And sometimes he would scream like a horse who'd stepped into a wolf trap. It was at those times Marie was grateful for his trunk of imported medicines. Unpredictable Loon had passed on to her what countless generations of Indian medicine women and men had learned about the healing properties of plants that European doctors had never seen, but the opium poppy didn't grow on this side of the ocean.

One night she carried a buffalo robe and some spare blankets upstairs and started to lay them out beside the bed. He said: "What are you doing?"

"Last night, every time I rolled over, you whimpered in your sleep. I think for now even the littlest bit of movement on the bed hurts your head. And I can't stop myself from moving around in my sleep, so—"

He furled the blankets open and patted the feather-bag mattress. "But I wouldn't have *been* asleep, and won't be tonight, if . . ." She left her blankets folded on the floor and crawled in beside him.

The next night, when she went up to bed he wasn't there. The children's bedroom doors were all closed and there was no sound of voices from behind them. She did a quick check of the spare bedrooms and then rushed back downstairs, as fast as she could rush without guttering out her candle. While she'd been busy in the kitchen he could've come downstairs and into his office without her hearing. But he wasn't there. She shone her candle into the corners of the parlor and then threw open the front door. She stood on the steps with her candle held high, wondering where to look or whether to call out for him and end up with the whole town beating the bushes. There were no sounds but the night sounds that had been here on this bend of the Assiniboine since before the river had a name: the peeping of tree frogs and crickets, the burble of the water making its way to the sea, the wind sighing in the trees . . . And then a voice wafted down out of the spangled sky: "Going for a torchlight run, Little Rabbit? You're too old for dancing in the moonlight. . . ."

She stepped down into the yard, turned around, and craned her neck back. Between her and the field of stars, a grid of the iron fence around the widow's walk showed itself against the white cloud of a billowing nightshirt. She went back inside and made her way upstairs, detouring into the bedroom to scoop up a blanket and the bedside chair. She needed the chair to stand on to reach the dangling thong of the trapdoor to the attic. Over the years it had grown even harder to reach as various members of her family steadily shortened it with knots so it wouldn't whop them on the forehead every time they walked down the hall.

As she stepped off the top step onto the attic floor, the counter-weighted trap swung shut behind her, sending up a gust of air that blew her candle out. But the hatch to the widow's walk was open, giving her a square of stars to guide her.

Wappeston was slumped against a corner of the railing, peering through the bars, apparently unaware of the fact that he was shivering in his nightshirt. She edged out onto the rim and closed the trap to make enough floor space for her to squat down beside him. She draped the blanket around his shoulders, scolding: "In case you ain't noticed, it gets cold when the sun goes down."

"Look who's talking." He lifted one blanket-winged arm to snuggle her in beside him. "I found myself feeling relatively painless and thought it was about time I took a stab at climbing out of bed before what muscles I have left atrophy. I saw him."

"Saw who?"

"Out there. . . ." He thrust his arm through the bars toward the void of the Place Where the Ghost Horse Runs. "I've been hearing him at night for some time now, but tonight I saw him. Sometimes he runs like the wind—no sound at all but the rush of his passing. Some might say it was just a trick of the moonlight, but it's a new moon tonight."

"Come to bed."

"Hm? Yes, I suppose you're right—that's enough exercise for one day."

A few days later he was well enough to start spending his days downstairs. The barriers at the ends of town came down. His eyes couldn't focus on print, so Marie or Maria Theresa or Marie Rose or Julie Rose would sit and read to him for hours, borrowing French books from the bishop or English ones from the Red River Library, which was the only lasting legacy of the officers of the Sixth Royals, besides a few more blue-eyed métis. In return for starting up the library, they'd coerced the Company into taking the tariff off cigars.

One afternoon while Marie was struggling with the words in *Gulliver's Travels*, Wappeston said: "Even though I'm doing it by proxy, I don't believe I've done this much reading since the day they handed me my cap and gown at Inverness. I'd forgotten how much I used to enjoy it." But that didn't soften the feeling of watching that roof-beam-shouldered body softening away in a chair by the fire.

He started to take walks outside, seeing how the crops were doing or sighing wistfully at his horses gamboling in the sun. The walks got longer and longer. One day when she thought he was still outside, she came across him sitting in his office studying a book: the big ledger of income and expenses that she'd been trying to keep up while he couldn't. He said: "No more reading duty for you and the girls; I can see quite clearly. Unfortunately, what I see is that we're broke."

"No, we're not."

"Well, I admit it wouldn't seem that way to most people, but we do live somewhat higher on the hog than most people, and I intend to keep on doing it. With the way we've been dipping into our capital, the interest is hardly enough to keep a dog alive. I think it's time we called in a few old cards from the redoubtable Sir George."

He stayed in his office for the rest of the day, scratching a quill across paper and humming to himself. When he was done he asked her to read it over before he sealed it up, to make sure that his eyes or his hand or his mind hadn't betrayed him. She had to admit it didn't read like a letter from a man who'd been flat on his back for a month.

Sir Geo. Simpson
Gov. of Rupert's Land
Dear Sir:

I fear, though I hope without sufficient ground, that this session may be your last for coming among us. I am therefore anxious to appeal once for all to your often tried kindness, because now the Council of Rupert's Land contains hardly any of my old friends.

I have long thought that I could promote the Company's best interests by trading again under its sanction. I was under this impression even before the competition of the Americans had begun to show itself across the lines; and if so, how much stronger must my opinion be now, when the competition has lasted so much longer, and spread so much farther, than could have been at first expected. In fact, the present state of things appears to be such as to render the assistance of individuals who can be depended on necessary to the Company; and at the same time it seems to remove the objection which certainly had weight some years back, that the employing of middlemen would tempt others to engage in the same business without authority. If this be so in general, I flatter myself that my services in this way might be more valuable than those of most other persons.

But to enable me to serve the Company with effect, I should require the command of a little capital. I see no other way of getting this but your powerful help. I should be glad to accept a composition in lieu of an annuity, the more so as very few indeed of those who know my claims are likely after this to have any voice in the management of affairs. All things considered, I should think that seven years of my present *income*, say, in round numbers £1,200, would be a reasonable amount, to be paid in such a way as may be agreed upon between us. I shall merely add that I do not wish to have the whole immediately, nor the whole in cash at all, but part in money and part in goods, say (first) £200 to be paid down in cash now, (secondly) Goods to the value of £500 at York Factory prices to be delivered this fall at York Factory, (thirdly) Goods to the value of £500 at

London prices to be sent out by the ship next year.
Hoping to see you personally soon,

> I have the Honor to be
> Dear Sir
> your ever grateful and obliged
> Humble Servant
> Cuthbert Grant.

When she told him that it seemed perfectly clear to her, he said, "Good," and reached for the sealing wax. "Oh, and perhaps you might mention to Daniel or Donald next time you see them that this should prove a reliable investment if they can free up some of the capital your father left."

"Sure. Did you want one of them to head it up? Or were you thinking of Pascal, or Charles? . . ."

"To head up what?"

"The trading party. Donald and Daniel'll want to know who you got in mind, if—"

"I thought you said that letter was lucid? *I'll* have to lead the expedition. That's the whole point."

She bit her lips together. She wasn't entirely sure that part of her urge to say "Don't be ridiculous" might not be coming from selfishness. As much as it pained her to see him incapacitated, as long as he was, he was hers alone.

As the leaves turned brittle and died and the nights grew colder, she couldn't deny that he appeared to be growing steadily spryer. She could tell he was lying at least a little, she just wasn't sure how much. She could see at times, if someone called his name from behind him, that he would fuse his spine and swivel his entire body rather than turning his head. And when Charles stopped by to see if they wanted him to pick anything up while he was running his dogs to Fort Garry, Wappeston said offhandedly: "You might ask Doctor Bunn if he has any extra laudanum he'd care to sell off."

"How much do you want?"

"As much as he can spare. The same goes for morphine. Better safe than . . ."

The Dumonts came to pay a call before setting off on one of their whims to go ice fishing on the Qu'Appelle lakes or moose hunting along the North Saskatchewan. They left Wappeston rubbing his hands together and chortling: "Well, well, well, well, well . . ."

"What's got you so Christmasy all of a sudden?"

"I think—I *think*—I can safely say that in not too many years the New Nation is going to find itself with a very effective new Chief."

"Who's that?" expecting him to reply "Aicawpow" or "Skakata-tow," both of whom she would've entrusted her family's lives to with-out batting an eye.

"Gabriel Dumont."

"Little Gabriel?"

"He's hardly so little anymore."

"He is compared to his brothers and—"

"Compared to his brothers and father and uncle, *I'm* little. He may not be all that prepossessing, and he's certainly rough around the edges, but he has it."

"Has what?"

"It's difficult to explain. . . . When I was at my best in the chiefing line, way back at the start, I didn't know what I was doing—that is, I didn't have any concept of myself as the Chief. There were simply things that had to be done, and I went ahead to do them and people followed me—a lot of people who showed a surprising amount of intelligence in other areas. 'Little' Gabriel has magnets in his eyes."

"He's just a boy! There's already men like Riel and James Sinclair and Pascal and—"

"Riel's a town man. Sinclair *wants* it so desperately he can't be trusted. Pascal only wants to get rich. Gabriel Dumont's one of the wild boys—genuine coin of the realm."

"What about your own sons? Or did you give a thought to them?"

"Several, actually. They're fine boys, and much too smart to follow in the footsteps they watched me trip and stumble and gyrate through. I'll lay you any odds you care to name, although I'm normally not a gambling man—"

"Ha!"

"At any rate, ten years from now—maybe less—you'll turn to me and admit I was right about Gabriel Dumont. What's that on the front of your dress?"

"What? Oaw! Stop that! . . ."

The new year was like the first winter they were married, in more ways than one. Once again she watched the ruined husk of a man knit itself back together again. Not so quickly as the first time, but just as steadily, and he was twice as old as he'd been then. In the spring, he felt robust enough to join Angus and Louis in the seeding. They'd had to do last fall's harvesting alone. On his way out the door, he bent to kiss her, bragging: "There, you see, Waposis? Given enough time and care, even this fat head can heal."

It seemed barely a moment later she heard Louis and Angus yelling: "Maman!" She ran to the door and threw it open. They were just coming into the barnyard from the pathway through the woods. Although her two youngest boys were almost men by now, it looked to be just about all they could do to drag their father along with one of them under each shoulder. The girls helped wrestle him upstairs and into bed.

The barricades on the road through Grantown went up again. His mind seemed to come and go. Marie found herself hoping for the times when he didn't seem to recognize them, because then he was less likely to wake up screaming in the night. Maria Theresa had a new baby, so she couldn't come over as often as she had last summer. But all Marie had to learn about the medicine chest was which dark liquid was laudanum and which white powder was morphine.

A letter arrived for "Cuthbert Grant (Grantown)" from "G. Simpson (Fort Garry)." Marie opened it in the kitchen. ". . . am very sorry to learn that the impaired state of your health prevents your coming down here and that consequently I shall not have the pleasure of seeing you this season. . . . I am not prepared to give you an immediate reply to the points you have brought under my notice in reference to your salary as Warden of the Plains. The arrangement to which you refer was made thirty years ago, & although I have in my mind a general recollection of the terms, it is necessary to refer to documents not in my possession here. . . . I shall look into the matter after my reutrn to Canada. . . . I am much obliged by your kind enquiries after my health, which I am obliged to say continues good. Wishing you a speedy recovery, I remain &c &c G. Simpson."

Marie had to restrain herself from ripping it apart and throwing the pieces in the fire. After all these years the little son of a bitch couldn't even be bothered to ride twenty miles. She folded it up into a square and put it away in a drawer where she wouldn't have to look at it.

CHAPTER 51

Grant was getting accustomed to being helpless. The notion didn't hold much appeal for him, but he didn't consciously consider it very often. He didn't consciously consider much of anything very often. He was too busy fighting against or suffering through the pain and the disorientation. It was impossible to gauge how much of the disorientation came from the drugs and alcohol that numbed the pain. He could see the pain. It was a green wolf. He watched it through the back of his head as it gnawed at the base of his skull—jagged orange teeth and red gums inside the green lips, with pink-and-white ribbing across the roof of its mouth when it opened its jaws to bite down.

Sometimes it left him alone and went chasing the white horse across the plains. He'd seen them once, the white streak and the green, running through the moonlight. Even from a quarter mile away, and with the window closed, he could still hear the hoofbeats and the panting.

Or perhaps he'd only dreamed he'd gotten out of bed to look out of the window. That was probably the case, since he couldn't remember a woman being in the room at the time. When he wasn't dreaming, there was always a woman in the room. At night she was Marie lying beside him. During the day the woman sat on a chair beside the bed and could be Marie or Maria Theresa or Mary Falcon or one of his other daughters or sisters. Sometimes there were two or three women at once, wrestling him into a clean nightshirt or propping him up to spoon soup into him. Sometimes he would blink his eyes and the woman on the chair would change from Mary beading a moccasin to Maria Theresa feeding his new grandson.

Two weeks after Marie had opened that horrible letter from that horrible little man, she was just finishing up in the kitchen and about to go upstairs to relieve Maria Theresa when Mary Falcon poked her head in the back door and said: "I've got the box of books from Fort Garry, but I can't carry them."

"Oh, damn—the boys are off fishing. . . ." With the barriers back up on the road, it wasn't just a question of bringing Mary's cart around to the back steps and maneuvering the box down. The men at the barricades would undoubtedly have made an exception in this case, but it didn't seem right when so many other people were going to so much trouble for his sake.

Mary said: "I'll go see if I can root out Pierriche or—"

"No need. Maria Theresa's upstairs. Between the three of us we should be able to manage."

"I think so. It ain't so much the books as they went and put them in this big wooden box. . . ."

"I'll be back down with Maria Theresa in a second. We can leave him alone for five minutes."

On her way up the stairs, she could hear his voice alternating with Maria Theresa's, so he was in one of his talking moods. Maria Theresa looked up at her as she came through the door, chirping brightly: "Me and Papa have been chattering away all afternoon." But from the strained look around her eyes, it hadn't exactly been a reassuring kind of chatter.

His eyes were wide open but cloudy. He grinned at Marie and said: "I've been hearing him again. Quite close this time. But no need for alarm—he was galloping. It's the walking you have to be wary of. Odin's eight-legged horse only plods along slowly, but no man can outrun him. I suppose it would have to be rewritten to twelve now, but the Vikings were somewhat more robust than these decadent times—it only took four of them."

"Could you lend me and Mary a hand with carrying in a box of books?" A week ago she would've tried to come up with some reply to what he'd said or at least clarify that it wasn't *his* hand she was asking for the loan of. But she had grown accustomed to assuming only his body was there.

Grant blinked and found himself in another dream. It had to be a dream, since there were no women in the room. Whoever had arranged the dream had been thoughtful enough to leave the window open and let in the sweet summer air. The breeze carried laughing voices in with it. Well, since it was a dream, he could do anything he wanted, such as bound out of bed and over to the window to see who was being so jovial and why.

The bound turned into a wallowing against waves of cotton and feathers. He would've thought that the least his imagination could do was dream up a place where he was healthy. He and the sheet and pillows cascaded off the bed and his head exploded against the floor.

There was a searing streak of green fur and broken yellow teeth.

Then it was gone and replaced by his three Maries—wife, daughter, and sister. They were trying to lift him back into the cloying bed. He wanted to go to the window. He tried to tell them so but kept losing his voice in the face of their sad looks. He tried to tell them not to be sad, just help him to the window. He struggled to his knees, and they supported him on his way, but then they always had.

He fell against the window frame and looked out. Ghost Horse Plains glowed like *sliobh grantia*—the Plain of the Sun. There were people walking along the road below the window: big Toussaint Lussier with his usual gaggle of trailing children hoping he might come across a pony, Euphrosme Grant, big with another eminent grandchild, Marguerite MacDougall with the bright scarf she wore to cover the place where the Sioux had scalped her. A mob of children were hunting tadpoles in the shallows of the Assiniboine.

Heads started to turn toward his window. The black eyes and the brown, the blue eyes and gray, all began to swell until they filled the sky. He glanced sideways at Marie propping up his shoulder, to see if she could see them, too. It was remarkable how she hadn't aged a day in thirty years. But it wasn't right that she should look so sad. He nodded his head toward the window to try to direct her attention to the eyes that filled it, so she could see there was nothing to be sad about. If anything, she should be astounded. All those eyes, and not one of them was hardened with wariness or distaste or mistrust of what they were looking at.

He thrust his arm out the window to touch them and realized just an instant too late. He should've known it would be lurking just outside the window frame, hugging the wall and waiting. There was a flash of green, and the yellow teeth scissored through his head.

Father LaFleche came quickly and too late. He asked Marie: "Did he make an act of contrition?"

"Yes."

"I hope, now that he's gone, you won't torture yourself with regret."

"Regret?"

"That you sacrificed your life to him."

"He's the one that's dead, Father."

"He gave his life to his people. He could not have done that if you hadn't given yours to him."

"We both did what we wanted to, Father. There's no martyrs here."

"If you approve, I would like to have his remains interred in the wall of the church. It's the way it's done with seigneurs in Quebec and France."

"He'd like that."

The next day she sat in the parlor with her hands slack in the lap of her black dress. They wouldn't let her do anything. His sisters and Maria Theresa had shaved him and dressed him, and their husbands had laid him in the coffin and carried it downstairs. Her daughters had taken charge of her kitchen. Pierriche and Charles were nailing down the lid. Toussaint Lussier was there as well. His nose had never straightened from the time Wappeston busted it, and he looked as though he hadn't stopped crying for the last twenty-four hours.

She pushed herself off her chair and shouted: "Stop!" Pierriche and Charles looked up from their hammers. "Wait. Don't close it yet. Pry it back open." They looked at each other, then at the floor.

She went upstairs. In the blanket box at the foot of the bed was her diary. The much spliced ball of knotted threads and sinews and beads and feathers of down and other markers had grown to the size of a baby's head. She started to unravel it and realized there was no need. She knew that in the center of it was the green bead she'd knotted in on the night Mister Grant had appeared in the doorway of the wedding at Red River; she knew where the blue and the black bead were strung together for Charles and Nancy, where the little white shell was strung on for the day she'd watched him fishing in the mist . . .

She carried the ball of beaded string back downstairs. Pierriche and Charles had pried the nails back out but left the lid in place. She said: "Take it off."

They'd dressed him in the rainbow coat she'd made for him. The girls hadn't done as good a job of shaving him as he used to do, but they hadn't had much practice. Someone who hadn't yet been perfectly Christianized—probably Pierriche—had laid his pistols and his spyglass across his chest. And they'd put coins over his eyes. Marie was willing to swear that in the last instant she'd seen life in those eyes, she'd seen that he'd finally worked up the courage to do the one thing he'd ever been too afraid to do—admit how much he was loved.

She snuggled her diary in beside that placid marble sculpture of a head and said: "All right, nail it shut. Oh—and there's only going to be four pallbearers."

Pierriche said: "He ain't ever been a light load to carry. . . ."

"That's the way he wanted it. Him and Odin."

Charles said: "Him and *who*?"

Pierriche cut him off with a wave of his hand. "If that's the way he wanted it—we got plenty enough strong fellows to pick from." Toussaint grinned hopefully through his tears.

It took two years for all the children left in the big white house to start families of their own. The scent of him in her bed grew fainter and fainter. The Cree and Saulteaux, and those métis who were fonder of a tingle across the back of the neck than theology, began to say that the white horse now had a rider.

The night after Julie Rose's wedding, Marie was wakened by a noise outside. She slipped out of bed and wafted down the stairs without a trace of heaviness in her bones. Waiting at the back steps was a pale horse with a dark rider who was beautiful and terrible. His shadowed face kept shifting from a young man to a worn-down old Chief, from the glitter-eyed totem standing alone between the circle of carts and the oncoming Sioux to the shuddering hulk spewing his fear out into Grant's Lake. His hand reached down and she took it, sailing up onto the back of the white horse as if she were made of air.

AUTHOR'S NOTE

It was while I was working on an earlier book involving Cuthbert Grant (*Red River Story*, available through your local bookseller, cheaper by the dozen, collect 'em, trade 'em with your friends . . .) that I came across the curious fact that his Christian name appears to have changed halfway through his life—from Cuthbert to Mister. Although there were a number of Grants (Richard Grant, Peter Grant, etc.) running Hudson's Bay Company posts in and around the Red River Valley in the middle decades of the nineteenth century, and many more salted in among the general population, if someone spoke of "Mister Grant" without specifying further, it was generally assumed that they were speaking of the Grant of Grantown.

I had generally assumed that this was a musty bit of a sidelight on a long-dead, relatively obscure local hero, until a book launch in Winnipeg for *Red River Story* (if your neighborhood bookseller has no copies in stock, I'm quite sure he or she would be delighted to order several for you). The entertainment for the evening, besides myself, was the Dakotah Ojibway Drum Society. (One of my prized possessions is a photograph of one of those stone-faced, burly young gentlemen actually *grinning* at me.) The chapter I read from as my part of the festivities was early in the story, when Grant was a young nincompoop of a junior clerk referred to only as "Grant" or "Cuthbert" or "You there!" But after I'd done reading, one of the drummers sidled up to my wife and asked: "Is this really a book about *Mister Grant?*"

This book required a good deal more filling in of blanks than *Red River Story* (have you memorized that yet?), because there is more documentation on Grant's doings during the few years on either side of Seven Oaks than the entire rest of his life. Various sources mention enough later events involving Grant that I think I can safely claim that most of the exterior incidents in this book, and many of the domestic ones, happened. Whether they happened exactly the way I described them is a moot point, because the original sources tend to be sketchy. For instance, the only reason we know Grant was involved in a Sioux war in 1842 is the offhanded "Grant has not yet returned from the War" in a letter from one fur trader to another. Then there is nothing until the preserved letters between Grant and the Sioux chiefs making peace.

Virtually nothing is known about Marie outside of her parentage, dates of birth and death and marriage and the relevant dates of some of her children—"some" because church fires destroyed many records in St. Boniface, and the parish registry of St. François Xavier didn't start up until the year little Nancy died on the night Charles was born. As to a physical description of Marie, there is only a twentieth-century writer's: "From her descendants, one gathers that she was a buxom lass. . . ." The only scrap of information regarding her domestic relations is that Grant's letter to James Hargrave regarding Willie McKay's proposal to Elisabeth makes it quite clear that Marie had evolved into someone who was perfectly capable of laying down the law to "the Chief of all the Half-Breeds." Other than those paltry facts, all I could do was imagine a seventeen-year-old "daughter of the country" who'd found herself married to Mister Grant and see where she went from there.

I wouldn't have been able even to start on this book, much less that earlier one (remember?), if it hadn't been for an amateur historian named Margaret Arnett MacLeod. Among her many other endeavors, including editing the letters of Letitia Hargrave and contributing to the delightful *Women of Red River*, Mrs. MacLeod also developed a passionate obsession with researching Cuthbert Grant. When someone asked me for an explanation for Mrs. MacLeod's obsession, since she wasn't a descendant of Grant's nor did she appear to have any other vested interest, the only theory I could come up with was the gap left in her life by her only son. Lieutenant Alan MacLeod was a World War I flyer and was unusual among recipients of the Victoria Cross in that it wasn't awarded posthumously. He came home to Winnipeg with all his arms and legs intact and died in the influenza epidemic of 1919.

Mrs. MacLeod's husband also died before his time. The result of Mrs. MacLeod's loneliness was a book entitled *Cuthbert Grant of Grantown* (well, snappy titles ain't exactly in the purview of scholastic publishing). It was written in collaboration with a budding young professional historian, because by that time she was unable to read her notes, her vision was so weak. The book has an interesting tension in it, because Margaret had a romantic concept of Grant, and her collaborator appears to have been rather, well . . . jealous.

Unfortunately there were further editions after Margaret MacLeod's death, allowing her collaborator (we used to shoot collaborators) to insert an introduction asserting that the dotty old half-blind lady's vision of Grant was flawed, because Grant was not, in fact, "heroic" (whatever that means). One reason given is that Grant "on occasion, at least, drank more than his position of responsibility allowed." Another is that Grant was used by the North West Company and the Hudson's Bay Company for their own ends, while "heroes, even when young, are not used; they pursue their own objects." I suppose we'll have to eliminate that brandy-sodden Churchill from the list of fit subjects for biography, not to mention that eager young Corsican who was so effectively used by Robespierre and by Joséphine de Beuharnais's sugar daddy.

The concept of Grant or anyone else as a "hero" seems a bit unhealthy to me to begin with. Heroes supposedly inspire us, but I think they tend rather to reinforce the notion that we small, frail, flawed human beings can do nothing but suffer through until some more-than-human hero appears to straighten out our lives for us. The redoubtable Mister Grant, like his successor Gabriel Dumont (featured in a book called Lord of the Plains by Alfred Silver, available through your local . . .), would not have interested me in the least if he hadn't been so obviously a very human being trying to blunder through as best he could, just like the rest of us.

Which brings up the question of how much evidence there is, if any, that the historical Grant bore any resemblance to the one in this book (and the earlier one, still available in the trade edition that is more attractive than the mass market and much more durable). In terms of his physical representation, there are two portraits in existence. One may be a copy of the other, as the pose is the same, or they both may be copies of a vanished original. Both show the same features—something resembling Robert Burns's illegitimate son by the queen of the Amazon—and the same suggestion of massive shoulders on a tall frame. But otherwise the effect is very different. One of them gives the impression of a head prefect who sings in the school choir and also captains the rugby team. As for the other one . . . A friend of mine whose first language is not English looked from one to the other and said: "This one, he eats meat."

There is a vague possibility that a painting of Paul Kane's contains another portrait of Grant, and the circumstances around that painting call up an aspect of the character I found lurking within the sketchy mentions of the chief of all the half-breeds. Kane traveled across western Rupert's Land in the 1840s and left a journal, sketches, and paintings that provide an invaluable, if somewhat romanticized, portrait of life in the *pays d'en haut*. He went out with the summer buffalo hunt and painted several pictures from that experience. In one of them there is a foreground figure of a large, tough-looking customer gazing out at the viewer from the saddle of a rather Arabian-looking buffalo runner. The features bear a battered resemblance to those in the head-and-shoulders portraits of young Cuthbert Grant. The eyes are exactly the same as those of the one who "eats meat"—large, black, unnerving, waiting placidly to see whether your hand will come out of your pocket with a hundred-pound note or a knife.

The strange circumstances around that painting are akin to Sherlock Holmes's "curious incident" of what the dog did in the night. Kane's journal is filled with anecdotes of the people he met on his travels. Whether Indian chiefs, chief factors, or wandering trappers, all were delighted by the opportunity to be memorialized by a real live painter and diarist from Toronto. But after many weeks of traveling with the buffalo hunt, all Kane could say was that "it was led by a Mister Grant."

It echoes a letter from an HBC officer to James Hargrave: "I corresponded with Grant, but . . . he writes but occasionally and with funny reluctance. Grant is a good fellow. I have met with none who possessed more bravery and personal resolution in time of danger, but that is the best that can be said of him." The scanty remnants of Grant's scanty correspondence show that he never lost that high Regency tone he learned in his youth and that he was subject to the occasional black depression. His last letter to Hargrave ends with: "I shall not attempt to intrude on your present time and give you nothing but dismal news."

I was also given a certain amount of confirmation for my notion of Grant from an unexpected source that had nothing to do with archival records. Maria Campbell is the writer of a marvelous book called *Halfbreed* and is also collecting folktales from around where she lives, a place called Gabriel's Crossing that once was the home of her great-aunt and -uncle, Madelaine and Gabriel Dumont. Despite the generations' worth of mythologizing, folktales tend to hold on to the essential character of the human grain of sand that first found its way into the oyster. I mentioned to Maria that what first interested me in the nineteenth-century Canadian West was the pair of men who were the bookends of the first métis nation, "Mister Grant" and "Uncle"

("Uncle Gabe lay in the shade, and the tales that he told made your blood run cold"). I added that they made an oddly balanced set of bookends, because Gabriel seemed to have been a simple man—though far from simpleminded—while Grant seemed a somewhat tortured soul. She said: "I think you're right."

That might seem like a rather off-handed nod of agreement, but in this business you got to take your confirmation where you can get it. Show me three original sources and two experts and I'll show you five different versions of what happened. A very authoritative scholar wrote that Adam Thom lost his case against the porch carpenter. I had written the chapter that way and then thought to dip back into *Four Recorders of Rupert's Land* by another amateur historian, Roy St. George Stubbs. There I found it stated that the porch carpenter's suit was dismissed. Although his credentials as a historian might not have been as impressive as the learned scholar's, I guessed Judge Stubbs might be more likely to know the difference between defendant and plaintiff.

But then everyone makes mistakes. Roy St. George Stubbs assumes that Dr. John Bunn, who served as recorder for a time, must have had some debilitating disease, because there are many references to "Old John Bunn" from a time when the doctor was still in his thirties. A quick glance through *Women of Red River* and *The Letters of Letitia Hargrave* garners several variations on "I mean Old John Bunn, Doctor Bunn's father."

Even dear old Margaret Arnett MacLeod went and assumed that Cuthbert Grant was the Grant in an incident that took place at Rainy River, on the old canoe route from the *pays d'en haut* to Montreal. Although it's true that Grant was traveling at the time, on his way back from England, his return was via Hudson's Bay, since he found Simpson's letter waiting for him at Norway House. That's one hell of a detour just to see a few thousand more spruce trees and mosquito bogs.

In fact, gentle reader, there is the possibility that there may even be a few slip-ups of minor details within lo these many hundreds of pages to your left. If such should prove to be the case, I will face up to it like a man and blame my editor, whose name and home telephone number are (DELETED).

I have fabricated the friendship between Grant and the Sutherlands, although there is no evidence to the contrary and they certainly knew one another. And Margaret Arnett MacLeod tells a tantalizing story that first got me thinking along those lines: "When Cuthbert McKay, son of Cuthbert Grant's daughter Elisabeth, used to walk along the bank of the Red River to attend college in Winnipeg, an old lady who was one of the original settlers would never let him pass without offering him some treat, saying, 'We all remember that we never slept quiet in our beds until your grandfather and his brave métis came to live near us.' '' Odds on that métis Catholics like the McKays would have resided on the St. Boniface side, and there was only one "old lady who was one of the original settlers" who lived on that bank of the Red.

Various historical characters such as George Simpson, Adam Thom, Louis Riel, Sr., etc., have been perforce portrayed as I imagined them to be seen from Marie's and Grant's points of view. But that doesn't mean they've been distorted beyond what their documented words and actions would suggest, just that we only encounter those facets of their characters that come out within the framework of this story. Simpson in particular was unquestionably a rather nasty bit of business, willing to put his employees through any kind of hell if it would increase profits by a few shillings and raise the London Committee's estimation of him. It always amazes me when I see a sentence or paragraph from Simpson's journals or correspondence quoted as a definitive source. Although it's true that Simpson was always very candid and pithy, particularly in his private "Character Book," his candid opinions had a habit of shifting to suit the circumstances of the moment. When Simpson was trying to convince the London Committee to hire Grant on as a clerk, his candid opinion was that Grant was a paragon of all earthly virtues. Barely a year later, after the New Year's attack on Grant made it obvious that Simpson had made a mistake, his candid opinion was that Grant was a tolerably good trader but only an indifferent clerk. A few years farther down the road, when Simpson began to see the need for a warden of the plains, Grant was suddenly a man of great ability and reliability.

The one piece of Simpson's writings that no one quotes at face value, the monumental tome that Adam Thom is assumed to have written for him, came back to haunt him. In 1857, when the Select Committee of the Imperial Parliament was exploring the question of whether the Company's charter should be renewed or whether Rupert's Land should be opened up for settlement, Sir George testified at length that the prairie country was a rock-strewn desert unfit for agriculture of any kind. Some members of the committee appear to have found it amusing to quote back glowing descriptions of the prairies as the potential granary of the empire, from *A Journey Round the World* by Sir George Simpson.

Adam Thom appears to have cut quite a swath in the ghostwriting vein. He is presumed to have authored a good deal of the *Durham Report*, which, for better or worse, shaped a good deal of Canadian history and is still doing so today. After his "retirement" he returned to England and finally devoted himself to his own book on the history of the world vis-à-vis the life span of our Lord—in between pursuing an endless lawsuit against his banker. Thom's literary labors culminated in the publication of *Emmanuel, Both the Germ and the Outcome of the Scriptural Alphabets, a Pentaglot Miniature*.

Maria Theresa was actually plain Maria, but after my editor had waded through hundreds of pages where the three most mentioned female characters were named Marie, Mary, and Maria . . . Maria Campbell informs me that a writer dealing with living métis families would encounter the same living problem—in fact, she has a younger sister named Maria Campbell.

Maria "Theresa" and Pascal Breland moved into the big white house in Grantown after Marie died. Maria inherited her father's medicine trunks and his rustic medical practice. She also grew very fat. One of her grandsons recollected that his special duty was to lift onto a chair whatever medicine box she needed to delve into. That same grandson apparently gave Mrs. MacLeod a detailed description of the house, which unfortunately didn't find its way into her book, so there's no way of knowing whether there was or wasn't a widow's walk on top. It's probably a bit of literary license, since it would've been a rather odd and fanciful notion for Grant to get into his head. Then again . . .

Pascal Breland became very prosperous and well respected, to a point: magistrate, member of the Manitoba legislature, and executive councillor of the North West Territories, which made him "the Honourable Pascal Breland." I say "to a point" because, unlike his father-in-law, Pascal appears to have had a knack for avoiding anything that looked like trouble. Whether during the Red River Rebellion of 1869–70 or the long years of agitation that led to the North West Rebellion of 1885, Pascal Breland always seemed to discover urgent business in another part of the country just before the organic fertilizer encountered the ventilating device. In the surviving photographs of the Brelands—although it's always hard to tell from old photographs—Pascal Breland appears to be a very handsome, self-possessed, well-preserved old gentleman, with a fat, hard-worn wife who does not look like a happy camper. The cemetery at St. Francis Xavier contains a large, imposing monument to "The Honourable Pascal Breland."

Beside it is a barely readable little eroded tombstone for "Maria Grant."

The mysterious General Dickson disappeared back into the mystery from whence he'd sprung, leaving only Pierre Falcon's song about the liberator's flamboyant departure from Grantown. James Sinclair, whom Margaret MacLeod's collaborator asserts would have made a much better chief of all the half-breeds than the old drunkard, never got a chance to prove it. He was killed in an Indian siege of Fort Walla Walla, where the Company had sent him to establish a British presence in the Oregon Territory by transplanting a batch of Red River métis. The siege was relieved by Phil Sheridan, he who once replied to a junior officer's questioning his policy of butchering Indian children as well as warriors: "Nits breed lice."

"Irish" Riel, in the last years of his life, swung around to Grant's point of view about the Company and Rupert's Land—or at least the point of view I've inferred from Grant's actions from 1823 to 1854. (One has to do a lot of inferring when it comes to someone who, unlike Louis Riel Sr. and Jr., seemed decidedly reluctant to express his innermost thoughts and motivations within hearing of someone who might write them down.) When the 1860s made it apparent that the Company's reign was about to be replaced by the only possible alternative, annexation by a foreign government, "Irish" began to think that maybe the Company wasn't so despotic after all.

Pierre Falcon lived into his eighties and continued to write songs. There is a family tradition that the old man had to be physically restrained from taking his gun and riding to Red River in 1870 to give the English a taste of Seven Oaks.

Alexander Ross, the sheriff of Red River, did write his book— several, in fact. Most of what we know of Grant's water mill project comes from a paragraph in Ross's *The Red River Settlement: Its Rise, Progress and Present State*. He twigs "Mr. Grant, chief of the half-breeds" with being "fond of notoriety" but ends with: "Everyone regretted the failure as a loss to the public, and still more on account of the projector himself, who was, on the whole, a generous and good-hearted fellow."

Some years ago a group of Winnipeggers clubbed together to rebuild Grant's Mill on Sturgeon Creek. Many visitors pass through unaware that the public-spirited Mister Grant was also the monster of Seven Oaks, just as many of the motorists streaming down Grant Avenue remain unaware that the road wasn't named after the president of a foreign country. Well, Cuthbert and Ulysses had at least one thing in common.

Grant's Mill grinds flour from spring thaw to freeze-up and is a fine piece of thoughtful reconstruction. However, a friend of mine who happens to be a millwright visited it shortly after its opening and grew very confused over the fact that the millstones seemed to be turning in the opposite direction from what their connection to the water-wheel would suggest. There was also this odd humming sound, not unlike an electric motor. . . . Perhaps my friend the millwright was still feeling the effects of the night before, or perhaps a century and a half of technological progress still hasn't solved the problem of building a water mill on Sturgeon Creek.

The Museum of Man and Nature in Winnipeg displays Grant's two medicine chests and the sword he got from General Dickson. Margaret Arnett MacLeod discovered the sword propped behind the kitchen door of one of Grant's descendants, who used it for clearing weeds. When I related that story to a friend with a military turn of mind, he replied that it made perfect sense. Cavalry sabers evolved for the purpose of chopping foot soldiers as one galloped by; the exact same principles of weight and balance would apply to chopping weeds as one strode by.

Many descendants of the original inhabitants of Grantown still live there, although the name of the place changed soon after Grant's death, first to St. François-Xavier and then anglicized to St. Francis Xavier. By the cutoff from the trans-Canada Highway is a life-size statue of a large, white, genderless horse. A plaque on its base thanks the distillers of White Horse Scotch, Glasgow, for underwriting the cost of the statue.

In the general vicinity of where the big white house once stood is a green prefab store. Down the road there is a lovely little park where a Red River cart stands in front of a dovetail-cornered, squared-log house with a delightful, matching, two-door outhouse. There was a plan afoot some years ago to turn the house into a museum housing artifacts such as Grant's writing desk, which resided in Ross House in Winnipeg, but I don't know how far the plan has progressed.

Between the Red River cart and the house stand two plaques com-memorating Pierre Falcon, one in French and one in English. No sign of a plaque in Cree. In front of the church next door is a bilingual plaque (French and English) commemorating Father Belcourt. On the other side of the road is a cairn for Cuthbert Grant, who never could get along with Father Belcourt. The inscription on the cairn says that Grant's was a life "dedicated to the native people of the West."

The aging church is a replacement for the much older one that burned down, the one that Wappeston was interred in the wall of. It seems that where the old church stood is where the paved highway was put through the center of town. Mister Grant lies under the highway. "Stranger, go tell the Spartans to soft-pedal it when they drive through here. . . ."

No book of this kind—hell, no book of any kind—gets written without the kind help of people whose names don't appear on the cover. The list could go on forever, but I'll restrict it to those whose contributions can be clearly defined. Elizabeth Blight of the Public Archives of Manitoba supplied me with information on Grant's portraits—although I suppose she's been repaid to a certain extent by the coincidence that an old friend of mine, John Wiznuk, was able to inform her that the lost portrait (the one that doesn't "eats meat") had somehow fumbled its way across the prairies and the Rockies to the Victoria Museum. Judith Hudson Beattie of the Hudson's Bay Company Archives cleared up my confusion about the HBC blanket point system by showing me that even the HBC ain't exactly sure. John Oleksiuk dug up (so to speak) the location of Grant's grave. Coincidentally, John Oleksiuk ran Mary Scorer's bookstore for many years, where the book launch with the Dakotah Ojibway Drum Society took place. Mary Scorer's Peguis Publishing reissued *Women of Red River* and many other books whose continued existence has made mine easier.

Well, and now we come to the odd feeling of bidding good-bye to a group of remarkable people I've traveled with for some ten years now—what with one book or script or another. Although they all died long before I was born, they've carried me a long ways, and I only hope I've done them some justice in return. They are the ones I owe the most debt to. One of them in particular, of course—the eternal orphan. Good night, Cuthbert.